PRAISE

"*If You Leave* is an engrossing, moving portrait of friendship and motherhood. Margaret Hutton is a gifted writer who knows how to convey human vulnerabilities and life's fragile connections to haunting effect."

—Jill McCorkle, author of *Old Crimes* and *Hieroglyphics*

"In Margaret Hutton's beautifully written novel, we meet Audrey and Lucille, friends driven apart by a secret, but then bound by an impossible request. *If You Leave* is a powerful and timely story, deeply examining the difficult choices women and mothers must make around issues of art and family and caretaking. I loved it."

—Jessica Francis Kane, author of *Rules for Visiting* and *Fonseca*

"Exquisite! With a painter's skill, Margaret Hutton builds up layers of longing worthy of Elizabeth Strout and William Trevor. On every page, *If You Leave* pits desire against duty, somehow convincing the reader to root for both. Each deftly drawn character wants the freedom to leave, but no one wants to be abandoned. Or, to quote the novel itself, 'Who's in charge of love? It's loose in the world, nobody steering it.'"

—Mary Kay Zuravleff, author of *American Ending*

"*If You Leave* is tender and razor-sharp, empathetic and unsentimental. Its evocation of wartime Washington, DC, captures brilliantly the texture of everyday life, both the limbo of waiting for the war's end and the pinched quality of women's lives. Margaret Hutton has written a wonderful novel about two indelible women, working through the meaning of motherhood and selfhood as the country changes around them. It's about betrayals and forgiveness, the necessity—and the costs—of leaving, about coming, however belatedly, into your own. Beautiful."

—Molly McCloskey, author of *Straying* and *Circles Around the Sun: In Search of a Lost Brother*

"*If You Leave* is an intellectual page-turner with a powerful emotional underbelly. The author's moral curiosity adds a unique richness to her depiction of choice and chance in two women's lives. Audrey, an artist, vacillates between responsibility to her talent and love of her family. Lucille, a fugitive turned stalker, offers as much as she takes away. As Hutton masterfully probes the selfishness and sacrifice that love and life demand from us all, she delivers an entirely fresh work of fiction."

—Boo Trundle, author of *The Daughter Ship*

"This sweeping, revelatory novel explores the complications of mothering and of everything that can come with it: a sense of obligation, resentment over personal sacrifices, and through all of this, an enduring bond of love. By immersing us in the lives and travails of the two women at the heart of the story, Hutton also considers the bonds of friendship, how far they can be tested, and how much we owe—or can expect from—others we've grown close to. With lyricism, insight, and compassion, *If You Leave* considers how seemingly broken relationships can mend, and how the most lasting or meaningful bonds aren't always forged by blood. The novel captivated me from the first page to the very end."

—Beth Castrodale, author of *The Inhabitants* and *I Mean You No Harm*

"'Loss often hides in the layers of color'—Margaret Hutton's exquisite debut novel sketches her characters and their impossible situations, then begins to paint them fully with intricate blendings, broad strokes, and smears off the paper. *If You Leave* follows two women who meet in Washington, DC, during the tumultuous years of World War II. Their choices in love, friendship, and motherhood keep them both bonded and bruised as the story builds, back and forth in time, ever confident, lovely, and disturbing."

—Kathleen Novak, author of *Come Back, I Love You [A Ghost Story]*

"*If You Leave* will crack your heart and repair it with transportive precision and luxurious prose. Steeped in themes of motherhood, abandonment, and loss, the novel spans three decades. Every character transcends the page and takes root in your bones. What may be more astonishing than the intoxicating writing is how the artful, elegant parts are balanced against the whole, a vibrant, well-paced story of the 'delicate fretwork' of female confidences turned tangled family saga."

—Laura Scalzo, author of *American Arcadia*

"*If You Leave* speaks to the deepest truth of maternal obligation, with its commensurate joys and frustrations, resentments, compromises, and bargains. Audrey's predicament captures the often unspoken reality of what it feels like to be a new mother for the first time. It happens in an instant and we spend the rest of our lives negotiating the losses and gains of that transformation. Audrey's struggle to remain true to her identity as an artist, while reluctantly surrendering to her role as mother, mirrors this cleaving of the self and the urgent, necessary effort to reconcile it."

—Alexandra Zapruder, author of *Twenty-Six Seconds* and *Salvaged Pages*

IF YOU LEAVE

Margaret Hutton

Regal House Publishing

Copyright © 2025 Margaret Hutton All rights reserved.

Published by
Regal House Publishing, LLC
Raleigh, NC 27605
All rights reserved

ISBN -13 (paperback): 9781646036417
ISBN -13 (epub): 9781646036424
Library of Congress Control Number: 2024951353

Cover images and design by © studiochi.art
Author photo by © Linda Fittante

The following is a work of fiction created by the author. All names, individuals, characters, places, items, brands, events, etc. are either the product of the author's imagination or are used fictitiously. Any resemblance to actual events, places, institutions, persons, current or past, is entirely coincidental.

All rights reserved. No part of this publication may be reproduced, stored in a retrieval system, or transmitted, in any form or by any means, electronic, mechanical, photocopying, recording, or otherwise, without the prior permission of Regal House Publishing.

All efforts were made to determine the copyright holders and obtain their permissions in any circumstance where copyrighted material was used. The publisher apologizes if any errors were made during this process, or if any omissions occurred. If noted, please contact the publisher and all efforts will be made to incorporate permissions in future editions.

Regal House Publishing supports rights of free expression and the value of copyright. The purpose of copyright is to encourage the creation of artistic works that enrich and define culture.

Printed in the United States of America

Regal House Publishing, LLC
https://regalhousepublishing.com

for Amelia

Stabat mater. Mothers can only stand.

—Anne Truitt, *Daybook*

1973

1

Audrey pushes the Hoover around the gallery before it opens, planning in her mind how to draw a value study of the light outside. The eastern sky, stark this morning, will require the lightest touch of graphite, but she'll press more firmly to convey the façades of buildings in shadow. There will be other variations she hasn't yet noticed, in the clouds and the storefront windows, for instance. She loves to do this, find the pattern of light and dark across a scene. It changes constantly, depending on the time of day, the season, her perspective.

But a customer raps his knuckles on the glass door. Vacuuming in plain view, she can't very well turn him away.

Halfway around the long and narrow room, he stops in front of her painting. His camel-hair coat, golden tan, has fallen open, and his arms hang slack at his sides. The canvas is large, four by six feet. Cutting a long diagonal across an expanse of water and horizon is a rowboat. It looks empty but for a bird perched on its gunwale. The palette is earthy browns and dark grays, subtle streaks of violet and blue in the sky and the bird's wing. Twilight colors. To look at the whole is both calming and unsettling. The piece has hung in the gallery off and on for years, never sold after its exhibition at the Corcoran, and now rests against the wall, on the floor. *The Wing.* Audrey usually doesn't notice the painting, just as she has ceased to see scuff marks along baseboards or broken sash cords in the house where she lives. She has been in the gallery often enough while someone studies her work to be inured to such scrutiny. But she does not want to watch, not today.

"I'm looking for something for my wife. Or for us. Our anniversary." The man smiles at Audrey, as though this declaration will evoke sympathy from her, a woman. A pair of aviator sunglasses dangles from his hand.

He has no way of knowing that she is planning to leave her own husband. There will be no more anniversaries. The decision is final, but as of yesterday's letter, her departure may be delayed. This troubled her long into the night, and she slept poorly. She smiles anyway. Selling a painting is about making people feel a certain way when they are in the gallery, the sensation they have while looking at the art, and she's determined to exude warmth.

"A piece of art can be such an expressive gift for a husband and wife," she says. "Something you both can enjoy for a lifetime, and an investment."

He moves on, saying nothing. To distract from her disappointment, she thinks of the apartment she's rented, how she must carefully choose the timing of when she tells Ben. Money from a sale would ensure she won't default on future rent; she has saved up three months' worth, no more. Her only regular income is from three days a week at this gallery, the same one where she first exhibited her own work, when it was on Connecticut Avenue. Several years ago Mr. Wooten relocated to Dupont Circle, after the original owner, a Belgian woman, passed away.

The customer pauses before each frame. Eighteenth-century French landscapes hang at spacious intervals alongside modern, abstract masses of color. The man steps gingerly around other paintings stacked against the wall.

"How many years?"

The man looks at her questioningly.

"Have you been married?"

"Ah, twenty-five."

"Such a big one!" She and Ben have been married twenty-eight years.

"We're here from Brazil on a long holiday," the man says. "I'm stationed there for work, but Washington is home."

"Were you born here? That's rare, a native."

"At Garfield Hospital. Closed down—thankfully, according to my mother. She says it was decrepit."

"Yes, I remember that one." Audrey resists thinking of the past but it arises anyway. "I donated blood there once, during the war. Once was enough." She laughs lightly.

The man returns to her painting. "Do you know anything about the artist?" She tries not to wince. She approaches the painting more closely, as if looking for the signature for the first time, though she signed it—signs all her work—on the back. Once there may have been a proper label attached to it, but such are the neglectful lapses of Mr. Wooten.

"The owner will know more. I like that, you know, the signature being less conspicuous. Would you like to see it on the wall?"

He nods, and she spreads her arms wide to remove an existing painting, places it on the floor, and then picks up *The Wing*, turning its backside to the man. "A. Bray," he says, and then rushes to relieve her of one end. As they struggle together to locate the hooks, the telephone rings.

"I'll find the CV," she says, heading toward the phone. But she's too late, there is only a dial tone. For a moment she feels the slightest pressure in her chest. A ringing phone will do that, make her think of Lake and whether she is in some kind of trouble.

"Please. We're collectors. Of a sort," he adds.

She hesitates over her file. She can't let him know that she is the artist—that the artist was vacuuming, though surely even male ones have swept the floors of their studios. But a client wants his romantic vision. She also knows it may be better to conceal, at least at first, that the artist is a woman. She is A.H. Bray on her curriculum vitae. And it is probably better that she wasn't able to answer the telephone, if it was in fact Lake, who never likes being put off.

"I have to tell you," Audrey says, pretending to read something on the desk, "a client is taking the work on approval this afternoon." She looks up at him, offering the two pages, the slim summary of her life, with the painting's price clipped to the top. A statement about the future cannot easily be called a lie—anything is possible.

He scans the pages, but she knows he can't absorb whatever is on them, especially as he digests the cost. Later he may closely read the list of where her work has hung—nowhere impressive besides the Corcoran. Mr. Wooten will return tomorrow, and he could close the sale. "Just overnight," she says. "Someone wants to try it in the night lighting. Of course, if he doesn't take it, we will allow you the same period of approval." She must remember to tell Mr. Wooten how she has stretched the truth.

They back up several steps to gain the best view of the painting. "I've always admired the mystery in this work."

"It has everything, doesn't it?" he says. "Fear, solace. Beauty, emptiness."

This statement summarizes, she believes, why the painting has never sold. No one wants to take this on. They want to gaze into it, they are curious about it, but they do not want to live with it.

"Would you like to bring your wife back tomorrow? Or is this going to be a surprise?" She smiles at him as she says this, her arms folded, while at the same time she gently, discreetly, presses the tender place on her chest. She had assumed that the next obstacle in her life—for there always had been one, such as her mother, who hadn't wanted her to leave home for college—would come from without. She knew there would be more pain, but she hadn't imagined it would come from within, her own cells turning on her. She'd had a scare. A lump detected, interminable waiting, the worst imagined but silently, to herself. With death sitting on her shoulder, she searched for the apartment. On the operating table, she waited as the excised tissue was examined. She would lose her breast by day's end, or not. Her health would be declared intact, or she would be physically altered, reduced, and face a long recovery, more treatment.

When the doctor delivered the good news, she wept her way out of the hospital. And then she signed a year lease.

"I'll want to share it with her," he says, his hands in his pockets, the pages folded under one arm. She wonders briefly what kind of wife will appreciate this painting as a gift—what it might mean between them. But this is not her business to know. She means to sell.

She put down the deposit on the apartment with money from her mother, whose frugality, in surviving on custards and bouillon till her end some hundred miles away in the small town of Ridgelea, achieved this small inheritance. Her medical bills had been a bit of a drain. A new roof too, but then Audrey and her sister had sold the house.

Her father, though—he had died last year with nothing. Leaving her mother, decades ago, to lead a separate life nearby cost him everything, it seemed. In a sense she had been waiting for his death, not wanting him to know that her marriage was ending. She didn't want to worry him. At their last visit, he said, "Don't die alone. I should have married again, even at my age."

"If I'm not here," Audrey says, "the owner will be. He can talk to you in greater detail about any aspect of the painting. Would you leave your contact information? We'll send you news on upcoming exhibitions." She and Mr. Wooten always write to visitors of the gallery. A handwritten note to impress a cordial feeling on a potential customer. Many visitors return only for conversation. What's the worst thing to come of it? If a sale happens, he has a piece of art on his wall with a pleasant association. She will reference Garfield Hospital, something clever about the modernized medical care in Washington, along with the art for sale. After hearing from her, maybe he will return.

"You've been most kind," he says, writing in their guest book. "I think my wife will very much like the painting, and the gallery."

She imagines how the sunlight streams through four windows—two east, two south—converging improbably into a singular pool on the wooden floor of her new corner apartment.

Light in a room. Lucille. Words from her letter that arrived yesterday, their implications, uncurl in her now. Her old friend from the war wrote that she is leaving her home in Pomona, North Carolina, returning to Washington, renting her own apartment. Almost thirty years she's been gone. Now Lucille says she has finished her nursing certification and will take care of old people here. Hard for Audrey to imagine. She hasn't seen her since that disastrous trip down with Lake. And at last Lake is grown, finally living on her own. She has a role in a theater production coming up, the first one in a long while.

The customer lingers on a pair of framed watercolors by the entrance.

Audrey straightens *The Wing*, slightly crooked after the inspection. One of the persons most relevant to the story is missing. Lucille. Lake's mother in absentia. Audrey didn't paint her for an obvious reason: She was not in the picture. But Audrey sees her, hovering outside its frame, each rare time she looks at the painting. For years she wished for her return, but not now. Too much damage done. She shifts her weight evenly between her legs—standing her ground. She won't let Lucille's arrival interfere with her move.

She goes to the door, holding it open for the customer, and he returns his sunglasses to his face, nodding goodbye. It happens fast, two men bumping into each other. "Excuse me," "Excuse me." A laugh she would recognize anywhere.

Daniel Brink fills the doorway, smiling at her. "Here you are."

She rushes toward him, no hesitation at all, wrapping her arms around his neck. "What a surprise. You're looking for art?"

"Not exactly. I was looking for *your* art, and went to Mrs. Moreau's old store. The watch repairman next door told me the gallery had moved here. I was looking for you."

"Come in. Look at this painting. I hope I've sold it. You're the one person who'll understand everything. I'll be so glad to finally let it all go."

He takes off his hat and stands beside her. Her focus goes to the interior of the boat, where she had played with perspective, what couldn't be seen with the naked eye through the boat's side. At first glance it looks like a tarp, or a blanket. She keeps looking. Loss often hides in the layers of color—what's been scraped off, painted over. But there it is, the faintest outline visible. An elbow, a face.

1944

2

She shouldn't have been surprised that the party was almost all women, taffeta and rouge everywhere. Only women worked in her office. She had rarely seen a man calling on anyone in her apartment building that first month in Washington. But now in her co-worker Irene's grand home—or rather Irene's parents' home—at a party replete with bourbon and scotch, trays of celery and olives and cheese, she had hoped to meet a few men. Irene introduced her to several women, but then turned back to a blue-clad Navy man. Making an introduction there would risk losing his attention. Audrey's roommate called this the government-girl's eight-to-one etiquette; she also used it as an excuse not to tag along tonight. Audrey should have insisted, but she knew invitations to parties—at least invitations for women—were rationed like everything else.

A breeze blew through the open windows, sweeping the curtains. It was a wet, cool night in late April. To avoid looking lonely—she wasn't but didn't like even the appearance—she filled a plate with shrimp, deviled eggs, toasted wafers. She stepped onto the side terrace, smelling the new earth that the rain had turned up. Slick black pavement, streetlights flickering, the gleam of chrome on passing cars. All around was novelty—this was what she had loved about leaving her small Virginia hometown and moving here, where trees grew in sidewalks and voices sang out around pianos, as with the bluesy "Cow-Cow Boogie" playing now. She didn't really mind that there was no one interesting to talk to. She wouldn't stay long. She would rather be at home, painting. Looking over the garden, she plotted a night scene like this, darkness yielding up its own shade of indigo. The sharp whiff of oil from the asphalt—like her tubes of paint.

And then the scent of tobacco. She smelled him first, his cigarette that he threw down, before she heard his footsteps up the walkway. A slight hush at the piano as everyone sighted a man at the door. If it had been a woman, the music might have grown louder. She turned to see a half dozen women plucking at his coat and chirping all around him.

A painting drew her back inside. She carried her plate, lighter now for the eggs she'd eaten, and stood in front of it. A woman alone in a café booth. Her dress was blue, and a gold locket hung in a V beneath her collar. Highlights in her hair, the same flecks of creamy yellow in her necklace. A bowl and a plate of bread on a table. On the booth's hook hung a coat and scarf, dark with rain, evident from a small puddle under them. All of it was painted with an intentional flatness; it was modern that way, along with its square frame. Nothing was modern about this home—or its owners, she suspected—but modernity crept in anyway. Art was rare in her own mother's house—only on the largest walls, and then flowers at the base of a mountain. Art as anodyne.

"You want to know what she's thinking about," a voice said behind her, "and I want to know what you're thinking about."

She might have given a little jump. How had he shaken loose so quickly? "I think you just answered your own question."

"Lucky guess," he said. His easy smile lingered. He had kind eyes and his hair was dark, slicked back.

"How do you know our host?"

"I don't know our host or anything about this woman in the painting. The lights were on, I saw a table set with food. A fellow's got to eat, isn't that what they say?"

He was a funny one, but she wouldn't give him a laugh, not yet.

"I know Irene's family," he went on, "her older brother. It's true I came for the food. She's got dull friends but splendid presentations like this. And I happen to know you're not one of her friends."

They looked over at Irene. "Oh, really? We're new friends. I work with her." She recognized others from the office—Beatrice, Mabel, and Constance, who was ashing her cigarette into the base of a palm plant. Irene was the only native she knew in town, and already Audrey relied on her for where to get the cheapest nylons, if they could be gotten, or the latest fashion in cartwheel hats. She had things the others didn't, like a well-stocked kitchen in which to make hams and pints of stew that she shared at work. In this way, she seemed more maternal, and more grown-up, throwing a large, formal party like this, even though she wasn't on her own. Not like Audrey wanted to be.

"That I would believe. They say you can't choose your family, but you also can't choose who you work with. No, if you were Irene's *old* friend, you'd be wearing a fitted jacket and some kind of skirt. They all talked beforehand, you see, about what they would wear, and how they would style their hair." He was gangly but made an elegant little box step as he talked. "You're from somewhere else."

"That's the first true thing you've said."

"I knew if I kept talking I'd get something right." He looked at her plate. "Plain shrimp? I've heard of people like you—no sauce, no condiment. Only the essence."

"You should get some food too, since that's why you came." They wandered closer to the buffet. "You know so much about me, what about you? What keeps you here when all the men have left?" The term *lesser men* came to mind, the ones the war didn't want.

"Nothing will much longer," he said, filling his plate. "I've just been commissioned as a surgeon."

She was starting to warm to him, could almost see herself encircled by his open, gesticulating arms, until he said that. A surgeon. Too eager to cut, all of them.

"I'm ruining the shrimp for you, aren't I? Just the mention of the word surgery does that."

"It's my mother I'm thinking of. She's had quite a lot of interaction with surgeons, and none of them have done her much good. But don't look so glum." She laughed. "It isn't like *you're* her surgeon. I'm sure you've got a better record than those old sawbones."

He cringed. "We all do our best. And you—a war transplant with an important job here in the capital. Coordinating the shipment of life-saving supplies, making sure everyone is paid on time." He wiped his mouth with a napkin.

"Something like that. In a dark, dank basement, I repair film. Reels of it confiscated from the Axis. A lot of it boring, but now and then we come across something disturbing."

"Ah, you're not so unlike a surgeon after all."

So clever. She couldn't think of a thing to reply. She felt the beady eyes of the other women in the room.

"I was just leaving when I came over here to look at the painting. It's been lovely meeting you."

"Have we met? You still haven't told me your name."

"Audrey."

"Audrey, leaving so soon? Let me, Ben, at least give you a lift home."

"But I'd be cutting the party short for you."

"If I want to come back, I will—how's that?"

"Let's go out another way. I wouldn't want to stir up any animosity for taking you away."

"You know an exit route?"

"I never go anywhere without one." She led him to the terrace, and he climbed down the brick side, then offered his hands to help her.

"Like two thieves," he said.

"Your coat," she called out as they crossed the street.

"If I don't return, Irene can take care of a coat. She'd like any excuse to call me."

"I'll bet."

His car's interior smelled like leather, the seats were burgundy. He asked about her mother, but she waved away the question. "I don't know how doctors manage. All that suffering you see, and you can't feel any of it."

When he asked about her work, she said she had a degree in studio art; her professor had told her about the job.

"I wouldn't have taken you for an artist. Maybe it's the high heels, your neat skirt. I'd like to see your work someday." She blushed at that, hoping he didn't notice in the dark car. They were parked in front of McLean Gardens, her red-brick apartment building for women working in the government.

She could have asked him in but didn't know what was proper. Would the front parlor be empty? And what if it was? Who might see them and would they care? They stayed in the car. He was thirty, older than he looked. He said both of his parents were deceased and he'd never been close to his younger brother. This singularity surprised her. She'd guessed a bevy of siblings around him, a boisterous, stern father above, a carping but generous mother behind. Maybe it was his effortless smile, his stance of open legs and animated arms. For her part, she said she rarely saw her sister, eight years older, married and a mother of three. She didn't mention that she'd never quite forgiven Viola for moving away, leaving Audrey alone with their ailing mother, her melancholy.

When the rain subsided, she said she should be going. He asked for her telephone number. They set out together from the car to the portico, fat raindrops starting again. "Your hair," he said, lifting his hand to touch it, then pulling away—his only tentative move of the night. She blushed again. She knew he meant the rain might ruin her hair, but she felt his gesture, for days afterward, like a kiss.

3

From her purse she pulled a soft leather-skinned book, a vial of water, her small palette of colors, and a brush. In the Corcoran's still rooms, empty but for an entire world within each frame, it was impossible to know a war was going on. There was something threatening in the quiet, the lie of it. Maybe it was wrong to care about beauty, to preserve it, at a time like this. She'd heard of museums being looted, art stolen, perhaps destroyed, in Europe. But she couldn't help wanting to draw something pleasing. And unlike the rest of the gallery, this room of student work featured paintings signed mostly by women. Women on the home front, who could enroll in classes that were likely taught by women. These weren't self-portraits by beginners, or the technical exercises of draped cloths with crosshatched, intricate folds. Some of them were astonishingly beautiful.

Standing before a cluster of rooftops, angles upon angles, shadows and light, sky and a tree, the paint thick and raw on the canvas, she laid her own lines, wet her brush. Wiping a strand of hair from her forehead with the back of her hand, she flushed warmly under her coat. Blue ran on the page, fast and concentrated. That wouldn't do. She turned her book so the side was now the top of the image—her mistake now an advantage—with a roofline on the crease of the binding.

Her professor had said of her art: *Done with a sure hand. You have talent.* Audrey had thrilled at these words—a frisson not unlike falling in love.

A feeling she knew, maybe for the first time. As she drew and painted, she imagined Ben shadowing her every move. Even now as she took off her coat and laid it on a bench in the center of the room, he was here. Why was that such a part of being in love, the importance of being seen? The lover as eyewitness, always privy to the most favorable angle—her cheek turned just so, eyes downcast, a coy smile. She had come here this morning because she had felt herself slipping, falling too easily into his gaze. All week she had preferred to lie in his arms, in her imagination, rather than paint.

She moved on to other shapes—a ballerina's foot, a pear, a doorway—filling three spreads before she'd made her way around the room. When would she call herself a true artist? When she first sold a painting, or first exhibited her work? Maybe her intense desire to draw defined her already.

And when would she see Ben again? After regular outings each weekend for more than a month, there had been silence from him since last Sunday's buffet of suckling pig. She painted several versions of the grisly piglet early in the week, then moved on to sketching Ben from memory. But when he didn't call, she spent the remaining evenings smoking ceaselessly in her room.

Two elderly men passed by the entrance, breaking the spell. No longer was the space hers. She sighed deeply, as if she'd forgotten to breathe while she worked. Gathering her things, she went outdoors, where sparrows and starlings called shrilly above the cars. Flowers on trees had come and gone; branches were fully leafed. In the sharpening light, she sketched the cornice of the gallery's rotunda, the head of Athena protruding from the main roofline, and one of the lions, the sleeping one, by the entrance. She walked north, past the Old Executive Office building, all self-consciousness lost. In the middle of a sidewalk, she sketched the bark of a tree, a crenellated awning, two Black men talking next to a telephone box. Along a sweet curve of New Hampshire Avenue, she paused to draw an iris bouquet, its stems stuffed through the mail slot of a townhouse. Such a wry, comical image—was it a gift, or the rejection of one? She kept walking, glad for her new shoes, wedges that didn't make her feet ache.

At a corner she drew a wrought-iron gate, its scrolls leading to circles, straight lines that landed in squares, arrow-tipped finials. Meager shrubbery against dingy brick buildings. A hospital, she saw now. And the sign: YOUR BLOOD CAN SAVE HIM! A pair of nurses approached the main gate, their white uniforms visible under capes. One heavy, the other slender—this one knitted as she walked, not dropping a stitch as she turned up the curved drive.

"Come, come. In before the lunch crowd," said the heavyset one, "and you'll avoid a line." Clearly the nurse assumed Audrey was there to donate blood. And hadn't Ben said that was the best thing she could do for the war effort? Walter Reed Hospital was always in need of blood— he had called it plasma, a word that made her queasy. But she had left her own mother, sick and bedridden, to be cared for by others so that she could come here to be an artist. Not to help with the war effort, though that was the pretense. New York would have been too costly to justify with the war going on. In Washington she was helping. Every weekday she rode a streetcar down to the Library of Congress, where she sat in a windowless room, inspecting, repairing, and cataloguing enemy film. For anyone she met, for her mother especially, this stated purpose was important. A reason greater than becoming an artist. But donating blood—Audrey would faint. Famished from the long walk, she thought to flag down a taxi.

Their backs to her, the nurses seemed to forget about her. But then the knitter turned around and, skillfully letting go her pale pink wool, summoned Audrey with her forefinger. Her expression, wisely soothing, didn't take account of Audrey's paintbrush and book. She seemed not to notice what Audrey was holding in her hands.

The room where blood would be taken—this seemed more and more certain—was on the right. "Along here," the thin nurse said, hanging up her cape and motioning for Audrey to sit against the wall in a wooden chair and wait her turn. She had a view of the whole room, a dozen white-dressed nurses hinged at the waist over rows of cots. A ghostly geometry. Her body heaved slightly with the smell of alcohol, the idea of needles pricking her skin. Bloodletting came to mind. It hadn't been too many years since such things were done. She tried squinting, blurring her vision. She could do this.

"Not like you're going to the leeches," the little nurse said, leading her by the elbow.

"You read my mind."

"All you girls think war is something that happens far, far away," she said, but kindly.

Lying on a cot, Audrey held her breath and closed her eyes. A nurse fingered the crook of her elbow for a vein. "You're a tough one," she said, "your veins buried deep." The needle stuck and then it didn't. Audrey exhaled, opened her eyes.

"Jellef's?"

The girl on the cot next to her was pointing to her shoes. "Your yellow wedges," she said. "I bought them at Jellef's on Thursday."

"Sale rack at Garfinckel's," Audrey said. "I can attest to their comfort. Not a blister after several miles."

"Mine are still in the box, so that's good to know. Who are you bleeding for?"

Audrey must have looked confused, because the girl answered her own question: "I've got a brother over there. This measly pint is the least I can do."

"I was recruited at the door, nearly against my will. I've heard it's one of the best things we can do." She wanted to bring Ben, with his medical clout, into the conversation, but she resisted. "And maybe this will help your brother—though I hope he never needs it. What do you hear from him? I'm Audrey, by the way."

Saltines and Dixie cups of water were brought around on trays.

"I'm Lucille. And I wish I heard from Jimmy more, but when he writes he always tells me he's getting plenty to eat." Her light, slightly frizzed hair was pulled away from her face by a gold metal clip with some rust showing through.

"Up slowly," the nurse said to Audrey, her grip perfunctory as she nodded toward the next person in line. "Take your time." To Lucille she said, "You don't look big enough to even be giving blood. You can't weigh but a pint yourself."

But it was Audrey who felt lightheaded. She righted herself by holding on to the cot. "I hope no one expects me to do that again." She was at least half a foot taller than Lucille.

"Maybe you need more to eat?" Lucille pulled a wax-paper-wrapped sandwich from her purse.

"Oh no—I won't take your lunch."

"Which way are you going? We could share." Two more women headed toward them to claim their spaces.

"I didn't think to bring anything. I've been sightseeing on my day off."

Lucille let out a small groan. Even though it was Saturday, her office required a full day; this was her lunch hour. Audrey's office let workers alternate Saturdays off each month. Walking a few blocks together before finding a grassy square, they exchanged this information easily, along with where they were from, their jobs, their living arrangements, all much the same line of talking Audrey had done with everyone she'd met since her arrival in Washington.

"You sound like you're from the South," she said.

"North Carolina," Lucille said. "Another country. But my father heard of the jobs program and signed me up. This sure beats starting off as a schoolteacher. You don't mind sitting on the ground, do you?"

"You probably have a soldier somewhere, someone besides your brother."

Lucille's mouth tightened. "No, not a soldier." She was freckled, with hooded small eyes.

"Ah, but someone."

"Someone"—Lucille handed Audrey half her sandwich, cream cheese and olive—"who no one wants me to have."

"Now, that sounds interesting."

"Or maybe that's a silly reason to want someone. Maybe that's why I do." Lucille bit into the sandwich. "Love him," she said, shielding her mouth as she ate.

"He's not married, is he?"

"You've heard too many soap operas."

"Then why's he off limits?"

"He's terribly old." Lucille shuddered in mock horror. "As my daddy would say."

"How old is 'terribly' old?"

"Old enough to be my father. What about you?"

"You're changing the subject."

"Forty-seven," Lucille whispered.

Audrey let out a laugh that she quickly cupped with her hand. That was old. "Decidedly May-December. Where on earth did you two meet?"

Lucille drew her chin back, looking offended. "In a tree." Then she started smiling, twirling strands of her hair as she talked about him, Arthur. She wasn't attractive in a conventional way, but her blue irises and her full dark mouth made Audrey want to look. She was sixteen, she was saying, when she'd climbed a tree to save her kitten, not realizing she couldn't manage her way down while holding it. Arthur climbed a ladder and reached through the leaves and branches to rescue them both.

"Very romantic."

"I miss home."

"Not me. I would have done anything to get away. Even decline a marriage proposal since it meant I might never leave."

"Doesn't sound like true love. Maybe a good story?"

"Not really. I don't much like disappointing people." In one way, turning Reginald down had felt like such a victory—Audrey couldn't stay in Ridgelea where he wanted to be. She would never have gotten out from under her mother's gloom and illness that swelled through the house after her father left. But thinking of Reginald pained her. When the undergrads and teachers thinned out at the boys' college across the lake in her hometown, he and a few others audited art classes on the girls' campus. Some nights they painted together. He rendered volcanoes on canvases, bright, thick blasts of color, and he listened to jazz. For a time she had welcomed his nearly wordless passion for her body, as prodigal and intense as the oils dripping from his brushes. After she refused his proposal, he joined the Navy. She was sorry for that.

"And you've no one here?" Lucille asked.

"If there were anyone, he would be leaving soon anyway. At least you don't have to worry about that. Best not to get attached, right?"

"Is that from handling film?" Lucille pointed to Audrey's fingers, stained with dark ink.

"I draw sometimes, for fun. Looks filthy." She held out her hands, large, thick-knuckled.

"You ever sell anything?"

"Someday, maybe. I'm not good enough yet."

"I'm not sure we're the best judges of what we do."

"What is it you want to do?"

"Not hunch over a typewriter like I will all afternoon. I want the simplest things. Fresh air, days like this, with children, lots of them, running around outside. Instead I'm in a building where each tiny window lets in enough air for a single lung. Luckily we're a nice group of girls, because we're all fighting for the same molecule of oxygen." Lucille stood, brushing crumbs from her skirt.

"I know what you mean. I can't turn around in my apartment without bumping into my roommate. Never mind trying to paint something without her leaning over my shoulder." Audrey pulled out a pen and a piece of scrap paper, wrote her office number and address on it. "I hope to run into you again sometime."

"Audrey Howell," Lucille read. "Don't you want this?" She was looking at the other side, a profile drawing of a soldier in his helmet. "That could be Jimmy. You're good."

Audrey shook her head.

"I'd give you my number but our offices are moving to the hinterlands soon—the Pentagon," said Lucille.

"I hear you'll have air conditioning." Audrey smiled. "Well, you know how to find me. Thanks for the sandwich. You really saved me."

"And I have a good story to explain why I'm late. So long."

Pear trees and spooked kittens, fresh air and children. The girl was so easy and natural, as if she had just sprung from this ground. And her simple wants. Audrey couldn't say what *she* wanted exactly, but it wasn't simple. It wasn't to be back at home with a passel of kids running around. She was different from other women in this way; she felt it keenly. Not lacking, but unique. Maybe Lucille understood that. Ben had noticed. She was glad she hadn't mentioned him, relieved for not getting carried away.

Oh, she still wanted him. She most certainly wanted his adoration of her, in a way she had never hoped for anyone else's. She wanted him—and more. Work, art, freedom, a bigger city—she wanted whatever was unlike anything she'd left behind.

Ben called later that day, making a date for mid-week. But when she showed up at his door, having insisted he not go out of his way to pick her up from work, he was still in his white lab coat, the expression on his face revealing he'd forgotten the time. "Hold on," he said, walking away, then waved his arm. "Come with me. You might as well see the train wreck." Only once had she been to his shingle-style house on this leafy street. He had come by it through his mother, who had died almost two years ago. Audrey knew he drove her car, that wine-dark Zephyr, ate off her china, and slept on his childhood sheets. She followed him upstairs but met a mountain of disorder at the top. Everything he'd emptied out of the linen and medicine closet at the end of the hall—towels, rolls of bandages, Mercurochrome, alcohol—lay strewn across the floor. He put his face in his hands. "I can't find it. My father's first aid kit from the first war. My mother told me it was here and to take it with me if I ever had to go."

"Have you gotten word?" She felt her stomach tighten. That's what this was about—he was leaving.

"No, nothing like that. I rushed home, realizing I'd never located it since she told me where it was before she died. I panicked."

"I'm sure it's here somewhere." She looked around. In this large house with its rooms full of drawers and closets, he might never find it.

He sat down on the end of one of the guest beds, crossing his legs and lighting a cigarette. His eyes were red; he might have been crying. "I should have taken more care. I never got to know him, you know. He made it through the war all right, which was why my mother wanted me to have his kit. But he came home to influenza. I was six. He died one day and the next I started first grade. I cried like a baby that first week at school. So my mother told me later."

Audrey smiled. She went to him, kissing his cheek.

"The worst day." He looked up at her, his eyes misting. "I lost a patient, right on the table. He bled out. I don't know what happened. Father of four."

"There are so many you've saved. Think of them."

He wrapped his arm around her waist, leaning into her. "I hope nothing ever happens to you."

She held him tighter and thought, yes, she wanted him—for keeps.

4

Wait for me. Arthur had told her one o'clock, after his appointment north of town but in time for a midday dinner, and so Lucille waited amid people coming and going through the hotel. The light bolting off the revolving glass entry doors, the slick shine of the marble floor, all the gloss and glare worked to fracture whatever surety she'd had about coming and telling him things he would not want to hear, things she didn't really want to say. She didn't want to wait, because the waiting was a dreading, the worst kind of waiting. It was already quarter past the hour.

Many times she had waited for him at the orchard's edge after seeing his hat left on his porch, a signal that he would meet her there. The trumpet vine up a poplar marked their private entrance to the woods, once full of trees cut down to build the orchard house, now thickened up again, wild and overgrown. Her father had never muddied his boots in the fields until that day. How many times had she heard him say to her brother, "Jimmy, you tell the men how to do the work, but you never, ever let them see you doing it yourself." But there was her father, something out of an inconceivable dream, past the rows of order—the progressive ripening from Baldwin to McIntosh, from older, larger trees to saplings, such care that went into it!—digging a hole with one of the men, next to a clump of trees turned on their sides, roots still in burlap. Lucille recognized his contradiction just as she and Arthur were leaving their own dream—their own dishonesty—with thistles and leaves they'd failed to brush off, walking out of darkness into light. They weren't holding hands; their paths might already have diverged by the time her father noticed them. But nothing was chaste about the woods behind them. Her father had his riding breeches on, his lace-up boots, and a bow tie. To use the shovel, he'd taken off his jacket with the carnation in the lapel, his signature.

"I will never tell your mother," he said later, his back turned to her as he stood behind his office desk, looking out the window. Sunlight, filled with dust motes, shone all around him. "You break her heart."

When her mother learned Lucille was leaving, she let out a piercing, single cry and then nothing, as if the pain was severe but had limits. Already she had a son at war. The cry seemed an acknowledgment of fact rather than an aspect of mourning. Now she would clothe and feed the third child remaining at home until she too departed, taking the dress on her back and the nourishment in her belly away.

Lucille had almost completed a business school certificate when her father insisted she leave home. Threw her out. He hadn't laid a hand on her, but that's how she felt, hurled in the air onto the concrete of Washington. She wouldn't sit for her exams at the business school, she wouldn't earn her certificate. First in the class, and salutatorian of her high school—none of that mattered. "You're on your own now," were his words. It had all happened so quickly, the wind knocked out of her, that even now she had to catch her breath thinking of it. She had cried to Arthur, "I won't ever be able to return."

"Time, give it time."

That was early spring, this was summer. She had not seen Arthur since, and she had worked hard to forget him, to turn herself against him. Despite the afternoon heat, she'd walked to the bus and then to the hotel, refusing his offer to pick her up at her apartment, unwilling to answer questions from her roommates regarding his age: Is this your father? Your uncle? Most of the time she forgot how old he was—he was all she had ever known. Her feet ached from the walk, but she didn't want to be sitting down, at a disadvantage, when he saw her. It would be quick, this dinner, and then Arthur would be on his way in a nursery truck, leftover shrubs and tree limbs springing from its bed, the debris of a farmer. A horticulturalist, he called himself.

And yet she had made herself as appealing as possible, rolling her hair last evening in preparation, and putting on a cotton-pique sundress and jacket, a pattern of flitting magenta butterflies. In front of the mirror, she had practiced her tongue against her palate, *Never. Not you. E-nough.* Whatever was asked, she would say no. Won't you write me back? No. When can I see you again? Never. Do you love me? No. The months since she had seen him had built up like a thick shellac. She could resist him.

Women in feathered hats and pearl-buttoned gloves swarmed around her, along with men in uniform or soft-pile suits, their tanned leather valises and plush millinery, their finely welted leather shoes. She never saw these things on the city streets, nor in Pomona. Moving closer to the reception area, as if to rub against such luxury, she fought an urge to stroke a rabbit's foot dangling from one of the luggage handles, for good luck, or courage.

And then there he was, lucent under the hotel lobby's spreading chandeliers. So familiar and thus welcome. She broke into a smile—that's how she felt, her resolve broken just by the sight of him. She'd half expected him in work pants and brogans caked with dirt, but he wore seersucker. He attended church, after all. The heat from outside drifted in with him: His lips were full and red with exertion, his forehead vulnerably damp and creased where his straw fedora had been. From his hand hung a frayed shopping bag. Pulled out of the safe grooves of her thoughts where he usually resided, he now was flung before her in a public way. She'd had nerve enough to come by only half believing he would be here. In her city. Standing on the same ground as she. Hearing the same words, the same music as she heard. Reaching out and touching her, if he dared.

He did, of course. He gripped her by both arms and pulled her into his warmth, unable to contain himself. It was this energy that she had never known what to do with. Something in Arthur allowed him to spill over like this and move her, as now, nearly to tears. When he pressed her head against his chest, she gave in to him.

"Shall we?" he said brightly, extending his arm and leading her to the restaurant that lay sunken in another great expanse behind the lobby. Passing the orchestra, three rows deep, he turned to survey the tables with white tablecloths, gilded bamboo-backed chairs, eight-armed candelabra on the piano—warming and overwhelming all at once. "I've never in all my life."

"Welcome to Washington."

He was still trim, with thinning, light-brown hair covering his head and skin golden-rose from the sun. The decades difference in ages, his forty-seven years to her twenty-one that always disappeared when they were together, seemed more obvious in the open like this. But no one stared. No one cared.

They sat. He crossed his legs and slung his elbow over the chair's back. "Relax," he said, nodding at how she leaned into the table and him, her hands hidden under her. "On the edge of your seat there, you look like you're about to fly away."

To read the menu, he put on spectacles, his hazel eyes blooming larger behind the magnified glass, and looked still younger. She waited for some whistling over the number of goblets at each place setting, or the prices, but none came. Elderly men in tails swirled, asking, "Water or tea, ma'am? Hot or iced? Lemon, ma'am?" against the sound of stringed instruments plucked in the background. She wanted to enjoy it.

"About to find out how the other half lives," Arthur said affably, closing his menu. He leaned over, touching her waist. "I was worried, after I heard about your appendix. Must have been scary. But you look well."

She had been scared, spending a week in the hospital, alone. Her roommates, Greta and Shirley, visited a few times, bringing cards from the office and a letter from Arthur, writing of this plan to visit. At first, she had savored her evasion of him. He couldn't find her if he wanted to. Days went by. But when she reread his words that recalled a particular afternoon on the banks of Buffalo Creek, grass against her legs, a single stalk across her cheek, she felt herself sinking, a familiar capitulation. Of course she would see him. Her short message, planning where to meet, would fit on a postcard, but a postcard was too easily read by others. In addition to a sealed envelope, a note required her signature, "fox," the name he called her after a female rodeo rider. The first time he saw Lucille she was stepping into his cupped hands—this was his story of their beginning—to rise onto the back of one of the farm's slow mares. She might have been five years old.

He was telling her how he hadn't fished on Lake Opora lately, nor had he been able to get to the coast—"all the accounts are still dried up thataways."

She wondered about her father—if anyone could detect any loss in him, her banishment. But Arthur wouldn't mention him. The two men lived parallel lives at the nursery. They had always stayed out of each other's way, and now more than ever. She thought of the peach trees sagging with fruit and the fallen pinkish-white apple blossoms blanketing the southwest corner, all since she'd been there last winter. By now much of the fruit was harvested. This was the time of year she and Jimmy bowled the rot of each crop down the rows. It was not improbable that she had, at one time or another, hung from branches in every tree. How beautiful her home was, and yet she couldn't remember ever remarking on that fact until she'd left it. Now it was all she told people when they asked where she was from.

"I have sad news," Arthur was saying when their iced tea arrived. "Liberty died. Her big heart gave out two weeks ago. I couldn't leave her much before now. I knew it was coming. Never again." She knew he meant he would not get another animal, he wouldn't have another thing die on him like that. He reached for Lucille's hand.

"I'm so sorry." Liberty had followed Arthur everywhere.

He went on to tell how he buried her next to other Pomona dogs that had died, after bathing her and covering her with a blanket she'd lain on in his truck. It was this care of animals that had astonished Lucille years before. The way he held her kitten in both hands, rubbing her fiercely, looking her in the eyes, whispering, had moved Lucille. To the men in her family, a barn cat was only as good as the last mouse it caught.

With Liberty gone, he was more alone than ever in his bungalow, since his wife's and son's deaths four years ago. "God, I'm a mess, aren't I?" he would say to Lucille, his drink sweating a ring of moisture into his tweed armchair. "This story will never change, so why do I keep telling it? You might change the story. You're my hope."

The way his sorrow overflowed into their time together had confused her. He had pursued Lucille before his wife, Maura, had died, and there had always been a firm line between the two, his family and Lucille. Was he crying over his love for his dead wife, whom he'd betrayed, or was he only mourning Peter? Or maybe he was grieving because he had loved neither enough.

She'd been such a stupid girl, thinking herself at the center of the scene. But it was when he sat crying that she felt his sorrow well up in her, as though it were her own.

For a while, one picture remained of Maura, her smile slightly out of focus, but then it was put away. She had thick alabaster wrists, exposed between her coat sleeves and gloved hands on the steering wheel when she drove Lucille home. She had hired Lucille to care for her aging mother in the afternoons. After Maura died, Arthur covered the mostly bare walls with images of fish, forests, and game, antlers smooth and fair as whittled birch. And horses. There were more pictures of horses than anything else. Lucille always associated the formerly blank walls with his wife, someone unfinished.

All she knew of his son, Peter, was the closed door to his bedroom. On top of Arthur's chest of drawers she'd once seen a pile of feathers and asked their purpose. "Peter collected them. Chicken feathers."

"What a band." He grinned now. He pulled his hand away, jiggling his leg like a boy.

What did Lucille know of inexpressible grief? There had been none in her family—unless you counted Jimmy, one bullet away from death on a battlefield. For her, other people's tragedies had always seemed open for dissection. In the past she had no shyness about asking Arthur the most morbid things. What had his son's and wife's bodies looked like, for instance, when he arrived at the scene of the accident. Not now. Losing her home had hurt. Her father's love retracted. Leaving Arthur. She reached for his hand.

"How were you able to finagle a trip to Rockville?"

"Finagle? Is that what you think I'd do for you? There was a problem with the last large order, so this was a hand delivery, a way of smoothing over our mistake. It always helps the relationship to meet face to face. Right, fox?"

He squeezed her hand, then let go.

"I'm glad you didn't drive all this way just for me. How long will it take you to get back tonight?"

"I won't be driving back tonight. When you told me where you wanted to meet, I booked a room."

"Here?"

"You don't think I paid top dollar? Everything's negotiable." He drank his tea.

Lucille tasted the bite of grilled steak in her mouth, the burnt-juicy flavor she'd missed for months. She chewed slowly. They had the whole night before them now, and she sank back in her seat with the realization. The words wouldn't come now, all she'd planned to say.

"I brought you something." He pulled a large box from the bag.

"This is too big. It's too much."

"Go on, open it."

She untied a red satin bow, rubbed her fingers across the raised Montaldo's sticker, and lifted the lid. Inside was a wide-brimmed straw hat, its shallow crown wreathed in daisies. It was lovely, a little of the countryside but sophisticated enough to wear here. He lifted it out and made to put it on her head.

"Let me take it to the ladies' room," she began. "It's wonderful, really. I adore it, but you shouldn't have."

"No, no, no, sit back down. You can try it on later."

"Are you sure?"

"Don't you like it?"

"Maybe we can sit by the pool later. I can wear it then."

"Now that I see you, I'm not even sure I want you to wear it." He tapped her nose with his finger. "Your freckles, they've up and left your face. All that office work."

"Well, that's a surefire way to make me put it on." She smiled. "I'll go ahead and be excused. Order me a gimlet, why don't you."

"Let's go upstairs first, then have a drink," he said, smiling.

"Soon," she said, already turning away.

5

The only vacant seats by the hotel swimming pool had no umbrellas, but Audrey welcomed the hot sun. After unspooling images all week at the bottom of the Jefferson Building, she felt like an undeveloped negative herself, undefined and translucent. Exposed to the light outdoors, and under Ben's gaze, she felt her flesh and features coming into focus.

"If you could have seen me, playing plumber at the house," he was saying. "It's not surgery, but it's not damn far off. I was laughing in spite of myself, with every tool around me."

His house had become familiar to her, a place she frequented in her mind more often than she'd visited. His surgical practice would soon give him up to the Navy, and in a matter of weeks, maybe more, he would go overseas, leaving Audrey and the house behind. Between her and Ben there wasn't an immediate branch of family nearby, which didn't bother her, complicated as her own family was. He answered to no one, there were no obligatory Sunday afternoon visits or errands. Instead the tall empty house beckoned at the end of their outings. In the daytime, light filled the house. French doors at one end led to more floor-to-ceiling windows, a slate-floored conservatory that would make a perfect studio. An easel set up in the northeastern corner, she could see it now. And in the evenings they watched for shooting stars from his back porch. Why shouldn't they spend time together, unchaperoned? They were lucky. Most couples she knew were courting in borrowed cars, behind dingy curtains in boardinghouse lobbies, or only in their minds, thoughts scratched out on sad, blue, tissue-thin pages. They could have drinks on his sleek sofa, set them aside and kiss for what seemed like hours. He could lead her upstairs to his bedroom.

Which he had not done. Lying next to him now, their lounge chairs touching, Audrey was aware of his hands, how they raked his wavy hair, still wet from the pool. A Doris Day song, "Bewitched, Bothered, and Bewildered," played faintly from the band indoors, and she gently beat her foot to the tune.

His hands had found their way to her before, after dancing, to her cheek, then neck, up from her fingertips to the crook of her arm, and then under her blouse, the lightest touch that left her wanting. He had experience, and in recognizing this, she admitted her own. It was impossible to think of these same hands now, his fingers absentmindedly sliding between wooden slats of his chair, with indifference.

"Two tonsillectomies," he was saying, recounting cases from the week. She thought of bodies he'd explored, cavities and vessels his fingers had probed, skin he had lacerated and sewn.

Doctors had taken her mother apart and tried to put her back together. None of them explained why she never got better. Her mother believed them all brilliant. Audrey tried not to think of her parents, knowing she would find them now as she had always found them. Her father had escaped from that irksome, stale air of her mother's house when Audrey was in high school. She had seen his boardinghouse room only once, his bone brush and bowl of shaving cream set like a still life on a small shelf above the sink, aglow under the only light in the room. She understood why he wished to live there. On any given morning he might stop by to drink a cup of coffee with her mother, then go around fixing small things in the house. Not because there wasn't help or money to fix them, but because there were other things he couldn't fix. Her mother lay in bed, her face furrowed and feverish, bobby pins holding little curls of hair tight above her ears, a tin of loose powder nearby, the bed banked by camphor, magnesium salts, and a dish of potpourri to cover the sour air. She was all vanity and its opposite. And in her needs, her demands, she had driven everyone away. Her two sisters, Audrey's aunts, lived nearby and tried to care for her, but they too had grown frustrated—and frightened—by her recurrent refusals to eat. Now it was only a hired nurse who endured her.

Audrey would never let anyone see her helpless.

People crowded around the pool, undressed out of the drabby blues and khakis the war had covered them in, desperate to idle in summer, early July. A girl sat down on the lounge chair next to Ben, and he watched her. She wore a white bathing suit, a little ribbon of purity against the color around the pool. It also suggested undergarments. She was small-boned with a boyish figure, and her coloring was neutral as bark. She was nearly unremarkable except for her smoothly sculpted nose and large, demonstrative eyes. She moved gracefully, her dainty fingers flicking down corners of her windblown towel and brushing stray hairs from her eyes. Ben still hadn't looked away.

"I see you," she said to him. "I do. She's beautiful. Go on, ask her for a swim."

"Aren't you in a mood all of a sudden?"

"Can't blame you if you want a little sip of her beauty. Isn't that what we're all thirsty for in this town? Say, aren't you going to get us one of those drinks with a little umbrella in it?" The pool gave a view over Rock Creek Park's trees, which looked soft enough to lie on. A breeze picked up and she lay back onto the warm chair. "Just keeping you on your toes."

He'd told her the other night, "I've been playing the same notes for years, the same kind of girls, dates, but I could never get the melody to resolve. Not the way it does with you." It had sounded so good to her, but maybe it was just one of his lines. His allure was just enough gallantry, not too much. That early trickling of attention from him had steadied into a gentle stream, but when she first asked Irene about him, her friend raised an eyebrow: "Confirmed bachelor, beware." Squinting into the sun, Audrey saw him still watching the girl.

He stood up and nodded toward the pool.

"I'm more reptile than fish," she said. "I like to bake in the sun, and I don't have gills." He reached for her hands anyway, pulling her up from her chair, and led her into the shallow end.

The girl in the white suit walked by, suspended like a strand of pearls out of the corner of Audrey's eye, but Audrey kept her eyes on Ben, who again reached for her, pulled her under to where they sat on the bottom of the pool and came up for air, the underwater silence slamming into the roar of broken water and poolside clamor. Down again, where he tugged playfully at her ankles, and up. But when she shot back to the surface, gasping, some shudder of fear ascended with her. She thought of the nitrate film she worked with, highly flammable. Because nitrate produced oxygen as it burned, it couldn't be put out once it caught fire. She'd heard of an entire reel burning underwater. She couldn't get the image out of her mind. A wheel of fire spinning to the bottom of the sea.

But Ben, who was not looking at anyone else but her, cradled her in his arms and spun her so that she skimmed across the water, like a ship circling the globe, which made him the world. When he left, only water would be between them, clear and traversable.

After changing into clothes for drinks indoors, they made for the hotel bar, where by late afternoon there was always a crowd, soldiers coming and going, dancing. They sat next to each other in a booth and he ordered gin and tonic for her and a bourbon and water for himself. Against one wall was the band, and already it was too loud to make out all of what he was saying. She followed the current, not so much his words. She knew he couldn't hear a thing, but that didn't stop him from calling out to other officers walking by. He never stopped smiling. "Hey you, Chuck, some girl's gonna need a shoeshine after you're done."

The music relaxed her. She swished her shoulders, shuffled her feet under the table, and lit a cigarette, waiting for him to finish another drink. She disliked it when people called Washington a small town. She was only a couple of hours from home in Ridgelea, but she might as well be in Paris.

When he led her toward the empty dance floor, he said into her ear, "Are you going to try to flip over my back tonight, like last time? Don't try anything fancy, this isn't a wrestling match."

Like a child, she couldn't contain her laughter. She felt herself losing her edges, even though what he said wasn't so funny, only a little funny. The band belted the first notes of a new tune. She trained her eye on his hand, keeping her feet moving, her hips tilting, their bodies turning toward and away from each other in a buried rhythm. She no longer knew where he left off and she began. His hand appeared and she reached for it, following where it went, over his head, hers, his shoulders, by his waist. She kept herself fairy-light, as though he were lifting her—and it seemed at moments they were aloft. This was the key, her lightness, his lead. She wished the girl in the white bathing suit could see them now. This was dancing. This was love.

The music ended, and during the lull their arms hung at their sides before a slower song began. He guided her to the edge of the now-thronged dance floor, where they swayed together, her head pressed to his shoulder. She knew this was the best time to ask him, here in the middle of the impersonal crowd, the question she felt was always fastened to them, like a tail to its kite: When are you leaving? And under that one lay a dozen more about their future. She had thought after giving up Reginald, and Ridgelea, she might never marry. She had been all right with that. But that was before Ben.

His chin rested lightly on her head, and when she pulled away he seemed in such a happy state of dreaming, his eyes closed; she couldn't ask him now. Another tune started up, this one a jitterbug, and everyone around them like jumping jacks. Pushing and pulling was how the dance went, and she thought that was his allure too, how he pushed and pulled back, offered himself, then withheld. No, she would wait.

They laughed at each other and others around them, faces filmy with sweat and an affect of seduction—or maybe just concentration, all energy shooting into their limbs. Audrey knew they were suspended in some artificial zone, free of the war, but still in jeopardy. She gave it her all, leaping into each step as hard as she could, nodding her head to the beat as if the beat pumped her own heart. Yes, being in this city was like being on vacation. Ben's reach for her now, twirling her in one spot, stunned and thrilled her like the dance floor undulating with men and women, the waves of sound coming toward her, the energy palpable and sustaining. She would never tire of it, of him.

When the notes softened and stretched, he said, "Let's go home," and even the suggestion that they shared a place called home sent her soaring. She glided on his arm toward the door. They wove through the tables, a faint applause for the band trailing behind, but she felt like it was meant for them.

6

Arthur had settled the bill and was waiting for her outside the ladies' room. They passed the band, making their way to a small booth with two drinks already on the table.

"You don't waste any time."

"What are nice hotels for? But I'm losing my patience, if that's what you mean." He smiled. When they were both seated again, he said, "It's time, you know."

"Time for what?"

"For us to marry."

"I'm here." She shook her head. Couldn't they just enjoy the night they had? "I have a job now."

"Voluntarily. Voluntarily," he said, stringing out the repetition. He looked weary, as though he'd worn himself down with this fact, the rejection within it.

"Not so. Why do you say that? You know I can't go home."

"My point exactly." He leaned in now, as if he had her on the end of one of his fishing lines. "What's the matter with my home?"

She had for years pictured his home as hers, his yard the one her children would skip through, swing in. But it would never happen, not while her father was alive. She had known Arthur would be hard for her family to accept, given how much older he was. Once she was through school, of marriageable age, and the war was over, the sentiment might change. He was a decent man, a widower now. But finally she understood there was more to her father's resistance.

"You've known my father a long time. Since you were both young."

When she added nothing more, he said, "Not everyone gets a second chance."

She didn't reply to that, but everyone they knew in this story had gotten exactly that. She had never talked to Arthur about his past with her father, how years ago they had loved the same woman, and she wasn't going to now. To do so would make her complicit in some sort of betrayal. She'd already been complicit enough. "He's not going to change his mind."

Dishes and flatware clanked. The music transitioned to a Cab Calloway tune and grew louder.

A photographer came along to take their picture. They tilted their heads together. "You're going to want this one," the girl said, grinning, but Lucille knew she said this to everyone. While Arthur paid, Lucille filled in only his name on the recipient line, not an address.

Lucille looked over the girl's shoulder to a couple stepping on the dance floor, spinning and twirling. They might have come from the pool, the girl's wet hair up in a chignon, her dress yellow. She moved like a buttery gem across the floor. A magnetic, unshifting space held them together, drawing Lucille in. The man pressed his face in to the girl's neck, eyes closed, and when he opened them, he smiled at Lucille. She looked away. It was the doctor, Ben Bray, who had removed her appendix. She shouldn't be surprised. At the hospital he was surrounded by recovering women who streamed out from him in every direction like blades on a fan. He had flirted with her, probably with all his patients. The couple spun and she caught a flash of the girl smiling—she knew her too. She couldn't remember her name just then, but it was the girl she'd met while donating blood.

"Anything is possible, fox. Look at how I love you."

When he said this, which wasn't infrequently, it touched her physically, hitting in a low, vital place.

"Come with me." He would sand away her surface, grind her down to tissue and bone. Many times she had ridden with him in his truck to the banks of Buffalo Creek, having told her mother she was studying the Treaty of Versailles with a classmate. Arthur and she fished together, cooking what they caught over an outdoor fire. By dark, she crept into his house unseen. Sitting on his lap, she cheered him when he was inconsolable, letting him hold her like the child he had lost. Other times she playfully shunned his grasp, inspiring a chase around the furniture, both of them in some primal stance, laughing, fierce, till he caught her in his embrace. What she would give to be back there again.

Now the war had happened to her. And to everyone, it seemed, but him.

"I want to stay here. This is a lovely spot."

The girl dancing with the doctor was wearing yellow shoes, the same cork-soled ones she was wearing when Lucille met her. They had talked about this, how she had bought them at Garfinckel's and Lucille had purchased the same pair from Jellef's. Her pair, still unworn, had been an indulgence that made her feel sick, even now. The girl's skin was the color of clouds shot through with sun, a golden cream. Her broad forehead, like an egg, should have been a detriment but wasn't. She had nearly fainted after giving blood, and Lucille gave away half her lunch, then proceeded to confess her life story, including her love for Arthur. Afterward, she tossed away the girl's number.

Lucille hadn't cared for how that felt, talking about Arthur, giving to a stranger what she'd worked so hard to keep to herself.

He placed his hand on her thigh now, and her face flushed at the prospect of someone noticing this, at her own liquidity under his touch. She didn't look back at the couple dancing; she suddenly didn't want to be seen. "Now," she said, squeezing Arthur's hand.

In the elevator, any uncertainty settled like silt at the bottom of a creek. Two drinks of gin had helped. She'd been alone with him before, but never far enough away from Pomona to be careless. An unintended gift of her father's. When they passed another couple on the same hall as Arthur's room, he greeted them with a smile—feigning legitimacy, his arm now proprietarily around her—as if to welcome other travelers, as if this were his home, as if she were his.

Once inside there was no pretense, certainly no legitimacy. There was speed and not a little force as he moved her closer to the bed, and then with a startling yank of the covers, they were on sheets. He moved smoothly now, and she wondered, as he unbuttoned her dress, kissing whatever shred of bare skin he could reach, how he wasn't interested in making love, only in this, whatever would keep her a virgin. His fingers strummed under her skirt, undoing her hosiery and garter with one deft strike, pushing them gently downward to loll about her ankles in submission. Then his spare touches, so spare. *Does this feel good?* Turning like a scope on her, only her, with his rough-shaven jaw against hers. She didn't mind it, that pleasure-pain rub. Never could she summon an outright affirmation—that would be the sound of guilt. But she closed her eyes to his gaze, to his careful placement of her hand on him, still half clothed. He took so little effort; not so much to ask. It came back to her, his smell, like linen from the line, of sun and earth embedded in the tiny recesses of his skin and now released with their friction. They ended, wilted with exhaustion, faces and legs lit by the moon outside the large window (curtains they'd not bothered to draw), Lucille sinking in the darkness, after the crest of pleasure she'd toppled, into a puddle of shame.

He whispered, "Come home to me, Lucille."

The only thing to do was let him hold her as he slept.

She stroked his head, remembering how in Pomona, after her accounting classes were over for the day, she always walked toward Mrs. Marshall's tailoring shop, which doubled as a lending library. Often she had a book to return or one she wanted to borrow. Lynne Marshall would be behind the counter working her sewing machine, sometimes with two curlers in her hair—no men ever came to the shop, for tailoring or for books. Then Lucille would say bye to Mrs. Marshall, who shouted over the hum of the machine but never lifted her eyes. It seemed necessary to conduct this routine each afternoon on her way to see Arthur. Passing through that shop was part of her becoming invisible.

He let out a long, falling sigh beside her.

Sometimes she lingered on the porch, leaning against the railing and reading the first page of her book. Then she continued walking to the K&W coffee shop, with an uneasy thrill, not unlike the feeling she got before taking a typing test, or diving from a boat into Lake Opora. In the parking lot, there would be his silver Oldsmobile, Arthur in the driver's seat. Before she spotted it, Lucille felt a surge of power, enough to keep walking past. She'd not yet put her eyes on the car, she'd only sensed its color and shape in her peripheral vision. But then a thing snagged at her, like a loop of her sweater's wool catching on a nail, and always she turned to meet Arthur.

Carefully, she rose from the bed. On a sheet of hotel stationery she wrote: *We must not see each other. This is for the best. Please don't make this any harder.* She took the bag with the hat; she wanted it, and part of her wanted him to think of her in it.

Down in the lobby the lone clerk told her all the taxis had gone home. She stared silently at him until he muttered something under his breath about young girls in the city and then picked up the phone.

1973

7

In the small theater, the lights are still up, the curtain down. Lucille chooses a seat far enough back so that anyone onstage—Lake, specifically—will not be able to make her out. She wears a beige peacoat, shapeless and shabby, with a dark-brown pocketbook strapped over her shoulder. Breathless, she clutches it on her lap. Her hair is still blond but shorter than when she last saw Lake; oversized, greenish-gray eyeglasses hide much of her face. She's also thirty pounds heavier. She hardly recognizes herself in the mirror—how could anyone else? Even so, she feels both tiny and exposed, like a moth trapped indoors.

This is as close as she has come to Lake since moving here more than a week ago. She has always known her address, having sent letter after letter—all returned, unread—to various apartments over the years. She has driven by her current one a few times, not yet hoping for an actual encounter. She needs more time to formulate a plan. What Lucille has focused on is settling, pinning herself down to one or two work obligations so that she will be compelled to stay. Loneliness, and the rebukes certain to come, will make remaining here difficult. She gave the doorman her name and number, along with a few letters of reference from former clients in Pomona. Already she has been paid to care for two infirm neighbors, including one she pushes in a wheelchair to a nearby park where they sit together. Sun on your face, the best medicine in the world, she says each day.

Although her letter to Audrey announced her impending arrival, she in fact left Pomona the day she mailed it. She had rented an apartment sight unseen. What did she really need, alone now? A television, to break the silence. A place to park her car. That was all, really. She didn't want to pay for any amenities, as the realtor called them, like the dishwasher Lucille has yet to turn on. One plate, one cup—two hands do the job.

Yesterday she called Audrey on the telephone, which is how she learned Lake is performing tonight in *The Cherry Orchard*—tonight plus three more shows this weekend. She had smiled inwardly, vainly, at this announcement, because of her own connection to an orchard, and the hope that there might be greater meaning in this coincidence.

Pomona doesn't have a theater, but Lucille read the play years ago because—well, a famous play about an orchard. She remembers being disappointed that the land was sold in the end and the owners were portrayed as frivolous people, full of histrionics and petty concerns. They weren't her people at all. She runs her finger down the names of characters. Certainly Lake won't play Madame Ranevsky; perhaps she's Varya, the adopted daughter. But no, the program lists Lake Bray as Charlotta. Lucille pledges to find the script in the public library. She must demonstrate an interest in such things. To understand Lake is to know something of these lights beaming onto the heavy velour curtain of gold, the communion between the viewers and actors—the electric anticipation of them both. Voices in the audience have spread out in a canopy of low-humming sound.

Audrey assured her that Lake knows nothing of her move. But if you have lost something, isn't a part of you always searching for it? When Lake showed up in Pomona ten years ago, Lucille wasn't surprised—she always carried an image of Lake in her mind, and there she was, only in the flesh. Might Lake always look for her on a crowded street, on the bus, in an audience? On her right is a slightly older man, his ankle crossed over his knee so that the crepe rubber sole of his shoe hovers by her thigh. She gently knocks her knee against it. He flinches but she's quick to smile. Lucille has vowed not to speak to anyone, not to call attention to herself, but as usual she gives in to this weakness. "Do you know anything about the play?" she asks.

"Only what my son has told me. He's one of the actors."

She wonders if the entire audience consists only of family members. "Wonderful, which one?"

"Let's see if I can pronounce his name." He laughs.

"Has he enjoyed it? Is he a full-time actor?" She suddenly has a rash of questions, next to this potential reserve of information. But the lights are dimming, the crowd hushing, and she misses the man's whispered response. Another man, younger, with a slender frame, takes the seat on her other side. Only now does she remove her large glasses, seeing the stage better without them. She has a plan to return to all three shows, and then maybe—maybe—after that final performance she will make her presence known. She pictures herself holding out a bouquet of roses to Lake.

On the telephone, Audrey said that Lake did not want them to attend. "'Don't come,' she told me and Ben. Not a good sign. She's not herself." When Lucille pressed, Audrey dismissed her: "I don't know what's going on with her." She was lucky to be talking with Audrey at all. Only since arriving in Washington has she started taking Lucille's calls again. For ten years—ten years!—Audrey hung up the phone as soon as she heard Lucille's voice. But last night after Lucille confided her own disappointments around her daughter Martha's wedding, how her sister had been more the mother of the bride than Lucille, Audrey had shared that Lake was back together with her boyfriend, Ray. "She broke up with him once before, which I didn't understand, but now she won't talk to me about him."

When Lucille told Eva, her younger sister, that she was leaving Pomona, they were walking into a fabric shop. Eva had been going over all the details—the basque waistline, the portrait neckline—of the wedding dress she was making for Martha. Now she was explaining how the bridesmaids would wear fur muffs with their dark-green velvet dresses. But it was hard to imagine a Christmas wedding with the heat swelling up from the black asphalt in the parking lot, Lucille said. She then casually dropped the news into the conversation. "Why now?" asked Eva.

Lucille couldn't give the real reason: After years of failed amends to Lake and Audrey by telephone and mail, she must be held accountable in person. Transplanting herself is her only hope.

Instead, she answered, "For one thing, everything is dying." She didn't just mean her husband, Arthur, who had passed away four years earlier. The textile mill had gone bankrupt; the town was emptying out. The school where she'd once taught was closed, the lending library gone. "You heard Martha say it: 'Mama, soon there'll be no more sick people to take care of.' And now she and Brody will leave too, after the wedding." Eva looked distressed at that fact. Single as she is, she might miss them the most.

Eva's looks could have enticed any man. And no doubt she had plenty of attention from the executives at the chemical corporation in nearby Gloucester where she typed up their correspondence and kept their appointment books. She had her job, her tidy, discrete shelter. She'd been their parents' favorite—the baby. Lucille remembers their mother telling Eva, "No one will ever dote on you the way we have."

Maybe she'd taken that to heart. In any case, all these years she didn't lack for filial companionship because she had Martha, who studied at her kitchen table most nights, lapping up her homemade soups and sweets. When Martha was born, Lucille was twenty-four and Evangeline, as she was called then—named by their mother for the poem—was only twelve, the age when most girls start noticing boys. But she claimed Martha as her own and began calling herself Eva.

As soon as they stepped into the cool store, Lucille thought of money. Air conditioning always did that. She'd never really let herself believe Arthur had any money, or that it had anything to do with her. He never said no when she wanted a new appliance, like a deep freezer, or when the linoleum needed changing out. But she asked for little, and finances were never discussed. Parcel after parcel of the nursery was sold from his sickbed, men coming in to shake hands on deals in his final months. The bit of land left, now leased for cattle and corn, brings in more money than she can spend; the profit from the sales is held in banks across the state or invested in the market. Like much else that is hers, she's hardly touched it.

"Where are you going to live?" Eva said.

"I'm moving to Washington." She smiled. Often a smile will stop an awkward line of questioning. "I know you don't want the house. I'm thinking of leasing the land but I want to keep the house." She dreams of a proper homecoming for Lake, holding this vision in her mind—Lake supping at her kitchen table, Lake tucked in a feather bed, Lake strolling through the remaining orchards under a lavender-pink sky.

It was clear from the way Eva's brow furrowed and she looked past Lucille, as if she didn't quite hear her, that this setting wouldn't do for this discussion. They would wring their hands over every little aspect of her plan before Lucille got out of town.

"Not before the wedding," Eva said. "And how are you going to 'close' it up? Remember last winter when vandals got into the Dodsons' farmhouse. Who'll look after all that?" She looked around the circular racks of hanging lace as if scanning the property.

"I'll figure it out. It won't be you."

"Yes, well, like I said, wait till the honeymoon's over. One less thing for them to think about."

Lucille had planned on that anyway, just as she had waited to see that her son, Clark, graduated from college last May. She'd started talking to other farmers about who might manage the land. But the house, she needs that to remain; she can't predict how things will work out for her in Washington.

Martha had been an easy child, a tractable teenager. She was a striver, getting all good marks in high school. But she often stayed out past her curfew with her then-boyfriend—a college-dropout who'd had run-ins with the law—driving around town in his Chevrolet convertible with a damaged muffler that announced him a block away. One night Lucille waited up, ready with threats as soon as she heard his car.

"I don't know why you're having such a fit," Martha hissed. "This is the first sign of motherly concern I've ever seen. Where have you been all my life?"

Was that true? Had her worries about a boy startled her into acting like a mother? Well, the wrong man could derail your life. She believes that.

But Lucille is far from the country of Pomona now, in a different kind of field. She holds her breath, casting a wide look over the rows of seats, the pairs of eyes fixed on the stage. She doesn't have to wait long before Lake appears, delivering that silly line, "My dog eats nuts too." She is so plain, and thin. The director may very well have chosen her for her youthfulness. But she is almost twenty-eight, not a child anymore. Soon, too soon, she is offstage, and Lucille wishes she'd bothered to read the summary of each act in the program so she'd have an idea when Charlotta is coming on again.

This effort for Lake to be someone else—Lucille must appreciate that. Maybe that was what Audrey meant when she said Lake might not have the "stamina" to be a performer. But perhaps such an exercise is a relief to Lake.

When she appears again, her line steals the scene. "If you let people kiss your hand, then they'll want your elbow, then your shoulder, and then..." Isn't that the truth, thinks Lucille; a line she could have used when she was younger. Gluttonous, she studies every gesture of Lake's, following her slippered feet and the lift of her hips as she sashays across the stage. Her voice is deeper than Lucille remembers. Dressed in white, tightly laced, Lake is an image of control that could spring loose at any moment. Lucille will not miss a word or look, any morsel.

Lake—Charlotta—opens the second act with a gun over her shoulder, lamenting that she does not know her age, how she always feels very young. "Who my parents were—perhaps they weren't married—I don't know." Lucille shrinks in her seat, hearing that. But then Lake bites into a cucumber and issues her line about the singers' sounding "like jackals." In her nervousness Lucille laughs out loud, a yelp of adulation; others laugh too. Lake has them eating out of her hand, Lucille thinks, and pride fills her for a joyous moment until she judges this ridiculous, feeling what other parents in the audience might feel, that this gift comes from her.

"I've nobody at all…and I don't know who I am or why I live," Charlotta carries on, which Lucille also finds unreasonable. She said her parents were circus performers. *You know who you are*, Lucille wants to say.

This is unsettling—Charlotta's aimless walking off the stage with a rifle over her shoulder. All part of the direction, Lucille tells herself, and she does not remember a gun going off in the play. She would remember that. She vaguely remembers a magic trick to come.

The fur muffs turned out to be a nice touch when on the day of the December wedding, snow flurries were spotted in the air. Down the aisle, Martha threaded her Alçenon-laced arm through Clark's, who was as snub-nosed as when he was eight. His girlfriend, Cissy, her hair dark and fringy, sat in the pews. They would be next, Lucille knew. In a long ultramarine dress with its torso made of tiny iridescent sequins, unearthed in a bin at a secondhand shop, she followed Brody's awkward footwork during their requisite dance. Even with a glass or two of punch, she kept her plans to herself.

When she finally did announce she was moving, everyone asked, "Why Washington?" It was true that she seldom mentioned living there. No one had ever really asked about that year. And what would she have told them? She might never tell them. She'd walked around Pomona all these years with her head held high, after marrying such an old man. People had not liked that. Perhaps Eva knew most—after all, she had, in a way, intervened to rescue Martha and, to a lesser extent, Clark. Maybe she sensed that when Lucille came home from Washington she was never going to be the same. But whatever Lucille had suffered, she tended to it privately, stoked it, burned it like fuel. That was how she withstood anybody's judgment. *You will never know what I had to do. You will never understand, better not to try. I wouldn't want you to understand.*

During intermission, the young man next to her leaves before she can speak to him, but when he returns, smelling of lavatory soap, she asks, "What do you think so far?" His sandy hair is thin on top, his cheeks lightly pocked.

"It's terrific. Funny and deep at the same time. My girlfriend's in it."

"Your girlfriend?" She smiles, her glasses back on, so she can see him clearly. He nods, and Lucille leans in. "Which one is she?"

"Anya."

She reclines back into her seat, disappointed he isn't Lake's boyfriend. Glad for the dimming lights, she turns her attention to the stage. But soon a boy in a beret emerges from a curtain pleat, announcing that the role of Charlotta will be acted by an understudy for the remainder of the play.

Lucille freezes. She hears a chair squeak, and a few rows ahead of her, on the far end of the aisle, a young man with neatly trimmed dark hair and rimless glasses walks to the exit. Maybe that's Lake's boyfriend going backstage. Ray—that's who Audrey mentioned over the phone, saying she was glad the two were back together. Lucille should follow him.

But her legs fail her. Eyes fixed on the stage, the actors moving and talking, she is stuck in a dream of running in place. Everyone else in the audience seemingly accepts this change. She didn't hear a rifle go off. No siren in the distance. The show must go on. But would it, if a cast member were seriously ill?

In the lobby, a man in a red vest is sweeping the concession-stand floor of popcorn, the smell still in the air. Outdoors the streetlights shine on nearly empty roads. The theater is on a large triangle of land, cut off from any urbanscape. She walks toward the rear, to what must be the stage door, but the handle is locked. Under a single floodlight, her breath clouds in the cold air, but under her coat she sweats. No ambulance comes, no one exits. She imagines Lake's face, hysterical and sobbing. Then she realizes she doesn't really know what the adult Lake looks like when she's crying.

Lucille should find a way backstage to make sure everything is all right; she could be useful there. Did the boy *say* someone was ill? She can't remember his exact words. Anyone else's mother would turn back to help. But instead she walks toward the dark, shivering, in search of her car.

1944

8

Bells chiming, carriage returns zinging, and keys clicking on twenty-five typewriters—the constant percussion of her Pentagon office left Lucille snappish at the end of each day. On one side of her, the girl wore earplugs, but Lucille refused because she didn't want to miss anything. Had she worn them she wouldn't have heard Lieutenant Colonel Houston, who'd been walking up and down the rows, call Madeleine into his office, or heard the girls whisper, "Dismissed!" Mad Madeleine had used the department's letterhead for revenge against an unfaithful boyfriend: *We write to inform you that you've been discharged from your post...*

Lucille would never have committed such a hoax, but sometimes she did want to run screaming down the aisles between desks to break the tedium.

On her other side was her roommate Greta, her head bobbing with the rhythm of her fingers, on one of which now sparkled a sweet round diamond in filigree. Last night her boyfriend from home, a new second lieutenant out of officer candidate school at Quantico, had proposed on the Lincoln steps. Below on the Potomac River, Tchaikovsky had streamed from a barge at the last Sunset Symphony of the season. She'd kept Lucille awake late into the night, rapturously recounting the romantics of it, but showed no sign of reduced clerical output today.

The women in Lucille's department were all in this together, with the exception of Miss Longhren, who was twice their age, working in the small adjoining room between two larger offices. Her desk was visible through the doorway; past that was another door to the lieutenant colonel's office. Yesterday Lucille had been the last to leave, and when she cut off the lights, she noticed the yellow beam coming from Miss Longhren's room. The colonel must already have left to have his evening meal of juicy pot roast, ladled out to him by his homemaker wife, their children tucked away under sheets pressed by that same wife. And here was Miss Longhren, taking care of things on this end. A green-glass lamp shone on an apron of papers, rows and rows of columns surrounding her. Lucille thought this the picture of loneliness.

The unity in the room comforted—that and air conditioning, at least on the days it worked. There was achievement too. Another row filled! Another letter completed! Another lunch break to anticipate—if one looked forward to tepid tea and soda crackers. Another evening listening to the radio and watching Shirley dress for dinner with either Harvey or Darrell. No matter the skewed ratio of men to women, her roommate managed the attentions of two vying for her company.

"I've been told there's quite a storm going on outside," Miss Longhren said from her doorway now. No one could see this for themselves. They were in the C ring, the darkest of the dark given that the A ring had windows onto an interior courtyard, and the outermost, or E, had windows to the rest of the world. The typists paused for a rare moment of quiet before chattering on about what the weather meant for their trip home. Everything would be delayed, no point in leaving now. Lucille waved Greta on. She would get ahead on tomorrow's work, type two more letters, maybe three.

But everyone had the same idea, and workers, along with men and women in uniform, clogged the corridors. A line was forming outside the barbershop and at the shoeshine stand as men waited for the rain to let up. It didn't help that many still lost their way in what had been nicknamed the concrete cobweb. Lucille knew her route only by passing a bank on one corner, where she stopped briefly to cash her paycheck, and a post office on another. At the exit, people stalled. She recognized him right away, his height separating him from the others: the doctor who had performed her appendectomy. Weeks had passed since she spotted him at the hotel bar. What an expression she must have on now, peckish and brittle as she felt. He smiled and made his way to her.

"What brings you here?" she said.

"Meetings all afternoon."

"They're sending you over?"

"So they say. They must be desperate, right?" He laughed. "I'm officially Lieutenant Commander Bray."

Others with umbrellas poised to open were lining up behind them, excusing themselves as they jostled to advance out the door.

"But call me Ben. And remind me—?"

"Lucille. It's nice to see you," she said too abruptly. She moved through the open doors, still feeling his gaze behind her like a warm hand.

"Lucille," he called, and again they blocked the flow of people, this time on the sidewalk. She raised her umbrella high above them both.

"May I?" he asked, relieving her of it. "How about a lift home? I'm over here." He pointed to the mass of automobiles but looked uncertain regarding a specific location.

Not waiting in the rain for the bus would be a relief. "I'm downtown. Could be out of your way."

"You stay here," he said, nodding toward the portico and handing back her umbrella.

She was glad not to be riding the bus home for another reason. A few days ago, two Black women—she didn't know their names, but recognized them from a pool of Ordance Department secretaries—had boarded the bus last, and one sat next to her. She was telling Lucille that when the building first opened, but was still under construction, they walked on wooden planks across mud to catch the bus. She'd ruined more than one pair of shoes. A baton smacked on the window next to Lucille. Both women jumped. A military policeman outside motioned for the woman to move to the back of the bus, but she kept talking as if she hadn't noticed. Another smack came on the window a row or two ahead, where the second woman sat. The sound terrified Lucille, but she too kept talking as if nothing were wrong. Why couldn't the men leave these women alone—they had waited in the long line like everyone else. Lucille knew it had taken a bloody struggle to integrate the cafeteria—this was before her office moved to the Pentagon—but apparently the buses made their own rules. Her stomach surged with panic. These women could get hurt.

When the policeman came on board, he ordered them both to the rear, but the woman's eyes stayed on Lucille, her voice at a whisper now and the bus silent. She wore a pearl brooch on her collar, and Lucille studied it, wondering if there was a message in it. For a split second, she saw herself using it against the officer. He stood over them for a full three minutes, delaying everyone. "Off," he finally said, and the two women stood up at the same time. Lucille watched them out the window, wondering how they would get home now, hoping another bus came soon. She had done nothing, and the nothingness felt as awful as her hate for the policeman, how when he leaned down to speak into the woman's ear, she could make out the dark stubble of his beard through his pasty skin.

But she mentioned none of this when Ben helped her into his car, a burgundy Lincoln-Zephyr. The only other fine automobile she'd ridden in had been Shirley's little coupe. His was roomier. The handles and knobs looked like brass.

"Why do you have a yellow ribbon tied to your antenna?"

"So I could find this car in that damn parking lot." He laughed—those dimples she'd noticed in the hospital on display again.

She gave him directions, but as soon as they were across the bridge, he suggested a drink. "We're hot and drenched, don't we deserve refreshment? A cordial—whatever that is." He pulled up in front of a set of heavy wooden doors with *Water Gate Inn* scripted across the large front window. "How does this look?"

"Like a place where horses are kept. Just the place for a cordial."

He smiled, holding the door for her. Inside, thick carpentry framed the windows and doors, and beams ran across the ceiling. "You said you were a farm girl, now I believe it. This place used to be stables. Now it's all Pennsylvania Dutch."

They chose a seat halfway toward the back, next to a cold fireplace lit with a few candles. Overhead fans ran on high. Old hobbyhorses, copper cookware, and dried corn husks hung from the ceiling; pewter pitchers lined the large mantel. If they ran out of things to say, they could find a topic on the wall.

She excused herself to call Shirley and Greta, but no one answered. Last night was Harvey, tonight must be Darrell. Maybe Greta stopped for groceries. When Lucille returned, a bowl of peanuts sat between them, and drinks, a gin and tonic for her.

"You must be going soon if you're meeting at the Pentagon."

"Who knows. These Navy ways are inscrutable. I have a colleague who was initially turned down for service and they're calling him now. They're getting to the dregs, and they'll get to me." He wiped his hand across his face with fatigue. Very handsome. "How've you been feeling?"

"Ah, that question again. No one's asked me that since I left the hospital. Good. They kept me so long the appendicitis seemed like ancient history by the time I left."

"Remind me where you and your hay-colored hair are from. Somewhere south."

"Hard not to notice. North Carolina."

He had his right ear turned toward her, and touched his left now. "I don't catch everything. Not a great loss, but if I'm not paying attention, I can miss some things."

"Or hear only what you want to hear."

"What my mother always said. Where in North Carolina?"

"You can't have heard of it. Pomona."

"The goddess of fruit trees."

"I'm impressed. My family helps run a nursery there. It started out as an orchard but it's grown. I've never had two days of rest in a row. Being in the hospital was nearly a treat, the last half anyway."

"You mentioned that, I remember. And your concern that donating blood had brought on the appendicitis." He laughed at her, as he had in the hospital. "There's no known cause of acute appendicitis, but I think we've ruled out blood donations." As if he'd gone too far, he added, "We had a few hens till I was about twelve, but that's as close as I got to your life."

"We have lots of those. Cattle and horses too." She listed some of the trees and shrubs they grew, running down the seasons for him.

"After our hen died, my mother put a bird feeder in our backyard. But your home sounds like a wildlife refuge. I can picture the frame house surviving the elements on a coat of white paint each year. The buds before the peaches. Your own Shangri-La."

She didn't understand the reference. Talking about Pomona made her think of Jimmy, a letter she should be writing to him instead of being here, and she sipped the gin and tonic to wash the taste of dust off her tongue. But Ben opened the menu and suggested the baked chicken. She had eaten every last peanut. *Dear Jimmy, Like you, I find myself desperate for a good meal.*

"Tell me about your friend from the other night. It was you I saw, wasn't it?" he said, without looking up from his menu.

"He's an old friend from home."

"A beau."

"An old beau."

"No longer, you mean? Or are you referring to his age?" He smiled sheepishly. "He might have been in the last war." The smile saved him from seeming cruel.

"The former. I didn't realize we were such an attraction. I didn't even think you saw me. And no, Arthur has never been in the military. He was turned down in '18 for a heart murmur."

She didn't ask about the woman he was with. It would have been natural, a jab when one was due. In the hospital she had asked him if he had any family. "No," he had said, "but don't feel sorry for me. I expect that'll make it easier to go—a clean cut."

She had wondered whether family sometimes did that, held one so tightly that leaving was as painful as surgery.

Out of curiosity, she later asked someone in a Navy pool to look at his file. Girls did it all the time in the office, and in easily half the cases they were glad they did. He wasn't married.

"Your old friend still looked rather content. You must have broken the news to him later."

She smiled, silent.

"You said you worked all the time. What sort of work does one do in Pomona when you're not tending to the trees?"

She was carving into her chicken. "The nursery work was the hard labor. The easy work was caring for Mrs. Causey in the afternoons, an old woman who owned most of the nursery land." The first few times she stayed with her, the woman tried to pay her to leave. But when Lucille insisted on staying—she wasn't that shortsighted—they came to an agreement. Lucille wasn't to tell anyone that Mrs. Causey smoked cigarettes in bed—or in the house at all. Her geranium-colored lips and beautiful white hair, in soft peaks like meringue against her pillow, seemed a kind of glamour triumphing over death.

It was dull work, sure. Lucille might play a few notes on the piano or wander through the house, taking in all its frippery, white crocheted runners on every chest, crystal droplets descending from each ceiling center. Sometimes she stayed outside longer than was necessary when emptying the ashtray. She poked around the chicken coop, disheartened when she found a smashed egg, accidentally stepped on by a hen, or she lounged on the striped cushioned wicker sofa on the porch, daydreaming. She told all this to Ben, the gin loosening her tongue.

"Daydreaming about what?" he asked.

She ignored the question. The daughter, Maura, was the reason Lucille had been called to take care of Mrs. Causey. For much of the morning and afternoon Maura took care of her mother but needed to be home for her son after school. "How she doted on that child,"

Lucille said, drinking from the refill of gin that had been placed in front of her.

At this point Ben interrupted to say how she should be a nurse. "Why aren't you helping out that way?"

Most of the lights had been turned off, and in the candlelight his dark eyes were merry, riveted.

"Because I can change a chamber pot? Shhh. That's not the point of this story. Thankfully, Mrs. Causey's house had a toilet under the stairs. It was tight for the two of us, but we managed."

The only excitement was *Lux Radio Theatre*—*Show Boat* and *Wuthering Heights*. Mrs. Causey demanded silence while they listened, unless she needed help firing her heavy nickel lighter.

"Don't think you're fooling anybody about her smoking," Maura told Lucille when she drove her home one day. Maura drove everywhere, even back and forth from her own house, half a mile away. She was dark-haired and sturdy, wearing printed scarves to keep her beauty-parlor hair dry on rainy days.

"Arthur said they should have moved Mrs. Causey in with them, and put the money they saved by not keeping up that old house into fixing her car—"

"Arthur?"

She hadn't meant to mention him. "I'll get to that," she said, thinking she would avoid talking about him altogether. She did not say that she'd happened into Mrs. Causey's cosmetics—her dressing table filled with powders and rouges—the first time Arthur kissed her. He entered through the enclosed porch that never warmed, where rocking chairs sat next to milk crates and an old hand-cranked wringer washer. He put his finger to his lips to silence Lucille, who was streaked with powder, pink up her cheeks and blue across her eyelids. He hung his hat on the handle, and with his other arm reached around her waist, kissing her painted lips until she felt a flood of livid pleasure. She didn't free herself until Mrs. Causey called her name.

Nor did she say that Mrs. Causey had told her that Hal Spence, Lucille's father, used to come calling on Maura. This astonished her. Later it explained everything. Her daddy bringing flowers for Maura Causey. Her daddy dancing with Maura Causey. But he didn't stand a chance after Arthur Lind came beating down the door, Mrs. Causey told her. "Not with those tiger eyes and apple cheeks of his. I told my husband it wasn't fair. Hal Spence had been working this land since he was twelve years old."

Lucille remembered this vividly, her exact words, because the fatal car accident was later that afternoon. "If they'd fixed her old Plymouth, it might not have stalled at a crossing," she said to Ben now. "A train killed her and Peter."

Ben threw his napkin onto the table. "That's the worst thing I've ever heard."

She nodded solemnly. But given all that had happened between her and Arthur, Lucille had hardened herself to the tragedy the same way she had when a lame horse she loved had to be put down. She wouldn't try to explain the fright—or thrill—of witnessing Arthur come apart.

She had rattled on and lost the point of the story. She might as well be talking to her brother for as little decorum as she'd shown. "So then I started cooking for the old lady too."

"Enter the bereft son-in-law and the young nursemaid," Ben said, circling his empty glass on the table. "I can put two and two together. He probably enjoyed some of those meals for Lady Causey."

"What, you think I was taken advantage of? I knew what I was doing."

"Maybe your sympathies were taken advantage of. The way he lost everything. I feel awful for the fellow."

But he hadn't lost everything. He still had her.

Ben opened his billfold and thumbed through the compartments, then clamped it shut. He looked alarmed. "I don't believe it, I've never done this. I left my cash envelope on my dresser. I'm terribly sorry."

"I have some money," she said, reaching for her pocketbook.

"We had an officers' luncheon today, or I would have noticed before. Banks close at five." He looked at his watch. "It's almost eight. And I've pushed dinner on you." He sighed loudly into his hands.

"Hardly. I would have eaten the napkin if we hadn't ordered something."

"We'll swing by my house before I take you home." She didn't argue. Rent was due at the end of the week.

He cut the engine without asking whether she wanted to come inside or wait in the car. They were in the middle of a conversation about what women would do in the war. She was arguing that women could do anything, they'd be in combat in this war or the next.

"I don't doubt it," he said. "Women can do anything. Fly planes."

"They're doing it now, you know, flying back and forth across the country. It's only a matter of time." The rain had stopped, but they dodged puddles up his walkway.

The house was large. A living room stretched long, and doorways hinted at rooms she couldn't see into. He started up the stairs, taking two at time. On top of an old dough box were bourbon bottles and crystal highball glasses, next to a record player. Albums lay in a messy pile beside the console. This was a home—wool carpeting, a cushion under her feet. She felt an inward lurch for the surrounding comforts, envy of the girl she'd seen dancing with Ben, the one with shoes from Garfinckel's. Maybe she had been here before. Lucille imagined hearing Marlene Dietrich's voice in this room.

He returned with the money, whistling a tune.

"My goodness, you really are a bachelor," she said, nodding at the albums.

"I do love music." Lifting a glass in the air, he said, "Shall we have one last drink?"

"Probably not. Thank you for this, though." She put the money in her pocketbook, but he moved to take it from her and set it on the coffee table. He leaned in to kiss her cheek, and she wasn't surprised. What took her breath away was that he didn't put his arms around her but kissed her neck instead, holding himself separate, so that if she wanted him to continue, she must move closer, which she did. There was such relief in feeling desire for someone else, like rain trilling through her, that she suppressed a laugh. Behind all these doorways, other possibilities of living existed, if she could just walk through them.

As he retraced his steps to his bedroom, she dragged a bit on his arm, finessing his insistence that she follow him. He unloosened her hands from the railing, pulling her lightly. She wondered what good could come of this, espaliered against the wall, shedding clothes. Arthur seemed another lifetime ago, but in a tender, sad way, he was with her too. There was the messy tumble of Ben's double bed—"Some officer you'll make; you need some basic training," she said, and he laughed. She felt the innocent curve of the cherry headboard he had lain against since he was a child. Baseball pennants and red and blue ribbons, shadowy dark, hung above a chest between two windows. The familiarity of this den of boyhood, so like Jimmy's, threatened to take the legs off her courage. She was trying to leave her youth behind.

Less than an hour later, when he finally lifted himself from her, she had her answer to the question of what good could come of this. The pain wasn't a surprise. The reward was in her loss of bearings, a reeling oblivion where, for once, she was flung free and all roads ahead were vacant, lit.

9

"Days," Audrey said aloud, and then pushed herself to finish the sentence. "How many days do you have left?" She and Ben were standing on his rear stoop, staring at the night sky. The harvest moon beamed low and colossal through the trees. Summer was over.

"I couldn't tell you if I knew. And I don't know." He caressed her arm lightly with his thumb.

"I could take care of things while you're gone."

"I could get called away at any time, you know."

"That's what worries me."

"So I better start telling you how to take care of things."

They saw it at the same time, a star shooting overhead, and cried out, pointing.

"I'll do whatever you need while you're gone," Audrey said.

"There's always speculation about which ships are due back in or how long it will take another to get ready. No one knows, not even the captain of the ship. But given what I've heard, I think it will be at least another month. I'm guessing four weeks and five days and seven hours and twenty-some minutes."

"All those 'ands.' You make it sound as if we have forever."

"You know the moon is always there, you just can't see it in its newest phase, between the earth and the sun. Remember that." He was still turned upward to the sky, searching. "How about two weeks from today—no, two weeks and a day, a Saturday, we get married? If you're still speaking to me, that is. Darling."

"Still speaking? What an irresistible proposal. Or was that in fact a proposal? Hard for me to tell." She pulled his hand to her neck, and he reached his arm around her. He always looked as though he had no idea what was about to happen; he was waiting, attentively, for it to be revealed, with that half grin and those wrinkles at the corners of his eyes, his head ducked almost submissively. Endearing, but maybe it was on account of his bad ear.

"A couple more weeks and you might decide you don't like this situation at all." He was kissing her forehead, her cheeks, her neck, her shoulder.

"But shouldn't I say yes first, before you suggest I change my mind? Or your mind." Oh, how jealous she'd been of every girl he'd looked at these last few months. All that was past.

"I'm here waiting for you to do that. I'll make some things official, of course," he said, taking her ring finger in his hand.

"A wedding. There's going to be a wedding."

"And you'll be in it."

"Yes, and you."

"I heard it. The girl said yes."

Ben asked a Navy chaplain to officiate, and a fellow doctor and his wife were their witnesses. Audrey wore an ivory peau-de-soie suit; Ben, his blue officer's uniform. It was better not to have time to plan a venue or invite guests. Her mother wouldn't have been able to make the trip but would have complained loudly if she was the only one who missed out. The truth was, Audrey felt that her father had already given her away earlier that year when he put her on the train to Washington, and she sped along, holding in her lap a little nosegay of camellias from her aunts. She was already betrothed to a new life. Ben was just the next natural part of that.

On their wedding night, she worried about pregnancy. "I have no family here," Audrey told him. "I wouldn't know what to do—who would help me?" They were lying in bed, his arm encircling her waist as if they were still dancing.

"Aren't there women you can hire to help you? I just read about funding for childcare centers. For wartime workers, like you."

"The only one I've heard about doesn't take infants. Besides, the Navy isn't going to feed a baby in the middle of the night."

"Are you saying you don't want children?"

"I'm just telling you—it would be complicated. Really, really hard. And I don't think my boss would like it. He let a woman go last month, and we all knew it was because she was seven months pregnant and it wouldn't do for her to work." She was carried away with listing inconveniences, but she hadn't answered the question. She didn't want children, not now. And she wasn't sure whether she ever would. They had never discussed this—like so many things.

"You don't need to work, you know. You'll have the regular Navy check, and there's money in the account for house expenses, anything the check won't cover. Money's no excuse. I've never heard of a woman worrying this way."

"You've never had to." Her voice sounded shrill, so she quieted. "All I'm asking is that we be careful, for now, until the war is over. What if something happens to you?"

"Nothing's going to happen to me."

"It's not like you'll be stationed in some hospital—you'll probably be on a ship, an easy target. Are you listening to me?"

He'd gotten up from the bed, and she heard the rustling of tin and paper, felt something laid on her stomach. "Enough, sweetheart. I think we're missing the point."

Later in the night he said, "They don't always hold, you know," teasing her in the grip of his arms.

The next morning Audrey retrieved her silk negligee from the floor and freshened herself in the bathroom before he woke. She brushed her teeth and dabbed rouge on her cheeks and lips, just enough color to define her. She was intent on Ben's not seeing her without makeup, but she didn't want him to notice it. She returned to bed, sliding into his half-sleeping arms.

They might have only a handful of days like this, off work, before he left. Today was for wallowing in domestic bliss. Any anxiety about their imminent separation came in the attention she gave, groping and fierce, trying to know him fully, impossibly, in the short time they had together. He didn't remark on her morning trip to the bathroom, but he seemed to notice everything else about her, even her earlobes. "Some of your best assets." He laughed, giving one a light fillip with his finger before holding it between his lips.

It amazed her, this new, irreversible intimacy in the broad daylight of a Sunday afternoon.

As they lingered in bed a new concern upstaged the pregnancy one.

"You know I can't cook," she told him.

"No? Not at all?"

"Can't cook a thing." The picture must be bleak for him: no children for now, useless in a kitchen.

"Well, if I'd known that…" he said, and pulled her close again, then moved them both to the edge of the bed. "There's always Hot Shoppes." He was downstairs before she could finish dressing. She took her time, buttoning her cotton dress, tying the bow at her waist, brushing her shoulder-length hair. Her life for now. Soon she smelled eggs frying. He could cook eggs.

What she learned of making a meal came from Ben's mother's *Joy of Cooking,* which looked like it had never been opened. She suspected, since seeing the cellar with its wall of canned fruits and vegetables—tomatoes, strawberry preserves, watermelon rind, all neatly labeled August 1942, the last good month his mother had before succumbing to the cancer—that the woman hadn't needed a book. "Are these still good to eat?" Audrey asked.

"You're really giving yourself away." Opening a jar labeled sour pickles, full of greenish-gold coins pressed against the glass, he said, "Hear that?" The tin top popped. "The sound of freshness." He pulled a slice out, dripping the juice on his tongue before eating it. "Delicious. The lady could can." Then he turned serious: "But don't eat from a jar that doesn't have a seal." Then, "How am I going to leave you here alone?"

He usually got home before she did, his office downtown at the university hospital and hers all the way to the Capitol. By the time she arrived he'd taken off his tie, had a drink, maybe even two, and was at ease, but hungry. She was cranky, he said, for the first thirty minutes after work, "from studying the enemy all day. Remember I'm not on their side!" And then he'd hold out his drink for her to have a few sips before he retreated to his wing chair in the living room, his cigarette smoke and newspaper a screen between them. She scanned the recipes for the shortest list of ingredients. Not coq au vin but braised chicken breasts. She unwrapped the raw chicken, pink juices splattering across the barely cut pages of the cookbook. Where was the joy in this?

It was the order of things that she always got wrong. She should have peeled the potatoes and carrots first, then layered them in the dish before placing the breasts on top so as not to overcook them. Ben would come in for another drink, looking not as worried as he should be as late as it was getting. He helped himself to a jar of peanuts and offered a handful to her. But she was too busy shoving the vegetables under the chicken and returning the dish to the oven. "I should have cut them into smaller pieces," she said.

"Cranky," he teased.

Setting the table, folding the napkins at their places, he at the head, she on his right, she told herself that this was her place, she would keep it. She could serve him a full meal, no parts burned or dried out, or even bloody as the meat had been the night before, a feast to fill him, keep him sated until he returned to her.

She wished for a way to preserve each of their married hours together before he received his orders. *Like your mother's preserves, our days sealed in jars to enjoy again later.* She held in her memory what she could: The way he put enough pepper on those eggs to make a fly sneeze, and his habit of sleeping with a pillow in his arms—always trading her in during the night, she told him, laughing. The times she bathed before bed while he sat on the closed commode, talking to her, drinking his scotch. The shocking sound of his early morning torrent of urine. The saddest hound-dog look he gave her over his newspaper when she complained, again, of their separate Christmases to come. "Hasn't each of these days been Christmas?" he said. She filled half a sketch pad with every angle of his profile, his sleeping head, his hands wrapped around his evening drink.

For a long stretch of time she would have to live wholly on gestures, on whispered words. Wasn't that always part of love, though, what you made out of these private expressions and signs, evidence the rest of the world couldn't see?

He initiated a fall cleanup of the yard by cutting back the large abelia in front of the conservatory where her easel stood, giving her more light. But that meant less privacy, a displeasure she didn't mention. He tended to the overgrown forsythia, now all woody-stemmed and bare, and told her where the lilies would come up, and the peonies. He pulled the neighbors' wisteria off the fence and the ivy off the mulberry. The latter was a large tree, a male without the messy fruit, he explained. He had planted spinach in the vegetable garden, mulching it over, and showed her how much to remove in the spring. "Pick the leaves as soon as you can grab them by your hand—too much taller and you're begging for rabbits. The tomatoes and beans, the zucchini, all that will have to wait till I return." In those moments she aspired to be a gardener.

But sometimes, when he confounded her by lighting a cigarette before he'd eaten first thing in the morning, or when he talked about how he was an atheist all through medical school—and wasn't sure he wasn't still—worry zipped through her. How well did she know him? What else might she find out that would make her want her to call the whole thing off? As she breathed next to him each night, breathing his breath, the intimacy overwhelmed her. They were part of each other now.

The effort of goodbye shaped every day; they believed it could be their last. There were smiles between them, quick hugs, and more instructions: garbage goes out on Mondays, milk comes on Wednesdays, who to call if the basement floods, numbers for a handyman. Through it all there was an element of their playing house, like children. He made lists on graph paper and used the little boxes to check items off, but he never remembered where he left them. When they turned up later, in the last of his laundry or between pages of a book, she glued them in her sketchbook, thinking his blocky capital letters a form of art: DETACH THE YARD HOSE BEFORE THE FIRST FREEZE. And CLEAR THE REAR DRAIN OF LEAVES AND DEBRIS.

His orders came on a weekend, and on a Monday morning he drove the two of them to the naval station. Outside the parked car, the overcast sky offered little distraction. There was no bright sun to defend themselves against, no shade in which to seek cover. Throughout the parking lot were clusters of people restrained—there were no outbursts, no scenes of loud crying. Other khaki-men, the name she called the officers, stood at the center of their families, full of anxious, overexposed faces, posing for photographs, eager to please.

"You should meet some of these women here," Ben said. "You might make a friend."

"I'm too sad to make a friend now," she said, almost pouting, but then added, "I have the number to the officers' club. I'll make an effort."

The plane was something to look at, awesome in its size. She remembered hearing about enlisted men, terrified before a transatlantic voyage: those in charge sometimes removed belts and ties from them, so they couldn't harm themselves. But she saw only officers, looking hopped-up and brave.

As if a silent sign had been made, the men began filing toward the plane. The last seconds amounted to a blur of lips grazing, his thumbs wiping tears away from her eyes, and words in her ear almost inaudible. She thought he said: "I'm leaving my heart here with you." But "heart" could have been another word.

Once he boarded, she panicked, thinking he had forgotten to give her the car keys, and in her rush to find them—he had left them in the ignition—she missed his takeoff. She was sorry she hadn't been part of the crowd, where he could watch her waving goodbye, blowing kisses.

There was more uneasiness as she started the engine; she hadn't driven a car since being in Washington. Stiff behind the wheel, she was two handed all the way back home. To avoid the empty house, she went to work, but at the end of the day, the house was empty *and* dark. She felt like an infant, coaxing herself back to sleep through that first night.

When, in those early weeks after he'd gone, uncertainty overwhelmed her about whether marrying him had been the right thing to do, it was his keen attention to the garden, as much as their intimacy, that she remembered. Such dear care for what one couldn't yet see in these fallow months. Surely he was a good man. And she painted like mad in the new studio. This was what she'd always wanted—space, time, light.

10

In the curve of the letter *C* of the Garfinckel's sign, a clump of dried grass and pine needles hung loosely, a pigeon's nest. Lucille was meeting Greta to shop for bridesmaid dresses after she had her wedding gown fitted. Lucille wasn't going to be in the wedding, in Wisconsin, but she'd offered to help find a dress that Greta would send home in different sizes.

Lucille arrived early, strolling through mannequins with padded shoulders. Under glass cases warm with light were coiled strands of pearls, bangles of Bakelite, vermeil pins, and bib necklaces. The perfume lady perked up when Lucille offered her wrist, but the scent was too musky, and once out of sight, she rubbed it off on her skirt. She wondered at the woman's job, in close proximity to such beauty she likely couldn't afford herself.

For weeks now Lucille had felt exceedingly airy, weightless. When she thought of Greta's leaving, it was with a small ache, but it measured less against the pit she'd felt riding the bus here in early spring, or when Jimmy said goodbye. Nor did Arthur hang like a shadow over her. When he called again, after her night with Ben, she told Shirley, "Say I don't want to talk to him." She wrote "return to sender" on his letters. The severance felt complete.

She hadn't heard from Ben. Leaving in that faint grainy morning light, she scribbled her number on a piece of paper and tucked it into his black oxford shoe. She flushed, remembering. She had also slid her bare feet across his bedroom carpet for one last caress with luxury. They had laughed easily together—at herself, her use of the word lallygagging; at him, the pompous way he said "aunt." Maybe any warmth she felt for him was because he wasn't Arthur. Maybe Ben had served his purpose.

To reach the shoe racks, she passed through rows of rich yellows and greens, fall clothes. Her eyes skimmed over the shoe stock quickly, searching out but not finding the skinny heels she liked, until she was homing in on a pair of red sandals on the sale rack.

"There you are," Greta said, rounding the rack corner. "I should have known."

"How was the fitting?"

"Terrific, except I'll have to skip every other meal from now till the wedding if I want to stay in the dress. What a fabulous sale." Her eyes glazed over, already lost in looking. Lucille had shopped with Greta before, and it was a dizzying, maniacal pursuit. Lucille stayed her course, ticking over the larger sizes, 9, 8, 7, and somewhere close to 6 she thought of dates, of days past, and how many days since her last period. She reached for the sandals and, checking the size, slipped one on her foot, walked toward the three-way mirror, and made a complete turn, all the while thinking back—if she could remember where, she could remember when.

"May I help you?" asked a saleswoman, her neck of powdery folds stretching toward Lucille.

"Very slick," Greta said, clutching three other samples to try herself.

"I like them too, but..." Even if it made sense to buy them on sale, Lucille couldn't justify buying them out of season. "I better not." She handed the sandals to the woman. "Where's your restroom?"

She wanted to look inside her underwear. If she couldn't remember the last period she had, wouldn't she be getting it soon? But when she was in the stall, she found nothing. She felt an odd mix of relief—at avoiding something unpleasant, bleeding—and doubt. Why wasn't she bleeding?

Greta held an armful of dresses for Lucille to try on. She pulled over her head a midnight-blue crepe and said to Greta through the curtain, "Hey, what night did we go to the Snake Pit with Mitchell and his crowd?" Lucille remembered now being at a dinner with Greta and her fiancé when she was completely without supplies.

"That must have been early August, because we'd just moved into the Pentagon." Greta buttoned her up the back. "It took us forever to get there after work, and by then everyone was drunk."

Lucille remembered stuffing toilet tissue in her undergarments and leaving early.

The blue wouldn't do, too military-like, said Greta. They went through the pile, Greta going back for a different size, another dress. They settled on one, cranberry colored with an empire waist. Lucille modeled it, spinning and flouncing in the mirror. "I'll remember you like this, and it'll be as if you're there with me," Greta said.

Then she held out a red wool pencil skirt. "Try this on. Only your little waist can squeeze into something this straight."

"Look at you, hunting for your trousseau but keeping an eye out for me."

Lucille took the skirt into the dressing room. Straightening herself before the mirror, she couldn't imagine anything was the matter. She saw herself fine, ruddy-faced, her freckles as pronounced as ever with all the walking to work she'd done the last month. She felt too good, better than usual. There'd been no morning sickness, no wooziness. Lifting her blouse now, she spanned her hand across her lower belly, which was flat, only the skin puckered with the appendectomy scar.

The skirt fit snugly, attractively. She could wear it to church now, in mid-September, and through the winter, maybe to a Christmas party.

On her bedside table she kept a little paper calendar, and before turning out her light that night, she flipped through the pages. Tomorrow's date was marked as Greta's departure. They'd already celebrated the last night out with the office, the last lunch, the last tea. Tomorrow Greta would board a train. Lucille's hospital stay was noted too, and Arthur's visit. She put a small *x* on the date she spent with Greta and Mitchell's friends. Earlier on the calendar were other lowercase *x*'s, a routine she observed her mother doing long before she understood what it meant. "It doesn't hurt to be able to plan a little," her mother had said. Forty-three days since her last period.

Lucille said nothing about her worry. She wasn't about to confess her night with Ben to Greta. Plenty she never admitted, including things she didn't know, like how to write a proper thank-you note, or what city the pope lived in. She was the same about money. She never mentioned that her family didn't have a telephone, or that she would never have been able to be a bridesmaid in Greta's wedding, had she been asked. She couldn't afford the dress.

Nor the skirt. She would never tell Greta how she folded it, narrow as a rolling pin, pressed it into her pocketbook, and took it home.

1973

11

Lucille walks down one wrong street and then another, losing sight of the theater. By the time she locates her car, she has traveled several blocks out of her way. She kneads the cold steering wheel with her hands. Surprising Lake tonight could have been disastrous; leaving her backstage may have been worse. The engine warm, she circles the theater. Still no activity. She pulls over and unfolds the map on the seat beside her. The trip to Audrey and Ben's house is at least twenty minutes. Running home to mommy and daddy, she thinks. She considers stopping to call. Maybe they already know what's wrong with Lake. But she doesn't want only information from them. Consolation—that's what she's after.

A green Cadillac is parked out front of their house, and light escapes the lowered window shades. Ben may not even know she's in town. She rings the bell and waits, knowing that whoever answers will have the advantage of the viewfinder, the little fisheye lens, like the one she has on her new apartment door. This door, however, has not always had one of those.

"It's Lucille," she says, not waiting for Ben's reaction. She doesn't want to hear that he doesn't recognize her or that he'd never expected to see her again. "I'm sorry to bother you all at night, but I went to see Lake in *The Cherry Orchard* and, well, she was wonderful, really good. Lake was. But then she didn't finish the show. An understudy came on. Have you heard from her?"

"Lucille," he nearly roars, as if he has heard nothing she has said. "What are you doing here?"

"Lucille," Audrey says from the stairs. "I didn't expect you—" Her voice is impatient.

"I'm so sorry, but I'm worried about Lake." She really should have called first, asked if it was all right for her to come.

Ben begins talking over her, filling in details for Audrey, and the two of them squint at her as if she might be a stray, maybe diseased.

"I thought you'd want to know."

"Could you turn down the television?" Audrey says to him and then turns to Lucille. "Did Lake see you? Did she know you were there?"

She shakes her head. "After you and I talked, I got it in my head that I could go watch her. I just wanted to see—"

Audrey frowns. "Really? What were you thinking? Do you think we need to go down there?"

"She didn't see *me*. I was careful about that. You mentioned a boyfriend—I think I saw him leave. Or is he an actor too?"

"Ray. Short fellow, with glasses?" says Audrey.

Lucille nods, explaining that she assumes he went backstage. "You haven't heard anything?" she asks again.

"Nothing. Do you think we should all go down there? You could drive us, Ben."

"That's a terrible idea."

Audrey glares at him, and Lucille looks at the floor.

"I'll go," he says. Ben is almost sixty, and though his hair has whitened and his face reddened, he still has a youthful wiriness. She avoids his gaze. Audrey's gray hair is a surprise, lighter than her former earth-brown color. Time has left its impress—that is what Lucille thinks when she sees her. *There* is time, in the color loss and the permanent lines across her forehead. But the broad and graceful way she carries herself quiets the room. She's barefoot, wearing a paint-marked smock.

Ben takes one last swallow of his drink and gets an overcoat from the front closet. "All the way down by Maine Avenue. Jesus." The door squeaks closed behind him.

They stand awkwardly under the dim light of the foyer. "I don't know what to think," Audrey says. "She's never happy, exactly, at least not with me. But she was doing so well, and we've all been absolutely elated about this role. Sometime since she started rehearsals, she got back together with Ray. I don't know if it's the production schedule or what, but she's this big around." She makes a circle with her thumb and forefinger. After turning on another lamp, she switches off the television.

Lucille is still standing with her coat on. This is the most Audrey has shared with her for so long that she hesitates to speak.

"You're welcome to wait and see what Ben reports. Have a seat. Sanka or...scotch?"

"I hope I haven't interrupted your work." But then, because she has imagined how much easier a reunion with Lake might be with Audrey and Ben here, she says, "Yes, Sanka, please. I have enough trouble sleeping." She chooses a seat facing the door—the one Lake might walk through any minute.

She notices two large rectangles on the wall. Paintings must have been removed recently, the yellow wall paint around them faded from the sun. There's what looks like a little spider in each dark space, where broken plaster branches out from the nail's hole.

Audrey sits across from her. Another long silence. "You look well," she says.

"You're a bad liar."

"I'll take that as a compliment."

Lucille lets the remark go, begins talking about her clients, one who is so sad she can't bear to have her curtains open. They talk about the wedding. "Not like the war, that's for sure. There was a live band at the reception. Martha's husband's family has money. You wouldn't believe the write-ups in the paper that named each kind of flower in the centerpieces at the bridal luncheons." But then she switches topics. "She's not going to want to see me."

"No." Audrey shakes her head. "That's true. I have to say, I'm shocked you would move here. Maybe you know what you're doing, but sometimes Lake doesn't want to see even us. I thought the show was giving her a place to...I don't know, direct her energy."

"What about this Ray?"

Audrey's brow furrows. "Ray Stapleton. I don't know. I used to think he was crazy about her. He served a year in Vietnam."

"He's not an actor?"

"No, an attorney, like his father."

"He looked more that type—I bet that's who I saw. Good-looking fellow. He sounds smart." She pauses awkwardly, out of things to say. "What about your paintings? Where are they?"

"You noticed. Ben hasn't."

"What do you mean, he hasn't noticed?"

Audrey firmly holds the chairs' arms, looking very much in control. "I've rented a studio for myself. And I'm slowly moving my work into it."

Lucille doesn't remember her ever being giddy for Ben. Perhaps she was incapable of seeing it. She always pictured Audrey as that solitary figure on the train from Virginia to Washington, in her young twenties, a bouquet of camellias in her lap. She described her arrival once, and Lucille has always seen her that way: resolute with desire, her future still ahead of her.

"I didn't know what I wanted," Audrey had said. "I just *wanted*."

She lights a cigarette now, lifting it elegantly into the air.

"Glad some things don't ever change."

"First and last one of the day. Pretty soon I'll be completely weaned. I had a health scare. I'm fine now." She waves away the smoke, along with any further questions. "But here's one thing that's changed. Daniel Brink came by the gallery a couple of days ago." She smiles for the first time.

"Daniel." He had loved Audrey. "When was the last time you'd seen him?"

"Long time ago, not since he married. That was a few years after the war. Apparently, his wife had been sick. She passed away last fall."

"And he was coming to tell you." Lucille smiles at Audrey, raising her eyebrows.

"You can imagine what good care he took of his wife. It was wonderful talking to him again."

"Maybe you'll stay in touch now."

"I hope." She shrugs.

"I was wondering—what has Lake been doing for money?"

"She hasn't asked you for any, has she?" Audrey looks stunned.

Lucille shakes her head.

"She has a job teaching drama, which was why the timing of this show at the end of the winter break worked so well. Her high school doesn't open until next week."

"Lake was good tonight. Maybe I was partial, but I thought the crowd loved her."

"She has talent. I agree. But can it sustain her, you know—is it enough? You need more than talent." She stubs out her cigarette and folds her arms. "Look, Lucille, the last thing we need is for you to make things worse for Lake. You've only been a source of sorrow—"

"I'm not going anywhere, I'm going to stay here and be a—" She almost says the word *mother*, but Audrey is looking at her with such contempt. "Eventually she'll understand everything."

"You better get it right this time."

When Ben returns he's alone. "Don't look at me like that," he says to Lucille and Audrey both. "I wasn't going to drag her back here. She didn't eat all day. She was nervous. She said she was fine by the last act and wanted to go on. Who does she think she is? Whatever her problem, it's not life-threatening."

"What about tomorrow's shows?" asks Lucille.

"That director—he's a real charmer. Told Lake and the understudy they both better be ready to walk on and he'd let them know an hour before. But I wouldn't let her up there after she pulled a stunt like that."

Audrey throws up her hands, as if to say to Lucille, *See? See what I'm dealing with?* She asks about Ray. "Was he there?"

"She'd sent him away by the time I saw her."

"He left her there?" Audrey shakes her head. "Nothing makes sense. But she'll call if anything is really wrong."

Ben freshens the drink he left on the mantel. The cup of Sanka Lucille holds has grown cold. She won't try to see the play again. Maybe she was the jinx. She should leave Lake alone, at least for now.

She lingers by the door, wanting something—maybe a promise that Audrey will call with news of Lake. But she won't stoop to ask. Audrey takes the cup from her, smiles wearily, opens the door for her. Audrey owes her nothing.

1944

12

Lucille had made a pact with herself regarding the skirt: If she was pregnant, she would walk back into Garfinckel's with it, try on something else in the dressing room, and leave both items behind. If she wasn't, she would return the tag along with cash payment to the service counter and wear the skirt every day for a week in honor of her future, set to rights.

It hung in her closet for weeks, the color muted in the shadows. When she finally pulled it off the hanger to wear it, she crushed the soft wool in her hands, as if to wring out some pleasure it would never bring.

Standing in front of the closet-door mirror, she pulled the zipper up its tracks. It ran smoothly, its brassy teeth in unison, but she felt a tightness, anticipating the worst. When the slide met the waistband, it stuck, and just when it seemed it wouldn't be forced, that there was nothing to be done about that indecent V in the middle of her back, she gave it another tug and it closed. The fit was smooth and straight, in fact, as a pencil. She'd lived on cottage cheese and Melba toast for the last week.

Inconclusive. There still had been no symptoms, not definitive ones anyway. If a rumbling stomach counted, then everyone must be pregnant. And no one had replaced Greta. Was this good fortune, not to have to pretend everything was fine for someone else? Maybe. Maybe not. This was the purgatorial balance in which Lucille woke, worked, barely ate, and slept. Would there be a baby, or not?

She didn't have to pretend much for Shirley, because they had never hit it off exactly. Her overstuffed closet and the cascading hats on her bureau—such riches were a wall to any real friendship. For Shirley, life was all fun and games, nothing serious about it. For instance, tonight she had invited five other women over for dinner without asking Lucille, forcing them all on a silly scavenger hunt around the apartment before dinner. Lucille hated games. Why should there be a winner and loser in frivolity? Life served that up on its own. She was eager for an excuse to exit when the first wave of nausea rippled through her. Nothing came up in the bathroom except another decisive wave. At least she was out of the game and in her bed. She rocked herself while the antics proceeded, Shirley's voice calling out, "You've won, you've won!"

Sitting on the edge of an exam table, Lucille listened to an older woman, Dr. Vandiver, explain her options.

"Not options," Lucille said. "I can't call them that."

"Recourse, then," the doctor said.

Clare Vandiver. The only female doctor Lucille had found in the telephone book. She was stocky, with a cap of white hair, and rocked up and down on her toes, maybe to give herself some height.

Lucille was wearing a wedding band from the five-and-dime—with so many men proposing every day, it wasn't hard to come by. The ring might be why she didn't sense any judgment, at first anyway, from the doctor. She made herself a few years older too, twenty-four, and said her husband was overseas in a military hospital. "He wrote to me that he might not make it home. I have no family here. I'll lose my job. I don't think I can take care of him and a baby too. And what if he doesn't make it? I won't be able to work." She ran the sentences together breathlessly.

"We can test you by sending your urine out. You've heard of this," Dr. Vandiver said. "Do you think we need to do that?"

"No sense in an animal dying when I know the answer."

"You don't want an exam then?"

"No need."

"Be careful not to gain much weight," Dr. Vandiver went on. "No more than fifteen pounds. As little as you are, maybe fewer. It'll make for a much easier delivery."

The doctor lifted her glasses, which hung from a chain around her neck, and put them on. She wrote something on a pad of paper. "There's a place, Penington, where you can live out the pregnancy."

Live out—what a strange phrase, like it would be a period of retirement, or survival. *Wait it out* was what she must mean. The doctor's rosy cheeks and white hair made Lucille think of Mrs. Claus. So that's what she delivered the rest of the year: babies, bad news, escape plans.

Lucille felt weak as straw. "Do you mind if I lie down?" She pulled her legs up and rested on her side, not waiting for an answer.

On the wall across from her hung a portrait of the Virgin Mary holding the Christ child. Mary's robe was the same blue as Dr. Vandiver's eyes. Everyone always said tell your troubles to Jesus. He knew more about trouble than anyone. Think of what he went through, dying on a cross, all his friends abandoning him, his mother weeping at his feet.

And then the doctor said, without Lucille's having to ask, "The only other option is Walsh. Larry Walsh. He's the only one who will do it and do it safely. Here's his number but you must call him after seven in the evening." She tore a paper off from her pad and handed it to Lucille. "I can tell from your face how desperate you are. I don't blame you. In your situation I might make up a good story too. If it's not all true, it might as well be."

"There's not a woman who'll do this?"

"I don't know one. Hard enough to work in this business as it is." Dr. Vandiver paused. "Do you have money?"

Even through her dizziness, Lucille read her look: *Probably not*. The people who need it most never have the money. "I have a job," Lucille said. "I can pay off whatever over time."

"It's not really something you could have saved up for, I realize, but this doctor can't send you bills. Paper trail, you see. Girls like you aren't good risks. You must have the money."

"I can get the money."

So many lies, like caged birds beating their wings inside her, all this time, had flown out. Who knew? She was capable of anything.

The following Saturday, she emerged from her cold and bare bedroom—it was November, but all warm days had to be over before the building manager turned on the heat. Shirley had said more than once: "Live here, why don't you? Hang a picture." Most mornings Lucille didn't bother to open her blinds.

A hollow fireplace centered the living area. Feeling forbidden but bold, she walked past it to Shirley's room, where a monogrammed pillow lay on the unmade bed and lotions and perfumes lined the vanity. She found her in the kitchen, the warmest room. "I need a hundred dollars," she announced to her roommate's back. Shirley was sitting at the table painting her nails from a bottle of red Cutex.

"Yeah, me too," she said, without turning around. Lucille stayed in the doorway, saying nothing. "You're not kidding, are you?"

Lucille wouldn't cry. She would not break down or get on her knees for Shirley.

"Oh, honey, don't look like that. Just don't. What for? What do you need all that money for?" She was waving her hands in the air, drying her fingernails.

"I hate coming to you like this. I'll pay you back."

"Oh, Lu, you're in trouble. I can tell. What'd you go and do?"

"It's going to be okay. I just don't have all the money. I have some of it—"

"You need even more than a hundred?"

"I just need a hundred from you." The sound of her voice, almost angry, surprised her. She could not contort herself into whatever shape of indebtedness was expected. She was acting as though she already had the cash in hand. And she knew she did, as soon as she asked. Shirley could not say no. Lucille saw how she might later resent Shirley for giving her the money. Gratitude might never mix with an act this unconscionable. "Please," she said, dropping her head in her hands to show that she could not countenance any more questions.

The address for Dr. Walsh was an apartment building. She hadn't thought of this possibility, that she wouldn't meet him in an office. The sun had been down for several hours. Open only during the day, businesses in this block of Fifteenth lowered their metal shutters at night. The street was eerily quiet. Inside, the lobby was dimly lit, empty of any furniture, nothing but a counter with a lamp hanging above, pigeonholes on the wall behind, no one behind the counter. She took the elevator up, a sluggish, jerky ride, and walked through the corridor, which smelled like cooked cabbage. She expected Dr. Walsh's wife to answer the door. At least she'd thought the voice on the phone had been his wife. When Lucille called him, a woman handed the phone over to Larry Walsh, who gave her the address and two commands: bring $150 in cash and throw away this phone number.

But it wasn't his home. The apartment was mostly empty, aside from a sofa in the living area. "Payment first," he said. A stethoscope hung around his neck. He laid the envelope of money she handed him on the sofa and led her to the bedroom, where dark wooden blinds covered two windows. There was an exam table, with two metal apparatuses at one end, what looked like a milking stool, and the floor covered by butcher paper.

Paper. Not butcher paper.

When he left her alone to undress, she moved methodically, folding her blouse and skirt and each undergarment into a crocheted shopping bag she'd brought. With each piece of clothing, she reminded herself what she wanted: riddance, a clean break. She wanted to work off her debt to Shirley and return home as soon as the war was over. But all day she'd told herself she didn't have to go through with this. Every step here she'd said that, over and over in her mind. A white ceramic bowl, like one used for mixing batter, sat on the papered floor alongside a row of stainless tools.

She wrapped herself in the cool cotton sheet he'd given her.

He was bald, freckled on his head, with black-framed glasses and the start of a hunch behind his neck. Maybe because she'd expected the medicinal atmosphere of an office, she smelled the wood of tongue depressors though none were in sight.

"Would you like some brandy?" He held out a small glass with a couple fingers' worth. He must have poured it in the kitchen. It burned her throat going down and she shuddered. He eyed her wedding band. "You're not trying to cover up something you shouldn't have done while your husband was away, are you?"

She shook her head. Her mother once said, "Men go to war to prove they're as tough as women in childbirth." Lucille leaned back onto the table.

"Put your feet in the stirrups."

Stirrups. She knew how to do that, though she'd had her feet in only one kind of stirrup back home. Now she wasn't in this room but playing at grooming horses with Jimmy, hiding. "Goldbricking," her father would say when he caught them goofing off. She went to light Jimmy's cigarette—"Let me, let me! I do so know how"—striking against the strip of friction, then holding the flame to the tobacco. She threw down the match, which caught on the straw and blazed. "Put it out," Jimmy said, but Lucille laughed. Jimmy stomped it out with his boots. "Stupid, you know that. You're stupid."

They both knew the story of their mother, how when she was a girl of seven she'd started a brush fire too close to the house and burned it down. The entire house. Things were always burning in the country, everything made of wood. Houses, brush, stables, chicken coops. Even things that weren't. Hearts. Our hearts *burned*. And lips. The angel who brought the burning coal to Isaiah's lips, *you are forgiven*.

Jimmy had known about Arthur, told her she was a fool then too, and threatened to tell her father. But then he'd left, drafted.

"First I'll examine you," the bald, bespectacled man said. "You'll feel my hand on your stomach, then pressure."

She picked a spot on the blank wall and made a picture of the orchard out her bedroom window—a monarch's view from a peasant's house, with acres of trees and shrubs split by dark rutted earth into rays of rich color, the greens and yellows and reds of early summer. The wall hadn't been painted in a while. Light black streaks showed where furniture used to be. A handprint. She looked away.

She did not want to die.

His hand went to her knee and she jumped. "Relax," he said.

She laughed nervously. He looked at her, or maybe past her. Her eyes had returned to the picture—the dimpled bottoms of yellow quince, the sculptured pruning of leaders and branches that let in more sunlight—when she felt something altogether different and a mix of anger and desire shot through her on the same current. She jumped again, this time shaking the whole table.

"Easy there, girl, I'm just having a little fun. You're no fool, not completely. You're coming along, and the sooner we get this done with, the better."

Sitting on his little stool, he leaned over his spread of instruments on the papered floor. She hoisted her left leg over to the right side in a soundless roll, the way she might turn a root sack into a hole. Her feet on the floor, she ran, grabbing her bag of clothes. She had wits enough about her to reach for the envelope on the sofa.

She needn't have run down the hall, taking the stairs five flights down, panting like an animal, dressed like someone in an asylum. At the bottom of the stairwell, she stopped to listen—nothing. The envelope was empty. She pressed her wet brow against it, crumpled it, and threw it on the ground.

At home, Shirley was lining her lips in front of her vanity mirror. Darrell was on his way over. "I'm going to have to break his heart tonight," she said. "My daddy says I have to return to West Virginia. I'll leave by Christmas. I hate leaving you in the lurch like this, Lu. I expect there are still dozens of girls who need a room. But this place is pricey. Maybe you need something cheaper?"

13

When Lucille started out on the bus it was twilight, that time of half-light before anyone had stopped their task to turn on a lamp. Against the pink horizon, buildings, houses, and trees were rising up in hulking shapes. From the stop on Connecticut Avenue she walked at a steady clip, but as soon as she turned onto Ben's street, with its sprawling houses and compact lawns, her knees went weak. She'd been full of conviction earlier, certain that talking to him was the right thing to do. She had found his street on a city map, traced the bus route here. Stars were barely out. The moon was thin as thread. What if he wasn't home?

In the biting cold and thickening dark, she shook so hard that she thought her heart might come loose. Perhaps this was how she would die.

What if he was home?

It wasn't courage that brought her to the city, though people always remarked on her gumption. She would never have had the courage to come here had she not been made to.

With the house in view, her dread lifted. All was dark. Encouraged, she kept walking downhill with an approach that an owner might take, as if this were her shelter to return to every day. Do I love him? She thought of how gingerly he had lifted the folds of her skirt onto her knee before closing the car door that night. The trees lined up neatly in their tree boxes along the quiet street. His car was at the curb, but a car outside didn't mean anyone was home, not when everyone was trying not to drive. She held on to the iron railing, its cold seeping through her thin wool glove, and walked up the steps to the covered porch, tucked away in the dark. The house was shingle-sided, with a screen door separating her from the main door, and paint coming away in thin matchstick strips. She blew on her hands, warming and readying herself. Though winter hadn't begun, it felt like the depths of it. She hadn't prepared for such cold, did not think she would need warm things because she'd always gotten by without. She stood longer, waiting for some sign. She opened the screen door and lifted the knocker, let it fall, then again.

The porch light came on, blinding her. She couldn't make out the face at the door. Lit from behind, it was in darkness. But she knew it was a woman. After a long, blank pause, she heard, "Lucille? Is that you?"

In that chock-full moment Lucille didn't know who was speaking in front of her, in Ben's house. Everything was wrong. The yellow light and its warmth drifting toward her when she was so cold, and the energy—the shrill voice—when she was so tired. But she knew something of this person, and with that knowledge came a wariness. She could not remember the woman's name. All Lucille could make out was a face pinched in query, not much else, until she saw the russet brown hair cut just past the woman's shoulders.

"Are you all right? You must be freezing out there. Come on in. You haven't got on a decent coat."

On the foyer table, a small lamp lit a row of leather gloves. Lucille had seen such a number of gloves only in a department store. Her mouth felt like cotton wool. She wouldn't look at herself in the long mirror bolted to the closet door. She looked back to the woman. "Audrey."

"I'd given up ever seeing you again. Goodness, wasn't it last May we met, now it's December. I've wondered how you were." Audrey wore a dress the color of plums, pleated at the bottom and fitted across her bust. She was much taller than Lucille, sturdy with soft edges, the way her hair curled under and the dress clung to her waist and chest.

"I found you."

"You did. How in the world?" She was taking off Lucille's coat and laying it across the radiator. Lucille shivered. She'd not wanted to give up her coat.

"It looked like no one was home." Words she didn't know existed flowed out of her. "I called your office, and they didn't have a number, only this address."

"Oh yes, I updated things when I moved in a few weeks ago. They should have my number, though—I'll have to remember to check that."

Ben has sold his house—that was Lucille's first thought. She would have to do this again, knock on another door.

Audrey led her into the dark living room. A dim light was on in an adjoining room through French doors. "I'd been painting in there," she said, now going to each lamp in the living room, switching it on. "I go round and do this every night, just to fill up the place." At first the dark room looked familiar, but as it brightened, Lucille didn't recognize the pale-yellow walls or blue velvet sofa.

"Thank you. I can't stay. I don't want to interrupt your evening. I just thought…" Lucille's voice trailed off. Impossible to explain why she was here. Tears thickened behind her eyes. She was hungry. She'd been too nervous to eat that last cracker in her pocket, now likely crushed as the coat lay folded on the radiator. There was a loud ticking, though Lucille didn't want to turn to look for it—she could not make another false move.

"Since Ben left, all I have to look forward to is the canvas. I've finished a half dozen and this one's almost done."

It was too late. She wouldn't have to face him after all.

"May I have a glass of water? I'm sorry to trouble you." Lucille's voice trembled. She partly wanted to be away from Audrey's eye and partly wanted time to consider the meaning of "since Ben left."

"Or is something hot better? I'll put on the kettle." The sound of running water, then: "Wait, we need something a little stronger to warm you up."

Lucille turned toward the ticking now, the tall grandfather clock. Marble candlesticks adorned the mantel, alongside the painting she remembered of full, feathery white peonies. This was Ben's house. Audrey lived here. She returned with two small cut glasses. "Sherry?" A gold band on her finger.

"You must have gotten married," Lucille said.

"In October. We were married only a few weeks before he received his orders. Here I am, another bereft war bride."

On the way here, Lucille had asked herself that ridiculous question, *Do I love him? What a stupid, stupid girl I am.*

"We met at a party," said Audrey, smiling for the first time. "Then we danced through the summer, and that was it."

Lucille noticed her quietness, the way she sat in the crease of the sofa's elbow, not moving, economical with her energy. She was plainer than Lucille first thought. Plainly perfect. "Isn't that how everyone decides to marry these days?"

"I've danced more in the last six months than I did all of college." Audrey reached into a side-table drawer for a package of cigarettes and held it out to Lucille.

"No, thank you." She was thinking she could corroborate that in some way. She had seen them dancing herself, a vision she had been disowning since Audrey answered the door.

"It's a bad habit, but when I'm not holding a paintbrush." Audrey smiled again, then lit one. "You still have the same job?"

"At the adjutant general's office, typing away." Lucille looked at her hands. "My fingers are so dry they might crack."

"And your brother?"

Lucille now remembered talking about Jimmy, the reason she was donating blood. "Still hearing from him, never as often as I'd like though. No news is good news, right? When will this war be over?"

"In some ways I feel it's just beginning, what with Ben's leaving."

"So you gave up your room at McLean Gardens? The town is full to the hilt. You must have made somebody's day."

"What about you? Where are you living?"

"In an apartment, nothing as grand as this. On Twelfth and M. But my roommates, one by one, are moving out." She rushed on with a new exuberance. "I need to make other arrangements. What did you do with your McLean Gardens spot? That's really what I wanted to reach you about, to see if you knew of anything to rent, just a room." She sipped the sherry, her hands calmer now. An explanation, a reason for being here.

"Oh, goodness, let me think. Nothing comes to mind, but I can ask in the office too. Even here I feel like I'm renting." She looked around the room. "This furniture—it's not mine. I've been cleaning things, trying to give the house a fresh start. Bought new pillows," she said, pointing to them. "But years have settled into this place."

"Tell me about the wedding," Lucille asked, even though she didn't want to hear. Effort was the best thing now, a cheery smile.

"Quick, tiny. Hardly what you'd call a wedding. It was still warm outside, then there was a cold snap and the leaves changed colors. Now they're gone and so is he. That's how fast it all happened."

"You must love him very much to do this. To marry and wait, I mean." A look on Audrey's face, a firmness or a worry, made Lucille wonder, does she? Does *she* love him?

"Yes, I just got a letter from him. After I read it, I felt like I'd eaten a meal but without any salt. I was full from hearing his voice, but unsatisfied without him beside me." She studied Lucille. "What about you—weren't you involved with someone?"

"No," she said without hesitation. And then, because she couldn't leave it at that, could never leave it at that—Arthur always over her shoulder—she said, "No, not overseas, back home. But that's over, for now anyway."

Audrey nodded sympathetically into the smoke. "Well, it's such an opportunity to be here, right? Like you said, it sure beats teaching school back home."

Had she really said that? She could think of much worse things.

"Hey—I probably shouldn't talk like this, I mean, I haven't thought it through, but whenever I open up the paper to the want ads, I do wonder. With all these empty bedrooms, I should put a sign up."

Lucille considered the pull to the yellow glow of the lamplight, the glass of sherry warming in her hand. She felt the air shift. "Well, if you did, I'd be most interested."

"I don't know what Ben would think," Audrey went on, renewed, as if Lucille hadn't spoken. "I don't think of it as mine to rent, you know. But it would surely help the cause, and otherwise, I'm not sure I'm doing much of anything for the war. I mean the film work, it's important, but it's hard to see how it helps anybody directly. I never was good at knitting balaclava helmets."

Lucille let the statements hang, as if to give them permanence. She took another sip of her sherry. "I didn't mean to keep you this long. Let me get your telephone number and I'll give you mine. We won't lose touch this time." She stood up and turned to fluff the pillow and smooth the seat cushion.

"Oh, leave that," Audrey said, but Lucille was already walking to the door, reaching into her pocketbook for a piece of paper to write on. They exchanged numbers, nearly losing their footing with the cold burst of wind through the door. "Not exactly weather to wear our yellow wedges in, is it?" Audrey smiled. "Let me drive you, please."

"You can't be wasting gasoline on me, not after all that war effort talk." Before Audrey could protest, Lucille careened down the steps and walkway, waving—almost happily—over her shoulder. "Thank you! Thank you!"

She was thanking her for help not yet delivered, only considered. She could not believe what she'd done, entreated Ben's wife.

Some part of her had known she would the moment she recognized Audrey's face.

&

Audrey returned to the little room where her painting was, a figurative, tonal study of lights and darks after Caravaggio, and saw how she had answered too much of it for the viewer. But her energy for it was gone now. She stretched out on the long velveteen sofa, the length of it luxurious and lonesome all at once. Her head ached, probably from the nitrate film—the headaches were unpredictable, but not serious—or the sherry. She had dreamed of this, living on her own, needing no one. Perfect independence. But every day was the same. A walk to the bus. The ride itself, with strangers. The walk home. Eggs or oatmeal, whichever she'd not eaten for breakfast. Painting, but no one saw her efforts. She had no subjects around her to draw. She liked doing solitary things in the company of others, like reading in the public library. She liked being alone. She didn't like being lonely.

Tonight someone had knocked on the door. The knock had frightened her. She didn't like living alone in fear. But she had opened the door and in walked Lucille, as radiant as if she were wearing those yellow shoes to match the golden highlights in her hair. She lit up the house.

Audrey would consider this—a tenant, maybe two.

14

The front hall was empty, silent, the sound perhaps of a family sleeping in far-off rooms. It was like that, a family's large home, smelling of detergent and wool, an ornate rug of reds and greens under her, dark chestnut moldings and banisters, a stuffed deer head at the top of the stairs.

Long before Dr. Vandiver ever mentioned Penington, when Lucille was tracking the paths of the army in the Philippines in the newspaper, thinking of Jimmy, she'd seen in the local section a photograph of three girls in the kitchen here, learning how to cook. The women—you couldn't tell if they were girls or women—all had their backsides to the camera. She remembered wondering at the awkwardness of photographing people who were trying to hide.

Now a young girl, not pregnant, or at least not visibly so, led Lucille down a hall and into an office where an older woman sat behind a desk. Mrs. Fleming, she said her name was, had dark hair, not yet graying, and wore a buttoned-up blouse, a bit of lace at the neck. How many frightened girls had succumbed to her soft, understanding gaze?

"How far along are you, dear?"

"Four months."

"We typically admit girls in their seventh month—that's when most aren't able to conceal their pregnancy any longer. And your family, where are they?"

"In North Carolina." Lucille needed a place to live now, not in three months, but she kept quiet.

"No one here to help you?"

"No."

"I welcome you to Penington. You've made a wise decision coming here. We can help you get set up when your baby comes. In the meantime, we'll keep you comfortable and fed. You'll meet lots of girls like yourself."

Lucille heard a crowd coming down the hall and turned her head to the doorway. Some of the girls were far along, wearing loose blouses.

"They're going for their afternoon outing," Mrs. Fleming said.

"Everyone gets plenty of fresh air—and companionship. You don't have to go through this alone, you know. Now, your family in North Carolina," she went on, "are they willing and able to help support you through this period?"

"How do you mean?"

"There are expenses related to staying here."

"Yes, of course," Lucille said without hesitation, though she hadn't thought of that. She'd thought this was a charity group. The charity of others would come to her rescue. The chimes of a grandfather clock went off, sounding just like the one at Audrey's. A somber, aching tone, but in a rhythm that made light of that tone. They waited for the quarters to play out. Weeks had passed and Audrey hadn't called her. Why would she, when she had her delicately stemmed sherry glasses and her long sofa of one unbroken cushion.

"We don't want this to be a burden for families," Mrs. Fleming was saying, "but not all the costs of caring for you are covered by our generous donors. There are also ways to work off any debt after the baby is born."

"I understand."

"We also work with outside agencies to find a couple wanting a newborn. You will make someone's dream come true, be assured of that. Many older women and men who are settled, with means, can provide things for this child if you cannot."

"You mean married couples."

"Married, yes."

"But there are so many women having babies while their husbands are in the service."

Mrs. Fleming—Hope Fleming, read the placard on her desk—said, "You've got a point, don't you. But the difference is that these women have family support around them—mothers or sisters—not to mention money, both of which will ease the difficulty of single parenting until their husbands return."

"And if they don't?" Lucille's voice rose.

Mrs. Fleming looked at her blankly.

"If their husbands don't return and they're left to parent alone? How is that different than my having a child now?"

"My dear, it comes down to economics, yours or someone else's. Doesn't it always? And not to be indelicate, but I believe we just confirmed that you have neither independent means nor means on which you can depend. Here are the details if you choose to spend the end of your pregnancy with us." She slid a piece of paper across the desk. "You won't be sorry. You will, in time, forget the difficulty of this decision."

"Do you have children, Mrs. Fleming?"

"I've been asked that question before. It's my policy not to answer it."

A cold silence descended. "Thank you for your time."

Mrs. Fleming led her back to the door, and Lucille felt at the height of control, saying yes, she would consider the opportunity of Penington, but she would not commit.

That feeling fell away as she descended the long set of stone steps. Had she any money, even the amount given up to Dr. Walsh weeks ago, she would be grateful for the chance. She looked back at the beautiful mansion that used to belong to a family. A lost home. No one would leave such a thing if they could afford to keep it up.

Whatever actions she'd taken thus far lacked any real deliberation. Like putting on shoes before going out in the cold. Stepping to the right in order to avoid a collision on the sidewalk. Every effort required the opposite of inertia—the production of energy—but not much and not with any joy. There was deep sadness. No satisfying resolution. Like taking one's own life must be. Tragic because compulsory. *You will, in time, forget the difficulty of the decision.* But there had not yet been anything like a decision. Decision involved choice, and there was none.

"Come with me to Lexington for Christmas," Shirley begged.

"You know I can't," Lucille said.

"There'll be parties, every night."

"You're telling me there are men left in Lexington."

"Handsome ones." Shirley winked. "My daddy's age."

Lucille didn't say she didn't need another one of those.

"I don't like leaving you here alone at the end of our lease like this. What are you going to do?"

"Don't worry about me. I'll figure it out." She did feel grateful, not for Shirley's money but for her insistence on being a friend.

"I'll leave my address, in case—"

"I'll send you the money. Don't worry about that either."

In the days running up to Christmas, without Shirley's comings and goings, the apartment was peaceful. The radiators hissed and clanked less with the heat turned down to save money. Keeping on the fewest lights possible, Lucille moved in the kitchen by the light of the open refrigerator, pulling out leftover meat from nights before, shredding it into chopped carrots, and heating both with water on the stove.

Most of the women in the typing pool who took more than two days off for Christmas did so without pay. There were several like Lucille who needed the money, and one of them, Helen, told her they could make a small bit selling chestnuts for a roaster outside the Mayflower Hotel on Christmas Eve day. At different corners of the building, each stood with a tray of little bags of nuts strapped around their necks. The roaster himself was across the street and down a block, doing a better business because the nuts were warmer, but she and Helen sold a few to the families and men staying at the hotel.

The trays brought to mind fruit picking, how a bag would be strapped around her neck, leaving her hands free to snap off each apple stem. You couldn't pull or yank—that might break the skin and rot the fruit or injure the bud of next year's fruit, hidden in each leaf spray. A thumb press might leave a yellow-brown bruise, and the pickings had to be poured softly into the field boxes. She pictured all this, a comfort, as she called out "Merry Christmas!"

"What are you doing later?" a man asked. He was tall with a thin mustache and bloodshot eyes. It was dark now, but she'd been advised to keep selling through the dinner hour. She had already dreamed of sitting inside the hotel next to its grandly lit tree, off her feet and warmed by a drink, but she said no, she couldn't, she had family at home. "You can never tell," he said.

The four dollars she earned went into an envelope for Shirley. At home, she closed the blinds against the wreathed streetlights below and didn't turn on the radio to hear carols.

The next day came wet with rain and clouds, and an ache in her neck. Walking aimlessly on quiet streets, she might have been in the country—an owl hooted high in a tree. Back in the apartment, she cleaned hair from the tub, wiped the fridge of moldy fruits, and mopped the floors. Saving the cleaning fee meant more cash for Shirley.

Lucille wrote home of how wonderful things were, the endless round of parties with sugar cookies and eggnog, her plans to attend the evening Christmas service at church. She wrote of turkey dinner with cranberries while she ate sardines and pineapple from a can. She described the tree she and her roommates put up, with gold tinsel garlands, and the snow that fell in a layer of gauze, how fast it melted on the warm sidewalks. Her inventions almost made her proud.

The only particle of truth was that she would go to church, only it would be a few days after Christmas, after work, when cries of children, unbearable to her just now, were less likely. Candles lit the altar, steps above the pews. Lucille saw no clergy, didn't want to meet anyone's solicitous eye. That would be too much. As would dropping to the kneeler. She'd never used one, but instinctively she knew the descent to her knees might draw out unending tears. She sat in the pew, the stained-glass windows dark with night. The organist finished practicing, and at first Lucille mourned the silence, but then she felt held by it, same as the music. Other people sat down, bowed their heads, crossed themselves, rose to leave. If they cried she didn't hear them.

She could see how this might become habit, retreating to cold, stony churches, except for what happened next.

While she was fumbling for her keys outside her apartment door, her phone rang. It rang with the persistence of Arthur, though this thought—it was a wish now—surprised her. Her mother had told her that he'd left Pomona, was on a long journey, hunting and fishing. He'd sold his land to her father. Her father's dream had come true, one of them anyway. Still she hurried, eager to hear his voice proving his infinite loyalty. She needed it badly just now.

But a woman said, "May I please speak with Lucille?"

"This is she."

"Oh, good. You're still here. I just returned to the house after being away," Audrey went on, "and I can't bear it, these empty rooms. Won't you rent one?"

"I'm not sure I can afford it."

"Don't worry about that, we'll work something out. Come as soon as you can." But she laughed as she said this, not sounding as desperate as she claimed.

15

It wasn't much of an adjustment, Lucille's moving in. Audrey had grown used to long baths, the kitchen empty of all but sunshine each morning, but these routines Lucille didn't disrupt. She didn't leave the bathroom sink streaked with toothpaste or her hosiery dripping from every bar like other roommates had. Those first cold nights in the house she slept with her window cracked, much to Audrey's bafflement more than anything. "I'd sleep outdoors if I could," Lucille said. Audrey's only moment of doubt came when she opened the front door to her and was reminded again how tiny Lucille was, how ungainly she felt beside her. But there was a fluidity to her movement, a lightness, that brought to mind the tree house Audrey's father had built years ago, high in a redbud, which became a refuge from her mother's sickly shadow. She loved its window, improbably sunlit in a yard otherwise thick with trees. Later, in her teens, curled in that surprise of light, she smoked cigarettes. She was back there again when Lucille tilted her head to one side, half closed her eyes, and opened her mouth wide with laughter.

Sharing a home with Lucille was nothing like living with her mother—there wasn't any neediness in her. Audrey would have smelled that from a distance; she would have barred the door if it came calling.

Lucille spent a long time walking through Audrey's studio, looking at but not touching the brushes and paint tubes, the chalky pastels and glue and ink bottles. When she got to the easel, a cluster of drawings clipped to it, she asked, "May I?" Audrey nodded and Lucille lifted each one. "I like your portraits best. I like everything. I've never known an artist."

"I still haven't sold anything."

"You probably haven't tried. Draw me," she said. "Don't you need a model? Go on, get your brush, or your charcoal—is that what you use?"

"I'm not really that kind of portrait painter."

"That's all right, don't try to flatter me. The last thing I want to be remembered for is trying to be pretty." Lucille mussed her hair and sat down in a ladderback chair.

Behind the easel, Audrey started making marks. She could almost feel the pencil touching Lucille, the slide of it across the paper, as if against her skin. Her thin arms formed a delicate geometry. "I know I'm really drawing when I forget that the line I'm making is forming a mouth. It's just a line, or a shape. I'm not drawing you, I'm delineating planes in space."

"Am I looking in the right spot? I have an itch."

"Hold on, almost there. Yes, a good spot. You've lost some of your accent," Audrey said.

"That's like saying I've lost a limb."

"You've still got enough, don't worry. Maybe it helped you sell some chestnuts at Christmas?"

Lucille laughed.

"Listen," Audrey said, "I haven't told my husband about your moving here. But I will. What's the worst thing he'll say? Tell me I have to have you out when he returns? Well, the war will be over then, and you won't be sticking around anyway. No, it'll all work out. He'll be glad I have some company. He can't do much about it, so far away, can he?"

"Let me know what he says. I don't want to be a bother."

Audrey turned the drawing toward Lucille to have a look.

"Yep. Definitely a mouth, and definitely mine. Like I said, you're good."

After Lucille had shopped for groceries a few times, she had everything she needed to prepare supper out of seemingly nothing. She never opened a cookbook. And each morning she brewed tea for them both, urging Audrey to sketch something or add to whatever she was working on. They started off on the same bus each day, parting ways at Foggy Bottom. But in the evenings, she walked in the neighborhood, and on the weekends, she walked in the woods. "You're like a houseplant," she told Audrey. "You just need the light from a warm sunny window, a few gulps of water a week. Not me."

Washington had wilderness, Audrey had noticed, but only from afar. "It's too cold!" she protested, but Lucille uncovered mismatched pairs of galoshes to put over their shoes and various overcoats and hats to layer on. "I look like a ragamuffin," Audrey said.

"The pine needles don't care." On a nearby trail, Lucille led her across stones and fallen timber that bridged streams, up and over tree roots. She showed her how to set the ball of her foot first when going downhill and how lichen on one side of a rock usually faced north. While Audrey sketched, Lucille lightly touched the whiskery pattern of frost on the edge of the creek, her moist breath billowing in front of her. "It's all for us," she said. Audrey had never had a friend like Lucille, who dragged her palm across tree bark, just to feel the tree. Audrey wondered, not without envy, what Lucille would reveal on canvas if she took up painting. On one of their walks through the neighborhood, a stray tabby followed them—or Lucille, rather—right into the house. "Out of nowhere he appeared," Audrey said.

"Maybe he's magic," Lucille replied. Thus Merlin took up residency.

Once when they walked through an open meadow on the edge of the woods, Lucille told Audrey how her father had called her "wild, untamable." Audrey asked why, but the wind picked up and she lost the rest of what Lucille said.

If Audrey was a houseplant, Lucille was a pungent scent in the woods that couldn't quite be located, or contained.

Eyeing the basket of yarn at one end of the sofa, Lucille asked, "Do you needlepoint?"

"Not a stitch. You?"

"Only clothes."

"I should have known. That long-waisted number with kick pleats, the likes of which I've never seen. I thought you had your own personal tailor."

"You know that's not true, since I only have three dresses."

The basket was Ben's mother's. "There aren't too many of her personal things just lying around. I hate to disturb them. That's the thing with a big house. Someone dies and you can close the door on their things and never have to throw them out. I don't think Ben's tossed her toothbrush."

"We should help him."

"Before he left, he said, 'Feel free to sort through anything and take what you like, donate the rest.' But I haven't had the heart. It's one thing to go through the belongings of a dead person you loved. Another to go through the bedroom of someone you never met. And none of it's in my way."

"But what if you want another boarder?"

That threw Audrey into action. She and Lucille laid dresses and gowns, fringed, beaded, and satiny, heavy things, on the high four-poster bed. Lucille insisted Audrey try them on but they were too snug. "You try," Audrey said, managing to button a scalloped-hem flapper dress only halfway.

"Oh no, I'd never have a place to wear them," Lucille said.

"She must have been some kind of socialite with this wardrobe."

"Must have been lonely, never marrying again."

"Or not," said Audrey. "Maybe she was lonely when she was married and only later, when Ben was nearly grown, maybe then she had the time of her life going to parties in all these dresses. You never know. I didn't want to get married, not till I met Ben. Now look at me, a matron at twenty-three."

"Any regrets?"

"Not yet." Audrey laughed. "I don't think I've been married long enough for any. My parents were miserable together. They live apart now—my father's in a boardinghouse, did I tell you? You're supposed to stay with someone in sickness and in health, but I don't know. Always on the outside of someone's affliction, not being able to understand or relate, feels..."

"Like despair, I would think. Heretical."

"You're right. Heresy. I've never put that word to it, but that's right."

"It's no picnic in Pomona," Lucille said. "My mother keeps the windows closed on Sundays so when neighbors walk past on the way to church they won't hear one of my father's rages."

Audrey felt a delicate fretwork being carved between them, full of transparencies and female confidences. "I think Ben will be a good husband, but I don't really know. We didn't have much time."

They moved on to drawers, collecting hair combs entangled with gray strands, dust-coated bottles of weakened cologne, photographs of unknown persons tied up in stained ribbons. They tried on clip-on ear bobs and rhinestone ring bracelets. In a pile of things Lucille had marked to throw away, Audrey spotted a brown-olive metal case. "Not this!" she gasped. In raised lettering the case said *First Aid Packet - U.S. Army*. "This is what he was looking for that day. I'd never seen him so sad. He'll be relieved that we found it, though I don't suppose it can be much of a talisman for him, since he's already over there." She looked over the things Lucille had culled, making sure they weren't of any value, and in the end she saved back more than she gave away. They mopped the wood floors, washed the windows, opened the curtains as wide as they would go, but the sun had already gone down.

"You should take this room, with its own bath," said Lucille.

"Maybe. I'm sentimental about our beginnings."

"Yes," said Lucille, "of course." She had pulled over her head and clothes a high-necked green taffeta gown that enwrapped her like the leaves on a tulip stem. The small lamps gave off light as lambent as candles. For a moment the air shimmered. Audrey adored her.

They laughed at how they didn't need a man then. Might never need one again, so sufficient they'd become, as women always did during war. A man blew in with his demands, stomping his feet clean at the door with his wish to be fed and cared for. But in spite of their beliefs, Daniel won Audrey over when he showed up at the house. The ad he answered hadn't stated women only, but Audrey and Lucille assumed only women were looking. He'd gone to college briefly before entering the service, but in Fort Jackson, the Army found something wrong with him. "I've never been sick a day in my life," he swore with a grin. Lucille said his drawl, different from hers but just as deep, made her feel more at home. He was only two years older than Audrey, and not much taller, though he'd already lost much of his hair. He'd driven all the way up here for a job only to learn it didn't exist, and walked around the corner to NBC, where he now worked writing copy.

"I don't make breakfast," Audrey told him, "though you're welcome to some shelf space and a corner in the refrigerator. And if you can mow the grass in the spring, I'll leave coffee for you to heat. The yardman my husband relied on must have enlisted—not a single leaf got raked in December." Audrey gave him the bedroom with its own sink and toilet.

"More than three of us? I don't think so," she said after that. "Three's a nice number."

"Sturdy enough for a stool," Lucille added.

Audrey believed they moved with an easy distance around one another, helped by the fact that Daniel kept odd hours. He told them he loved living with two women, their fragrant sprays, little hats with veils, and pealing laughter—a sound so foreign in his childhood that every single time he heard it now, he sat up and wondered at what it could possibly mean.

But sometimes at night, Audrey heard a stirring in the house, and once she came down the stairs only far enough to discover Lucille in her nightgown, her backside a silhouette, staring out the windows. Just standing in the moonlight. Lucille would be up before Audrey, making their tea. Audrey wondered if she ever slept. On the weekends, Lucille seemed more and more content to spend time by herself in her bedroom. "I love dawn and twilight, give me midnight too. Afternoons, you can have them," she said lightly.

For weeks Lucille had dressed out of her suitcase. As long as she didn't hang up her clothes—including her three belted dresses that would give a bit, concealing as she grew—or put them in drawers, she was only visiting, stopping over, on a journey that hadn't ended. But with Daniel boarding too, her station seemed more official, and she spread her things around the room. Mercifully it was not the same one where she'd spent the night with Ben. She would have found a way to refuse that. She might never sleep in a bedroom this large and lavish again, with floor-to-ceiling drapes and crown molding; she tried to savor it. She was awfully tired. She knew this was partly because of the baby, five months along now. But she had become so adept at denying its existence, she had nearly convinced herself. She hadn't felt any movement. The effort to hold in the truth was what exhausted her. Yes, that was what felt heavy, carrying around this lie. She pulled the rabbit's foot off her suitcase—she'd gotten one for herself—and sat on the bed tearing at its fur till it came out in clumps.

How could she be a decent person, and so duplicitous? Who did she think she was, imposing on the wife of this baby's father? She could hardly express the thought to herself. She wasn't a criminal. She was kind to animals and strangers. Of course, she could think of many examples when this hadn't been true, plenty of sins of omission. She used to dump out Jimmy's tobacco on the roadside when she was mad at him, though this was nothing compared to the fact that she hadn't written to him in months. She didn't know what to write of her life now. And Arthur. A welter of faults where he was concerned. She had not yet managed to return the red skirt to Garfinckel's. But still—nothing had foretold this daily deceit of living with Audrey.

She picked up a photograph of Ben as a boy with his dog and placed it in the bottom of a bureau drawer.

This was temporary, only for a couple of months.

No one needed to know her predicament—she'd gained only six pounds.

She would save seventy dollars. The rent Audrey charged wasn't even a third of what the apartment had cost. She had nearly repaid her debt to Shirley. The rest would carry her to Penington.

1973

16

In passing, Audrey has mentioned a new studio to Ben. He grunted, asked why, then poured a scotch. She was relieved. He has always been generous in a spatial way, letting her take over various rooms in their house to make art—a tolerance that kept her at home. She didn't name a starting date, nor did she call it a "studio apartment." She has not yet said this will be the beginning of a separation. But today she's determined to move her supplies before he returns from work—before he begins drinking and her commotion causes a scene—and she tosses tubes of paints, inks, brushes, adhesives, lacquers, and brayers of all sizes into boxes. She is eager to begin working in the new space during the day. Her clothes, other items—the final announcement of her leaving—will happen in the next week or two.

The front door opens and she hears Lake's voice, laughter, another woman's, rich and deep, joined to it. Prudy, Lake's voice coach. Prudy has known Lake since she was a baby. Audrey goes to listen at the top of the stairs. They rarely practice here since Lake lives on her own, though Audrey wishes they would. She likes to hear them. She hasn't seen Lake in nearly a week, since before the play. She tried calling several times, but they spoke only once, long enough for Audrey to determine Lake was all right. Audrey has not yet asked directly about the performance, nor mentioned Lucille.

She hesitates to interrupt the lesson, but if she doesn't say hello now, Lake might sneak out without speaking to her at all. When Audrey reaches the bottom step, they hush. Lake is standing by the piano, engulfed by her cobalt-blue coat, her head a slight, protruding nodule.

"Hello," Audrey tries cheerfully. "Take your coat off, stay a while." Lake's shoulder-length brown hair is parted down the middle, held back on either side in combs. She's pretty when she tries, with her small, unpronounced nose, thick lashes. But today she looks wan, no makeup. Prudy pulls her hands from the keyboard. Her face is thinner, her hair pulled back tightly from her face. Out the row of windows, the sky hangs low and gray. "Good to see you, Prudy."

"You too."

"I got so chilled last night, I can't get warm," Lake says. "They turned off the heat in my building."

"In the whole building?"

"I don't know for sure, I haven't talked to anyone else."

"Oh, Lake, did you not pay the bill?"

"I paid it today," she says distractedly, her attention back to Prudy.

Audrey is skeptical. "I want to talk to you, okay? I'll be upstairs, cleaning out." She raises her eyebrows at Prudy, who never takes sides where Lake is concerned and only smiles, running her hands, left over right, up the keys.

Audrey wonders why, if Ray is back in Lake's life, Lake slept in her cold apartment and not in his. Young people do that now, sleep together without worry, live together without being married. Once, when Lake was still living at home, Audrey heard the cries and moans of their lovemaking. Mortified, she went outdoors, shivering without her coat on. She waited, smoking a cigarette, until a sufficient period of time had passed. Already she had spotted the compact of pills, like a rotary phone dial, in Lake's bathroom and had asked her if she thought sleeping with Ray—she called it "having sexual intercourse"—was a good idea. "My mother used to say, 'Why buy the cow when the milk is free.'"

"Your people sound like country bumpkins."

"And your generation thinks you invented sex."

"I'm pretty clear evidence that my generation did not invent sex 'out of wedlock,' as you like to say."

Since high school, Lake has had several boyfriends, progressively derelict in their grooming, the last one bearded, with tangled shoulder-length hair. Ray's clean-shaven face and wire-rimmed glasses surprised Audrey. He was pointy—his nose, his elbows, even his careful speech. Lake had gone to college nearby and taken on acting roles around town; a friend had introduced her to Ray, who worked in his father's law practice. At some point during law school he served in Vietnam. So many boys Lake's age had been called up or had dodged. While she wished Lake had more girlfriends, Audrey liked his quiet intelligence and steady presence in Lake's life. She did not like—though privately she understood the thrill of it—his motorcycle, and how in the warmer months the two of them rode around town on it.

She found relief in someone else's caring for Lake—it wasn't only up to Audrey anymore. Once she came up behind them on the living-room sofa, the television volume down low, the two of them talking. They never stopped talking. Turned toward each other, their knees hinged together so they formed an open book. He beamed at her as she spoke. Audrey's breath caught with jealousy, watching them. Or not jealousy exactly, but loss—the feeling of having something once and squandering it. Daniel.

During Lake and Ray's brief hiatus, Lake's sadness fell back to Audrey. She was the one Lake called when she walked out of rehearsals because the director had said her style was "reductive," and when her car broke down, and when she was awake at two a.m., crying for some reason she was unable to name. "Homesick," she said on one of those occasions. "I feel homesick." Audrey assumed more time would allow Lake to heal, instead of considering that time was giving whatever was wrong with Lake a chance to burrow deeper, setting tracks into clay, hardening to stone.

An hour has passed when Lake enters the studio, still wearing her coat. "Wow. You really are cleaning out. I noticed two paintings missing downstairs."

"I'm moving to a new studio."

"Why, with all this room, do you need a new studio?" The blue in Lake's coat sharpens her blue eyes and the dark shadows underneath.

"It'll be better to get out of the house each day. Separate work from home." She could tell Lake now, before she tells Ben.

"What'll you do with this room?"

"Whatever your father wants to do with it." She says this lightly, breaking down her large wooden easel so it can be carried.

"Will that painting go too?" Lake points to one of a river oxbowing into two separate bodies of water. The whole composition makes a maudlin face, with a crescent of land in the lower corner.

"I don't know what to do with half of those." The worst part of the cleanup has been encountering her old work, reconciling her revulsion to it with her reluctance to discard it.

"I'd like it."

"You would? Here, take it." She hands it to Lake, seeing again the colors of autumn leaves, outlines of clouds on the water. "Like you," she says, "a lake, a sky garden." She laughs. "I remember when you almost took scissors to this." She had found eight-year-old Lake underneath her drafting table, cutting up sketches for it.

"It was just another coloring book to me," she says. "You acted like I'd taken a knife to a Rembrandt."

"I didn't know what you'd gotten hold of."

"Wait, this is the one I want." Lake lifts a large watercolor of pears—vivid orange and brown, yellow and green—hanging so thick and heavy they bend the bough, with a dark grafting scar down the branch. Audrey had transcribed the painting from trees she saw when she walked the orchards, alone in Pomona that one time she took Lake down there. The scars, abstractly beautiful, she remembered thinking, were necessary to save the fruit. More than that, they sweetened it.

"Take it. Take both of them. Makes me happy for you to have them. I sold a painting at the gallery a while ago, did I tell you? The one the Corcoran exhibited." She had painted both the pears and *The Wing*, her last realistic works, just after their trip to Pomona, though she doesn't speak of that now. Lake hadn't gone to the exhibition, and while Audrey hadn't kept the painting out of view on purpose, she has never known how Lake might react. One more reason to be rid of it. She peels flakes of pigment from her fingers. Mr. Wooten had been as surprised as she was that a diplomat in Brazil wanted the painting. But it was no more than a transaction to her now. She has enough money to sever the bonds of marriage.

For years, she kept up with the no-fault divorce laws, her eye on California, scanning the newspaper for a wave of legal changes moving eastward. Whenever other women murmured that a divorce could be had, as if there was nothing to it, she couldn't bring herself to ask further. In a town of attorneys she'd been hard pressed to think of one she'd feel comfortable consulting. She certainly couldn't go to anyone in Ray's practice, not when Lake was still involved with him. The lawyer she hired had trouble meeting her eyes as he laid out the process, but she reminded herself she wanted advice, not approval. All she needed was a voluntary separation of eighteen months. What had to be proven was living apart.

"Now's a good time to clean out your room. I'm dropping some things at Goodwill soon."

Lake sets the pear painting at her feet, signaling she'll stay longer, and twists her hair into a knot on the back of her head. "So much junk in there I don't know what to do with. Things I don't want, but don't want to give up."

"Like this." Audrey empties a flour sack full of colored glass onto her table. "You remember our days at the beach?" Arguments between her and Ben came easily at the end of long, sweltering days she spent at home with Lake when she was small. Sometimes Audrey retaliated by driving Lake to Rehoboth the next day after Ben left for work. In a perturbed, removed silence, she would cross the Bay Bridge, Lake beside her, her head resting on her raveled blanket. The bridge was more than four miles long, and while Lake slept, Audrey imagined a hot burst of wind or a pelting rain heaving them to the right, their wheels spinning through the air, stilled by the waters below. She would never. But she wondered, what if?

They sprawled their towels, buckets, and shovels on the uncrowded beach, along with sandwiches she'd made and a thermos of iced lemonade. In the shallow tide, they sat for hours, the receding waves sucking their bottoms deeper and deeper into the sand, little oceans of their own filling up around them. Their hands like claws, they dug for shells, fashioned wet sandcastles. Sunlight spangled the underside of cresting waves. Audrey stared at the horizon, sure it held an answer. She just couldn't see it yet.

Later they'd search up and down the surf for sea glass, jade and amber. If their trip followed a storm, all the better were the findings. Lake skipped ahead. Already Audrey lamented the inevitable day she stopped skipping everywhere—on this beach, any sidewalk, or to the refrigerator for a glass of milk. What else expressed such oblivious joy? The search was a happy contest—each cheered when the other found an unusual color, like a soft yellow or once a cornflower blue. Now Audrey runs her fingers across the weathered, safe edges and holds up a kelly-green piece to the light.

Usually she drove home after sunset, but a few times, when she'd thought ahead and had enough cash, she checked them into a motel— scaring the hell out of Ben, she hoped, that they might not return. One evening she and Lake, side by side, hammered out their dinner at an old crab shack and gorged on sweet hushpuppies dipped in butter. The finer hair framing Lake's face had turned golden. Audrey wiped off the light film of white zinc oxide still on Lake's nose, and Lake let her. Audrey had nothing to compare this child to, couldn't know how good she was but knew it anyhow. She leaned over to kiss her cheek, pink with sun.

At dusk, a sword of orange light came through the almost-closed curtains of their motel room. Lying next to each other, not minding the sandy sheets, they encircled and twisted their hands, their disembodied, dancing fingers "like little flames," Lake whispered. Mesmerized, they didn't stop till the sun fell below the horizon. Their arms heavy and tired, Lake folded hers under her like a bird and went to sleep.

Still holding the green glass up to the light, Audrey says, "Maybe we can go again this summer." When Lake doesn't answer, Audrey says, "I think I've been a good mother. I tried to make a home."

"What's a home anyway? I've been asking myself that today, now that I don't want to go to my cold one. Maybe it's a place where you count on things not to change."

"We did that for you," Audrey says, adding, "but you're grown now." She could speak tonight, force the issue. "I didn't say I was a perfect mother. A presence—I've decided that's the most a mother can be. Maybe an example of how to live. Though I know I haven't modeled everything well." She smiles, expecting Lake's agreement, but Lake is looking off into space, her slight overbite pronounced in profile.

Audrey goes on. "I've been trying to call you, see how the show went. We did what you asked and didn't come."

"I bombed. I don't know what happened, but I couldn't go on. I couldn't breathe. They hate me."

"That's not what I heard. I heard you were marvelous. No one hates you. Why do you say that?"

"Who said I was marvelous?"

"Lucille saw you. She was there. Didn't she tell you?"

Anger flashes across Lake's face. "Lucille? Why was she there? And why didn't you tell me?" She is calculating as she speaks. "Then you know how the show went."

"I didn't know she went until after the fact. I assumed she—"

"Would suddenly show up in my life and do the right thing? Giving her a little too much credit, aren't you?"

"—was in touch with you now. Please don't yell at me. Lucille has moved back to Washington for one reason, and one reason only. She doesn't know how to approach you."

"You could have cut her off."

"You know I tried that. She didn't ask me if she could move here. A lot of time has passed. She seems serious about staying here."

The front door opens downstairs, and they watch each other. Ben does not call out a greeting. Audrey follows his predictable path through the house: his keys dropped on the radiator cover, the squeak of the closet door where he hangs his coat, a bottle of scotch plunked on the counter, ice cracking in its metal tray. When she hears that sound, it's like nails down a chalkboard.

She hasn't reached out to Daniel, though she knows how. She doesn't want to make this about him. One step at a time. She begins stacking her spiral-bound sketchbooks. "Prudy seems well."

"She's struggling, I think," Lake says. "Did you know the riots tore up her street? The riots from five years ago? Today she told me she'd moved. I can't believe I didn't know that."

Prudy, the real constant in Lake's life.

She is a Black woman who once lived—maybe still does—with a white man named Lon. Audrey was told this years ago, but not by Prudy. Once she saw him pick her up from a voice lesson. She didn't know what Ben would think—they both knew Lon's family; she and Ben had first met at his family's home, at his sister Irene's party—and Audrey felt protective of Prudy. She didn't need judgment, or trouble. Audrey has always been in awe of their love, the idea of it anyway, persisting against the world. She wants to ask Prudy if they're still together but never does. Shouldn't she already know who Prudy lives with?

"I'm afraid there's a lot we don't know."

"Did *you* know she moved?" Lake asks.

Hearing the two laugh easily together earlier, how much they share, Audrey senses something wasted. Or something she'd overlooked in Prudy, as if a sheer hung between them. She doesn't remember clearly the time around the riots. Five years ago she was trying to keep up with the Washington colorists, a so-called school of artists, and she did for a moment, dabbling in stripes, before returning to her abstract figures. She and Prudy must have talked about what was happening at the time.

"I don't know, really. She's private," Audrey says.

"With you she is."

"I never see her anymore, so how could I know? She does seem a bit, I don't know, somber. Though you two always laugh a lot together."

"She wants me to ask if you have any odd jobs for her. I think she's having to piece work together. She hasn't had anything regular since the Conservatory went under." Audrey feels a twinge of sadness, hearing that things are hard for Prudy and Lon. His family has done everything to make it so.

"She can help me move and organize." Audrey almost says "move out" but catches herself. "I'll call her."

"I came up here to ask you if I can stay here for a couple of days until the heat is turned back on. The super couldn't guarantee it would be working by tonight."

Audrey hesitates a second too long, considering what will be delayed.

"What, all the rooms are suddenly full?"

Audrey closes her eyes slowly, opens them again, forces a smile. "Of course you can stay here."

"You know what I've been thinking? It would have been better if Lucille had given me to a stranger, someone who really wanted a child. Not her friend, somebody who couldn't say no. That's what Dad said—you couldn't say no to her."

Like lashes, the words sting Audrey. She stands, pointing her finger to the ground, emphasizing each word. "You can't stay here and talk to me like that. I won't allow it." She takes a breath. "Is that what he said? When exactly did he finally explain himself to you?"

"Years ago. And years too late." Lake swings a leg over her knee, and only then does Audrey notice her feet, sockless, in rubber wavy-soled lace-ups. A bruise spreads from the top of her right foot like a wet-into-wet watercolor bloom, bluish purple. "Lake, what happened? That looks awful."

"Oh, that. A while ago. Ray accidentally ran over it on his motorcycle."

"Ran over your foot? Why would he do that? Let me see it, take off your shoe."

"I was standing beside him, saying goodbye, when he drove off. It's not as bad as it looks."

"It's not broken? You should have your father look at it."

"It happened a week ago. If it were broken, I wouldn't be able to walk."

"Come on, I want him to see it." Audrey motions to the door, watching Lake as she stands up.

"See, I'm not even limping, I'm fine."

Downstairs, Ben is settled in his chair, the television on, his highball already half empty. "I thought I heard you up there," he says to Lake.

"Take a look at her foot, see how bruised it is. Should she be on crutches?"

Lake tells the motorcycle story. "He didn't mean to do it. Audrey is making such a big deal about it. It's really nobody's business."

"Well, she's right about one thing, that's a hell of a bruise. Did you ever ice it? That's not going away for a long time," Ben says, running his thumb and forefinger along the sides of Lake's foot. "You got lucky. How many times do I have to say it, stay away from his damn motorcycle." He returns to his chair and sips his drink. Lake joins him in front of the TV.

In the kitchen Audrey adds water to a pot of green beans. Pulling dishes down, she catches her distraught reflection in a dinner plate, tiny fissures in the white porcelain. This is what she dreaded about Lucille's return: Lake's meanness, her ingratitude, whatever is in her that can never be made whole, all of it disturbed again. She was easy to love when she was a baby, as babies are. Audrey has tried, she has!

She is ready to leave, to hand Lake over, like the painting of the boat, her old work, this house—"to be done with all of it." There, she's said it out loud, into the rising steam.

In the morning, Audrey comes quietly down, and when she opens the kitchen door, Lake jumps, spilling coffee on the floor.

"Let me get that," Audrey says, and wipes up the spill. "Did you sleep okay?"

"Better. Where's Dad?"

"I need to wake him up."

"You wake him up?"

"Every day. And he's never happy about it."

Lake covers her mouth, full of toast. "You can't do that forever, you know."

Audrey searches Lake's face. All her stridency, any scaffolding from yesterday, has vanished. Lake pours herself another cup, her hand faltering, her shoulders a bit crumpled. She takes small, weak sips.

"Something is hurting you, I think," Audrey whispers. "I don't know what, but it is."

Lake presses her fingers into her closed eyes, sighing. "How many chances do you give someone?"

"That depends." Audrey is thinking of Lucille.

"But you've stayed all these years."

Audrey takes a deep breath, stunned, and grips Lake by the shoulders. "For you, I did." She puts her arms around her, holds her for a moment. But then she pulls back and looks her in the eye. "Why would you follow *my* example? That part of my life—don't model that."

1945

17

In February Audrey asked Lucille to give her a haircut. "Chop it all off, I want a bob." She had a towel around her shoulders as if they were in a salon. "These are in good shape." She snipped a few wet strands with an old pair of hair scissors she'd found in a drawer.

"Wait, not so fast." Lucille rolled under the ends of Audrey's shoulder-length hair to mimic a shorter cut. "All right," she said approvingly. "This is good timing for a new look. Have a seat." She clipped up a few sections of hair. "Because I'm going to take you to a gallery, right on the Avenue. You've seen it, in the window there's a still-life drawing. A pitcher, a bowl, and a knife." She marked where three inches of hair would come off. "This good?"

Audrey nodded.

"I already talked to the owner, a nice Belgian lady. She wants to see your work."

Audrey jerked her head.

"Hey, that could have been your ear."

"I don't have anything ready to sell. What on earth would she want?"

"She'll decide. What do you think, somebody's going to see a painting of yours through the window here? She'll work out pricing with you. She gets a cut of whatever you sell. Didn't they teach you any of this in college?"

"None of it's good enough yet. It's too early to sell anything."

"You just have to pretend the work isn't yours, separate yourself from it," Lucille went on. "The lady thought I was from Australia—she couldn't place my accent at all."

"Selling my art—that feels like losing a limb to me."

"Luckily you have more than a few paintings. Plenty of limbs."

The next night an ice storm brought the power down. They'd been sent home early from work on slickening streets, even Daniel from the newsroom. Lucille started dinner over the gas stove, and Daniel built a fire and filled old kerosene lamps. They closed the doors off to the kitchen and living room to trap the heat. In front of the hearth, Audrey set a card table, covering it with one of Ben's mother's tablecloths, lighting candles in her silver candlesticks. An occasional cloud passed over the moon, but mostly the night outside was bright. Audrey brandished a bottle of gin and the syphon. "Ben'll know exactly how much fun we had when he comes home to an empty liquor cabinet," she said, delivering a drink to Daniel at the piano.

When she asked him about the day's news, Lucille called out, "Wait, what? The cook misses everything. Say it again."

He shook his head, playing a minor scale up and down the keyboard. "No news. Troops are still on Iwo Jima." They'd all read of the island landing and the fighting that had gone on for days.

"What'd you see on the projector today, Audie?"

"This week we had some German folk singers in costume. Also the Bolshoi Ballet in Tokyo. And then there was something unintelligible, which we translated as 'The Famous Purple Hood'—though of course we have no idea the color of anything."

"Meanwhile, our men are watching Betty Grable," Lucille said.

They served themselves creamed chicken on toast, carrying their plates to the table. "Mmmm, this is delicious, Lucille," Daniel said. "Wasn't long ago we were all eating like this, no electricity. A good night for stories." He had already told them how his aunt and uncle raised him, how he hated the country. Talk like that miffed Lucille, but she kept quiet. "Did I ever tell you about the king snake on our porch? One came right up while Uncle Godfrey was sitting in a rocking chair, and went on into the bedroom, and then came right out again a few minutes later. He kept rocking, watching it chew on a weed in the yard. A few minutes later that king snake came back on the porch and into the bedroom, then out again to the same, certain weed. Four or five times the snake did this before he slithered off for good. When Uncle Godfrey went back to the bedroom, he didn't see anything wrong. But later that night he pulled back the covers to find a dead snake coiled up—the biggest copperhead he'd ever seen."

"I'll never sleep now, thanks a lot," Audrey said. Daniel laughed.

The candles dripped and dripped on the cloth, but no one minded.

Lucille couldn't have said how he got from one story to the next, but it reminded her of home, how certain men talked and expected you to listen. Women didn't do this; women never stopped working long enough to tell a story. Often you were entertained, like now. She knew, too, that he talked on as a way of holding Audrey's attention. He'd told Lucille, "Before Audrey ever mentioned a husband overseas, I'd already hung my trousers and settled my shoes in her closet. My heart started breaking before she even said hello that first day."

When he mentioned earning extra money picking cotton in nearby fields, Lucille told them how she and her brother had done the same every September. She wore a big wide-brimmed hat pulled way down, a handkerchief at her neck and rags tied around her wrists, gloves with fingers cut off, and overalls. When she got so hot she couldn't bear it, she jumped in the lake and then started working again. "My daddy threatened to send me over to some cornfields to scare the crows." Everybody laughed.

After they washed the dishes, Audrey and Lucille sat shoulder to shoulder with Daniel on the piano bench. Lucille couldn't carry a tune and Audrey only thought she could, but Daniel could sing in a deep baritone, and he could play. They knew all the words to Johnny Mercer's "G.I. Jive." She and Audrey danced the lindy hop till a candle tipped and Audrey righted it, and then he slowed the tempo on "Don't Fence Me In," which they all sang as loudly as they could.

"One for Ben," Daniel shouted, and they went straight into "The Song of the Seabees" and "Praise the Lord, Pass the Ammunition."

Somewhere in the middle of this one, Audrey clutched her hand, saying, "My ring." She'd taken it off to wash dishes and set it above the sink, but when she went to look now it wasn't there. All three of them took lamps and candles back to the kitchen and shone them on the sink and the linoleum floor. Lucille got down on her hands and knees and felt with her hands, and Audrey did the same. "Found it," she said.

"Ben might be a little unhappier about that than the booze," said Daniel.

"I have to stop doing that, taking it off to wash."

Daniel had walked to the front window and was looking out at snow falling. "Let's sled down the hill," he said, and for once Audrey was game, but Lucille hesitated. She barely took care to nourish her pregnancy with food, but sledding was more dangerous. If she lost the baby here, now, everything would unravel.

But wasn't that what she wanted, an out? She would be careful. Besides, didn't she take a risk every time she crossed the street?

They dug around in the basement—"like marauders!" said Daniel—

and found a Radio Flyer, and then pulled apart a box of glassware and a hatbox to use for two more sleds.

There weren't any cars at this hour, and the road was still a sheet of ice underneath the powdery snow. They each took one run at a time, waiting at the bottom of the hill for the others. She shouldn't have worried, the incline wasn't steep enough to gain much speed. Crunching back up the yards of frozen grass to start again, she tingled at the fresh cold around her, at home outside. "If we don't go to sleep, we never have to wake up," Lucille said.

"Let's never go to sleep," said Daniel, snowflakes in his lashes.

When they were back inside, they moved the table away and pulled up the chairs and sofa closer to the fire, which Daniel built up. He passed around one last pour, now bourbon, and told a story of Depression times, about a poor woman who'd knocked on their door and asked for "grease." His aunt didn't know what she meant at first but eventually gave her a bowl of bacon drippings, and the woman stood in the yard eating it like it was pudding.

"To be so hungry," Audrey said.

One of the last things Daniel said before he fell asleep, drained of inhibition, was: "I got to town too late for you, ladies. I got scooped." He smiled at Lucille, but she knew he was talking about Audrey.

⁓

Audrey stared into the fire, following its flames and sparks as the others dozed off. The woman asking for grease—she pictured her thin as a corn husk. Her own mother had a policy of never answering the door to strangers. Even the Fuller Brush salesman, with his hairbrushes and brooms, would peer through the windows to see if anyone was home and receive no response. Once he had two children in the car. Audrey later wondered if that was because they had no mother or home. "They'll want something" her mother had said, "that we can't give them."

Opening her door to Lucille was one of the best decisions Audrey had ever made. These were some of her happiest days, living like a family without the burden of one.

She hauled blankets from an upstairs chest and covered Daniel. Lying on the sofa, his mouth agape, he looked vulnerable as a baby bird.

Lucille, rosy and fleshier than when she first moved in, seemed happier too. Maybe she thrived by cooking for the people around her.

Audrey took special care with her, in case she was dreaming that Audrey suspected her of taking the ring, because she had, for one shameful second. Now she hoped Lucille felt the weight of the wool on her feet, then her chest, the flush of air over her face like an apology.

※

Lucille chose what was going in the portfolio sleeve, all figurative paintings and drawings. She and Audrey each wore one of Ben's mother's fox-fur-trimmed jackets, ill-fitting but adding a patina of maturity as they walked up to the Avenue. Mrs. Moreau, the gallery owner, tweaked Lucille's cheek between her thumb and forefinger. "A genuine Southern belle, the first I've met!

"You are the artist?" She studied Audrey, who nodded but whose tongue may as well have been cut out. Lucille laid the canvases and papers on a long table. Mrs. Moreau hovered over one in a series of portraits. "And you're the subject," she said to Lucille. In the painting, Lucille was perched on the edge of a table, leaning forward with her legs dangling beneath, her arms straight beside her so that her shoulders pitched toward her ears.

"Unsettling," Mrs. Moreau said, "a woman staring you down."

"Can you sell it?" Lucille asked.

"The fewer the lines on the face, the more troubling the thoughts underneath."

"You don't have anything like it," Lucille said, looking around. She smiled faintly at Audrey over Mrs. Moreau's head.

"Sixty days, then we'll see. The most I could get is thirty dollars. I take ten percent."

On the walk home, Lucille said, "Thirty dollars! Did you hear that? Audrey, you're brilliant. Nobody wants a painting of a stranger—of me!—on their wall unless they see something else, something vital in it. Now, that's a different thing entirely."

On the first day of March, Lucille cleaned up the garden, trimming back the roses along the fence and up the house trellis, and the lilac bush by the alley steps. Later that night Audrey wrote Ben a letter, telling him about it. The two of them had planned this, Audrey explained, to think only of each other last thing at night, putting their thoughts down on paper and mailing them each week. Lucille had noticed that the daily writing had dropped off over time, but the weekly letter still went out, always signed, "All that land between you and me, all that ocean—sending you the same mass of love." She had read these words over Audrey's shoulder one night. Audrey believed he was, like Jimmy, in the Pacific, sent over as late as he'd been. Now she read aloud: *Dear Ben, You owe any success in the garden to our boarder who wears a big shade hat, bobbing like a flower herself around the garden. She brings little sprays of hellebores into the house, putting them in the silver tops of your liquor bottles. Snowdrops have sprouted all over. She says it won't be long before the reddish stalks of peonies come up, then burst with pink or white blooms that drag their stems to the ground.*

Lucille listened quietly, never letting on that she wouldn't be here to see them.

There was a scene Lucille continued to play in her head, foolish and fantastical.

A spring day in the not-so-distant future with a piercing blue sky and bright grass, yellow daffodils nodding in front yards, welcoming soldiers home. The war is over. Lucille is in the house alone while her newborn baby is sleeping. She has opened the windows, and curtains dance through them. From the living room, she notices a man in uniform coming down the hill. She knows him immediately and rushes to greet him. He registers surprise at first, then recognition and even joy. She puts her arms around him, accompanying him inside. Wordlessly, she leads him upstairs by the hand.

Then what? That was as far as she got. More often than not, all the daydream consisted of was Ben walking down the street, Lucille watching him expectantly from the other side of the glass, his knowledge of the baby and reaction still to come before the dream dissolved.

The reality was this: She couldn't stay here. Never intended to stay this long. And when she told Audrey and Daniel she was leaving, she wanted it to be quick. No drawn-out departure, no cajoling or wailing, no promises to visit and write. She couldn't promise anything.

In her free time, she cooked food and froze it for them. Scalloped crab meat, soups, Boston baked beans, pork and parsnip stew. They wouldn't starve without her. If they noticed she'd gained any weight, her time in the kitchen explained it.

But when she made her announcement, they raised their arms in protest. "Oh, you can't!" and "Why now?"

"My father's not well. He's had to slow down, and I'm needed."

"I thought you'd stay forever," Audrey said, her eyes teary. "What about your job here?"

Lucille thought: *Don't, please don't.* Pulling a shepherd's pie out of the oven, she said, "I let the office know yesterday. I'm one less person they'll have to let go when the war is over." Then she looked at Audrey straight on. "You and me, we were always just filling in."

When she'd told Miss Longhren, the woman stood up from her desk and walked around to face her. "I think it's fine that you're leaving. I don't know how you girls do it, moving far away from home. Your families will be so pleased to have you back."

Then she did an odd thing. She pressed her hand against the fabric of Lucille's jacket and skirt to her belly. Quick and light as a butterfly's, so brief and without effect, her touch couldn't be proven. It might have been a question. Or a blessing. Had Miss Longhren, in her youth, hidden a baby somewhere in this world without anyone knowing? Maybe. The idea comforted. An image of her under the glow of her little desk lamp accompanied Lucille and her suitcase on yet another bus, this one down to Penington.

18

If Mrs. Fleming, the housemother of Penington, felt any triumph at Lucille's return, her face didn't show it. In her long skirt she led Lucille up to a room with a window between twin metal-framed beds. The unoccupied half for Lucille was bleakly austere, but the other side was in disarray. The covers were mostly off the bed, clothes and books strewn on top, and a woman was ranting as she looked for something she'd misplaced. "Paula, I give you three minutes to tidy your space or be charged with five demerits," said Mrs. Fleming, explaining the system to Lucille. Paula, a short, thick-middled woman with dark straight hair tucked behind her ears, a few years older than Lucille, glared at them doubtfully.

"This is Audrey," Mrs. Fleming said, and Lucille winced at the name. During the intake process, Mrs. Fleming had asked if she wanted to use her real name. She said no, and Audrey's was the first one that came to mind.

After Mrs. Fleming left, Paula asked, "Where are you from?"

"Wichita."

"Right. And I'm from Bangalore." She found what she was looking for, a notebook of poems she'd written. "If I lost those..." But she didn't finish her thought, busy restoring order to her side of the room.

When Lucille turned to her unpacking, Paula said, "It's all right. We all lie in here. And Mrs. Fleming's bark is worse than her bite, don't let her scare you. Apparently, she had to really tighten things up after a gang of girls climbed down the fire escape in the middle of the night last year. Are you going to keep your baby? If you even have one. You barely look pregnant."

"I haven't decided what to do."

"Me either. I could go back to work and board the baby while I earn enough money to pay back Penington. And then pretend to be someone else in another state."

"There's adoption. Mrs. Fleming could probably talk me into that."

"Why would you let somebody talk you into anything? Haven't you been down that road before?"

One of the girls—there were twenty at that time—couldn't have been older than fifteen. She'd not stopped crying, Paula said, for two weeks, and Mrs. Fleming mothered her more, allowing her to shadow her throughout the day. The girl loved the huge laundry facility underground; the women who ran the steam irons took her under their care, and she stopped her crying. The other faces around the three dining tables weren't so much unhappy as they were vacant, a look Lucille recognized in the mirror.

In one way, it was the most honest house in which she'd ever lived. For days she felt a reprieve after the effort, such dissembling, during her stay with Audrey. None of the girls pretended anything here, especially joy. They didn't attempt to like each other, incapable as they were of making lasting friendships. How could they attach with all their practice of detachment—from their babies, their families, the fathers of their children. They were polite. Politeness wasn't a pretense but a way to avoid additional injury. Piddling things might set a girl off. For instance, Paula yelled when somebody used her talcum powder, never mind that she'd left it on the bathroom sink. Or another girl lashed out about being shorted on custard. But people on the outside did this all the time: admitted outrage at the smallest thing while never acknowledging their real grief. Here, a girl's true torment, her hopelessly pregnant state, was always on display.

Tales of how best to induce labor circulated frequently, from the outlandish, such as licking the inner bark of sassafras, as evidenced by the stripped tree on the rear property, to the well-storied castor oil and enemas. At Penington there was an entire wing devoted to preparing for delivery so the girls could leave quietly at any time. One rumor Lucille couldn't verify was that she would be blindfolded during labor. She hoped it was true. Questions that she hadn't addressed in her first discussion with Mrs. Fleming, such as what would happen after the delivery of the baby, came up regularly now. She had envisioned a clandestine handoff, but she found out she was required to return to Penington, remaining with her baby, helped by nurses, for at least two more weeks. If she did want to relinquish the child, she would have to appear before a court.

Falling asleep at night, she listened for the sound of babies crying, but they must have been too far away.

More than a month after Lucille arrived, news came over the radio that Roosevelt had died. The group instinct was to look outside, confirming the world's end with the sight of scorched timber and earth, but all they found was the greening of April, blooming tulips. Perhaps it wasn't true—the world was too beautiful. But by nightfall, Truman had been sworn in; Roosevelt was indeed dead. In an ordinary home, they might have dispersed to neighbors or nearby shops for comfort and information, but at Penington, everyone stayed put. Lucille thought of Audrey, likely hearing the news alone, Daniel not home from work. She imagined a yelp escaping—sometimes Audrey did that, emitted something wild from her otherwise impermeable façade. Mrs. Fleming; Miss Kent, the housekeeper; and Miss Roland, the cook, looked shaken but restrained themselves. Quiet tears streamed down their faces, and they tried gently to shush any voices that spoke over the announcer's. But the girls—their tears hardly needed an excuse to flow. His was the only president's name they remembered hearing spoken, the perfect repository for every regret that had come before. They wailed, inconsolably.

Glum before, Lucille thought, glummer now.

After a six-thirty breakfast every morning, a sign-up sheet went around on which the girls marked their preferred activities for the day. In addition to chores, they could take a turn at the piano, learn practical sewing or some other needlework, prepare meals with Miss Roland, or weed the Victory Garden.

Hours on end a girl called Edna worked herself up at the piano with two tunes, alternating between "Come Thou Fount of Every Blessing" and "Don't Sit Under the Apple Tree (With Anyone Else But Me)." She convulsed with such force through the latter that she put Lucille in mind of an exorcism.

Gardening outdoors—the best way to escape the music.

While weeding, Lucille imagined an eager couple who might want her baby—the mother in a sky-blue suit and pillbox hat, the father a bigwig on the Hill. She pictured her return to Pomona, how grateful she would be for the overbearing sun, her fatigued muscles after hours of sorting peaches from the grader into boxes. She hoped, tossing down handfuls of compost, that she and Audrey would visit each other in the years to come.

Lucille felt as though she were out in the country, with so few houses on that side of town and fewer cars, and this assuaged a worry that she might see anyone from her former life. Today it was warm, two geese hovering above on the light breeze, only a few dogwoods and redbuds open. To hide their condition, she and the rest of the girls wore coats, despite the mild weather, on their way to an ice cream parlor. Rarely were they allowed to go into the neighborhood, and then only in a group to discourage meeting any boyfriends. Until now Lucille had never, not once, accepted the offer of an outing. She hadn't wanted to take the risk.

And there, on the sidewalk in front of her, was the reason. She recognized Daniel at once, even though he wore a hat covering his balding head. His brown suit and yellow tie were familiar, but something else identified him, the slant of his shoulders, one higher than the other. The details quivered into an awareness that stopped her cold.

They looked at each other for a moment. She braced to hear her name called—though it would have been the wrong one—and she kept her expression frozen, forbidding. He nodded at her but kept looking, eliciting an elbow from Paula, until finally he moved to one side of the walkway, letting the group pass. Lucille quickened her step.

"I think you have an admirer," said Paula.

"No," Lucille whispered back. "He definitely had his eye on you."

◈

Audrey couldn't stay in the house with only Daniel for much longer. Without Lucille, the two of them had moved through the rooms as if there were a fragile, barely visible bubble between them. His presence loomed behind his slightly open bedroom door or when he sat reading in the living room. They ate supper together once or twice a week on his nights off, but he knew she was looking for another tenant. This time her ad specified only females. Two called. She had set up an appointment to meet Minta from Iowa when Daniel came home with news.

He'd seen Lucille. She hadn't gone home. She hadn't left Washington at all.

He sat, guttering like a blown-out candle. "She wasn't ten feet from me. With a gaggle of women. The strangest thing is that they *all* had wedding bands on. I was beginning to feel sorry for myself—had every eligible young woman left town?" His face reddened. "Then I recognized her. You must have known."

"Oh, Daniel, I don't believe it."

"I kept walking until I found a drugstore. I asked the pharmacist about that group of girls who all looked alike, as though they lived in the same place, maybe. Did he have any idea where that might be? 'Penington,' he said. 'One of the homes for fallen women.'"

Fallen women. Daniel's shoulders caved in as he told her. He was taking the news as she was. He felt it too, betrayed. "You didn't know? I was sure you did. Thought maybe the two of you didn't want *me* to know."

She shook her head. "She's not who she said she was."

Lucille's eyes had pleaded with him, Daniel went on. It was probably a plea for silence, but it looked a lot like a plea for help.

Audrey reconsidered everything Lucille had told her, especially what she knew of Arthur—not much. Lucille had a post office box because of her frequent moves and didn't receive mail at the house, but she never spoke of letters from him. He didn't call as far as Audrey knew. Her mind raced. Maybe Lucille had been involved with someone else. What did she really know about her anyway?

But to run away and have a baby in some institution?

Audrey had been the one who'd called and asked if she wanted to rent a room. Lucille had mentioned it, but only that one time when she'd so oddly shown up on the doorstep, shaking with cold. She had wanted a place to live, hadn't she, even if in the most roundabout way? But Lucille hadn't accepted Audrey's offer until she negotiated a better price. She never begged, she never seemed terribly in need.

Or pregnant.

For several nights afterward Audrey imagined Lucille lying in a strange house full of unwed mothers and their infants, who were wanted perhaps by them but no one else in their families. Often the same thing, these mothers and babies—unwanted children.

On her way home from work a few days later Audrey noticed that the painting of Lucille was no longer in the gallery's window. She told Daniel what she was going to do.

"What makes you think she'll come with you?" he said.

"Now I know the truth. She didn't want to tell me earlier. She was ashamed. But there's no reason for that now."

Audrey parked in front of Penington. The red-bricked fortress, such an unlikely home with turrets surging into the air, must always have had other aspirations, like all its inhabitants. At the door, she said that she wanted to see Lucille Spence—she was Lucille's sister.

"There's no one here by that name."

"Are you sure?"

"Hold on just a minute, please."

Audrey waited so long she began to wonder if Daniel had been mistaken. But eventually a woman introduced herself as Mrs. Fleming. "I found your sister. She said she had no family here." Audrey and Mrs. Fleming sat across from each other, on opposite sides of her desk.

"Well, you can imagine why, under the circumstances. But I'm prepared to care for this child and her," Audrey insisted. "Let's settle whatever she owes now."

Audrey rushed Lucille with a kiss on her cheek, but Lucille didn't look her in the eye. She looked plumper. No makeup, not that she wore much anyway. She gave a parting hug to a girl with dark, unwashed hair.

On the car ride home, Lucille said, "I cannot repay you," and "I will have to give up this baby. You know that." She stared out the window with an unpleasant look on her face. Audrey thought she might be sick.

"Mrs. Moreau left a message," Audrey said. "The painting sold."

"Did you get paid?"

"Not yet."

"You have to go collect," Lucille said weakly, still staring out the window.

"Are you going to tell me any more about this?"

Lucille closed her eyes. "That's why I left, so I wouldn't have to."

Only once did Audrey see Lucille ungirded, acknowledging what grew inside her. Audrey was painting quietly in her studio (a landscape now, maybe always a landscape, she was so frustrated by the rendering of shadows on faces), and Lucille had come in from one of her walks. She hung her coat in the hall closet, closed the door, and looked into the full-length mirror bolted to the outside. She must have believed herself the only one home. She smoothed over her round stomach, cradling it. Audrey watched from her doorway, the way she'd begun watching everything Lucille did. She had almost eluded her gaze forever, but now Audrey followed her every motion, amazed at what she could know and not know about someone. With an anguished face, Lucille took the hem of the skirt and wrapped it tighter and tighter as if to make a knot around her belly.

Audrey moved away from the studio door, dropping her brush on the floor as a warning. Lucille called out hello, then bounded up the stairs.

※

With the announcement of Germany's surrender, she heard Daniel's and Audrey's marching through the house, imagined their little flags waving, heard their singing at the piano. Lucille didn't come out of her room. The end of the war was near. It should mark the end of time she'd served in her father's eyes. Sentence complete. She'd never felt more imprisoned.

When she finally emerged, Audrey started talking of plans. "When the baby comes, you can stay here for as long as you need," she said, but Lucille knew that meant until Ben came home. "Then you can stay right here in town. Wouldn't Miss Longhren—isn't that her name?—wouldn't she be pleased to find something for you? Downtown might be too expensive, but some girls in my office live in Petworth, or even out in Rockville. You could find a place of your own and a way to board the baby with another woman until—"

"Until what, Audrey? Until I strike gold with my shovel? Stop acting as if everybody has money like you."

She didn't mean to snap like that, but the offers to help were a kind of pressure. She was sinking under it.

19

Lucille was lucky in one way, that her water broke on a weekday, after Audrey left for work. She had planned to slink off like an animal, like the cows her father had told her about.

"Cows have to fight off other cows from the herd. Another maternal cow will try to claim the calf for itself," he had said, adding, "You don't want to know about lions."

"What about lions?"

"Some other time." He laughed.

"Tell me."

And he told her how the lioness always goes off, because when a new lion is coming into his own, he has to leave his own herd and take over another one. The first thing he does is eat the cubs that aren't his.

Though Audrey had offered to come home at any hour, Lucille hadn't wanted her gawking. Now she was scared. She stood in the bathroom, waiting to be sick, but nothing happened. She phoned for Dr. Vandiver, but another doctor, Busick, was covering for her. "Come in when your contractions are fifteen minutes apart," he said, "not before."

She cleaned all over the house, taking ammonia and newsprint to the windows. She went outside and cut peonies, filling the rooms with vases until the house looked positively funereal. One last thrust of energy, as if she might never do anything useful again in her life. She thought of Jimmy, wishing Germany's surrender meant he was closer to safety, even if he was likely in the Pacific. She wanted to think of his well-being, not her own. The sun went on shining despite her rising panic. She was so alone. Think of all the women who had given birth. She took down the Bible. Moses's mother came to mind, but she couldn't find much of a story around her. The crucifixion verses in the Gospels—she was after that feeling of being totally forsaken. She knew it now, didn't she? Had she really thought she was different from everyone who came before her, slipping through the years without ever feeling nailed to wood?

Finally she wrote a note: *At the hospital, no need to come. Will call with news!* She left the house around five, walking to the bus stop, though her contractions weren't yet twenty minutes apart. She couldn't risk Audrey's coming home and insisting on going with her.

In a wheelchair, like Lucille, another woman in labor waited for the elevator. She wore a bright floral print, and her thin, dark eyebrows drew together in a single line each time she grimaced in pain. What Lucille had to look forward to. The woman's husband kissed her goodbye on her cheek. Nurses wheeled them into the elevator, turning them to face the doors. Now Lucille could only hear the woman's panting.

She'd learned a few things from the girls at Penington. She would be given a shot in the arm and likely wouldn't remember anything. She was awake long enough to see another drawing of baby Jesus and Mary on the wall opposite her bed. Lucille's sorrow, another's solace. Instead of studying the nativity, she'd read all the versions of the crucifixion, noting the blankness around the words. It was hard to say exactly what was going on while Jesus hung there, dying. Where was his mother in all of this? Mary was there only once, in John's telling. She'd abandoned him, hadn't she? This astonished Lucille now, for the one person she wanted most was her own mother. *Mother,* she cried quietly as she lay in pain, *where are you?*

She woke into a quiet, dark nothingness, her insides like a tomb, carved out. Her eyes adjusted to the morning light. The holy mother and child staring her down again. She thought of the men standing around the cross, jeering, casting lots for clothing, and the women weeping. She thought of her own witnesses: Dr. Busick's wrinkled, dark face—as if he'd been a ranch hand all his life and not delivering babies indoors—and the various nurses who were in and out. The one with the gap-toothed smile was Mary Magdalene. The doctor was more like a Roman soldier.

The humiliation of her legs spread in stirrups.

A large, gaping wound, and then reported new life.

Worse than crucifixion.

Mother, where are you?

When they brought the swaddled baby to her, she corrected her longing. This was what she wanted, not her mother. This baby girl with a smear of berry lips and blue eyes, fleshy cheeks. What was essential had been restored. It was as if something missing all her life had found its way back to her. What had been parted from her, she would always crave its return. Parturition—she thought back to Latin class. She couldn't be sure of the word's roots, but in her hazy consciousness, the work was clearly in the parting. What labor it was to part. Holding this bundled baby, she was devastatingly whole. She traced the creases of her legs, the chapped center of her mouth; she ran the edge of her nail into the lines of the baby's feet and followed the swirl of hair on her crown. She understood the great mystery of being now, what all mothers since the beginning of time have known. How the world works, and how someone comes into it. Love. Then the nurses insisted she get some sleep and took the baby out of her arms, parting them once more.

She had thought through everything. She had imagined nothing.

Somehow she knew that memories, the ones that have never been recalled, are the most pure and accurate. To remember was to alter, or taint. Lucille refused. Somewhere in her was that feeling of first holding her child. She never relived it, never examined it, but left it perfectly preserved, precious as ancient spider silk embalmed in amber. Whenever she went to the edge of this unsummonable memory, she took comfort that it was something no one could touch, or take away.

Audrey came to see her, with arms full of hydrangeas, each of the five days she was in the hospital. She said she had diapers stacked up, pins, little soft sleepers for when the baby came home. She'd been asking around at work for names of baby nurses.

"I didn't take you for a saint when I first met you," Lucille said. "I'm rethinking that." Her legs could barely hold her when she first put her feet on the ground. Everything was new, even walking. She took laps around the maternity ward with Audrey's help.

"What will you call her?"

"Lake," Lucille whispered softly, tugging at Audrey's arm. She had seen the name in a family Bible long ago, always knew she wanted to use it. Now the mystery in it seemed right, a word that conveyed clarity in its particular substance, but its overall form was often opaque. It hinted at something larger than herself.

Audrey leaned toward her as if she hadn't heard correctly. That was okay. The name still felt like a secret. Lucille didn't repeat it.

The same way a newborn falls in love with its mother, Lucille fell in love with her nurses, especially the kind ones. Mrs. Hodges was one of these, with an upturned nose, round eyes, and skin softer for its wrinkles. Each time she came in her room, she brought simple observations about the weather and chatter about her sons. Her love for them. One was on his way home from Europe and one was probably in Japan. It was this one whom Lucille learned so much about—his love for mashed potatoes and playing the banjo, details she carried with her forever, never certain he returned home.

Because Lucille came from Penington, Mrs. Hodges must have known not to pry. She gently suggested a telegram to the family. "No need," said Lucille. Before bringing the baby and a bottle of formula, Mrs. Hodges always asked, "Do you want to feed her?" in case Lucille had changed her mind since the last feeding. She never did, but she appreciated the acknowledgment that someone else could feed her child, keep her alive. When the western sun shifted in the afternoons, Mrs. Hodges always tilted the louvers so the light was out of Lucille's face, directed up toward the ceiling, where it glowed.

Lucille had slunk off here to this hospital den, like the lionesses. She was safe, she dreamed, thinking of her father.

"How do you know about the animals?" she'd asked him, a long time ago.

"Because once I was king of the jungle," he roared and, making bear arms, embraced her, swinging her until she squealed, "Stop, put me down!" But he kept spinning and tickling her. She couldn't stop laughing, gasping for air. When she woke, she wasn't sure whether that had been her father or Arthur.

Once when she woke, Dr. Vandiver was sitting upright, asleep in a chair against a nearby wall. Susurrous noises came from her mouth every so often.

When she opened her eyes and found Lucille looking at her, the doctor smiled. "You were sleeping, so I closed my eyes. Boy, I must have been tired. I wanted to see how you're doing."

Lucille smiled back at her.

"You have a beautiful baby girl. I saw her in the nursery."

"Thank you, doctor."

"You caused quite a ruckus, I heard."

"I didn't realize. There was so much blood afterward—hadn't expected that. I almost fainted in the bathroom."

"It's okay."

They sat in silence for several moments. "Do you have children?"

A long while passed before Dr. Vandiver said, "No," as though this question, one she must have answered a thousand times, depleted her. "Never have."

All those babies into the world, and not one to keep. Lucille said, "I don't think I can breastfeed. My milk—"

"Oh, that's all right. I know mothers who wouldn't think of it these days." She brushed her white, fluffy hair out of her eyes and stood, straightening her white coat.

She might have stayed for a quarter of an hour, this doctor whom Lucille had seen now only twice. But the image of Dr. Vandiver resting vertically by her side came to Lucille countless times during her life— the attending physician, she always thought. Watching over her.

Lucille's milk finally came in, a sensation that reminded her of tears welling up. But she'd already made her decision about breastfeeding. Mrs. Hodges brought her little bundles of ice to place on her chest.

On the last day, in the last hour, she slipped Lake's tiny, bare arms into a batiste gown that Audrey had brought just for this occasion. Lucille asked Mrs. Hodges about the woman who'd arrived on the elevator with her. "In the pink-flowered dress, remember? Those pencil-thin brows. Did she have a girl or a boy?"

At first Mrs. Hodges shook her head, as if she didn't know. But then she slowed her movement. She'd taken Lucille's blood pressure and was hanging the meter and tube carefully over a pole. "Stillborn," she said.

Lucille felt that sensation of tears welling up. She needed to talk to the woman. She had lost her baby, just like Lucille was going to lose hers. She would tell the woman in the flowered dress with pencil-thin eyebrows, the husband who kissed her on the cheek, "Here. Take. Love." She would give Lake to a stranger, someone who had surely yearned for a child.

"Do you know her name?"

Mrs. Hodges was helping fold her things into a suitcase. Her eyes went to the ceiling, thinking. "I don't. I wasn't her nurse."

"Could we find out, you think?"

Mrs. Hodges never answered. Audrey, together with Daniel, was in the doorway, smiling, calling out in a singsong voice and waving her arms, "Time to come home, it's homecoming day for Baby Lake."

20

All of Lucille's energy before and after giving birth, everything she'd been holding in, seemed to leak out of her now that she was back at Audrey's. Incapable of the slightest stir for hours at a time, she rarely held Lake unless she was feeding her. Every maternal feature had receded—her bursting bosoms, her abdomen, her care. She changed diapers, she washed at the sink and tub—like a soldier, that's how she looked. Since she left the hospital, her face had become stark and severe with a facile flatness that Audrey wanted to capture. Like a bleak landscape, a morose face was easier to depict. She asked Lucille—heartlessly, she knew, as soon as the words were out—if she could draw her. Lucille didn't answer; she lay there, acquiescent.

Apparently, however, she noticed the pink peonies, dying on their stems in the yard below, and tried to rescue them. She wrapped the remaining blooms in dampened diaper cloths for the baby nurse to take home. Prudy, carrying the dripping stems on her way out each afternoon, reported this to Audrey. She had arrived the same day Lucille and Lake came home from the hospital. "Where's my baby? Hand me the baby," Prudy had said, smiling—the most demanding words she'd yet spoken. Early on, Audrey pulled her aside and told her Lucille's story. "I'm so glad you told me. The way she carries on about those flowers. I knew something was wrong." From then on Audrey and Prudy checked in at the end of each day. How do you think Lucille is? Did she hold the baby? Did she get out of bed? Gently swinging Lake in her arms, Prudy would give Audrey a concerned, conspiratorial look, shaking her head sadly. She seemed a baby herself at nineteen years old, four years younger than Audrey. But she knew everything—how to swaddle, feed, burp, bathe. And sing. "His eye is on the sparrow and I know he watches me"—her voice carried softly through the house. She worked days and nights for a week, and then only days when Audrey went to work.

All the while Lucille was at Penington, here again, and then in the hospital, Audrey painted. She had a stack of work almost ready for Mrs. Moreau, who had asked for more. But the canvases went unfinished when Audrey took over caring for Lake in the evenings. She kept thinking she would get back into the studio, just for a few minutes even, to touch up something on one or redo a corner in another. During the day, ideas came to her and she made quick sketches. Maybe she would find a few hours on the weekend. But that time didn't come. She didn't mind, rubbing Lake's tiny nub of a nose with her own, smitten by her fragile fingers. "You are a lump of sugar!" she said, burrowing into her neck. If Lucille let her cry too long or held her limply in the crook of her elbow, in danger of dropping her, Audrey was there with outstretched arms. After nights of being wakened by the baby and going to Lucille's room to feed her, Audrey moved the bassinet to the sewing room between them. Her mother had made child-rearing look difficult, but it was simple, she saw now. Maybe she did want a child of her own. She would think of this, holding Lake under her tiny arms and bobbing her on her lap, and then she would remember something she wanted to create, a collage of Lake's little figure, for instance, using old fabric she'd spotted in the sewing room.

Easy, yes, if you didn't want to do anything else.

What she also wanted was the return of her vacant friend. She was a shell of herself. Is that what happens, she wondered, to other mothers? A baby supplants the mother's body for so long the mother never returns?

Sometimes Audrey felt the sting of Lucille's remark about money right on her face, where she'd felt it land. Audrey had read Ben's ledger books. He was a weak manager, but hidden in the blanks, where he was disorganized and lax, were means. The house was paid for, his check came from the Navy every month, as did Audrey's salary from the Archives film job. There was the boarding rent—at first a bit from Lucille, then Daniel's came regularly. If Lucille had help to support herself and this child, she could start over. Audrey again brought up the idea of moving. "You can pay me back in a year or two. Or never." If Lucille didn't want to stay in Washington, think of the places she could go: Richmond, Boston, St. Louis. She seemed to perk up, hearing how easily she could reinvent herself. Audrey had written to the Chamber of Commerce of each city, inquiring about jobs. Now the envelopes were coming in.

※

But a veil had fallen between Lucille and the world. What was right in front of her—her baby—darkness shrouded. Days felt like nights, and nights the same. The hospital had been a hideaway where she was Lake's mother. No one knew how she'd got there. No one knew she couldn't go on being Lake's mother. Now she couldn't pretend. She walked in her sleep at all hours and once found herself in Audrey's room, sitting on the edge of her bed. It must have been night because the shades were almost all the way down over the open windows and the attic fan pulled in the lightest breeze.

"Lucille?" Audrey startled and reached for her wrist. "Is that you?"

"Help me find a place for her to go."

Audrey sat up. "We talked about this. I can help support you. You'll get a job."

When you find out—she didn't say it out loud—*when Ben comes home all your generosity will vanish.*

"Are you worried about what people think, is that it? Husbands are dying overseas every day. Nobody needs to know you never had one."

"Don't you see, though, that question will never go away if I raise her. 'That woman on her own'—how many times will I be asked about her father?" She could barely feel them, tears coming down her cheeks. She couldn't put faith in a secret. Every secret she'd wanted to keep had been found out.

"Why can't you go to the father? He should be helping."

Lucille almost said his name. But Audrey's face was so sweet and dear—she saw it in the dark, that brow furrowed with love and concern.

"I love Arthur," she said. "I've never loved anyone else. But he would never… My family would never… You saw all those girls at Penington. Like me. My father isn't a bad person. It's me. I am."

She felt Audrey's arms around her, rocking her.

"You little bird, you. We will figure this out."

And for a few minutes more she let Audrey hold her, believing.

"It's your mother," the voice said over the telephone, but Lucille heard, "Your brother has died," before any more words were spoken.

"Jimmy," her mother said. "Come home." There were other details and plans exchanged. Neither cried, not wanting to waste the money it took for the phone call.

Instead of going to Audrey with the news, Lucille left through the front door as though nothing had happened. She took her old route to the post office. A slight wind pushed the warm air around. She needed to move, step through sorrow, waves of it gathering at her feet. As she lay in bed the last few weeks, it had pooled around her like a poison.

But Mr. Walt behind the counter didn't have a letter from Jimmy. Her post office box was empty. Light rain outside began to streak the windows. Lucille started to cry. "I'm sorry," she said.

"I seem to have this effect on people," Mr. Walt said. "It goes with the territory. You're not the first, not even the first today."

Next door to the post office was a florist, and that day a clown—a clown!—stood in front, holding a bouquet. As she passed by him, he offered the flowers, but she held her hand up in protest until she saw his own painted-on sad eyes and accepted a red carnation. She walked home and left it on Audrey's kitchen counter. The house was still. She stood at the back door, holding it open with her foot, smoking one of Audrey's cigarettes, which she never did.

She pulled diapers off the line and folded them, then washed the bottles in the sink. Upstairs the baby was still sleeping and Audrey's door was closed; maybe she was resting after what had been a sleepless night for them all. Lucille began sorting through her things. She took several dresses off hangers, two pairs of pumps, an extra pair of gloves. Letters from Jimmy. There was so little to take. She made her bed. In her purse she felt a few coins for bus fare; the bills in her wallet would cover her train ticket.

Then she went into the baby's room. A rattle that Audrey had bought lay on the dresser; the baby hadn't even held it yet. Lucille thought of cutting a little bit of her sparse, fuzzy hair. Instead, she unfolded a clean blanket from a stack and laid it across the bed. She picked up the baby, hoping not to frighten her out of sleep and feeling cruel when she did, and changed her on the large wooden desk. She still didn't know what color her eyes would be. Then she wrapped her in the new blanket. She carried her into her room, taking the old blanket with her and packing it in the corner of her suitcase.

Audrey called her name, and Lucille closed her eyes. "I'm in here."

Audrey came through the door, bright with anticipation, probably happy to hear Lucille moving around. But the open suitcase stopped her. "What are you doing?"

"Jimmy. In Okinawa."

"Oh God." Audrey hugged her and the baby.

"I don't want to go home."

"Of course you don't. It's a sad journey."

"I haven't written him, not in all this time. I didn't know what to say. How could I have neglected him like that? I am a terrible, selfish—"

"No, no, don't talk like that."

"I can't take the baby."

"We'll keep her, Prudy and I."

"I've started to pack."

"So soon—today?"

"I'm catching the bus to the station. I'll leave everything you need." I owe you, Lucille wanted to say. Instead she said, "You're better at this than I am." She handed the baby to Audrey.

"Prudy's better than both of us."

At the door, Lucille said, "You keep holding her. You hold her so I don't have to give her back to you." She began to cry again.

The baby's eyes were still droopy with sleep, but it wouldn't be long before she began crying of hunger. She wore a terry sleeper, too big for her, but in a matter of days she would outgrow it. Lucille pressed her lips to her forehead.

Audrey placed her hand on Lucille's cheek. "Don't worry. We'll be fine."

"I know. You will. It's not you I'm worried about."

1973

21

After dark, Lucille parks her car across the street from Lake's apartment and cuts the engine. The grand colonial, with a rounded, shallow-stepped portico, looks like a home for a single family. This confused her at first until she observed, on previous nights, different people coming and going and corresponding windows lighting and darkening. After examining the mailboxes, hanging by the front door like little black clutch purses, she knows Lake lives in number three. Because the second-story window on the right has been dark for the last two days, is still dark with no sign of Lake, she believes this is her apartment. She waits, the car's interior growing colder; she can see her own breath. A few days ago she left a note in Lake's mailbox, with her phone number, but she hasn't heard anything, nor has Lake answered when she has telephoned.

A figure moves in front of the house. She can tell it's a man with long and wiry legs. He paces back and forth, turning at intervals to look up at the windows. She follows the orange ember of his cigarette, an arc from his thigh to his mouth. He leans against a light-colored Volkswagen. He's the boyfriend she saw leave the play. Ray.

She rolls down her window, craning her neck out. "Hey, I remember you."

Now he's the startled one, squinting in the dark.

"From *The Cherry Orchard*." She waves and smiles. "I saw you there."

He steps a few feet closer, his hands deep in his front pockets. "No."

"Your girlfriend then—Charlotta, right?" She can see this knowledge unnerves him. "I never had the chance to speak to you—"

"About what?"

"I know Charlotta too. Lake, I mean."

"Have you been watching us or something. That's kind of weird, lady."

"I'm Lake's mother." Her eyes sting, watering in the cold.

"No, you're—"

"Lucille." She wants very much for this name to register, positively or negatively. She wants him to have heard she exists, and watching her name work itself through his mind, she is gratified. His eyes narrow on her.

"Looks like you're having a hard time getting in touch with her too," she says. She steps out of the car.

"I guess you could say that."

"Does she disappear often, without letting you know where she is? I've been trying to reach her for a few days now."

"I think she's there, actually." He looks back to the house. "But yeah, you could say she hasn't had the best role model for sticking around."

Shame, almost pleasurable, spreads through her chest to her upper arms—pleasurable because she prefers this sensation to the numbing emptiness she is used to. "We know why she might not want to see me, but what about you? You're a little old to be throwing rocks at her window." Above him, Lake's window lights up. "Though it is romantic, your playing Romeo out here."

He tosses his cigarette to the ground, extinguishing it with his loafered toe. He wears a suit underneath his jacket, and the combination of professional attire with his windbreaker makes him seem younger, vulnerable.

What a pair the two of them make out here, in the dark, trying to woo Lake from the shadows. His devotion is undeniable. "I like you," she says. "I can tell you care about Lake. You wouldn't be here like this if you didn't."

He crosses his arms, puts his thumb between his teeth. "Yeah, that's right, I do." They're standing in the street, but a car turns, lighting up Lucille, and they move to the edge of the yard.

"Could you talk to her for me? I don't want anything from her, I just want to talk. Explain. I have years of explaining to do." The car passes.

"I can try." Ray turns up the walkway, toward the house.

"She's tough, I know. Understandably."

The front door opens, and Lake's tiny figure, backlit, speaks so softly that Lucille can't hear her. Ray is already inside the house. The two embrace, more words are exchanged. "Lake," she calls, starting up the walkway, her hand lurching high in the air. She is incapable of moving fast. The door shuts, but not before Ray's hand waves in return.

An ally, she hopes.

The next morning she sits, feeling bruised, on a small sofa in her client's apartment. She isn't expected to talk to Brenda Ordway or do much of anything except attend and record. These mostly passive things she can manage. She knows when she is unwanted—that's what she'd been last night at Lake's. And Lucille isn't wanted by Brenda either. But for once she welcomes the silent, indifferent hours she will spend here, a few buildings over from her own, in a nursing home. The blinds are drawn in the room. Faint as a shadow, Brenda lies in a recliner with her sunglasses on, as always, a wool blanket pulled up to her chin. In her eighties, she has recently lost her husband to a long illness. Her children, believing she has fallen into a stupor of mourning for their father, insisted she move here. Lucille is not as sure of the cause of their mother's sadness. Brenda has nothing to look forward to—a sad fact. But Lucille knows better than anyone how people shield their griefs and regrets, how private they remain. It's astounding what people manage to cover up. That the children want to romanticize their mother's desolation Lucille finds touching. She doesn't argue.

Brenda has the care of the staff. They help her dress and escort her to meals in the dining room downstairs; if she needs assistance, she presses a button. Her two daughters and two sons, thinking she will improve if she has someone to talk to, hired Lucille for three afternoons a week. No particular skill is required, only a willingness to spend time in someone else's home. And people don't mind Lucille in their homes. After every visit with Brenda, Lucille leaves a note for her daughter, Roxanne, explaining what she and Brenda have done and talked about and any concerns. The message is nearly always the same.

During their first few visits, Lucille attempted to open the blinds but Brenda objected. "If you're going to wear those sunglasses, we need to find you a lounge chair by a pool." Lucille laughed. Brenda didn't smile. Only once has Lucille seen her without them on, and then her eyes were shut, tiny dark seams. But Lucille wonders if Brenda watches her from behind the dark glasses while she wanders around and studies photographs: Brenda as a girl with braids; as a young bride, full-faced and serene-looking, with darker hair; as a middle-aged mother with eyes behind other glasses and a heft that has since disappeared.

Lucille hopes the same will happen to her, cells and pounds vanishing. How has this extra flesh settled on her in the first place? A building up of something: muscle from planting the fields and steering a tractor, a shell hardening over in the sun. Each year there is more of her, as if she's been picking up heavy things along the way, storing them on her person. Her hair is the only thing she's let go of. After years of it thinning and losing curl, she's cut it to her chin. That returned some spring to it. But if anything she looks heavier with shorter hair.

Or has she simply filled a nagging emptiness with sweets. She does that—craves sweet things and gives in to the craving. She feels along the cabinet shelf now for a caramel chew; she ate the last of them a few days ago, but given her short reach, she may have missed one. Nothing there.

One of the last coherent things her husband, Arthur, said to her before he became bedridden was, "You walk different. You didn't used to walk like that."

"Like what?"

She thought he would shrug, give it up, but he imitated her by walking across the room, holding his arms stiffly out from his sides. Her weight made her move differently. It was an ugly thing for him to do.

Lucille hasn't made any friends, not that she's had much opportunity. Roxanne, Brenda's daughter, might make a sandwich for Lucille and eat at the oilcloth-covered table with her, friend-like. While her mother is in the next room, Roxanne might confess in a whisper what she has never told anyone outside her family, how she visited her mother no more than a handful of times in two decades. Now she sleeps with her at night, the old woman barely breathing in bed next to her, with Roxanne's hand on her arm, or hip—wanting to make up for her spiteful abandonment.

But Lucille can't be called a friend. After the coffin goes in the ground she'll be only as good as a dead person's clothes, a reminder of all Roxanne has lost in her mother. Lucille knows this from Arthur's death. At first she had taken comfort in his barn jacket or rain slicker to step outside, like wrapping part of him around her. But his closetful of clothes, the encumbered coat rack—these had a gravity of their own, pulling her down with each sighting. After that first year, she hauled everything to the Salvation Army.

Lucille has never succeeded in persuading Brenda outdoors. Sometimes she reads to her from scientific journals on the coffee table until she hears a soft snore. But today she makes little effort, weary from rejection. A door closing in one's face, like last night—it's difficult not to feel that.

"Ouch," Brenda says, motionless.

"Mrs. Ordway, what hurts?" She doesn't get an answer. She has heard these complaints before and is fairly certain they have no physical cause, but she asks anyway. Lifting the blanket, she uncovers Brenda's feet and holds them in her hands. The only offense of Brenda's that Lucille has learned from Roxanne is that her mother did not like being a housewife or staying at home with the children. Four kids, and the only part she enjoyed had been the baby years. Once they could all walk, she went back to school, got her doctorate in biology, and taught at a local college. Those kids didn't like that—nobody else's mother was doing that. Lucille rubs the bottom of Brenda's feet, which are flat and bulky in thick socks.

For any aged or ailing flesh, Lucille feels pity. She feels sorry for the pruned skin or, more specifically, the revulsion it churns up in others. She can do this, touch what is abhorrent to the rest of the world.

Whenever Lucille hears the unconscious ramblings of the elderly, which usually run deep and narrow but not wide, she wonders what she might say when her time comes. What nonsense, and what obsessions, might be laid bare.

"Ouch," Brenda says again.

Lucille knows the answer. It is the same story she always tells the people for whom she works. *When I was a young woman I came here during the war...* Every time she starts, she thinks she can't possibly repeat it all, from beginning to end, one more time. She cannot. But a few sentences in, some turn of phrase, or a detail, a fresh insight, comforts her, and once again she is seduced by her own telling.

In the end, which version of the story will remain? And who will be there to hear it? Not Arthur, though that had been understood. When they married, he had been almost her age now, forty-nine. He was always going to leave the world first. She had nursed him till he died. Nursed him to death—some days she felt that. Her hands holding his head up, forcing him to drink, turning him in bed to avoid sores, her oppressive presence. She wondered if he closed his eyes weeks before he died because he didn't want to listen to her anymore.

Her son, Clark, would come to her bedside, and his girlfriend, Cissy. They would make the drive on the interstate. Though she couldn't be sure Clark would stay long in a hospital or a home like this. Her lawyer son-in-law, Brody, might send his well-wishes over the phone, and her daughter Martha would come, though it would take time, half the country away. Would she get close, though? Would she stay for long?

And Lake. Not now—not today she wouldn't come. But maybe someday.

Lucille had in fact gotten a decent look at Lake in that porch-lit doorway—or maybe her imagination filled in some details during the night. Maybe she dreamed that Lake's silky hair slid out of combs and clips. That was the style, same with her blouse, roomy and ill-fitting, nearly falling off her shoulders, her skirt loose and billowy, her face pale against her darker hair. She slipped away before Lucille could meet her eyes. But Ray got through, and maybe he'll get through to Lake on Lucille's behalf.

Another notion comes to her, rising up like sap as though it has been there, waiting. She will find him. Shouldn't be hard, with his father's name on the law firm. Stapleton.

Ten years ago, Lake showed up in Pomona after being on a wild bender out west at the end of high school. Lucille did not do the right thing. Lake lay in her arms then—impossible to imagine now—and Lucille... Well, she can't form a verb in her mind, it's too painful. She has a shadowy notion of walking out of the water, toward the sound of Arthur's voice calling her. But she doesn't have words for what she did that day, only for everything that came before. Explaining that part of her past makes her feel better, like a little hit of sugar each time. And the effect is similar, short-lived. She always yearns for another hit.

"I want to warn you," Brenda says after a long silence. "This could happen to you."

She's not exactly sure what Brenda means. If she's talking about losing the will to live, Lucille has already experienced that. After Arthur died, before deciding to come here, all those unopened letters returned from Lake piling up around her, she had believed her life was over. But instead she says, "I know, Mrs. Ordway. I expect it will."

Flesh—it does sicken her a bit. She's taken off one of Brenda's socks and holds her foot, threaded with purple veins on top but chalky along the sole's edge. The odors of the body; long, thickened nails; thinned, matted hair when it goes unwashed. These things make it harder for Lucille to get out of bed some days. But the elderly, with their porous and baggy memory, always listen to Lucille's story with the same patience, as if hearing it for the first time. She goes to rub Brenda's shoulders.

Years ago, I lived not far from here...

When her time is up at Brenda's and she exits the building onto the sidewalk, she will feel as if she has come out of a dark mine. The sunlight will seem unbearable, but only briefly.

1945

22

The baby's cries woke Audrey, pulling her as if with a rope from the dream of her former life, the one she wanted. She was in a cornfield, far away from her childhood home, when she saw Ben. It must have been before they were married because his hair was longer, his bangs falling in a wave on his forehead like they did when she first met him. Up close she saw his just-shaven neck and its reddened crease where the collar of his shirt chafed, and the little nick of a childhood scar under his left eye from a ricocheting BB gun pellet. Even in the dream she felt gratitude for this vision, somehow knowing that such details were no longer available to her in her waking life. She had nearly forgotten his face.

When she fully awoke, fear stiffened her, and her heart beat wildly in the awareness that this instead—a baby crying the next room over and she the one responsible for it—was her life.

She wouldn't be able to go back to sleep, even though her body ached from doing what it did not want to do. The cries had cranked up like the monotonous sound of pistons under a car hood, up and down in the cylinder. If only the cries could be switched off as easily. She might have let them go on longer but for her concern about waking Daniel. In her robe and slippers, she opened the door onto what had once been a sewing room, Ben's mother's. She thought, as she had every time she entered the room since the baby came, how much it lacked. On a desk was an old wicker bassinet, likely Ben's as a baby, which Audrey had found in the basement. There was no soothing wind-up music box or even a stuffed animal. As soon as she had time, she told herself, she would purchase soft articles. Softness—that would help keep the baby from waking, and a rocker would help get her back to sleep. Arms and legs had come loose from the muslin blanket. Audrey gathered the baby in a bundle, pressing her head into her shoulder.

She hadn't mixed a bottle before going to bed. To do so would have been an admission that this baby wasn't going anywhere, that she would still be here when Audrey woke up in the morning, or more likely night. Past Daniel's closed bedroom door they went, she shushing the baby, then down the stairs. In the living room, with its spread of five windows giving onto the street, she paused, watching for headlights, what surely would be the baby's mother's anxious return. But when Audrey looked out into the black night, all she saw was her own reflection, a baby in her arms.

She'd not yet learned how to manage an infant with one hand and accomplish anything like mixing formula with the other, so she laid her on the floor of the living room and swaddled her waving arms—like a choir conductor's, Prudy had said. She had taught Audrey how to do this, explaining that snugness was soothing to an infant; without it, a limb was apt to flail about and needlessly initiate another crying jag. Audrey went to mix the formula in a bottle and warm it in a pot of water.

Thank God for Prudy. Everyone was relieved when she'd walked in the front door a month ago. She had no child of her own, no younger siblings, evidence to Audrey that a woman either has a maternal instinct or not. Experience hardly mattered.

The simmering water jostled the bottle and she pulled it out, then went to pick up the baby, whispering, "What am I going to do with you?" until it was a song, up and down on her toes. "What-what am I gonna do with you? Stuck to me like glue-oo. How do I undo?" She prodded the bottle's nipple into the baby's mouth until she drank.

Lucille had left for her brother's funeral, delayed on her behalf, last Saturday. She was to be gone four nights, back on Wednesday. Everyone had agreed, Audrey especially, that it would be easier for the baby to stay here, with her at night and Prudy during the day.

No one spoke the obvious, that Lucille had not yet told her parents she'd had a baby.

When Audrey was coming home from work Wednesday, hearing Prudy's singing on the sidewalk before she even reached the front door, her heart sank. They nervously passed the baby back and forth in silence, Audrey clinging to what she believed were natural laws governing mothers and their children. Lucille would return. But Prudy finally said, "I thought she would have at least called by now to ask about her." Audrey didn't validate that with a comment. She was thinking she would never forgive Lucille for this, devising all sorts of invective for when she did show up.

Friday afternoon, when there was still no sign of her, again it was Prudy who had the courage to speak first. She was wiping a cloth in the valley between black and white keys, sounding faint notes, when she said quietly, "Miss Audrey, I don't think she's coming back." Audrey almost didn't hear her, but when the words registered, she handed the baby on her shoulder to Prudy.

"Stay right there," she called out on her way up the stairs. She hadn't gone into Lucille's room yet, though now she wondered why not, why she had continued to protect her privacy after she left. Or even before, when she was a boarder, paying rent. Always respectful of her, Audrey placed whatever of her laundry was left on the line outside her door, never venturing in unless Lucille was there, and knocking first. But hadn't Audrey a right to know what was going on in that room, in her own house, hers and Ben's? After Lucille stopped working, she walked. Up to the main avenues and back again, her gloveless hands shoved in her pockets, her purse dangling from her wrist. She had no money to purchase anything, Audrey was sure of that. Once she found Lucille asleep on her side on a blanket in the yard. A blanket she kept on the line through the rain to dry in the sun. She was gone more than she was present, so there was plenty of opportunity to check the room for neatness and order. But the walking had stopped with the birth. Everything had stopped. Toward the end of her stay, for weeks, really, Lucille never left the house.

Audrey opened the bedroom door now onto a wave of hot, stale air. Lucille had left at midday, with the blinds raised. At first Audrey only looked, as if the mystery of Lucille could be solved in her displayed belongings. The bed was made in its yellow cotton spread, the white fringe hanging mostly straight, but one edge was wrinkled where Lucille had last sat. On top of the covered pillows was a white satin one, creased from sleep. Hydrangeas from the garden rotted in a glass jar on the dresser. Tucked underneath a small clock with an illuminated dial were a few unframed photographs of her typing pool.

Inside the closet was the faintest odor of Lucille, a sweet floral scent. Fingering the pockets of a few hanging clothes, Audrey found only an eyebrow pencil and a book of matches marked Wardman Park; a price tag was still strung to a straight red skirt. Her large straw hat, the one she'd worn to coax Ben's flowers into existence again, lay on the shelf above the hanging clothes, and on the floor were three pairs of shoes, one still in a box. Those yellow wedges, unworn.

Slips, girdles with suspender clips, brassieres were jumbled in a drawer, along with a bandage stiff and dark that Lucille had used to cut off her milk. No letters. The baby's hospital bracelet, her first fingernail clippings, things that Audrey, not Lucille, had seen to saving, were not there. Those were small enough to fit in a purse.

Lucille had left nothing she couldn't live without. The record from the doctor's office where Lake had her first check-up at four weeks—eight pounds, eight ounces—lay next to the dead flowers. There was even the thin wedding band on the nightstand, beside a box of neatly stacked handkerchiefs, the cheap kind from the five-and-dime, and an issue of *Collier's*. When she was fully pregnant, Lucille had worn the ring each time she went out of the house. A bowl of gold wedding bands had sat on the foyer credenza at Penington, like peppermints you picked up on the way out of a restaurant, she had said.

Audrey started flinging sheets off the bed and opening drawers she'd cleaned out herself six months ago so that Lucille could take up residence. She found the photograph of Ben as a boy, with his dog on hind legs, held upright by his paws. They were the same height. She hadn't moved that to a drawer, Lucille must have.

Prudy was coming up the stairs, calling, "Miss Audrey, are you all right?" Her eyes searched the room. "Come, hold the baby."

The baby this, the baby that. Audrey couldn't even think the baby's name, let alone speak it. But Lucille's name—that one she was muttering over and over, as if it were fuel propelling her around the room, chucking the contents of drawers, sweeping her hands under the bed and mattress, swiping at her own flyaway hair.

She stopped, sinking onto her knees. "You're not going to leave too, are you, Prudy? Then we'll be in real trouble. Where is her telephone number? Lucille's. Do you remember where we put it?"

In that moment, *we* became the operative pronoun, because she was not, she told herself, in this predicament alone. Whizzing past Prudy and the baby, clenching her skirt, she ran downstairs. Lucille had written her number on a label she'd peeled off an empty vegetable can, and Audrey had set the can aside for the tin drive. She rifled through useless items in the telephone-book drawer—scraps of paper, food-splattered recipes, broken pencils, misplaced screws—until she found it, something formerly of no value, now as precious as a book of ration coupons for gasoline.

She called upstairs, "It's all right. You can go home now. I'm sorry to have kept you this long." Prudy wouldn't return till Monday. What was one weekend? It wasn't as if Audrey hadn't done this before—for six nights, to be exact.

Prudy came down, the baby apparently in her bassinet, and opened the door to the basement. Her recent habit was to change her clothes next to the washing machine and ironing board before walking to the bus. When Prudy cared for Lake that first week, she slept upstairs and used any bathroom in the house. This wasn't Mississippi. For weeks Audrey wondered about her shift in routine.

"We'll be fine," Audrey said now.

"I know you will, Miss Audrey. Tell Miss Lucille she's got a good baby."

"Call me Audrey, please. We're practically the same age, for goodness' sake."

"All right then," Prudy said, taking her authority and knowledge down the dark stairs.

A truck drove past—such a lonely sound now, the approach and retreat of a vehicle that didn't stop. Audrey held the label in one hand, the other pressed to the telephone.

What would she say?

"Lucille, you forgot something."

"Lucille, you left your baby."

Or she could try a subtler tack: "Is everything all right? I want to make sure you're all right."

She'd never heard of a mother leaving her baby, so she couldn't say for sure what might bring such a mother back. But she'd heard of fathers who left their families in the middle of the night, in the middle of the day, left them standing in the middle of town waiting to be picked up and never came back for them. There was discreet planning in these disappearances, an intended permanence. These were people who did not want to return.

Her own father had left when her mother was on the shortest of trips to see a childhood friend, the only trip Audrey had ever known her mother to take alone. She returned to a bare chest of drawers, a half-cleared closet, a few knickknacks gone, and an empty bed. How many years had he waited for her rare absence to make his move?

In all the varieties of leaving she'd heard, she'd never known of someone being brought back by a telephone call.

She dialed the number on the back of the label and waited. After one ring, a man's voice said, "Pomona Nursery."

"Wrong number," Audrey said. "My apologies." Lucille hadn't given her a house number, it dawned on Audrey, because she didn't have one. "Would you by chance know how to reach Lucille Spence?"

"We can get a message to her house, if that's what you need."

Audrey read out her telephone number, even spelled out her name so there would be no mistake. "Please ask her to call me."

The bottle empty, the baby's mouth slack with satisfaction, Audrey carried her up the stairs. She felt the slightest burp, then the warm run of vomit down her neck and through her nightgown. Quickly, impatiently, she moved through the cleanup, trying not to breathe in the smell of yeasty formula. Wetting, wiping, drying, then a clean diaper, and finally a return to the bassinet.

She cleaned herself up and put a fresh nightgown on. She lay awake for a long time, restless. When crows roused her in the morning, her sheets and coverlet were in a heap, her nightgown damp with sweat, as if she had fought with Lucille in her sleep. The crows got louder. Panic-dreaming that they were pecking and slivering the baby's face to bits, Audrey rushed to her room. She found the baby crying but her face unharmed. Only then could she say it, sighing with relief into her baby-girl neck, "Lake, Baby Lake."

The new life for whom she now found herself responsible was, of course, the opposite of death. With birth, nothing was missed, yearned for, or expected to be as it had once been. Upon waking each day, Audrey had to relearn this new, needy presence in the world.

But with death, you waited for the deceased to walk through the door any minute. You listened for someone on the stairs, thinking you heard her whistling a tune; or the phone rang and you believed, if only for a second, it could be her. Not that Audrey had known death firsthand, but her father's departure had been that. After Ben left, she focused on the slightest reminders of his absence: ashes in the fireplace from fires they'd warmed by together, his cigarette butts that for days she hesitated to throw out, his empty slippers just under his side of the bed.

Still, nothing came close to Lucille's absence—no return call yet—and the heightened expectancy that followed. Daily it happened for

Audrey. There's Lucille coming through the door, breathless from her hours-long walking, a regular flâneuse, that girl.

A faint sound of music from upstairs might make Audrey first think of Lucille—until she remembered Daniel.

A light bass thud at the bottom of the steps—Lucille, is that you? But it was Merlin, the cat.

Each night Lake started out in the bassinet, but now—two weeks after Lucille's departure—when Lake woke to be fed, Audrey pulled her into bed with her. All mothers would do this if fathers weren't in their beds. This was special knowledge, she was sure, understood by certain women all over the country these days.

After Lake's feeding, Audrey lay awake, ruminating on the idea that Lucille hadn't wanted to leave. The leaving wasn't planned. She'd had to go home for her brother's funeral—an event that came only a few days before the Japanese surrendered Okinawa. She'd been devastated by grief, not plotting some sinister deception. Even if she'd wanted to, she wouldn't have just left. But now that she was there, with her parents, other family, their sadness, her old town, it was the returning she couldn't manage. Audrey knew how an old place worked on you, how you stepped through the back door of your parents' home and became like a child again.

Audrey had felt such pity for her and her plight, how Lucille's father had exiled her from some kind of paradise. Maybe the peach trees, with their tangy-grass smell, their fringy leaves that Lucille had described, maybe they held her there. Audrey could see that point of view, out of some narrow corner of her eye.

But if she blinked it was gone, along with that tender feeling for Lake that Audrey had after her dream of crows. A whiteout kind of rage overtook her, obliterating all hope of joining Lucille's side. How could she have duped Audrey like this, how could she have trashed Audrey's generosity and sympathy and aid? It was worse than biting the hand that feeds you. Lucille still held her by the jaws.

No, she didn't think Lucille was dead. Good as dead, maybe, but a dead person would have loosened her grip.

The day she ransacked Lucille's room, Audrey found a scrap of paper. The handwriting reminded her of the kind that young girls practiced when they were learning cursive, discovering who they were. They wrote their full names over and over, as if their identity were in those curves and dashes and tails, as if the trajectory of their lives might be read in streaks of graphite.

If they wrote a boy's name, it meant something else. A schoolgirl's crush. A healthy obsession. Or love.

Written on a piece of ruled and folded paper, as though torn from an old lesson booklet, was *Lucille Spence*, three times. At the bottom of the page was *Benjamin Randolph Bray*, written once. Underneath it was his street's name and the cross street.

Audrey didn't think Lucille knew Ben, but she'd never thought to ask her in their months together. Audrey had told her his name; Lucille had seen his photographs in the house. Surely she would have said something if she'd met him. Nothing explained this discovery. Audrey laid out all the collected items, like puzzle pieces that didn't fit, on the chest in Lucille's room. Her remains, she thought of them. And then she closed the door on them.

23

The morning was a scorcher, eighty-five degrees before nine o'clock. Sweat dripped through the mesh of Audrey's stockings. Walking from the streetcar to the Library of Congress, not even a block, she blotted her face with a handkerchief, sure she was wiping off all her makeup. Ahead she saw Irene, a penciled line up the back of her legs to suggest nylons. Audrey would never draw attention to her own shapeless legs that way. Tree trunks, a boy had called them in sixth grade. Better to sweat.

They were both headed to the basement—relief from the heat was coming, in exchange for natural light. These past few weeks, caring for Lake, Audrey took comfort in her job no matter the weather. She wanted to call out to Irene, she wanted a moment alone with her to tell her all that had happened, but Irene fell into step with another co-worker, Beatrice, and Audrey didn't want to hear Beatrice's told-you-so's. She had never met Lucille but distrusted anyone who would take a room without telling you she was pregnant.

At her workstation, Audrey emptied the next canister in line, unfurling the film onto the two rewind reels. Carefully she turned the hand crank on the spindle, spreading the film above the light table, then peered through her eye loupe to magnify each frame. Gently wiping her lint cloth across each foot or so, she felt for damage. On her first day she had put the film on the projector and watched it shred to bits because she hadn't first inspected for torn sprockets. Where there were tears, she placed splicing tape; every few canisters she'd have to cut out a bad frame and splice two good ones together. She'd likely find other imperfections on the same reel—each canister was typically either flawless or not. She wrote notes in longhand as she inspected, first listing the country of origin. They were all Japanese since V-E Day in May—no need to study old enemies. She recorded the condition of the film and marked the number on the counter, the length. Then she was ready to watch.

Standing at the projector, she determined whether the film was of training sequences, a battle, or troop movements, along with any geographical details, including the weather. Her report would be sent to the military to determine whether the film contained anything worth their time. Maybe the film she was looking at right now, men marching in rows, rifles at rigid degrees, then breaking out of formation and aiming in one direction—maybe this would be the one that ended the war. She would never know. But she was grateful for the immersive, methodical distraction of the work.

The twelve o'clock bell broke her trance. No one dared suffer the heat outdoors, where it felt hot enough for the film to go up in flames. Instead, everybody headed for the restroom upstairs with its bright light, marble and terrazzo floor, and walls almost as cool as their basement office. This restroom also had a pea-green leatherette couch, in case someone wanted to take a nap (which Audrey had done more than once in the last month). They kicked off their shoes and draped their hosiery and dresses carefully on hangers. Beatrice stood in the mirror, re-pinning her wilted curls, and Mabel sprinkled talcum on her chest and arms. In their long white slips they repaired to the larger space of the bathroom, the spotless, gleaming bathroom of all places, where they lay on the floor or leaned against cold radiators and windowsills and chilly lavatories, pulling their sandwiches from wax-paper wrapping, and ate. Constance ate faster than everyone else, eager to light her cigarette, but politely she waited till the rest were done, and then they all smoked, the added heat of their flaming matchsticks be damned.

Irene was Audrey's closest friend—resourceful and practical Irene, the confidante for all the women, but therein lay the problem. Audrey hadn't managed a moment alone with her. When she told her she was marrying Ben, Irene had looked taken aback. "You did it, wow! I never thought he'd marry." Audrey detected a hint of jealousy under the shock, as if she'd landed the last remaining bachelor. But Irene was the quiet center, the one who organized birthdays and celebrations, and she'd held a bridal shower for Audrey in this same room—more a trousseau outfitting because there wasn't a piece of silver or glassware that Audrey needed in Ben's mother's house. She'd modeled shiny, shimmery white negligees last fall, strutting up and down the marble alley.

She appreciated the Irenes of the world, who fed and cared for others, always anticipating their needs. Until recently she'd clung to an expectation of women around her carrying life forward in this most basic way, relieving her of the same obligation. Just now Irene was passing out slices of applesauce cake sweetened with honey. But lately she was fixed on moving out of her parents' house, and Audrey wondered, if she told her that Lucille was gone, whether she would want to take her place.

After the baby came, Irene was the one who had given Prudy's name to Audrey. But since then Irene had been oddly reserved with questions about Lake, uninterested in finding out how Prudy was getting along.

"How's that baby?" Mabel asked, licking cake crumbs from her mouth.

"Growing. Hungry all the time."

"How's Lucille?" Beatrice said, lining her eyebrows in the mirror.

"I wouldn't know."

"What d'you mean?" Irene asked.

"I mean I haven't seen her in a month."

"But you said Baby Lake is growing." Constance put out her cigarette under the running tap.

"That's true, but not with her mama around. Lucille left."

They all moved closer, either by craning, leaning, or stepping—it was nearly balletic the way the conversation turned.

"It's been awful," Audrey said. "Lucille left for her brother's funeral and she hasn't been back."

The questions sprang at her:

"Has she called?"

"Have you called?"

"Have you told Ben?"

"What are you going to do?"

Then: "What kind of mother does that?"

"You need to find Lucille."

"There are laws against this."

"Poor Lake."

"You would take care of her if it came to that, right?" Mabel said. "You want a baby, don't you?"

The bell for everyone to return to work sounded, and they hurried into their girdles and dresses, the air thick with talcum powder. The time for any helpful advice was finished, and Audrey felt even worse.

On the bus home, she asked Irene if she was still thinking of moving out. "I have an empty room now."

Irene shook her head. "No, thanks. This war can't last forever—I'm saving up for a place of my own." Her gloved hands gripped the handles of her red leather purse in her lap. "I don't know how to say this, so I'll just come out with it. Prudy has ruined my brother's life by getting involved with him." She went on. It all started before the war when Lon and Prudy were still in school—as children they had all played together; Irene had loved Prudy, she insisted—and the family had hoped time and distance would pull them apart. But Lon came home early from the service with a hand injury and was seeing her again. He wasn't working. "When you first called me, asking for help, I wanted to help you, I knew you were in a jam. But I also wanted to help Prudy's family; her mother lost her job over this. That's how much I cared." She pulled a handkerchief from her purse and dabbed at her nose. "I also thought... I don't know. That a job like this would...hold her back." Audrey felt herself stiffen; she crossed her arms. But Irene continued to pour out a stream of grief next to her, finally coming to her point: "You must let Prudy go, please. It's hurting my family, your supporting her like this—"

"Irene, I'm not supporting her. She works hard."

"But without a job she'll come to her senses. Especially if she knows why you let her go."

Audrey turned toward the aisle and looked around—she felt an impulse to move to another seat. "This is wrong, what you're saying. I'm sorry your family is distraught, but I'm not firing Prudy over this. What she does on her own time is her business." But she was also thinking: *I need Prudy. Prudy is good. Lake loves Prudy.* Irene looked like she was going to say more but then turned toward the open window, the wind blowing back her hair.

Audrey often forgot Prudy was in the house on the rare occasions they overlapped. When Lake napped, Prudy would do some light housekeeping. If there was something extra needed, like cleaning the oven or the lawn furniture, Prudy took it on. Audrey always knew where she had been that day. The tin cans and Mason jars holding brushes would be slightly shifted, or the paints, in sequence of the color spectrum, out of order. Audrey would shift them back. A triangle of candles on the mantel might be pressed together into a clover, and Audrey would separate them. Back and forth, a trace of tension acted out between them. But oh how Lake loved her, crying out for her when she woke, nuzzling her sleepy head into Prudy's neck.

One afternoon, Prudy handed her to Audrey, saying, "Here's your mama. Here she is."

"We can't tell her that, Prudy." Audrey held Lake up, her little hands and feet wiggling. "Call me Audie. Your mama is Lucille and one day you're gonna meet her."

But what if Prudy wasn't needed much longer? That might be a good thing for her. She was clearly overqualified for the work. Lying in bed later that night, stroking Lake's neck, willing her back to sleep, Audrey began to mull over a plan that someone had thrown out during lunch last week in that barrage of disbelief. She wasn't sure whose voice it was, but she bet on Irene's. Once the helper, now the saboteur. But who else besides a native would know the name of the local orphanage? "Take her to Hillcrest Children's Village," the voice said. "Those little Tudor-style cottages look lovely."

The plan agitated Audrey so much that she got up from the bed, as though acting out the scene she'd constructed, and went downstairs to the sofa, feeling the cool distance between her and the baby. Lake stayed asleep, even alone in the empty bed. It could be done. Audrey could leave the child asleep in its carrier on the building's stoop, a warm night like this, and return to the car she'd left idling. The baby would be embraced by a ready family, dozens of brothers and sisters to hold her. Hillcrest might know of couples wanting a child. Such a match could happen within hours, and that would be the end of it. Audrey wouldn't have to meet anyone, explain anything. The baby wasn't hers to explain.

There were other things she wanted to do besides rinse out diapers in toilets, soak them in the disinfectant pail, and hang them to dry on the line.

Sleepless early mornings like these she looked for Daniel's hat on the hall tree to see if he was home yet, though it was almost always a sign he was already in his room. But that night his footsteps sounded on the walkway through the open window, then the brass knob turned. She rested in the arm of the sofa, her feet tucked beside her.

"Good evening," she said quietly.

"Good morning," he said, not startled by Audrey's voice, as though he knew, even in the dark house, that she waited for him and had done so before.

"How was your day? Your night?"

"Not the biggest news day, but maybe that's a good one. Everyone's got their eyes on Potsdam in Germany. Did you see that the Louvre opened up recently? I meant to tell you that earlier. Happy news, right?"

"Very happy," she said, touched that he had thought of her.

He sat, then stood. "Sherry for you, Audrey?"

He drew her name out like it was a hill he was rolling down. His voice was deep, never halting. Her mother, in her polite way, would call his accent "country." Audrey pictured it coming not from a box in his throat but from a dirt road, far south.

"Please," she said. They had done this all spring, shared a drink together while Lucille drank iced tea by the gallon. But when the baby came, Daniel had tilted away from them. Now, without Lucille, there was the same awkwardness there had been when she was at Penington.

He set their two drinks down now, hers on a dainty stem, his in a jelly jar. They sat in silence a few moments before he asked, "What do you think your husband will say about Lake's being here?"

His question jarred her for a moment but shouldn't have. He was always direct. "So many questions. Has anyone told you you'd make a great reporter?" She smiled, then took a sip, feeling the drink warm her. "I hope it doesn't come to that. But I don't know what he'll say about anything, even your being here. He didn't exactly know I was going to do this, open up his house to strangers. He might not like any of it."

Daniel nodded. "Why'd you do it, then, when you knew he might not like it?"

"When you've been married only a short time, you're not sure what your husband will like. He might have liked it less if I were out roving around town for company."

"You've never roved in your life. I'm sure he knows that," Daniel said, laughing. He jumped slightly, as though remembering something, then reached into his briefcase. "I picked up the mail on my way out this afternoon by mistake. Here it is."

She flipped through the stack, and when she came to the manila envelope, its flap sealed and the brown cord wrapped around the button, she knew at once it was a gift she was due. The outside of the envelope read *Mrs. Benjamin Bray* in a lovely Palmer hand that Audrey recognized. There was no other address on the face of it, only a postmark from the infamous town, Pomona, NC. This name was as evocative of Lucille as if she herself had arrived on the doorstep, her hair frizzy from the humidity, her white-gloved hand plopping down what she called her "pocketbook" on the floor beside her.

But inside were only five loose-leaf pages, mostly blank, barely a sentence on each page.

Dear Audrey,
I am
Dear Audrey,
By now you must have realized
Dear Audrey,
Please know it's with deep remorse that I write
Dear Audrey,
The rains have rotted the peach harvest and today is the first sighting of sunshine in a week. The mosquitoes are like vultures over all us farm hands.
Dear Audrey,
I wish

The pages were out of order—the first was the Saturday prior, and the last was a week before that—but no matter. The message was the same.

It was as if a switch had been hit, red heat coursing through her body. "I think the right thing to do is to take the baby to an orphanage."

"An orphanage?" He whistled. "Now, why would you do that?"

She handed him the letters and waited for him to finish reading.

"She can't expect us to raise it," she said. "You want to raise this baby girl?"

The only light on him shone from the kitchen, half his face in shadow. His silence deepened the darkness, and she couldn't tell if he was looking at her. "I would, if it came to that."

"Oh, you people who always say what you would or wouldn't do in someone else's shoes." She sighed, stopping herself from saying what she wanted: *You make me sick.*

"Look, you have everything here a child needs—"

"Except its mother."

"That baby doesn't know any different. You've been with her from the day she was born. You're going to pass her off to strangers now? From where I'm sitting, this is a sweet home." He stopped, as if he didn't want to say more. "Why don't you go down there, try to find her?

That town of, what, a hundred people—someone will know where she is. What's stopping you from going after her?"

"This matters to you."

"It matters to you, doesn't it? You've taken on the responsibility for now, anyway. I know Lucille. I spent time with her too." Then he added, "I miss her too." He lit a cigarette, aiming his exhale away from her. "Maybe she was never going to stay, no matter what we did. Listen, people have always worked this out," he went on. "Parents get sick, they die, they go broke. That's happened since the beginning of time. And people who knew them took care of their babies. You know who raised me. A great-aunt and -uncle. I'm not sure my parents had spoken more than five words to that aunt, my grandmother's sister-in-law. And I was miserable half the time, or thought I was. I came to hate the sound of her slippers slapping her heels as she plodded around. How she made me chop wood all afternoon because she wanted me out of the house." His voice grew quiet. "I'd lay down my life for her now. Thank God no one dragged me off to some orphanage. I'm glad I had a link back to my beginning, as true a birthright as there is." He sounded steady and reasonable, not at all what Audrey was feeling. "I can't tell you what to do, shouldn't try. I feel for you, being put out like this, I really do. But you'll figure out the right thing," he added.

The next day she tried calling Lucille again, but the telephone rang and rang, apparently no one there to answer it.

More than a week later when Audrey came home, exhausted, pulling off her shoes and rubbing her feet, Prudy told her that Lake, who was recovering from a mild cold, was sleeping but she'd been fussy all day. "Wake her up soon or you'll be up all night." That was the last thing Audrey wanted to do. She didn't want to wake the baby. She couldn't bear asking for its conscious presence when it was sleeping. She wanted it to sleep always when she was home—that was the truth of it.

Prudy seemed in a hurry to leave, agitated, when she suddenly turned, her hands clasped in front of her. For a moment, Audrey thought she might start singing. "I feel awful about this, Audrey, but you need to know. My mother says you need time to find someone to help you. I'm going to school soon, full-time. In a few weeks I start at the Washington Conservatory of Music. I just got my acceptance letter."

Audrey sank back in her chair. This was a rehearsed speech, all right, and the earnestness of it—and its message—almost brought tears to her eyes. "Oh, Prudy, that's wonderful news. I've heard of the Conservatory. It's a fine institution. Of course you must go." But she leaned over then, folding herself over her knees, and put her tired face into her hands, resting for a minute. When she looked up, Prudy was still there.

"Are you all right?"

"Just a headache. Probably the nitrate," she said. "A few more weeks, you say? I'll figure something out." She managed a smile. "Your mother must be so proud."

Prudy straightened, gathering up her height. She was proud of herself, Audrey saw. It was her voice after all.

Audrey was wide awake now, thinking of work, how she would keep it up, whether she could find someone quickly to take care of Lake. Anger at Lucille, a well-worn pathway by now, blazed through her. Could she not count on anyone? Why had she thought Prudy was different, that she wouldn't leave too? Audrey, like Irene, had underestimated her.

She walked upstairs in the dark. It was hotter on the second floor. She switched on the attic fan, its slow rumble evening out to a steady murmur. Lake was sleeping, but her back was damp with sweat, and soon she was making little darts of sound. Audrey tried swinging her in cradled arms, something she'd seen Prudy do, but the crying persisted.

Trying to cool down her cheeks, red with fever, Audrey bathed her in the bathroom sink. She covered each ear as she poured cups of water over her head, which Lake could now hold steady on her own. She hadn't been baptized yet, and Audrey regretted that. The umbilical spot was still pink, a trace of Lake and Lucille's conjoined flesh, now severed. That traumatic first wound. But nothing compared to the second injury, being unyoked from your mother's skin, smell, voice, the outline of her face, the taste of her fingers. Lucille's gentle handoff, her quiet absence, reflected none of this violence—or the third hurt to come, that of comprehension.

Audrey dried the baby off and buttoned her in a clean sleeper. Downstairs she crushed aspirin with the back of a spoon and stirred it with applesauce, feeding the mixture to Lake. The two of them lay down, and Audrey slept a drop at a time. They were like a fly to flypaper, sticking together through the night.

In the morning Lake was limp as a noodle, her cheeks enflamed again, and now her lips bluish. "I hear her wheezing, I think you should call the doctor," Prudy said as soon as she arrived.

Audrey called in to work, telling them she had a family emergency, then found the number of Dr. Keith, who had seen Lake for her checkup in June. Over the phone his questions were routine: "What's her birthdate?" Audrey had to think about this. "Getting plenty of sleep?" he asked, chuckling. "How long has she had a fever? What have you given her for it? Is she eating? How long has she been wheezing?" Apparently she said enough to concern him. "You should have brought her in at once. I'll meet you at George Washington."

Prudy helped her pack. Audrey would have liked her to come, but Prudy wouldn't be allowed in a hospital for whites only. Neither of them mentioned this. Alone in the car, Lake in the carrier next to her, the truth became obvious. Babies got sick, they couldn't tell you what hurt or how severely, their illness went untreated or treated incorrectly. The chances seemed suddenly great that Lake would die.

What if this baby, over whom she wasn't even an official guardian, died? She hadn't asked for this responsibility—it terrified her, thinking of her guilt if something happened to Lake.

In the waiting room, Lake made loud bellowing sounds; despite the discomfort they suggested, their robustness gave Audrey hope. The mothers in the room looked on sympathetically. The day was hot, but a wind banged Venetian blinds in and out of the open window. It was getting close to Lake's feeding time, and Prudy had thought of this. Audrey tried holding a bottle to Lake's mouth, but she would have none of it, and soon her head drooped again on Audrey's shoulder. On the admission form, she left the father's name blank, filling in the mother's as "Lucille Spence" and writing "Lake Spence, female, born May 9, 1945." She was almost three months old.

Audrey had accompanied Lucille to Lake's first appointment and remembered Dr. Keith as impatient, rushing them through the checkup, but he ministered tenderly now, inspecting Lake's tiny fingers for any tinge of blueness. "I suspect pneumonia," he said. "We'll admit her and start her on sulfonamides. You can't stay in the room with her, so you might get more rest at home. This can be serious."

"When can I see her again?"

"Tomorrow, if we can tell she's responding to the treatment." His eyes were tired. "You should get some sleep. A woman on your own, you need it."

There it was in his tone, the judgment Lucille had feared.

After his exam, a nurse took Lake from Audrey's arms and made to deliver the bottle of formula. "She hasn't eaten, she won't eat!" Audrey called, but the nurse was already down the hall.

Before leading her back to the waiting area, Dr. Keith said, "Miss Spence, when you come back tomorrow, ask for the nurse who checked you in. Sheldon's her name."

Outside Audrey put on sunglasses. The street was busy. She crossed into a commercial area, passing a shoe repair shop, its oily smell of polish and leather, before walking into a jewelry store. She stood in front of an electric fan, not caring that it blew her hair and dress askew. "May I help you?" a woman asked from behind the counter. Audrey thanked her and walked outside.

What was being asked of Audrey was too great.

In a drugstore, she strolled down an aisle of tweezers and hairspray. There was an underlying scent of menthol. Flags for sale, a surplus after the Fourth of July, hung in the still air above her. The only customer at the counter, she ordered lemonade. A man pushed a broom along the wooden floors, and a woman quietly organized pipes in a display case behind the counter. Cars sputtered to a stop at the corner.

"Hotter than a firecracker out there," the woman said.

Audrey wasn't capable of caring for a baby, especially without Prudy. People died from pneumonia every day, but she hadn't even thought to ask Dr. Keith about the danger. In the waiting room, she'd wished for paper and pen to draw the woman across from her—never mind that Lake lay sick in her arms.

The glass of lemonade had a tiny chip in the edge that Audrey rubbed with her finger. She lit a cigarette, but the smoke and sour lemons left a bad taste in her mouth and she snuffed it out. Her leg, crossed over her knee, bobbed up and down. She held the glass at her wrists to cool herself off.

She stood up, pulling her cotton skirt from where it stuck to her legs. She did not want to be a mother, not like this. Lake was safer than safe. She would get better where she was. No one would let harm come to her in the hospital. That's where you went when you'd been harmed. It had everything she needed. It was really the perfect place.

Someone in that hospital would take Lake in. Maybe it would be Dr. Keith himself, whose ample hands had examined her, his two fingers over her heart, his thumbs gently lifting her eyelids. He understood the burden was too much. When he'd called Audrey "Miss Spence," she had almost pleaded with him. *Please, help.* Perhaps Nurse Sheldon, her voice as sharp as those pricked corners on her cap, would take pity on Lake. Or maybe somebody in that waiting room, after losing a loved one, would carry Lake home.

These were Audrey's thoughts as she drove away from the hospital. As soon as she knew Lake was well enough—and she would tend to her the best she could until then—she would notify the hospital of the situation or take Lake to Hillcrest.

When she got home, she called Pomona Nursery. Again, a man answered.

"I'm trying to reach Lucille Spence. This is Audrey Bray."

"I passed along your last message," said the man. "I'll try again."

"Is this Arthur?"

"Yes, Arthur Lind."

Audrey held her breath, daring herself to say more.

"Tell her it's urgent."

She went to bed before she heard Daniel coming home, and fell asleep imagining his face when he learned she'd given Lake up—a face in retreat after being struck. But with her decision, she felt the heavy wooden planks that had weighed her down for weeks, pressing her cheek into gravel, lifting. After so many sleepless nights that summer, she slept hard.

Daniel, however, was waiting for her when she woke in the morning. At the bottom of the steps, he held out coffee for her, the newspaper in his hand. He looked concerned. "Where's Lake?"

She started to tell him about the fever, stumbling over her explanation of Lake's stay in the hospital last night, Prudy's upcoming departure, but he interrupted. "Let's go see her. Right now. I've got some news that'll make her feel better." He was giddy, waving the newspaper's front page in front of her, but she couldn't make out the meaning. "I almost woke you up last night to tell you. The war's going to be over soon. Everything has changed. We just dropped an atomic bomb on Japan."

She couldn't move for a minute, astonished by what had happened and what he was suggesting.

"Come on, what are you waiting for? And Lucille called last night. Didn't you hear the phone ringing off the hook? Said you'd left an urgent message. Now I understand why."

And that was how she was driven back to the hospital, back into caring, for the time being at least, for Lake, whose fever had broken.

1973

24

Driving downtown, Lucille considers passing by her old apartment on Twelfth and M before going to Ray's law firm, but thinks better of it. She has no way of knowing whether he'll arrive before the firm opens for business. And besides, isn't her return to the city enough, just being here? Must her penance involve revisiting every corner and room that held only suffering? She cannot remember one happy day in that apartment.

This idea to approach Ray and befriend him came to her days ago but still feels impulsive. She should have called him on the phone at work. Told him she was going to be down that way. Said: *I think I can help*. She hasn't planned what she'll say—that might look too rehearsed. She is good on her feet, always has been, despite contrary evidence with Lake. She can't wait outside; a mild sleet is coming down. Entering the large office building, she is swept up with everyone arriving at work, each with a job to do. Yes, she has a job to do.

Wearing a gray wool dress under her coat, not her nursing whites, she hopes to blend in while she waits outside the firm's wooden doors on the second floor. She was right not to take any detours. She almost misses him, briskly as he's moving. He carries a briefcase but is hatless, unlike the older men filing in. He seems to look right through her, but she waves her hand in front of him. "Ray! Remember me?"

Pale, his nose red from the cold, he is taller than she remembers. He doesn't smile, but he doesn't try to avoid her either. He looks almost relieved when she explains herself: "I was down this way, have an appointment a few floors up, when I noticed your name on the directory. Thought I'd check in with you, see how your night with Lake went."

With both hands he clutches the handle of his briefcase, bouncing it lightly against his thighs. "At first we got along fine, but then she called everything off."

"Everything? What exactly was on?"

"I mean she doesn't want to see me anymore." He blinks—tears, she thinks, but then light reflects off his glasses, hiding his eyes.

"Did you have a chance to ask her whether she'd see me?"

"No, she doesn't want that either." He sighs loudly. "Look, she told me not to come around anymore. Said she asked her neighbors to tell her if they see me. She said, 'You're creeping me out.' That's the expression she used, after knowing me all this time."

"Goodness, that does sound definitive. But don't give up, Ray. Doesn't she work at a school? You could always visit her there."

"I think we need to get away. I wish I could have a few days with her somewhere, away from—"

"You think there's someone else she's interested in."

"I don't want to think about that." He holds a hank of hair, lifting it off his forehead. His fingers are long and slender. "I love her too much to think about that."

She frowns with sympathy at him. "How long has it been, a week? You've given her some time." She touches him lightly on his shoulder, like she might Clark, her son. "She's probably wondering what you're up to." Looking at her watch, sticking to her original story, she says, "I have to go. Here's my telephone number. Call me if I can help. I can tell you care about her."

He walks with her to the bank of elevators. "Nice to see you," he offers. But when she presses the down button, he says, "I thought you were going up." She only nods, coolly correcting her mistake with another press of a button.

She wouldn't want to oppose him in a court of law.

※

All morning and into the afternoon, Audrey empties her and Ben's bedroom. With Prudy's help, she pulls clothes from the closet, folds blouses and sweaters, adds to stacks designated as "keep," "donate," "alter." At the rear of the closet, used solely by Audrey for years, are shelves cut at an angle deep into the hipped roof. She finds a hatbox full of old photos—they could be useful for her work—and boxes of gloves and shoes she hasn't seen since the 1940s. Ivory satin pumps she wore at her wedding go in the donation pile. The yellow wedges from her first job in Washington do too, though she hesitates over them for a moment. She rises slowly from her knees to carry a load across the room, but Prudy moves like a teen, hoisting the "keep" pile in her arms.

"Want me to hang these back up?"

"Oh no, thank you."

Prudy looks puzzled.

"I might as well tell you. I'm moving to an apartment. I'm—we're—separating."

Prudy lays the clothes back on the bed. "Oh. That is something. I'm sorry."

"It's okay. You know better than anybody. This has been a long time coming…undone." She has practiced many times what she'll say to Ben. She has not figured out how to string two sentences together about this for anyone else.

They lapse into silence, hauling boxes of clothes, which will go into her new chest of drawers, and bags, which she'll donate or consign. Everything must be packed and moved into her car by nightfall. First thing in the morning she'll tell him her plans; she will avoid the word *divorce*, for now. Her suitcases—outfits for a few days, her toiletries—and the stack of hanging clothes can wait till then. Prudy, who is always singing, never without a verse on her lips, is quiet as they make trips up and down the stairs, and her silence feels uncomfortable. As though it's meant for Audrey.

"Have you been performing lately?" Audrey asks.

"I sang at a place called Bohemian Caverns a few weeks ago. You heard of it?"

"Yes! That's incredible, Prudy."

"Lake came—it was a little thing. Headliner wasn't any more well-known than me." She laughs.

This fact surprises Audrey, Lake's watching Prudy sing in a nightclub, not telling her. "Do you think Lake is all right? She talks to you more than she does me, that's for sure."

"I told her, don't get hitched to somebody back from war." She is re-folding a stack of sweaters into a paper bag. "Those boys are too beaten down after something like that. That's the mistake I made, getting tied up with somebody wrecked by the last war."

"I didn't know that was the case, Prudy. Was that Lon? Are you still with him?"

"No, not for a while now. We just about undid each other."

"I'm sorry to hear that. But I'm glad Lake can talk to you."

"Everything to do with love is easier said than done. Who's in charge of love? It's loose in the world, nobody steering it. She says Ray is bound to her—how did she put it?—like a heavy perfume. I didn't like to hear that."

"She said that? I thought he adored her, didn't you?" She hasn't known what to make of Lake's statement about chances in the kitchen that morning, but it nags her. Lake hasn't made any long-term commitment to Ray. There's no need for her to give him numerous chances.

"I don't know. Maybe. Seems to me everybody has the right to be left alone."

"That's what she wants?" They're standing in the entrance hall now, winded after another flight of stairs.

"Better talk to her. She's tried to break things off with him. That's all I know." They set their bags down, sorting others around the door. They need to make one more trip to Audrey's car. She looks at her watch. The delivery truck of furniture arrives at her apartment in an hour.

The TV is silently on and visible from the entrance hall. An advertisement for the evening news is showing Nixon in front of the White House, following his inauguration this past weekend. Audrey has avoided thinking about him, cannot believe he won sixty percent of the popular vote and, she suspects, Ben's vote. In past years, she's gone to the ceremonies, but she didn't mind missing this one. A name appears on the screen and her hand goes over her mouth. She can't look away.

"There's Daniel! Do you remember him? He's on TV."

Prudy turns, a smile spreading across her face. "I do, I do. Look at Daniel."

"It's been one thing to hear him on the radio all these years, but to see him on the screen! He didn't tell me that—I saw him recently—he didn't mention he was going to be an anchor now."

Age has filled him out. His lack of hair gives him an elegance never achieved by shaggier cuts so in vogue. The camera shifts to justices in black robes. She lingers, waiting for him to come back, but a soap opera returns. She hurries to catch up to Prudy.

Ben has used the guest-room closet for years, and standing before her now-empty one, Audrey has a fleeting inclination to help him by moving his clothes here.

Such thoughts—vestiges of her ingrained, dutiful ways.

Another thought is to search his clothes for evidence of what could be helpful. She might have found it years ago but never looked. This could be her last chance. She remembers where she was when she realized Ben's infidelity. Late one night she picked up the ringing telephone from their bedroom at the same time Ben answered downstairs. Only Ben said hello. Audrey heard a woman's voice, familiar—his nurse, Jeanne. Whenever Audrey saw her, say, at a small dinner for their medical practice, she noticed Jeanne watching him. Not only looking at him when he spoke but watching him when he fell quiet. She saw this now, in the instant she heard Jeanne's voice, and a slight electric current rolled through her body. Before he served in the Navy, Ben had dated her, before he married Audrey. He was almost always summoned the nights he was on call. Audrey had no idea if that was typical. But on this call Jeanne said, "I'll see you there," sounding urgent—a tone perhaps fitting for a medical emergency but for its swagger.

Audrey waited for Ben to leave and then turned on every light in the house. Each lamp and fixture blasted inhospitably. For so long she had lived as a foreigner in a hostile place, calling it home. *His house, his child.* She might as well have been hoping the planet Mercury could be hers. Faces and figures of women he'd ogled before they were married, and even since, flared in her memory. Oh, he loved women. Walking through the house again, she paused in the doorframes as one might do during an earthquake. By the time the sun came up, she had adjusted to the brightness.

No longer did she require herself to be a devoted wife. She felt herself rationing emotion for Ben, even for Lake (though if she was honest, rationing had begun long ago). She finished work that composed an art show she held in their home; she invited everyone she knew, except for people in Ben's practice. She quit picking his clothes off the floor. And over time, without any declaration, she stopped sleeping in the same bed as he, at least nights when he drank heavily. By this time, that was most. She didn't make a show of separate bedrooms, there was no conversation. She just found herself a different bed to sleep in each night: sometimes Lake's, rarely Lucille's, most often Daniel's. It was a threadbare comfort, laying her head where his had been, but she seemed to sleep better. She hadn't spoken to him in so long. Occasionally she looked up his address. Once she drove by his house and eyed a swing set between his and his neighbor's yards. A football on the front lawn. Children.

Even now she isn't angry enough, or cold-blooded enough, or whatever it takes to level a charge of adultery. The accusation might convince Ben she's serious about a divorce. She has never gone through the pockets of his trousers and suit jackets. At the time she told herself it wasn't because she doubted his unfaithfulness. She didn't. Proof would only hurt worse. Maybe it still would.

Neither Audrey nor Prudy hears Lake coming up the steps, despite her breathlessness at the bedroom door. Her face is blanched and her lips pale from the cold. "I need to stay here again."

"What happened?" Audrey says, on her feet to get a good look at her. "Are you okay?"

"Ray came to the school, pretending to be a parent. The principal ordered him off the premises. The whole thing was humiliating." She pauses, noticing the boxes and suitcases. "What's going on here?"

"Hold on, finish what happened."

"I'll take these down," Prudy says, lifting two more bags.

"Ray left, but I could tell he was in one of his rages." Lake sinks down on the bed. "I don't know where to go."

"You're right, you shouldn't go home. We need to let his office know what he's doing. Call his father." Audrey looks at her watch and starts hauling bags into the hallway. "You've got to stay away from him."

"What do you think I've been doing?" she says. Her expression flattens into helplessness. "What is all this?"

"The studio," Audrey starts slowly, but she doesn't have much time. If she misses the furniture truck in front of her apartment, they'll leave everything on the street. "It's more than the studio I'm moving. I'm moving to an apartment. Your father and I—we're going to live apart now."

"When were you planning on letting me know?"

"I thought I should let him know first. I haven't yet... I—"

"I can't believe the timing of this."

"I'm sorry."

Lake walks to the window, quietly looking out. "I just need something to hold together right now."

"This is hard for everyone. I know you're upset—"

"You two have never been happy together. I know that better than anyone."

"What is it you want me to do? I think I've done a lot."

"Because you've had to."

"This is about Ben and me. I'm not leaving *you*."

"But all this time you've wanted to leave us. Haven't you? I can feel it; I knew when you were cleaning out your studio. This—this weight has been lifted off you, and you're so…happy." Lake turns now, crying.

"Oh, Lake." Audrey puts down the bag of shoes and rocks her gently in a hug. "Come with me. I'm running out of time to meet the truck. Let's go to the apartment. I need your help."

Prudy waits by the door with the last of the bags. Audrey wonders what she overheard from Lake, who is already outside in the warming car. Prudy's look says: *Why can't you give Lake what she needs?* For a minute, Audrey is embarrassed, but she says, "You may be gone by the time I finish unpacking. We'll stay in touch." She wants to say: *You have been the glue for so long.* She puts her arms around her, something she has never done, but Prudy's body feels rigid. Audrey steps away with a half wave, and is out the door.

"This is a joy to Bée and me. I'm not leaving, Sue."

"But all this time we've wanted to have you. I wish you'd consented. If I knew where you_'d been and what your studies... This—this weight has been lifted off you, and you're so — happy." Lake turns away, crying.

"Oh, Lake," Audrey puts down the bag of shoes and packs her can of painting. "Come with me. There's lamp oil of mine to use. The trunk. Let's go to the parsonage. I need your help."

"Push on…" Lake nods with the heart of the bag. Audrey wanders after her overboard. It isn't Lake, who is already outside, in the excitement of Pugh's book even, that wants to see Lake near the candle for a moment.

Audrey comes back and calls the aunt. "Audrey," he's gone by the time I finish myself up. "We'll manage to watch." The aunt is sorry because even she for a time. She puts her hand on his hip. "So it is long since she had never aloud, but Pugh's book is dear to her." Audrey steps away with a half smile, and it is time he drew.

1945

25

That Audrey reached Arthur on the telephone and called him by name must have rattled Lucille, because she phoned again the next evening. Her voice was soft, contrite.

"I'm sorry I haven't called. How is Lake? Is she all right?"

"She's—" Audrey stopped. "Do you know how lucky you are that I've kept her with me? She's in the hospital. I can either leave her there or take her to Hillcrest, an orphanage." She paused to catch her breath. "You decide."

"What?"

"That's right, she has pneumonia. The drugs are working, and her fever has come down. But you can't just abandon your child like this."

"Audrey, please." Lucille was crying now. "Please don't leave her. We can work this out. I've been so worried knowing what I'm doing to you, but I had no idea."

"There are people who think I should have you arrested."

"I can't explain everything just now, but I need time. More time to work everything out. Can you help a little longer?"

"How much longer?" asked Audrey.

"I don't know. I couldn't possibly come before Christmas. I need to get settled, on my feet. I've applied for a teaching job, to make some money." When Audrey didn't say anything, she added, "With Jimmy gone, my mother will fall apart if I bring a baby home. I wish I were there with you."

"Prudy is going back to school, so I don't know who's going to look after Lake."

"I'm so sorry. Please don't leave her," Lucille said, her voice barely a whisper.

"When Ben comes home, what do you expect me to tell him?"

There was a long pause.

"You better not let so much time pass before calling again," Audrey went on. "The next time I get somebody from the nursery on the line, no telling what I'll say."

"Audrey—"

"What?"

"Audrey, please forgive me. I'm sorry for everything."

❧

When Lucille returned home after calling Audrey, it wasn't yet suppertime, but her father was in the house. Something was wrong. Her sister, Evangeline, rushed onto the porch to greet her, her braids flying at Lucille's cheek. As always, she thought: my first baby. Then she heard his yelling. She held her hands over Evangeline's ears. He had noticed signs of fire blight on the pears in the spring, but all the measures to contain it by pruning and disinfecting the trees had failed. Now he raged about black streaks under the bark, the leaves charred, the crop lost. She and Evangeline moved through the gloomy parlor, always unused, with its Victorian horsehair sofa and the out-of-tune melodeon. A long table of military blue stretched empty in the dining room. Chairs had been shoved, presumably by their father, to the walls. They avoided his warpath by going upstairs. Evangeline huddled against Lucille, who read aloud from *Emily of New Moon*, a buffer against his shouting. Lucille couldn't make out her mother's voice but imagined her placating gestures and quietly argued reason, the same tactics she used to soothe a child.

Later Lucille went to sleep in Jimmy's room—her room now, despite its sadness. Jimmy's old saxophone leaned in the corner, his fingerprints and lip prints still on it. No curtains hung over the window, which she opened to let in fresh air. She pulled Lake's blanket from the drawer and lay down in the dark with it. Lucille's own smallness, with which she'd been born, had never gone completely away under this roof. She wept, thinking of Lake sick, in the hospital, and of the burden she'd laid on Audrey. She prayed that Audrey wouldn't desert Lake, as she had.

By now the blanket had the smell of the farmhouse, nothing of Lake.

That was the last of their father's yelling any of them would hear. A week later, he was talking to his foreman, Bryant, in the lee of a tractor on a blustery day. He leaned his arm against the large wheel as they calculated slimmer profits. He had always said that Bryant, a man whose grandfather had been a slave in these parts, knew more about planting than he did; not only that, Bryant could tally bushels and pounds and dollars faster than you could say chrysanthemum. Her father's arm went limp, then his clipboard of invoices fell, and he followed to the ground. Bryant shouted for help, a crowd of men came running, those who were back from lunch, and someone went to tell her mother, who was cooking in the house alone. Before she even followed her husband to the hospital, she went to tell Arthur Lind, who had returned for Jimmy's funeral. Besides Bryant, who had accompanied her husband, Arthur was the one person she trusted to keep things running in an emergency.

His speech lost from the stroke, Lucille's father now needed constant care. Her mother would manage most of it while Lucille taught school during the week. On the weekends, she helped out more. "Why doesn't Lucille have to go to church?" Evangeline complained.

"And leave your daddy here all alone?" her mother said.

The kitchen to themselves, Lucille cut apple slices and shelled peas, chattering to her father. He sat in an armchair in the corner of the kitchen, blocking the cupboard. Dishes were now cleaned and returned to their place settings, not stored; he needed watching and this was the best room for that. "I've got to make my lesson plan for tomorrow, go ahead now, eat up. I always loved that school, you know I did. The polished floors, the sound of the bell. I didn't mind those mill kids; maybe you tried to make us think we were better than them." She turned down the radio, a sermon she was talking over. "But we weren't. On April Fool's Day I'm going to give everyone bad marks. That'll put a smile on their faces when I let them in on the joke. And when the class starts reading Longfellow's *Evangeline, A Tale of Acadie*, I'm going to bring Evangeline to class, dress her in a bonnet and gown."

She liked this kind of talking—not with him, at him, as he used to do to her.

Later, after supper, her mother cleaned the kitchen while Lucille tended to him again. She helped him in the bathroom, disrobed him, removed his slippers, guided him to bed. He wasn't stooped to the earth the way other men became bent by their labor. He had resisted gravity like a sorghum stalk—until that day by the tractor. She said his prayers for him and hummed a verse of a hymn. She was always gentle. But now that he had no power over her, she whispered in his ear things she'd told no one, pulling back to assess his reaction after every declaration. The two dimensions of her life nearly met then, but there was only his slackened cheek, his lost eyes.

It had been, continued to be, a year of sorrows. Leaving Lake, losing Jimmy. The two couldn't be teased out from one another to be properly reckoned with. Now the pear trees ruined, her father unreachable, Lucille wondered if this was life: each new grief dredging up the old, keeping it fresh, so while she mourned the last, she was always mourning the first.

At Jimmy's funeral the singsong lilt and six-eight time of "In the Garden" cradled her like a swing. The sight of Arthur consoled her too, though a beard obscured his mouth, so Lucille couldn't tell if he sang. What showed of his face looked bludgeoned by his own cumulative losses. He later expressed his condolences to her and her mother but said nothing to her impenetrable father. Approaching him would be like knocking into a wall. Those two had spoken their last words to each other.

For weeks after Jimmy's death, Lucille got nothing but silence from Arthur too, though she saw him more frequently after her father's stroke. He was running the business again, and he always tipped his hat, nodding to her as he would to anyone. Many afternoons she passed by him sitting on the Boyds' porch with Teddy. Teddy had returned from the war with only one of his legs, and now instead of working he looked out at everyone else using their legs to walk by. She'd not known Arthur and the family were friends, though everyone within a two-mile radius was friendly. But no one had much liked Teddy before the war. He was in steady trouble and had once sold the family's single piece of silver to pay a gambling debt. All was forgiven now, life having punished him enough. She was jealous almost; she wished she were on the porch next to Arthur. Each time she walked by she felt a desire to know what they said. She wanted to hear Arthur speak. She simply wanted to be within range of his voice. They lifted their hands in greeting as she passed.

Nights, she tossed and turned, until a truth slowly surfaced like old roots of a tree.

Early one evening, she held her shoes in one hand and walked barefoot in the ruts between plantings, all the way to the end of the orchard. From here she looked back at the spreading land, the rows of trees—lavender in this light—a few bees still pricking at lingering flowers: she would never take any of it for granted again. Even the silence. But the apple trees, heavy with unripened fruit now—she regarded them differently. The way the workers broke the branches as they grew, twisting and turning them downward so the fruit was easier to pick. Or how they cut the limbs that grew too vertically, spreading them for a wider crotch, letting in more light, spurring the tree to fruit more heavily. These were things done since the beginning of time, but now the sight grieved her.

She took the path, withered and grown over with honeysuckle, that she used to travel to Mrs. Causey's house, finding the rocks on one side, the crating shed on another side, the same rivulet of water. She knocked and said Arthur's name so as not to frighten him. He came to the door without turning on a light. "Is everything all right?" he said. He'd shaved his beard, years off his face.

"Yes. Well, you know as well as I do how things are."

"I didn't think you were going to stick around this long."

"I could say the same for you. I'm teaching now up at Springs."

He nodded. He'd worked off his sorrow—"tripled sorrow," he said, "after losing you too"—by sleeping under the stars, and now the trees had come back to life for him.

"The mill kids, they don't always like to listen to me."

"You're not singing to them, are you?"

She shooed away his insult.

"Then you should be all right."

"I don't know about that. There's something wrong with me."

"Me. That's what's wrong with you." And he opened his door to her.

They talked for several hours that evening, in the half dark, only the smallest of lamps on to keep the temperature down. He told her how, to heal the heart she'd broken, he risked his life jumping freight trains across the prairie. It was as if she hadn't gone a day without seeing him. She wanted to tell him about Lake. She wanted to know if he would help her. She didn't ask outright. Not: would you raise this child with me? She told him about all the people she'd met in Washington, then mentioned one who was in a particular kind of trouble.

"Some people have it hard," he said, eyeing her over his spectacles. "I never wanted that to happen to you. Made sure it didn't. She made a bad decision there, don't you think?"

Her inexperience had always seemed precious to him. She saw it had a practical side and felt a flash of love for him in that. She'd given away what was precious. He wouldn't like that, though she couldn't imagine how exactly he would express his disgust.

Or was it her own disgust for what she had done?

"Seems like the man who got her into this fix," he went on, "ought to be the one to get her out."

"What if he's married now?"

He whistled, shaking his head. "Like I said, some people have it harder than others."

"Maybe if she starts out on her own, she'll meet somebody who'll take in the child."

"Could be a lot to ask."

She felt uncomfortable, the way he was watching her now. "I just feel so sorry for her," she added.

"Name's not Audrey, is it?"

She waved away his question and changed the subject. What did he think about turning over the pear crop to landscaping inventory?

"Oh, we're going to save some pears. No doubt about it. Bryant's already got a crew busy grafting."

26

The Japanese surrender didn't come until almost a week after a second atomic bomb was dropped. They hinted at giving up, but on their terms; the Allies insisted on theirs. What if, after all this, troops were required to invade Japan? Daily there were false reports of Hirohito's conditions. To Audrey, the suspense felt like dread. She couldn't stop thinking of Ben. He could already be on his way home. Would she even recognize his voice if he called from the front door? At the only officers' wives luncheon she attended, she learned that if he was in the Pacific, his ship was probably cleaning up, going round to the vanquished islands, finding prisoners of war and retrieving whatever materiel and weaponry could be found. She wondered what it would feel like to be held by him after all this time. She should tell him everything, and soon.

She had kept her head down at work for the rest of August, in front of the viewfinder, frame after frame sliding across the screen. Talking to Lucille, hearing her suffer, had quelled her anger. Mad as Audrey was, she didn't want to hurt her. But nothing felt resolved. A few times she misplaced an entire deck of reels, putting them under the wrong country, and it took the office all morning to sort out her mistake. She began sketching the Japanese soldiers she saw in the films during the day. She perceived their hands and noses, all their features, only as edges and angles, dark and light, the negative spaces equal to the rest. She had pages of them, and when her book fell open once during lunch, Irene looked shocked. "I don't think you should be doing that."

"Doing what?"

"Drawing them. The enemy. You're making them into something... beautiful."

"Need help?" Daniel leaned against the doorway of the bedroom, his jacket slung over one shoulder, a drink in his other hand.

"Frankly, you don't look much like you're ready to help." Audrey smiled. Over the sound of the sewing machine pedals she hadn't heard him come up the stairs. She was stitching together heavy chintz fabric to hang on rings and rods that lay all across the floor. Lake, who was lying between them on a blanket, grabbing her toes, was going to have a proper nursery soon. Earlier that day Audrey had found a rocker—long ago concealed by her blank stretched canvases, in the corner of her studio—and moved it here; the desk was now across the hall. She draped the finished curtains across the bed.

"When I'm not holding a drink, I can be pretty handy. One summer I even wired a whole house. I bet there's a hand drill in the basement."

Minutes later he was holding a stepladder and toolbox.

"The hospital stay had one good effect—she's slept through the night ever since. She doesn't disturb you in the mornings, I hope." This close she could see a little spot on his neck where he'd cut himself shaving.

"She's not a bother. I miss Prudy's singing to her, playing the piano. Some of my favorite hours." He unfolded a ruler and climbed the ladder.

"She did that? I didn't even know she could play. Didn't that wake you?"

"Very peacefully. She knows every gospel hymn I've never heard, and the few I have. Her voice has such…power. I know she draws a crowd to church, and one day, who knows, we might see her name in lights." He made the first hole for the bracket.

"I wish I'd heard her sing more." Lake burbled little sounds from her blanket. "Maybe I'll go to one of the Conservatory concerts. I couldn't find anyone full time—no one like Prudy, that is. And the sitter I hired could work only through September," Audrey said, her voice drifting. "I'm sounding sorry for myself, after being home only a week." She hadn't told anyone at work the reason for leaving, not wanting Irene to know something that could be used against Prudy. Saying goodbye wasn't hard. The office was winding down; no one would have a job after the holidays.

"It's a lot of change." He moved the ladder to the next bracket. "I'll keep my job, but I've started looking for another place to live. Any day now your doctor's going to come through that door, wanting to be king of the castle again."

"I think we'll have some notice. Ben says he'll send a telegram."

"I can't wait for a telegram. I have to find another boardinghouse. But it won't be like this."

"Not much else to miss now that Prudy's voice is gone."

He stepped down and stood inches from her face for a second too long. "I wouldn't say that. I wouldn't say that at all." Then he turned back to the window, closing the ladder.

Nothing occurred except in her mind, a stainless kiss between them, a rupture in the unwavering air. She clasped her hands under her breast as if holding a soft animal. The knowledge that such a thing was possible was new, and the relationship, for her part at least, altered.

She left him to finish the second window and measure the rods before trimming them. She would thread the pins tomorrow; they could hang the curtains later.

By the time he joined her for dinner, she had already fed Lake and put her to bed. She asked him what she had always wanted to know: "Why didn't the Army take you?" They had the dining room to themselves, all the lights out but the wall sconces dimly glowing.

He told her about the diagnosis of a kidney ailment, how he didn't even think it was true, he was fine. At first he'd been outraged that he couldn't fight. "But I've interviewed so many guys at Walter Reed, seen their disfigurement and heartache up close. If I'd gone overseas and been wounded, I wouldn't have handled that well. Not half as well as most of them. I don't have any regrets."

She kept pressing. "And your parents. What happened to them?"

He leaned back, tilting the chair on its rear legs, his arms like wings behind his head. "My father clocked out of work, took his last check with him, and never came back. My mother never recovered. 'Went away,' as they say. To a home. I've seen her a few times. Twice in fact. One of those times she spoke to me and said, 'You look like him. Short, too. Bless your heart.'" He laughed.

When he set his chair right again, Audrey touched his arm. He shook his head. "No, I'm like you. Don't feel sorry for me."

She didn't know how he knew that—something she hadn't known. He saw right through her.

After dinner, he thumbed through the drawings on her easel—a half-peeled orange, a can opener, little exercises she did every few days. She resisted the impulse to cover them. He studied the faces of Lucille for a long time, saying nothing. She waited for a reproach. Instead he said, "I'd almost forgot. I only remembered how happy she was with us." Then he came upon a drawing of a Japanese soldier in front of a campfire offering food to the viewer. It was detailed, tightly crosshatched in places—she'd spent a long time on it, trying to get his expression right, a worried kindness, and the way he held out a bowl, a spoon extended. Daniel took a step backward.

"Not the usual depiction, I know. But this is what I look at all day. It's hard to hold them…apart all the time."

"It's extraordinary, the generosity."

"His?"

"Yours."

They sat together on the side stoop of concrete, where grass had eluded his lawnmower blades all summer and now rose up high against the steps. The night was cool and quiet, cicadas having died off or gone underground, like the fireflies—Daniel called them lightning bugs. When the dark got even denser, they both sat back, awed by the stars above the highest tree branches, a net of lights, and rabbits skittering across the yard. He pointed out the start of leaf spot spreading through a hedge close enough to touch. They did not touch each other. They moved inside to listen to Count Basie under those big black windows that still hadn't yielded the headlights of a car bringing Lucille home to her baby. He poured jiggers of rum; they each smoked more than one cigarette. She didn't want to be the first to quit the night. They stayed awake past twelve, just talking. "You did tell your husband you have a man living here, right?"

"I mentioned a few boarders." She smiled. "I only recently wrote him about Lake, and I haven't heard back from him yet. But after I told him about Lucille and you, he said, 'You better be making good money,' and 'All of 'em better be gone when I land.'" She imitated him in a gruff voice, and Daniel laughed with her.

She didn't think he took her seriously, but soon he leaned over and kissed her cheek. "Night, Audrey."

Avoiding the hallway upstairs—the dreaded awkwardness of the hallway—she waited to hear his door close before stubbing out her last cigarette. She tiptoed past his room. In her own bed, she couldn't sleep, straining at the slightest creak in the old house. She wanted to believe he was awake too, thinking of her.

By the next morning the curtains in the nursery had been hung—he must have done that. His door was open, which it usually wasn't this early. Her first thought was that she must comb her hair before seeing him. Inside his neat and tidy room, not even a hat was on show. She opened his closet door, now a small dark cave, and buckled at her waist.

He was gone. She sat on his bed and didn't move for a long time. Then she lay curled on her side, growing used to the emptiness. She had hoped for a continuance, a development, but without indiscretion. What would that have been? She didn't want to live here without him.

But he was no longer here to judge whatever happened next with Lake. She slowly walked downstairs and dialed the number she knew from memory.

27

Audrey was one of a handful of white people at a church on Eleventh Street, sitting on the back pew of Lincoln Congregational. She read through the program with teary eyes. The Washington Conservatory of Music was performing Samuel Coleridge-Taylor settings, all Negro spirituals. She felt uncomfortable, but she was there to see Prudy. The men and women on the altar were singing "Wade in the Water." She didn't hear the words, but the music buoyed her. Lake was at home with a sitter. Audrey's mind was elsewhere.

When she had called the nursery and Arthur answered, he surprised her by saying, "Hold on." She waited for several minutes, realizing what Lucille had done. *If she calls again, come find me immediately.*

Lucille was breathless on the phone when she said hello. "Is Lake all right? Is everything okay?"

"Yes, she's fine. You have to come get her, Lucille. I've been patient. I've given her a good home for many months. But your time's up."

Lucille cleared her throat. "There's something you should know, but I haven't known how to tell you. Do you remember how I said I'd spent some time in the hospital late that first spring?"

"Yes, why?"

"I met Ben. He was my doctor. I knew he wasn't married, and so when he asked me out for a drink, I went. I was so eager to break away—you have no idea."

Audrey's mind went dark. She couldn't hear anything clearly, but Lucille kept talking, on and on about her *sadness,* her *despair* that drove her to the desperate point of knocking on his front door. It was Ben she was looking for when she showed up that day in December. She'd needed to talk to him, to tell him about the baby. His baby. *Lake is Ben's.*

The sentences came in painful waves, ramming against Audrey, flattening her against the wall. She slid down, her legs splayed out in front of her. What had she missed? Why had no one told her about this? Was she crazy?

No, Lucille was crazy. Prudy could corroborate that. She and Prudy had spent hours discussing her state of mind after she left. Prudy needed to hear this. Audrey managed to stand to hang up the phone but not fast enough, not before Lucille asked: "Will you be her guardian?"

"You don't know what you're saying, Lucille. This is absurd. You know I can't do that. Not after what you've just told me." With each statement her voice got softer, more incredulous, until she dropped the phone, left it hanging, spinning on its cord. She should leave Lake napping upstairs, walk out of the house, and never return.

But instead she went to look in on her. She might suddenly recognize some mark of Ben on her face. The child was awake, sitting up in her crib, rubbing her nose, then her hair, puffing it up on one side. It was light like Lucille's and so were her irises, but these could still change. Maybe he was there in the more rounded shape of her eyes. Oh, Audrey might drive herself mad hunting for him now.

She called the Conservatory, but Prudy couldn't be reached. "She's in rehearsals." The man on the line was friendly. "You should come hear her tonight."

Once she was in the church, she thought people would stare at her, maybe ask her to leave. But of course everyone was focused on the altar. Voices rose up around Audrey, the ones in her head. *Not fit to be a mother. How did this happen? I must have done something wrong. What was it? Marry Ben, yes, that's what. And I went around collecting people to live with me so I didn't have to face the fact that I'm doomed to live with someone I barely know for the rest of my life.* Audrey made out Prudy on the second row, her hair braided and pinned to the back of her head, her dark eyebrows raising and lowering with the notes. She could even make out the tension in her fists, how she sang with all her strength. High and low the voices went, all the odd details coming back to Audrey: Ben's name in Lucille's handwriting, his childhood photo that she'd put out of sight, the bizarre way she had tracked Audrey down to the house. She wanted to ask Prudy, "Did you know? Did she ever say anything to you?" The chorus was finishing "The Stones Are Very Hard."

Then Prudy stepped out from the risers, and a light shone on her. *Sometimes I feel like a motherless child,* she sang, a cappella. She swayed from side to side, the way the sea might rock her. *A long way from home.* Her floor-length white dress, more white and dark suits behind her, looked like it was from the previous century. But this kind of music Audrey had never heard—it must be the sound of the future. It was only eight or nine lines, and it was over in less than a minute. Audrey knew what the song was about. Being severed from your home, your mother. Sold into slavery. All the motherless children out there in the world. With Prudy's pure voice, the shape and sound of the words, Audrey felt like something had been rinsed out of her. She looked around. People were weeping.

When the concert was over, she made her way to congratulate Prudy. Others were crowding around. "You were wonderful! Tears," she said, streaming her fingers down her face.

"Give that precious Lake a hug from me," Prudy said.

Audrey squeezed her hand, promising she would.

Daniel returned—his voice anyway. A few weeks after he moved out, it came over the evening radio broadcast when she was in the kitchen washing dishes, and a shiver went through her. He'd been promoted apparently. He'd clipped his vowels, making them stand up straighter, but it was his same thick stewy speech. She didn't even hear what he said but focused on his sound, like notes of a stringed instrument.

Daniel would help her reason out how this had happened, how she should move forward. She wouldn't have to hide anything from him. She called him at NBC, and when he answered, she said, "You left without saying goodbye."

"We're talking now. Looks like we didn't need goodbye."

"I need to see you."

She'd found a young girl who lived down the street to babysit after school while Lake napped. Usually Audrey ran errands, but this afternoon she met Daniel at an old French brasserie near his office. For a moment before sitting down, he took her hand, then hung her coat. Everything poured out, and he let it come, no questions.

"I'm scared, I don't know. I'm scared of myself. Nothing is what it seems. You said I would do the right thing, but I don't know what that is. Or if I can."

"Wait and see," he said. "A lot of this is out of your control. Ben didn't do anything wrong exactly—this happened before you were married. See what he does now. Has he answered your last letter?"

"No. His last letter suggests he could be in Seattle any day, then on his way here."

"You have to give him a chance. He might make everything right."

"You would, I know you would."

He frowned at her. "I thought you didn't like it when people talked about what they would do in another's shoes."

"Can we stay in touch? Please."

"We are." He touched her hand again. "We will."

She avoided making plans with her mother for the Thanksgiving holiday by telling her Ben might be coming home. But as the days approached without definitive word of his arrival, she had to come up with another excuse. She couldn't very well bring Lake without explaining too much—and that would unleash opinion she wasn't ready to withstand. "Remember Lucille, my friend, the boarder? She's got some kind of awful flu and needs help with her baby. Timing is terrible, I know."

"What, miss Thanksgiving? You can't do that. Viola's coming, her whole brood, even your father is planning on eating with us."

"I'm so sorry, but I can't leave."

"But when am I going to see you?" The question pitched high. Audrey felt herself in her mother's stuffy, hot bedroom, the radiator valves opened all the way. There was the whole day of her mother, the whole world of her, hardly larger than the bed. A sickle path cut in the carpet, gone from green to a gray ring, around her bed to the bathroom, back to the bed, out to the kitchen and back. Such was the orbit she made a dozen times each day. So many steps taken in this one room, with no place left for her father to stand.

"I don't feel well myself. The last thing you all need is for me to give you the flu."

"Oh no, don't bring me that." She changed the subject. "That neighbor's dog never stops barking."

And, "I have this burning in my chest that won't go away."

Audrey held the receiver against her ear, listening, the least she could do.

"These...aspirations you had," her mother went on, seeming to search for the right words, "the reasons you went to Washington. Are they turning out as you expected? They usually don't, you know."

When Audrey didn't answer, her mother said, "There's no one to talk to now."

"How can you say that? Your sisters." In the next room Lake was crying out, awake from her nap.

"These same walls."

She imagined herself on the edge of her mother's bed, what she had come to think of as furniture of entrapment. She had avoided it the last years she lived at home. And she was not going to see her mother for Thanksgiving. Whatever her aspirations were, then or now, they would always lead her away from Ridgelea. What mother didn't ache when the distance between her and her daughter stretched like taffy and then broke off? This time she let her mother's warm hands cup her face. "I'll be better about writing and calling."

"Please do," her mother said. "And whatever is going on with that baby, I think you're in over your head."

1973

28

The few pieces of new furniture arrive at the Cairo, the tallest residential structure in the city. With the movers' help, Lake and Audrey take boxes up in the elevator to the sixth floor. It's a ten-minute walk to Mr. Wooten's gallery, she tells Lake, a perfect location. But after the movers finish sliding the bed between the two walls of the tiny second room and are out of sight, Lake says, "Too bad there's only one way in and out." And, "A walk-in kitchen—you might not have room for that teakettle I noticed you swiped."

"Most important," Audrey says, "I have room for you. Here's the daybed you can sleep on when you visit." Objectively the place is dismal. Boxes, most unopened, cover the walkable space. The walls are bleak, lit by only one table lamp on the floor. "Not quite as exotic as Egypt."

But it's mine, she thinks, and I shall love it.

The longer they stay, the more relaxed Lake seems, even sleepy, legs stretched out in front of her. In her lap is a portfolio of drawings.

"God knows what you're finding there. I feel like I could still toss half that work."

"I've never seen these."

Audrey looks over Lake's shoulder at all the old drawings and sketches, even a few linen boards, of Lucille. In fact, the sleeve is labeled "Lucille." "I tried to keep a neat little file of her, didn't I? You look like her, you know. I never really wanted to admit that."

"This hardly looks like her now."

"Take one."

"It's just a piece of art," Lake says. "Could be anybody, right?" She slips one from the pile and sets it aside.

All day an elusive, pale sun has lit the sky into one unbroken cloud. Now, with the windows uncovered, the sky has flattened into dark and intruded. "Come sit," she says, tapping the daybed. "How worried are you? About Ray, I mean."

The mention of him sends the slightest twitch through Lake. "He's not a bad person, I know he's not. But he got so jealous, thought I was falling for someone in the company. He's obsessed."

"Were you falling?"

"No. Not at first. Not falling for someone, but now that Ray has done what he's done, I don't know what to think. I loved him." Tears fill her eyes.

"What else has he done? Has he hurt you?"

Lake shakes her head. "But I don't know, he might. I mean—he hurts *things*. He threw a sugar bowl when I told him I was trying out for a role that would take me to the Soviet Union. What's to stop him from distinguishing me from a thing when he's having one of his rages?"

"And your foot."

"I don't think he meant to run over it. But he was mad then too."

"Oh, Lake, I thought he adored you. All his attention. I thought he was madly in love with you."

"Madly something. He has to know where I am every minute. It's exhausting."

"He has this peaceful Arlo Guthrie thing about him, with his guitar and all. How does someone with that gentle voice—"

"Maybe you were seeing what you wanted to see. Ray's like one of those rubber-band-propelled airplanes. Wound tight until he's in flight and soon crashes." Then she adds, "But I fell for it too, his Arlo side." She scratches her face hard, leaving a red mark. "'You're going to be sorry.' That's the last thing he said before he left the school."

Audrey doesn't like hearing Ray's threat. In the car, her thoughts flit about, nerves churn in her stomach. She'll have an hour or so to organize whatever bits are left, sweep the studio, make one last pass through the medicine cabinets and closets before Ben returns from work. She won't announce anything till morning, after Lake has gone to work. He won't notice what's missing.

She pats Lake's knee beside her and suggests she stay with her at the Cairo, where Ray won't be able to find her. But Lake has fallen quiet. Audrey considers her distress earlier that day. Lake needs something from her, but what? Audrey wishes she had told Lake that she loved her, words they rarely say to each other anymore. She's been trying to hold these two needs straight, parallel like the headlights on the road in front of her: her departure and Lake's well-being.

"I love you, Lake."

Lake smiles weakly and sighs but says nothing.

Their front porch is lit. Prudy must have switched the light on before leaving. But then Audrey notices Ben's car.

Approaching the porch, she sees her metal armature on the top step. She'd left the model in her studio, not sure whether she wanted to bring it with her. One leg is awry, an arm bent behind the wiry head. This pose recalls for her the nude women pictured in magazines she once found in Ben's bureau. The women's faces were beautiful—hadn't Marilyn Monroe posed in a magazine like this?—but who really noticed with such large breasts exposed and legs suggestively spread. Even she felt a swell of arousal. But the access to this material was startling—in her and Ben's bedroom no less. Surely her father never had such access. The stirring she felt turned to revulsion for Ben.

There he is, opening the front door in his shirtsleeves, no coat. He grabs the armature by its waist, and suddenly she's gripped by fear. Anger contorts his face.

"What are you doing out here in the cold?" she asks gently.

"What am I doing? What are you doing, sneaking off like this? You think you can just move everything on your own and tell Prudy about it, not me?" He's screaming now, and she walks toward him slowly, trying to calm him with her outstretched arms.

He swings the figure like a baseball bat at the air.

"Dad, Dad—stop!"

He looks at Lake blankly.

"I was going to tell you," Audrey says. "I'm sorry you heard it from Prudy. She had no right—"

He jerks away from Audrey and in a final strike smashes the armature against the trunk of a birch tree. An arm breaks off into the mass of ivy beneath.

"Don't blame her. What was she supposed to say when I asked why your packed suitcases were in the hallway?"

She has forgotten all about her suitcases, her pile of hanging clothes.

"I've seen your empty closet. Just yesterday you were...making sandwiches for us, and today...you're walking out? Who the hell are you? Do I even know you? I always thought you were a cold fish, I really thought so, I had come to accept that. But even fish bleed. You're bloodless."

"Where's Prudy?"

"I told her to go home."

"Come inside, Dad. I'll make dinner. I'm staying here tonight anyway."

"We can talk later," Audrey says. She can't stay in the house with him enraged like this. He may have started drinking already. "I'll sleep at the apartment tonight."

"Oh no, you don't. I've called my lawyer."

"Ben—what? We don't need a lawyer now. I'm just talking about a separation, not divorce. You don't have to do this now." She thought she'd live apart from him before filing for divorce. But he has to be the one in the driver's seat.

"He's meeting us at his office now," he says, flinging the hall closet open.

He puts his arms through his coat and gropes for his gloves and hat at the top of the closet. "Come on," he says, digging his fingers into her back, pushing her through the front door.

Lake follows them out. "I'll go with you—"

"Absolutely not. This is between us."

Audrey turns briefly, holding up a weary, ashamed hand, signaling Lake to stay.

After a few silent moments speeding down Connecticut Avenue, gripping the wheel, Ben says, "I would have never left you."

"Maybe you should have." Then, quietly, she says, "I'm grateful you didn't."

"You've been lying about your studio. Your studio apartment. How could I have been so stupid? Can you really say you feel nothing for me? For our life? To throw it away like this means you're throwing away almost thirty years."

"I lived those years. I gave them to you and Lake. Starting something new doesn't erase all that. This is about the future." She holds tightly to the door's arm rest.

"The future I'm getting ready to retire for. The one I was going to spend with you."

"Oh, Ben. Your retirement was never going to be about me."

"Why didn't you tell me how you felt?"

"When have we ever talked about how I feel? We're all organs to you. Organs don't feel, they just—serve a purpose."

He rubs his eye with the heel of his hand; he's crying. Has she ever seen him cry? Once, when Lake left home in high school and they couldn't find her, he had wept then.

"Who else have you told about this? Jesus, Audrey, I don't know anyone who's divorced. What wife does this?"

His voice has climbed back to a screaming pitch when she sees a dog, or a fox—it is low to the ground and has pointed ears—run into the lane of traffic. "Watch out," she yells. And then she reaches across the seat and clutches the steering wheel, pulling it to the right. The car wheels ram into the curb, spinning the car backward, slowed slightly by an elm tree grown thick and close to the road. By some miracle no one is in the lane behind them.

Not that Audrey notices any of this in that moment. She has pumped the floorboard of the car with her foot over and over, slamming on phantom brakes. All she senses now in the stillness is a shooting rod of pain, ripping from her foot to her hip. She moans, breathy little grunts. Ben's face droops with shock. Not a scratch on him. He isn't yet moving with the cool care of a surgeon. But he does, soon enough.

Later, in the emergency room, she asks that the overhead light be cut off, as if darkness, in the same way it softens the sharp edges of rooflines and mountain peaks, will blunt her pain. But with the slightest movement, like hot grease in a tilted pan, pain spills into another corner—a vein, a muscle fiber. It collects around her knee, that great hinge she suspects has come loose. She pictures every cell expanding with pain, and how the pain loiters in the spaces between each cell. Words don't stand up to the sensation. Finally the lights are out. The sound of nurses' voices, like paper, rustles above her. Someone to talk to.

"I wanted to hurt him in that instant," she whispers. "For one second. I wanted to ruin him. I've never felt like that before." What she says isn't wholly true. She has never felt that way about anyone else, but she has felt that way for years.

In her confused state, Audrey thinks this woman beside her is a nurse who wants to take her pulse. She offers her arm.

The woman holds her hand. "It's me, Lucille."

Audrey manages a half laugh, able now to distinguish her white uniform. "I've never seen you in your...getup. What are you doing here?"

"Doing what I do, thanks to Lake. I went by your house and found her in an absolute panic because the hospital had just called. I was going to stop off at home first, but then I had a glimpse of Ben's green Cadillac, wrapped around a tree. I knew I better get here fast."

"He's fine, isn't he?"

"What was that about wanting to hurt him? He has a few bumps and bruises, not as many as you. That was a healthy elm you all tried to take out." Lucille laughs. "One of the few in town. Shame on you. But I took a good look at it. A few scratches, that's all. It'll outlive us." She puts her hand lightly on Audrey's leg. "They're going to set this leg and operate on your pelvis and send you home on crutches."

"Pelvis?" Audrey tries to sit up, but Lucille shakes her head.

"You have a hip fracture."

"I can't go back there with him. I need to be in my own apartment."

"What apartment? What are you talking about?"

Audrey shuts her eyes. She hasn't wanted anyone, least of all Lucille, to witness whatever ugliness might ensue. "I'm leaving Ben. I've been moving out. He found out today."

"You can't get along by yourself now."

"I'm not going back to his house."

"You'll be here a while longer. And after that I can stay with you till you're walking. I can help."

Audrey doesn't know how to respond. She's not sure which is worse: returning to Ben's, or depending on Lucille—on anyone—for anything.

Lake stands by Audrey's bedside and calls her by a name she never uses anymore, Dee-Dee. She cries, Audrey knows, because she has never seen her or Ben suffer. That is a hard thing, to see a parent weak and in pain before they are old.

"I'm okay," Audrey tells her. "I'll be fine. Have you seen your father?"

"Only long enough for him to order me around. He asked me to bring you a few things from those suitcases. He told me the house will be mine."

This takes Audrey a minute to process. What she's giving up will be someone else's—Lake's. Of course.

"I think he said that so I'll stay with him longer. He's terrified to be alone."

"You saw Lucille?"

"Why won't she leave us alone? I can't stand her—we have nothing in common, nothing to talk about."

"You don't know her." Audrey turns her head away from Lake, closing her eyes. "She used to be different. This isn't her nature. What happened went against her nature." She almost sings the next words, settling into sleep. "When I met her, I thought: I've been so still, and a tiny bird has lighted on my hand."

"You should have known better. Birds fly away."

1945

29

The shock of Lucille's confession hadn't worn off by the time Ben's telegram arrived. His ship had disembarked in Seattle, and in two days he would land by plane at the naval station in Washington. That same day his last letter arrived, finally responding to hers: "Not what I'd hoped for…but your happiness… This mother will return for her child in due course—the optimal course." Audrey felt nothing reading these words now, and threw the letter in the trash. With a numbed efficiency, she moved any sign of a baby upstairs—diapers, toys, Lake's Binky. She hired a sitter who planned to take Lake to where her friend worked a few streets over, caring for another baby. They might have lunch there and stay until Audrey phoned. A pot roast was cooking in the oven.

Audrey wasn't sure why she was making such an effort to delay any meeting between Ben and Lake. And indeed every moment was an effort. She felt like a mule forced uphill. Slowly she screwed on the backs of her pearl earrings. She pulled on her gloves, tightening them finger by finger. She didn't bother with cologne, only a quick dab of lipstick. She took each turn slowly, lingering at every stoplight. By the time she arrived, the plane had landed.

In the twelve months since he had been deployed, a reception room had been built, but there wasn't any waiting. Men in uniform were already descending from the plane, but none of them was Ben. What if he wasn't on the plane or, more terrible, he was so changed she didn't recognize him. He was the last off. He wasn't thinner, as she expected, though when she thought of it, she realized he would have eaten three regular meals, more than he usually bothered to do for himself at home.

He stumbled a bit, his leg veering off course and then swinging back in front of his other leg before he reached to hold the arm of the man beside him. Maybe he was drunk. As he got closer, he looked at her with a first-date shyness, chin tucked and eyes sideways at her, still holding on. "Vertigo. I've got vertigo. It's nothing."

When they embraced, she cried. She couldn't help herself. She guided them toward the driver's side of the car, but he said, "Drive us home, will you." He didn't let go of her arm in the car, explaining that the vertigo had come only after landing in Seattle. "It happens sometimes to sailors," he said. He laid his head back and closed his eyes. "I'm so glad to be here, it's a shame I can't even look around. I don't want you to have to pull over."

When they opened the front door to the house, she tasted the same fermented, appley odor of his childhood home, along with the roasting meat. He set down his duffel bags, and she led him through each room. Everything was just as he'd left it. Propped against her easel in the studio was a drawing of him she'd made from a photograph, also clipped to the board. He smiled. "Who is that good-looking devil?"

The dining room table was set for two. In the kitchen she grew talkative, nervous now: "Oh, you should have seen the place with two boarders, cluttered with tea tins and bread covering the counters. I think we survived on peanut butter and Ritz crackers."

But Ben wasn't interested in talking. He led her upstairs, past the guest room, the one Daniel had lived in, where a wooden nativity set and boxes of glittered balls for the Christmas tree now covered his bed.

Lake's door was closed. "But you don't feel well," Audrey protested, aware that the sitter and Lake must already be back, that the sitter was likely rocking Lake, who might cry out at any moment.

"This will make me feel better," he said.

None of his jubilance lost to vertigo, he squeezed her tighter and tighter, breathing in her neck as if she were oxygen itself, kissing her again until there was no place on her skin unkissed. Mixed with pleasure was a grinding anger in her groin. The anger didn't diminish the pleasure; it may have heightened it. The strangeness of intimacy nearly made her laugh. Later, calmly lying with him, his arm cradling her neck, she felt herself being swayed, the way she had in their first days, and never by anyone else. The memory of that feeling had sustained her, and now it was fresh again as he tenderly lifted her arm above her head, telling her how beautiful it was, "Such a delicacy, like a frog leg."

"Now that's a way to charm a girl, tell her she looks like a frog." Audrey laughed.

"I've lost my touch."

"I didn't say that." She smiled, resting her head on his chest.

One night, Lucille had said. *A bachelor's last carousal.* Drifting off, Audrey pushed her name away.

Noises came from the next room, and her body tensed, separated from his, though he still held her. She looked at the clock. They'd had an hour and a half together.

"What is it?"

"I think they're here. The sitter and the baby. They were supposed to be out, but I hear them."

"I'm sure she won't mind getting paid a bit more." He kissed her shoulder. "Let her handle it."

"What will you do tomorrow?" She was trying to imagine him around while she carried on her routine with Lake, whose cries she heard distinctly now.

"I've got to go through the discharge process at the station. I should check in at the hospital. Or I might find something to do in the yard." He stood up now with a towel around him, in front of the window. His back was narrow, and there were moles and freckles she didn't remember.

"Oh, goodness, don't look outside. You'll find plenty to do, I'm afraid. Months of neglect out there." She kept talking while she buttoned her dress. "Let's go see Lake."

He leaned on the sill. Outside, the wide-spreading mulberry tree had shed leaves all across the yard. He sat back down on the bed. Now she could make out the sitter's voice.

"This is goddamned awful." He sank back into the bed. "I can't operate like this. I just need to sleep. I will meet her. I will. I'll do whatever you say." He closed his eyes.

She closed the curtains, carefully pressing together the two panels until they met, blocking out the light.

The next morning, Ben rose before she did. She'd been up half the night with Lake, who wouldn't sleep after napping too long yesterday, and Audrey dozed until she heard her. On their way down to the kitchen, she saw Ben through the staircase window. He was heaving the earth around in the yard—weeds with cloddy roots. He moved large stones that formed a border around the grass to one spot and then another. Nothing apparently was as he wanted. He gripped a fence post and looked up at the sky; starlings whirled above him.

She carried Lake to the back stoop, letting the screen door slam behind them. Ben looked up from his raking. Under clouds, her view of him was clear.

"Steady ground," he said. "There's nothing like it after a ship and dark quarters. This is where I need to be." He wiped his face on the shoulder of his barn jacket.

The air was chilled and heavy with coming rain. Audrey curved her shoulders around Lake, warming her. Above them more birds swooped into flight. He still hadn't looked at Lake, and Audrey made their way toward him. *Look at her.*

Finally, he smiled a gentle, resigned smile, dropped his rake, and patted her on the head. "This is the girl, eh—the one I've heard so much about. I'm Dr. Bray, Lake, it's a pleasure to meet you. You are a cute thing, you know that. Such a little thing." He turned back to his work. "I'm done with the Navy, by the way."

"You decided to turn everything in? Last time you wrote, you weren't sure."

"It wasn't a big decision. I sure as hell don't want to step back on a ship."

"I'm glad you've made up your mind." This was how it would go, Ben making decisions on his own, no input from her.

"I've put too much into my practice here. Besides, in the military you can't just have a conversation and resolve anything man to man. Layers of procedure and bureaucracy. And it damn near drove me crazy to take orders from someone less competent than I am."

"Ah, the real rub."

She was relieved he didn't mention the matted-over vegetable garden. She didn't want Lake to carry the blame for that.

In an hour he was back in bed, a pail on the floor beside him. The next day he tried driving to the office but returned within a couple of hours, and for several days thereafter he stared blankly at a fixed spot on the wall, clinging to his pillow. Shutting his eyes became a torment, lest the spinning begin. In time he moved about the house in his bathrobe, weakly groping. "It's like a hand is pressed on my head, forcing me to the ground." Audrey thought how apt this description was for both of them.

He resisted speaking to Lake, or even about her, unless Audrey held her in front of him and he had no choice. Maybe for that reason, she held her more now. But she also tried to order their routine so Lake wasn't in his way. They ate earlier in the evenings, for instance, so he wouldn't have to wait while she fed her in the high chair. Again, why she tried to appease him was unclear. When Lake was fussy, yelping over a dropped bottle or wanting more food, Ben eyed Audrey wearily, as if to say, *Come on, you've got to be kidding me.*

She almost blurted out Lucille's name, but something held her back. If she didn't address the problem, it might change on its own, like weather. Not telling him what she knew was giving Audrey a railing of her own to hold—a way to steady herself in those first uncertain weeks.

A part of her had begun to think it would be too easy if he knew Lake was his. He should be forced to accept her the way Audrey had been forced.

Feeling was returning but in unexpected ways. She felt a push and pull, away and in, like blood through her heart. She wanted to be with Ben, and yet she wished he'd never come home. She saw no way to reconcile this. She loved Lake, but she hated how she had come into her life. Audrey wanted to leave, but she saw no way to leave the two of them.

And Daniel, he was a railing too, if only in her mind. She hadn't called again. And he would never. But his voice over the radio—even when other people were in the room, she kept one ear out, listening, embraced.

One morning Ben declared himself vertigo free, sitting up in bed and swinging his legs out to the floor. Dizziness gone, his focus sharpened. "Enough, Audrey," he said. "Enough. Why should I go along with this? You want to keep this child? Who is this mother? Where is she?"

"Good question. She's not much of a mother, is she? And I can't just write a letter to the Navy and be done with this child. Besides, we have the means." She waited. "The war has been hard on everyone."

"And now it's over. We get to resume life, pick up where we left off. The world is safe. The Depression, the war—all of that's in the rearview."

"If you think it's easy to give up a child after holding her all this time, you need to start holding her." She held Lake out to him.

But he brushed past her. "I'm going to work."

On Christmas Eve day, they purchased a tree from a filling station where Fraser firs had been trucked in from western Maryland. Christmas shone weakly through the dreary weather: the swish of tires on wet pavement, the bright colored lights of the tree lot blowing in the wind, streetlamp decorations circled in misty halos. Somewhere the tinkling of a Salvation Army bell. Above them the sky was a broad slate of clouds.

At home, they sheared the long, curved branches, strung the colored lights first, then his mother's ornaments. "Let's go hear Truman at the tree-lighting ceremony," he said.

"And take Lake? We'll have to wake her up."

He'd forgotten about her, and the forgetting, or the fact that she was still here, put him in a foul mood. He didn't speak till halfway through dinner, which was nothing but crab soup, because Audrey was also cooking for the next day's big meal. "Do you have an address for that woman? Does she write or call? Or even care?" He blew on the soup to cool it, eyeing her.

"She's done both. She'll keep in touch."

"Listen, I'm as sympathetic as the next guy, but—"

"It'll take you about six and a half hours to drive her down there. Longer on the train."

After dinner she heard him breaking ice in the sink before putting it in a glass and pouring bourbon over it. He calmed down. She put Lake to bed and later found him in his chair, reading his old Christmas books that she'd stacked by the hearth. He read *Twas the Night Before Christmas* aloud to her; whole verses he knew by memory.

When he was finished, he said, "Let's have a dozen more of our own."

On Christmas morning, Audrey thought of Daniel, wondering whether he was alone, hoping he wasn't. She was in the kitchen scooping out the cream that had collected on top of the bottles of milk and whipping it into butter to make biscuits. One of Ben's uncles was coming down from Baltimore that morning, but the rain was probably slowing him. She wore her apron with felt holly leaves sewn across the hem. They had talked of going to a church service later—Ben liked carols.

"Let's open presents," he called.

Back in late October, near their wedding anniversary and before her call with Lucille, she'd bought gifts for him: a new razor set, a leather belt, a pair of binoculars. She'd felt heady with frivolous spending and realized now, watching him unwrap his presents, that the feeling had gone the way of the money.

He retrieved a square package under the tree, in wrapping she didn't recognize. His gift was a Leica, gorgeous chrome and black. He showed her how to load the film, though she already knew. She took a photo of him in profile, looking through the binoculars, and one of Lake by the tree, her first photograph, strands of tinsel dangling from her mouth.

When Uncle Charles arrived, he wasn't alone, and Audrey hastily set another place. A woman—she might have been a few years older than Audrey—clutched his arm. "Look at this old house, I wanted to show it to Dorothy here, where I grew up." He was only eight years Ben's senior, and they'd overlapped here as boys. Dorothy was blond and tall, jittery, with an overdone mouth and a sideways gaze. He gave her a tour of the house, his hand on her waist, stopping at every photograph on the wall, calling out names and dates of relatives. "They don't build them like this anymore," he said, stroking the molding around the doorway, as if it were the hind of a horse.

No one paid much attention to Lake. When his uncle looked surprised to meet her, Ben said: "We're helping out Audrey's friend from the war." Everyone ate and complimented the food, the conversation flowing between Ben and Charles, from Truman and Stalin to the housing boom to the economy. Dorothy cleaned her plate quickly, then reapplied her lipstick in her compact mirror.

Afterward, Audrey washed the dishes—no offer to help from Dorothy—and left a few pots to soak. Though she rarely smoked during the day, she lit a cigarette now, while Lake sat on the floor by the tree, crinkling wrapping paper between her hands. Charles too found his after-meal reward in tobacco. He lit and relit his pipe, making neat piles of his matchsticks. Dorothy studied her nails. Lake began grasping at the branches of the tree and tugged an ornament off. Ben flinched the first time, but the second time he raised his hand, a newspaper folded in it, and made as if he was going to strike at her.

"What are you doing?" Audrey cried. He tucked the newspaper under his arm, like a dog tucking his tail between his legs. "She's not a fly to be swatted at!"

Charles hardly raised his eyes, instead searching his pipe for a shred of tobacco to burn.

"While you've been doing the dishes, this child has tried to pull every goddamned decoration off the tree. What do you want me to do?"

Incensed, she carried Lake upstairs. Daniel would never act that way. The contrast between the two men lunged at her. Diapers, pins, a few sleepers—what else would she need? "Stop that," Audrey snapped, swapping a soggy piece of wrapping paper in her mouth for a pacifier.

Downstairs again, she pulled out a map of the southeastern United States from a kitchen drawer. With a black marker, she drew a line from Washington down to the middle of North Carolina. Pomona wasn't on the map but Gloucester was, the adjacent town Lucille had mentioned. She loaded up the bag with bottles of milk, little jars of food. Charles was standing in the living room, saying it was time for them to be getting on the road. Audrey ignored him, marching to Ben with Lake and the bag on one side, holding out the map with her other hand.

"What are you doing?" Ben asked.

"You wanted to know how to get there. I think this is a fine time to go. Shouldn't be too hard to find her on Christmas Day."

When he didn't move, she said, "Go on, get moving. You've been wanting to do this."

He sighed loudly. "Our apologies. It's been a pleasure having you." He shook his uncle's hand. Audrey gave Charles a starchy smile and went to open the door for everyone. For the first time the girl, Dorothy, looked her in the eye. It gave Audrey an eerie feeling. They were like two cars on the highway, glancing off each other before heading for their own separate disasters.

"It's Christmas, Audrey," Ben said when their guests reached their car. "Why are you doing this?"

"This is the worst Christmas Day of my life," she said, loud enough for everyone to hear. "You have ruined it. Get your coat on."

Instead he closed the door and slipped the bag from Audrey's shoulder. He took Lake from her arms and placed her in her playpen. He started cleaning up the wrapping paper off the floor and took it to the kitchen bin.

"Those terrible people," Audrey said. Tears streamed down her face.

When he returned, he said, "Her teeth weren't real. Were they real? I thought they might come out with the pecan pie."

"Maybe that's why she couldn't talk!" Audrey started laughing in spite of her anger. "And the way he was palming the furniture, like he was trading livestock."

"What the hell was he building over there with those matchsticks?" Ben wiped his face in embarrassment. "He was like an eight-year-old with Lincoln Logs. He has a wife, five children he's estranged from. I had no idea he was bringing anyone. I only knew he'd hit some hard times." He bent over the record player, putting on an Artie Shaw song. "Come here," he said. He held her head in his hands, then softly pressed her collar down and thumbed her earlobe. "There's nothing a little dancing won't fix."

For a long time, she thought of that first year as Ben's falling. His vertigo and recovery happened periodically, analogous to what was happening between him and the child. But later she realized it was the same for her. It was the time of *her* falling—into a sort of trap, laid by others she had loved—and adjusting. His dizzy imbalance was an affliction she wasn't outside of. She understood exactly what he meant when he said his brain was adapting. "Getting used to being off balance by doing some trick to make me think I'm balanced." And each time the onset of vertigo seemed a necessary misery he must endure as his body made some gradual acclimation to Lake. He and Audrey would default to an almost speechless tension during these episodes, uncertain whether he would remain chronically besieged or forever removed. But each time he recovered and she grew more used to what her life might be, the horns, like a long sigh, would start up on the record player, and they would dance.

30

Lucille wrote in her letter about her class of fifth graders—midget tyrants, all of them! She'd been lucky to get the job before earning her certification, but that just showed how desperate the schools were. This was Lucille's second letter regarding a visit. The first was the request itself along with some cash. She had her own money again, but it didn't yet come with more freedom. Her father had recently suffered a stroke. Her mother, caring for him around the clock, needed the weekend respites provided by Lucille, so there was no chance of a trip before summer recess. Unfortunately, she would miss Lake's first birthday.

Before these two letters there had come a half dozen apologies, inquiries on Audrey's state of mind, and more contrition regarding her request that Audrey be guardian, but there was no hint of that here. Instead she rambled on about how she was explaining her visit to her mother: "I need to say a proper goodbye, I need to collect the rest of my things. A holiday. People do that, you know, go look at the historical sites, like the Washington Monument, and Lindbergh's plane, and the First Ladies' gowns."

"Look at? Fiddlesticks!" her mother said, no patience for that kind of idleness, reported Lucille.

She had given up pleading. She was making light of everything. "June 15th. I'll be there by noon." Audrey didn't like the way she sounded. So presumptuous.

Nothing in her letters suggested Lucille was coming to retrieve Lake, but Ben was sure she would. "Finally, this ordeal will be over," he said. He would let this Lucille woman know, with his stern lack of interest, how he felt about the matter. He wouldn't be rude, but no goodwill would flow from him. He would convey his irritation by his unwillingness to engage, his refusal to smile. Then he would ask a lot of difficult questions.

Audrey nodded as he said all this.

Lake was wearing a white sailor dress for the occasion, a navy ribbon down her back. The three of them, Lake in Audrey's arms, greeted Lucille. She barely glanced at Audrey and Ben before locking eyes on Lake and reaching for her. At first Audrey took this as an inclusive gesture and moved to return Lucille's embrace, but Lucille's arms narrowed on Lake, who had turned into a limpet. She clung to Audrey, who peeled her little arms and legs off, passing her to Lucille.

Audrey had imagined an awkward introduction to Ben, silent servings of tea, a reticence between estranged mother and child. How wrong she'd been. No one else seemed to be in the room besides Lake, certainly not Ben. Audrey had her eye on him too, as he listed slightly against the doorframe. She'd never seen him blush, but he was crimson now, retreating to the perimeter. He recognized Lucille, all right.

Audrey suggested she and Ben take a walk, but as they changed shoes, Lake flailed about. Lucille held her more tightly in her arms, but Lake would have none of it, arching her back in big slinging motions, her face red and hot.

"I'm sorry, she must be coming down with something. She's not herself," Audrey said. All false, but she wanted the bungling moment to pass. "Go to your mama, Baby Lake. This is your mama—Lucille. We've talked about this." Audrey spoke loudly over Lake's cries, stroking her thrashing head. Having an audience felt awkward, and these commands had an ersatz firmness. "It's better if we just slip out," she said, biting her lip. "But watch her closely. She just started walking a couple of weeks ago."

⁂

Lucille waved them out the door. Relieved they had avoided a scene, for now anyway, she bounced Lake on her knees and hip, pointing to this and that with perfect distraction: the bird out the open window; Audrey's paintings, propped around the studio—Lucille could see she hadn't added any in the last year; and Merlin, sprawled in a patch of sun on the floor. Rooting around in kitchen drawers, she found a pair of scissors. She would need these later. Soon Lake was wiggling out of her arms, walking unsteadily through the kitchen. Lucille had missed her first steps—of course she had. She led Lake outdoors, never letting go her hand, the garden in full bloom. Lucille named the flowers she'd nurtured, even the clover, a thick carpet into which Lake sank.

Exhausted, Lake had run out of noise and only listened. Lucille carried her again, telling her about the flypaper hanging in strips above her kitchen sink, the large stove with jelly bubbling over, the infinite dust that came in from the orchards. As they made their way around the yard, she spoke of her mother's long white hair that no one ever saw because she wore it up every day of her life, working in the kitchen, in the fields. She opened a jar of honey she'd brought from the orchard and spooned a bit out to Lake now. That got a big smile. She named apples, pears, peaches, plums. "Anytime you eat a piece of fruit, remember me," she said, laughing. She hoped these sights, sounds, and smells might lodge in Lake, the same way she herself had dreamed at night whole rooms she'd never entered, faces she'd never known.

She told her all the details about her life except Arthur. She'd told no one about his proposal, which had come more than a month ago. She hadn't answered him yet. There were things to account for—how she would care for her parents, for one. While she was here, holding Lake's cheek to hers, savoring every touch, she held Arthur in her mind too. Weighing, considering.

Back indoors, she acted out what she always did in her relentless dream of Lake, day or night. She lifted her into the ray of light shining through the window, saying aloud, "Isn't she lovely?"

✥

"Aren't you afraid she'll leave with her?" Ben asked. They were approaching the Avenue, each emphatically alone as they walked.

"Isn't that what you want?"

He was silent for a long while. "I know her."

Audrey said nothing at first, then, "I know you do. She told me you were the father. Not at first. After she left."

He paused in his stride but she kept walking. Incongruously stiff in the warming air, his arms were tight against his sides, his hands deep in his pockets. "I had no idea."

"Of course you didn't."

"I don't know what this means." He stopped in front of a bench and sat down. She sat apart from him. They stared straight ahead. Then he put his hands over his ears. "I lost two patients this week, you know."

"No, I didn't know." She felt an ache for him. "This situation with Lake isn't news to me, I've had time for it to sink in." She was thinking of the awkward moments at the door, reasoning out Lucille's actions. To engage in conversation with Audrey and Ben was to acknowledge this absurd tableau: someone else raising her child, Ben in her presence for the first time since becoming the father. But Audrey had been her friend—couldn't she acknowledge that?

After a few minutes he got up, walked across the street to the liquor store, and came out with a brown bag. He hadn't stopped shaking his head.

"That's a good solution."

"I was going to buy it anyway." He gestured for them to walk.

They followed stepping stones that ran alongside the house. Audrey peered over the hydrangeas, just now flowering, and looked in at Lucille and Lake, visible through the window. She was intruding upon something private. Lucille might take Lake with her, she just might. Her eyes were closed. She was gently pressing Lake's head into the curve of her neck, swaying.

When they walked into the house, Lucille was feeding Lake a piece of shortbread, spilling crumbs and pretending to bite them off the front of Lake's dress. The child squealed with delight. Audrey went to fetch the small suitcase in which she'd gathered most of Lucille's clothing and effects, from the yellow wedges and straw hat to the matchbooks. "Remember to take this with you later," she said, setting it off in a corner. She had her camera strapped around her neck. "Let's take a picture."

"For Chrissakes, Audrey," Ben said.

In the photograph of them sitting on the sofa, Lake is looking up at Lucille, pulling on her hair, but if there was any pain Lucille didn't show it. Crumbs could be seen on Lake's mouth, down her dress.

Audrey was getting ready to ask if Lucille wanted to see Lake's nursery, but Lucille had stood and was carefully setting the cushion into the sofa's corner, as though to remove any trace of herself. She lifted Lake off the sofa and handed her to Audrey. And then she picked up the suitcase and began walking to the door. Ben held it open. Audrey was astounded.

"What? That's it, you're leaving already? Lucille!" Now she sounded like her own plaintive mother, but she didn't care. She handed Lake to Ben who, for only the second time, took her in his arms.

"Am I the only one who cares about this child?" Audrey had followed Lucille onto the sidewalk and now held one arm out to Ben and one to her. Lucille turned, setting down the suitcase.

"You know I care or I wouldn't have come. I just—"

"Just wanted a little romp around the room and then to be on your merry way?"

"—didn't leave enough time for a longer visit. I had no idea what to expect. From the looks of things, neither did Ben."

"Ben! I wasn't going to do everything," Audrey said. "I wasn't going to be the one to take care of this child for you and for him, and then be the one to tell him too. That's a little too much to ask, don't you think?" She said this with a half laugh. "Some things the two of you will have to work out yourselves."

"You know I *can't* care for her. Look at you. You and Ben. You have everything. She loves you. She is attached—"

"If you leave now, that's it. Don't come back." Audrey said these words slowly, each one with a little punch.

Lucille's face went blank. "Don't say that, Audrey, please. You don't mean that."

"Now I'm like you, am I, not ever saying what I mean—the truth?"

Lucille's hand went to her throat. She clasped the luggage handle again and, leaning to one side as she went, carried it up the hill.

"Why didn't you tell me?" Ben said that evening, after they'd hardly spoken over dinner. He had looked incredulous all afternoon, hardly blinking except in the severest light.

"Don't you start."

"I would have liked some warning."

"Warning?" Audrey waved her fork in the air. "I would have appreciated one myself."

"But now—this situation. You've got it all wrapped up, both of you. *Fait accompli.*"

"Both of *us*. How about you two—I'd say it was a fait accompli a long time ago. Not once have you looked at this from anyone's point of view but your own, not even that child's," she said, pointing her finger upstairs. "You're feeling stuck? We're all stuck. I'll tell you something else I'm not going to do for you. I will not be the one who breaks that baby girl's heart and tells her the truth about this whole situation."

She'd beaten him back down into silence, but she couldn't stop. "You never even cared enough to find out this woman's full name or anything about her. I don't know what I expected today, but not this. You know what attracted me to you? Your openness, your candor. But now I understand—you can be so open because you're hollow."

By this time he'd left the table and she was shouting up the stairs. It wasn't until the next day that she noticed Merlin's food was untouched. Had he slunk away with all the goings-on yesterday? she asked Ben. She couldn't remember the last time she'd seen him, and this acknowledgment worried them both. They called his name all over the house, in the yard, down the street. "Maybe he left with Lucille," Ben said.

"A cat on the train? I don't think so." She paused. "But I've never known a cat like that. He was devoted to her, that's for sure."

※

On the train back to Pomona, Lucille pulled the small bag of shortbread out of her purse. She had meant to leave it with the honey but forgot. She slowly ate every last piece.

She shouldn't have gone. Audrey rarely answered a letter, so Lucille had no idea what to expect, and Ben acted as if he didn't know who she was at first. She didn't figure in their world. Lake was walking; she already had a will of her own. She had seemed happy, healthy, loved. Lucille rested in that for a moment.

She had wanted to see her, hold her, never let her go, but there at the end, the impossibility overwhelmed her. In the days leading up to the visit, she had thought more and more of bringing Lake home with her. But what would her mother do if Lucille returned with a baby on her hip? Same as what she always would have done last May or June, or now, a year later. Nothing had changed. She would cry out, "Your brother gone, your father wasting, and here you come with this—this shame!"

Lucille had chosen a seat on the right-hand side to watch the setting sun as they moved southward. To discourage company, she placed her pocketbook on the seat beside her. It was a brown wool jersey, too dark for this summer day, but it was the only one she owned. She kept important items hidden in it. In case of a fairy tale, when she was called to claim Lake as her own, she would produce the hospital identification bracelet. If ever she had to explain why she carried a newborn's bracelet with the same last name as hers, she would make up a story with someone else at the center, the kind of truth mired in all great stories. The lock of hair, cut just hours before and tucked in an envelope, might prove a connection; she imagined a day when scientists could use strands of hair to prove kinship.

The name *Lake* worked likewise, a secret capable of being decoded by tracing her mother's side in the family Bible to *Lake Stansfield Carlisle*, born 1821, died 1887, three generations back. A name for her child she'd chosen while still a child.

And then there was the name defined. Lake: water in the middle of land, cut off from any source. Of great depths, always seeking the darkest place, in the heaviness of the earth.

She had thought that an encounter with Lake—even a painful one—would heal the emptiness. As with a field that burns, then flourishes.

Sunbeams sliced brightly through the trees as the passing landscape darkened. Don't look directly at the sun, Lucille heard her mother's voice saying, it'll blind you. She blinked back tears, rocked by the rhythm of the train. Stands of pines close to the tracks came into focus before blurring away, blackish barns there, now gone, like her vision of Lake, looping through her mind, fading.

She was twenty-two, not yet twenty-three years old.

"Look who's here," her mother called, padding alongside her father into the kitchen. She might have been referring to Lucille or her father. His eyes—you could hardly make them out for all the squinting he'd done in the sun—showed no sign of recognition. Her mother had continued to pin a carnation on his lapel every morning. Today's was red.

"You got in all right," her mother said, more a statement than a question. She would not inquire about her visit. She never asked questions. There was her mother's world of Pomona, and there was the outer, parallel world, which might as well be a fiction. Though the house had been electrified more than five years ago, a glass oil lamp had been left on the kitchen table from the night before; next to it a romance novel lay open, face-down. Even when the other world punctured this one, like Jimmy's dying in the war, Lucille knew that the greater grief had been when he left her world. That didn't mean she didn't grieve his death, but it was not a fresh grief. Lucille began to see how she could live like her mother in one dimension, here on these twenty-eight acres, separate from another fixed dimension, where she forever held her child in her arms in a distant window's light, and the two might never touch.

When she told her mother that she was going to marry Arthur Lind, her mother laughed. "Why, you'll be caring for him, already so old, all your married days. You're getting some practice, girl, yes, you are." She was dragging a sudsy rag across the linoleum floor of their kitchen, a towel rolled under her knees. "Help me here," she said, pointing to the bucket in the sink. "Stop, stop. Don't walk across it wet. All these men coming back home, just starting out and looking for a wife. And here you want one whose life is behind him." Then she added, "But he's a man. If a man lives long enough, he's often granted a second bloom."

Lucille didn't remind her that only one fellow had asked her to ride into town for a movie, a boy who had come home only to leave again, to go to school on the GI bill. "I'm not so foolish as to lay my livelihood at the whim of weather," he'd said. He wanted to build things, to be an engineer. "The future's in helicopters." Driving past cornfields, he made a gesture with his hands of plucking something up, moving it a few inches in space, and setting it back down.

She had been under a kind of siege not to love Arthur. Since her father's stroke—an obstacle cleared—she had discovered tenderness and occasional bliss. By now she knew that the great concern of her own life would not be love for a man. If she went ahead with the marriage, seeing Lake would become more improbable, given how difficult a trip was even now. Once she had to account to Arthur fully, she might never get away. There might be other children, untold responsibilities. Perhaps not her own money. This was the bargain—and the consolation when she recalled Audrey's ire, her demand that she never return.

She called the preacher, ordered the cake. Making her own wedding dress nearly did her in. Heaps of white silk in her lap, spreading across the floor, engulfed her in the days before the ceremony. Her mother didn't help—her way of objecting to the union. It was the last piece of clothing Lucille ever sewed.

The wedding was in their church, the Methodist one. Evangeline, the young maid of honor, held her hand down the aisle, and Lucille carried a bouquet of dahlias, hydrangeas, and roses. Arthur wore stephanotis on his lapel. They had family and a few friends back to the house, and paid Mrs. Stockdale from town to watch her father, though everyone laughed that they best be watching each other, old as she was. He was no different than he'd been at Jimmy's funeral: his heart broken once, now cleaved in two.

But the other part of the bargain, the surprise clause Lucille hadn't factored in, was Lake's ever-presence. Out the corner of Lucille's eye, Lake was a guest at the wedding, white smocking across her chest, tiny legs dangling from the pew. The child never left her side, not really. She was in Lucille's thoughts at first light, in her dreams at night, her shadow in the kitchen, the ghost with whom conversation never ceased.

"Talking to myself," Lucille said when anyone overheard.

1973

31

"There are a few things I want you to bring from the kitchen and bathroom when you pick up my suitcases." Flat on her back, Audrey holds a pad in the air, writing a list.

Lucille doesn't mind being ordered around. She is glad to be here, needed. While still in the hospital, Audrey accepted her offer of help—which she couldn't have refused from the looks of the new apartment: canvas rolls, art supplies, unpacked boxes, furniture strewn about. It was hard enough to walk from one side of the apartment to the other, never mind on crutches. At first they related to each other as if on the teeth of connected gears. If Lucille came near for too long, Audrey sent her spinning away. But Lucille persevered, hauling groceries up, preparing every meal, rubbing analgesic creams behind Audrey's knee. In unpacking her apartment, they are uncovering a lot of the past, but they discuss it lightly, as if it's a piece of art they're appreciating from a distance.

"Daniel," Lucille says, "have you seen him again?"

"No."

"You should reach out to him," she says. "It's the seventies. You can call a man. Not like the old days. He told me once that his heart was broken before you ever uttered the first hello at your door. You must have known that." She paused, then went on. "I don't even know how you met Ben."

"I don't know how you met Ben."

"Yes, you do. Appendicitis."

"Ah, right. He took out something useless."

"He saved my life," Lucille says. "I remember seeing him dancing one night at a hotel. I didn't speak to him, just saw him from afar." As soon as she says this, she regrets it, remembering how she saw Audrey too. Lucille can't admit this now, not when she's so close to earning Audrey's trust.

"You're talking about the Omni? Before we were married, we went dancing there all the time. And swimming. You had already met him then?"

"This was after my appendectomy—"

"Maybe we were all there the same night," says Audrey. "It sort of gives you chills...how we were bound to meet again."

"It was a small town then," Lucille says and lets it go at that.

"The girl I worked with, Irene. She's how we found Prudy, remember? She warned me to stay away from him. I didn't listen."

Lucille hasn't stopped moving, sweeping out the living area's corners with a broom, stirring the vegetable soup in the kitchen, and then back to Audrey's side. After a while she asks, almost shyly, "Did you want children?" She doesn't say "children of your own" or "more children."

Audrey takes a minute, thinking. "No one has ever asked me this. Yes. Probably more than I admitted. We tried for years. But I talked myself out of it. I was too sad. And I decided it was okay, I would create other things."

"In my experience more children didn't make up for any loss."

Audrey hands her the list. She rubs her hip, taking shallow breaths.

"Can opener? Band-Aids?" Lucille raises her eyebrows. "You want me to go rummaging through drawers and cabinets?"

"He won't be in the kitchen this early in the day. I'm hoping Lake is there. She can help you get anything out of the bathroom upstairs."

"You can buy these things at the drugstore, or down the block at the hardware—"

"Money. It all costs money."

"Mmm," Lucille says, trying not to show any satisfaction at this. Audrey, who's never had to consider money in her life, feeling strapped. "I'll do my best."

"Be sure and give Lake my new number. I reached her yesterday for a minute, and she plans to visit this afternoon. But I want to know how you think she's doing."

If Ben gives her a hard time, she'll produce Audrey's key. Even though she's justified in being there, she braces herself. She can't know whether he's home because his car, badly damaged, has either been sent to a wreckage heap or is being repaired. She looks for Ray's Volkswagen, but doesn't see it. He called last week, letting her know his visit to Lake's school hadn't gone well, his voice sounding small and defeated. Before Lucille left Audrey's, she telephoned him from the lobby, encouraging him to meet her at the house now. The three of them could talk together. A little more effort from him wouldn't hurt.

"Any advice for me?" she asked.

"Stop explaining. She doesn't want to hear it anymore."

Lucille considers this now. Tiny needles all over—she feels them on her palms, behind her knees. She wipes sweat from her upper lip before she knocks. But there's no answer. The doorknob turns easily. The first thing she sees is herself, a reflection of her plump cheeks in the full-length mirror opposite the front door. Her reflection first and then the smell of a former life—something like sour apples and musted-over old wood, not unpleasant. Surveying the living room, she feels the quiet order in the books arranged on tables at slight angles, bowls precisely off-center. The suitcases are by the front door. Before she starts looking for items on the list, she tiptoes through the living room, the dining room, and the kitchen, taking in everything in the bright light of day, all that she couldn't absorb the night she was here with Audrey and Ben after Lake's performance.

This house is like a museum. Nothing has changed except where Audrey has removed her paintings. She never cared for the household arts, and the rooms look much as they always have. The weather station hangs in the entrance hall, and there are iron sconces, oval mirrors, and a fringe lampshade in the living room—all in the same place, Lucille assumes, when Ben grew up here.

This unchanging accumulation feels cluttered yet vacant, empty of them as a couple, of Audrey. Maybe she was always a kind of tenant too.

Lucille finds one alteration, a small, newly enclosed den, where Lake is asleep on the sofa. A yellow afghan is pulled up to her chin. If Lake ever went out in the sun maybe her skin would freckle like Lucille's. But her face is pale, with faint purplish-red veins crossing her eyelids. Her lips are dark, berryish, and her hairline begins in a slight point in the center of her forehead—features Lucille stores away. She holds her breath, watching.

A long time passes like this: her eyes fixed on Lake, Lake perfectly still. Lucille resists an urge to place her hand on Lake's forehead. She would like to brush strands of hair away, feel for warmth to make sure she's well. But she doesn't dare. The grandfather clock ticks. She begins to hum softly the tune of Brahms's "Lullaby" and sings a few lines.

"Lake, honey," she whispers. "I don't want to disturb you, I've come to get a few of Audrey's things."

As if bitten by something at her feet, Lake scrambles to sit up. "You scared me."

"I didn't mean to."

"That song—I've heard it before." She frowns.

"You had a music box that played that tune."

Lake's face goes cold, revealing nothing. "Does Ben know you're here?"

"Nobody answered when I knocked, so I let myself in."

"Has he been calling over to Audrey's?"

"Her phone just got hooked up yesterday. Maybe that's a good thing?" She hands Lake a note with the new telephone number. "She's looking forward to seeing you later."

Lake's attention goes out the window. Lucille recognizes this despondency and wonders, for a second, if the girl might be pregnant, if that was the problem with Ray or her fainting during the play. "I know you're not happy to see me. You're not in any real trouble, are you?"

"No."

"Have you been staying here?"

"I sleep better here. I needed a break."

"From Ray?"

Lake looks at her sharply. "Why do you say that?"

"I don't know. He seemed quite devoted the night I met him."

"Let's just say he makes a good first impression." Lake puts her feet on the floor. She's wearing a chocolate-brown leather jacket that makes a squishy sound as she moves. Lucille thinks of veterans who careen around the country on motorcycles. The leather is supposed to protect them when they fall, helping them skid across the pavement.

"I loved seeing you in *The Cherry Orchard*. You were like a…star."

"It's odd you were there without my knowing it. Much as I've imagined what it would be like if you were there."

Lucille's heart quickens at hearing that. "How's teaching? You know I was a teacher once, I loved it, those little kids…" She risks talking too much, taking any thread of acceptance until nothing is left on the spool.

"I'd rather be acting myself, not sopping up kids' tears over lost leading roles or begging art teachers to make cardboard sets."

"Lake," Ben calls down the stairs. "Is that you? Is Audrey here?"

"He doesn't stop talking about her," Lake says quietly.

From the bottom of the stairs Lucille calls up, "It's Lucille." Silence conveys his disappointment. To Lake she says, "What's next? Do you have another role coming up?"

She shrugs. "I'm auditioning for a part in *Our Town*. The theater company is taking it to the Soviet Union, to Moscow."

"To Moscow?" Lucille laughs and reaches for Lake's arm. "Honey, you don't want to go to Moscow. Not now, when I just—"

Lake pulls her arm away, frowning.

"I just mean—what about your life here? I've had this idea that we could visit my home, for real this time. I could show you everything, start at the beginning. Ray could come too. It might be good for the two of you—"

"This is really too much," Lake says.

Ben lands from the stairs with a thump, walking with a cane. He has on a pressed shirt and trousers, and his hair is wet. Old Spice is in the air.

"Come to pay your respects to the abandoned lot, have you?"

"Just here for the suitcases and a few odds and ends," Lucille says, her eyes on Lake. There's a knock on the door, and Lake goes to answer it.

"Can't you talk her into coming home?" Ben is saying. "Why would she leave now, after all this time?" He leans both hands on his cane, which is too short for him.

"Shhh," Lucille says, trying to hear what Ray is saying. But soon Lake pulls the door closed behind her. Lucille watches through the window, Lake zipping up her jacket as they approach his motorcycle. They face each other, not smiling. She wonders why Ray didn't come inside, where they could all talk. She might have been able to help him.

"It's like she took something—like this chair," Ben says, pointing to the ladder-back next to the fireplace. "It's like she took something that worked perfectly well and smashed it to pieces." A lock of his wet hair comes loose.

Lucille hears him, but she's not listening. She's in a hurry to complete her assignment from Audrey and leave. Outside she'll be able to tell what's going on between Ray and Lake.

"Audrey sent me here," Lucille says. "You don't mind if I pull a few items from your bathroom and the kitchen? She says you have two can openers." She starts up the stairs, not waiting for a response. Searching through the cabinet, she is thinking about the house in Pomona, how in a bathroom like this, the view out the window is of trees. She wants Lake to have that experience, feeling like she is held by the branches, even if it's on a dark winter afternoon, like today. Maybe snow will fall soon on Pomona.

Retrieving an electric blanket from the linen closet takes a bit of time, and when Lucille comes downstairs, Ray's and Lake's voices are coming from the den. She dodges another appeal from Ben—"Won't she at least see me?"—and with one hand rummages through a couple of kitchen drawers, stacking on the blanket what she needs. Her arms full, she peeks around the corner. Ray is smiling, playing at putting a helmet on Lake. She shakes her hair out like the Breck girl before strapping it on her head.

Better to leave them alone just now. They need time to themselves. Lucille had told Ray that Pomona might be the perfect place.

1947-1963

32

Ben liked being behind the wheel of his 1942 Lincoln-Zephyr on the fifteen-minute drive to his office each morning. He liked driving: The carefree feel of one hand on the steering wheel and the other out the window, the croon of the radio at his fingertips, the rush of speed in certain stretches of unceasing road. He relished the quiet cushion between him and the world at the beginning and end of days full of relentless intimacies, surgeries. He'd discouraged the purchase any earlier, holding out for the Liquimatic transmission—and he was glad for it, coasting along now. But he always started the engine with a tinge of regret. His mother had been eager for a new car, but because of his stalling, she enjoyed only two rides before being given her death sentence. The first drive was home after the sale, and the second to the doctor who delivered her diagnosis.

His model wasn't made anymore. Although a car was a foolish place to put money, everyone had come back from the war and done just that. Drive a new one off the lot and the next day you might as well chop off the back seat, because you were driving a car half the value. But this car would last him years longer. With his mother gone, he had moved back into his childhood home and waited. Bided his time for some kind of transformation of himself into head of a family, and of the house for that future family, even as he moved from woman to woman, and tried out each bed in a different room each night. Unlike Goldilocks, he found none of them just right. Marrying Audrey, of course, had ended all that.

In the operating room, Jeanne, who had been one of those women, held the body on the table open in a three-inch square with retractors. He'd severed the peritoneum, followed the ascending colon down to the cecum, and had his fingers on the small reddish bulge of the appendix now. Emergency operations he liked the least, not knowing who was behind the draping. It was a man—appendectomies usually were—age forty-eight. That's all Ben had, age, dimensions of 172 pounds and five feet eleven, blood pressure figures, and the fellow's list of complaints in his chart. He'd never met the guy healthy. He liked to know to whom—or to what quality of life—he was restoring the body. Was he giving a tenor another chance to sing, a mother a chance to continue mothering? He'd dreamt about this, cutting out his mother's growth from its surrounding tissue. The patient's life interested him, not in any selfless way; it simply mattered to him in a way that baseball statistics did not. And yet Audrey had pointed out to him just this morning that when he told her what was on his schedule, he always referred to the procedure or the organ of the body. "I have a cholecystectomy today" or "a colon resection tomorrow."

He had dreaded seeing Jeanne when he returned from the Pacific. She'd stayed with the practice while he was gone; he had hoped she wouldn't. Before his tour, when he told her he was marrying Audrey, he hadn't looked away fast enough. Her face flinched with pain. She'd known he might not marry her, but she'd been sure he wasn't going to marry anyone else.

The slurpy sound of her suctioning the fluid around the mesoappendix filled the room. He clamped the base of the appendiceal artery and made his incision. Then he sewed a purse-string suture around the protruding base. She tucked the stump inside, and he pulled the thread tightly around it. She clipped the thread. An appendectomy's recovery was brief. This man would be just another name in the composition book he kept concealed in his sock drawer. Lives saved, and unsaved. The shorter list weighed more heavily on him. He knew this kind of attachment made him different from other surgeons, who went into surgery expressly to save people without having to deal with them. Find the problem. Cut it out. Sew him up. Send him home. Ben appreciated the brevity of the relationship, but while a patient was under his care, he cared. He ligated the mesentery end with three knots.

Jeanne hadn't looked at him yet. He hated her unreadable, blue-eyed stare from above the surgical mask. There had been times in the past when, if he didn't speak to her gently enough, there were consequences. She wouldn't let him make a mistake, but there might be a coldness, or an unnerving deliberateness in the time she took to respond. She was the one who'd found the job for him. She'd assisted him during a few procedures—maybe his first hernia—so she knew how he worked, and she'd mentioned him to her boss as an able resident. He was sure she regretted that now.

And last night after they had gotten through a messy trauma case, a knife wound too close to the carotid artery, he had reached for her hand, drawing her close in. Only for one moment. Innocent. She had pulled away, told him he needed to get a hold of himself. He was paying for that now.

He crushed the base of the appendix, ligating it with three more knots, then snipped it off. He, who had no desire ever to leave Washington, never fully understood why Audrey had moved here, but it wasn't to land a man. She was the woman least interested in him that evening he met her. Irene, the hostess and Audrey's co-worker, had later said, "Good luck to you. She's a tough nut to crack." Back then it was easy to get a woman's attention—one woman looking at you was all you needed to attract another.

He'd stayed a bachelor so long in part because he'd thought the revelation of a wife would come to him like a thunderbolt. Instead, the Navy summoned him to a ship and he grasped at the closest anchor around. He had wanted much more as a child. A mother *and* a father, a slew of brothers and sisters.

But she *was* more. He remembered thinking as he twirled her on the dance floor: I want *this*. He couldn't envision a life without her. Her quiet passion for her work, the way she glided around their house in paint-blurred aprons, her eyes glazed over with distraction—she awed him. And when her passion turned on him—her brown eyes brightening, focusing, as if she were the surgeon doing a thoracotomy, seeing through his layers of lab coat and starched shirt and undershirt to something he'd always meant to keep hidden—he recognized it as love.

During their courtship, she never wanted him to pick her up at the trolley stop downtown and drive her the rest of the way home. "I don't like the idea of you waiting on me," she said. That same independence had turned into something obdurate. She'd not wanted to try for a child when they had the chance before he left. Now she was so flinty he could strike a match on her. He wanted to shake her: "You opened up the house like a goddamned hotel and let a man sleep in my mother's bed. You're mad at *me?*"

"Dr. Bray." The scrub nurse handed him the electric cautery, and Jeanne was looking daggers at him. He could do this in his sleep. He held the metal to the stump of the appendix. He'd cut someone open in order to save him—that's what he did, removed the hazard. It lay on the tray, the vermiform—worm-shaped—appendix. It was on the low end of normal size, three centimeters. He thought of the seemingly useless worms in his garden. Just because the medical community had not found a use for the appendix didn't mean there wasn't one.

A daughter. He still couldn't believe it. The sight of her had embarrassed him—her pulsing, wiggling flesh on Audrey's hip. For months, whenever he saw her, a florid guilt filled him up. She didn't look like him. She was fair, a tinge of red in her fine hair, blue eyes. And now she ran circles around him in their house. She squealed with delight when he walked through the door each night.

He'd removed her mother's appendix on this very table. When he saw her in his front hall, he recognized the same look of strained will from the night he brought her home, her chin tucked, bullish, being drawn into something despite the risk. Earlier, in the restaurant, she'd not stopped talking in her almost stupid-sounding country voice, making light of caring for that old woman and explaining her suitor, an older man, his tragedy. He'd heard plenty of confessions from his patients over the years—hers, too, was a kind of confession. But he'd been wrong about her. Blood on the sheet stunned him, left him ruing his judgment.

When he recognized her, he reached for the open door to steady himself—but the door wasn't a steady thing, and he had to catch himself as it swung.

He knew Audrey must have relished his near swoon. "I wasn't going to figure out everything for you two," she'd said in smoldering tone. "Hadn't I done enough for you already?" He would have liked a little less generosity. What if she'd never opened the door to the woman in the first place?

He was talking about his own flesh and blood. He could hear his mother say that about him and his brother: "You're my own flesh and blood, all I've got." He had always thought of the loss of his father as a hole in his life where flesh and blood should have been. He'd always told himself that no one should create holes intentionally. Unless there was no other choice but to go in and operate, no holes.

And Lake might be all he got. Months and months of trying—good God, they were going on two years now, and Audrey still not pregnant.

His breath came evenly again. Sometimes, in the middle of an operation, even one he knew he could do in his sleep, he caught himself holding his breath over what was before him, the guts, the thing he'd trained himself not to see. He had sutured the internal oblique and was now on to the top skin, pushing the hooked needle through, pulling the thread. He was ready for a cigarette. Push, pull. Binding, tying it up.

He wanted to make it a legal thing, this blood, his blood. That's it, he said to himself, giving a final tug—that's the only way to heal an open wound.

The scrub nurse, her eyes above her mask beady at him too—maybe that was his least favorite thing about the operating room—had hardly finished pulling off his gown when he reached for the pack in his breast pocket and took off down the hall to smoke.

33

Objects penetrate one another… They do not cease to live, you understand… They spread imperceptibly around them by intimate reflections, as we do by our looks and our words…

Audrey breathed in gummy paints and faint turpentine. This was what she needed, to be in her studio with words once spoken by this lonely old artist, Cézanne, to his friend Gasquet. In a used bookstore, Ben had found this study of Cézanne's life, full of his conversations, in the original French. She didn't know the language well, but she loved the heft of the book, the thick pages with their edges cut. Here and there, penciled in the margins, a few lines had been translated into English.

She clipped a print of an early Mont Sainte-Victoire painting to the corner of her easel, placed a small blank canvas panel in the center. Each fold of the mountain seeped into the next. Fastening her eyes to one of the slopes, she blindly followed its contour with a pencil on the canvas until it led to another, as if she were tracing these descents with her finger.

A knock came at the door and with it a flash of impatience. A perfect moment interrupted. Lake had been sitting at her feet peacefully. A miracle, Audrey had been thinking, a jolly miracle that this little imp would strike a black Conté crayon on a piece of newsprint with such diligence for this many consecutive minutes. Though when she peered down now, trying to ignore the knock, the crayon was in Lake's mouth. *I will play dumb if you play dumb,* thought Audrey. Another knock, and Lake looked up at her, waiting. She scooped her up and went to answer the door.

It was the neighbor across the street, Nancy. "I saw you through your window, so I knew you were home." Little Mel shivered beside her, buttoned up to his chin in a wool coat, a knitted hat pulled down past his ears. After the war, the houses around Audrey and Ben's home filled up with newlyweds and their babies. An elderly couple across the street had sold their house to Nancy and Mark Dudrow.

"Come in, come in," said Audrey. She didn't want to see Nancy Dudrow. She did not want to see anyone, but here was Nancy with her son, wanting something.

"Company," Nancy said. Her bulging cheeks, maybe swollen from the cold, forced her mouth into a lollipop shape. "We just want a little company, and I saw you there staring into space. I knew you weren't busy."

The two of them followed her in, and Audrey quickened her step to the studio to shut the door. She didn't want anyone else to see her work, its marks like dirty fingernail scrapings.

At her heels, Mel asked, "Want to know the color of my new Erector set?"

"Coffee, I can make a new pot," offered Audrey before she could say something rude. "Blue?"

"Only if you're going to anyway."

"And some milk for you, Mel?"

"Red. Do you got any orange juice?"

Audrey looked at Lake sternly, as if to say, *Don't ever act like that in someone else's home.* She kissed her cheek before putting her down.

"Mel, don't be impolite. Mrs. Bray has offered you milk. Yes, please, or no, thank you."

While Audrey waited for the coffee to brew, she watched Nancy walking around the room, inspecting books on the shelf and art on the wall, handling objects as she pleased. An antique candle snuffer, a miniature porcelain shoe, a china plate painted with a peacock. She turned over each piece in her hand as if determining its origin or value. When Audrey returned with two cups of coffee, Nancy asked, "Is this yours, did you paint it?" She pointed to a portrait of Lucille above the record player, one that Mrs. Moreau hadn't selected to sell. Audrey had hung it after Lucille's visit. She knew it was odd—Lucille literally hanging around them all. But she told herself it was for Lake's benefit. "Who is she?"

"That's Lake's mother. Her name is Lucille."

"Her mother? I thought—are you related to Lucille?"

"I'm Lake's stepmother." She meant the old sense of stepmother. She'd settled this in her mind. "Step" had its root in the word for loss, for orphan. Audrey reached to stroke what little hair Lake had. "My little foundling, that's right. There she was one morning, tucked in a wheelbarrow outside."

Lake crinkled her face. "Not me." She was still dressed in floral-printed, footed pajamas.

"I'm teasing you," Audrey said, down to her.

"Ben is very lucky to have married you," Nancy said. Audrey saw her calculating all the possibilities concerning the status of the woman she now believed was Ben's first wife. Deceased? Remarried? Audrey smiled, a trick she'd learned from Lucille. A smile, the bigger the better, could halt a conversation.

"Well, we've been bored out of our gourds, haven't we, Mel? We were wondering if you wanted to walk to the park with us, or else swing on our tire in the backyard."

Audrey pursed her lips in an effort not to frown. She didn't want to leave the house now. She didn't want to give up Cézanne and the prospect of painting Mont Sainte-Victoire to the edges of the canvas by lunchtime. Lake, however, brightened at the idea. But Audrey was in charge. In loco parentis.

"I'm afraid I can't go anywhere this morning," Audrey said. "The handyman is coming to fix a leaky radiator, and I just put a roast in." Lies, both of them. Lake had started Mel on a loop around the house; the center rooms, the living room and dining room, could be circled, and this was like open road for Mel.

"Oh," Nancy said with disappointment. "We could take her with us, I suppose."

"Are you sure?"

"I better get used to watching two." Nancy placed her hands on her stomach. "You can't tell, can you? Due in June."

It stung, this announcement. *But it is the reflection which is enveloping, the light…is the envelope…*

Nancy was pregnant. Of course she was. All married women get pregnant—and some who aren't married. Audrey turned her gaze out the window. "You look radiant," she brought herself to say.

"Radiant! I feel pillaged. I've never been so sick; I've been living on black coffee."

"Mark must be thrilled." They drank their coffee while Mel and Lake sheared corners like critters in pursuit.

"Do you think you'll have another?" Nancy said. "I mean, a child of your own?"

"We've tried," Audrey said, feeling her cheeks flame, a surge of heat all through her body. She looked back to the white sky through the panes, the Ligustrum hedge almost black in the wintry stark light. "We're trying."

Two days ago Audrey learned again what she had been learning for years, that she was not pregnant. There was no possibility of becoming pregnant for many more days. She had, in those moments of rubbing her hand along the mountain in southern France, forgotten that. At one time she'd been certain she had not wanted to be a mother. But how do you know what you want until you have it, or can't have it? And then it's too late. Ben had made clear he wanted children to fill up this big house. This house, with its huge granite fireplace, deeply set bench seats, its wide-arched openings, longed for more. But she couldn't produce it. Ben's legal effort to claim paternity of Lake would be finalized in a few months. There was such shame in her body failing her like this. What was wrong with her? Her mother, lying in bed, flashed before her. Had her mother felt shame at her body failing her?

Oh, my poor mother.

But even her mother had ultimately given birth to two children. *The seed cannot gain purchase.* Somewhere Audrey had heard this phrase in relation to a miscarriage. But in her own case, there wasn't even proof of a seed. There was nothing.

Finally Audrey said out loud to Lake, "Let's get you changed so you can go to the park."

Upstairs, she knew her lie about the roast would easily be detected if Nancy ventured into the kitchen, but what did she care? Perhaps Lake shouldn't go with them. Mel was a little brute—a year older, a good twenty pounds heavier, with a militant pout on his mouth. He would boss her around while Nancy stood by, clutching her belly, too preoccupied with her condition to defend Lake.

"You sure you want to go outside?" Audrey asked, pulling an undershirt over Lake's head. "It's cold."

Lake folded her arms over her chest, and her teeth chattered. Audrey pulled on another top. "You take me," Lake said.

"You'll have more fun with a friend."

Little Jack Jingle
He used to live single
But when he got tired of this kind of life
He left off being single and lived with his wife.

Lake had returned unscathed from the park and napped, and now was groggy on the sofa, warm against Audrey as she read nursery rhymes. Audrey had painted the mountain. Every so often she peered into her studio to see it. Her admiration would diminish in a few days, inadequacy settling in its place. A light came on across the street in Nancy's house. Audrey turned on the lamp beside her and reached for her sketch pad and pencil.

"Dee-Dee—" Lake couldn't say Audrey, and Audrey had never considered that Lake should call her Mother, or Mama, or Mommy. The words didn't feel natural to her. Audrey and Ben were Dee-Dee and Daddy. "I want a banana."

"You want a banana? I can get you a banana."

"Wanna play house."

"You want to play house? Let's go play house."

"Where's Daddy?"

"Where's Daddy? Daddy's still at work, lambkin."

Concentrating on her pad, Audrey didn't rise to meet any of these requests. She was drawing Lake's profile, shading in the darkest crevices of her ear, leaving the paper white where the lamp shined brightest on her hair. Audrey's pencil followed light into dark and out again, scanning the pattern of value across her cheek, still chapped from the cold day, to her slight pucker of lips.

All afternoon Audrey had been bothered by how flippantly she'd told Nancy about Lucille. And in front of Lake, who rarely heard Audrey mention her name. Although much distressed her about Lucille's visit, a few times she had pointed to the sailor dress with the long ribbon down the back in Lake's closet. "You wore it to see your mother, remember?" Every so often, she pulled out the photo she'd taken and showed it to Lake. Audrey didn't believe in secrets. She hadn't spoken to Lucille in the two years since, but she read her letters. She always passed on the gifts she mailed. A little wooden music box had arrived a few months ago—another occasion for talking about her. But that time Audrey called her "my friend from the war." To keep talking about a mother who wasn't there—that was too painful. She still believed it was up to Ben and Lucille to tell Lake the truth, to explain why her mother wasn't in her life. Without Lucille's presence, Audrey was pressed to make up stories, excuses. She hadn't made another close friend; someone like Nancy Dudrow was a reminder that she might not. For a moment she wished Lucille were here right now to tell her whether any paintings in her studio were worth selling. But she already had another child. She had done what Audrey said—words that now weighed heavy with regret on her. Lucille had not returned.

Across the street and through the Dudrows' front window sat little Mel, a speck of color at the breakfast room table. It was time for Lake to eat.

In the kitchen Audrey peeled and sliced a banana and chopped leaves of spinach to boil. The phone rang. It was Ben. He'd been walking out of his office when the hospital called. Tonight would be a late one, he said.

Mark's car pulled up across the street, his lights shut off.

A couple of weeks ago, after Audrey and Ben's last effort, he had turned away from her in bed. "We could adopt," he said.

"Haven't I already done that?"

Nancy opened her front door, embracing Mark.

Audrey heated a slice of meatloaf under the broiler and fed herself and Lake chunks of it, with the spinach and banana. When a light went on upstairs across the street, Mel's, Audrey carried Lake to her room and turned on the light. She sounded out the words of *The Poky Little Puppy*. She would do anything for Lake to learn to read early, to lose herself in storybooks. She went downstairs to leave a light on for Ben, looking one more time at her small painting, still pleased.

From her own unlit bedroom, she saw Mark and Nancy's light come on. She waited for it to go dark before falling asleep, thinking of how he doted on her. If Nancy's cocktail wasn't to her liking, he poured it out and mixed a new one, stirring it with his finger and then licking the finger to test for himself.

After Ben slid into bed beside her, waking her by fluffing pillows and adjusting covers, she thought, as she had just after they married, of their shared breath at night. What once felt like sustenance now felt like deprivation. What had once attracted her now seemed a defect: the softness in his shoulders, how he craned to hear what she was saying. Since Lucille visited, something weak in him had been unclothed, like his lean chest. Audrey lay there, her thoughts twisting back to Mark and Nancy. Mark held his own reflection too long in their entrance-hall mirror whenever he came over. He was servile and effete. She didn't want him, or what they had—but *they* wanted what they had.

She hovered her hand over Ben's pale and bony shoulder, exposed above the covers. Close enough to feel his warmth, she hesitated a moment, then pulled away.

She had spoken to Daniel recently. Urges to talk to him overcame her, and every so often she asked to see him. She just wanted to be with him and talk, and feel an old peace that she felt only with him. They met at the National Gallery and walked through an exhibit of Whistler prints. She told him about Lucille's long-ago visit and the letdown that followed. "It's like I've been putting him through trials all this time," she said, "and he keeps failing."

"But now he's going to make things official with Lake," Daniel said. "Isn't that what you want?"

She sighed and put her arm through his, walking on. "Yes, you're right."

He stopped and turned to her. "I wanted to see you today because I wanted to tell you." They were in front of a print of Venice, two arched doorways. "Audrey. I'm getting married." He smiled, the way a man in love should smile, and she wiped her eyes and laughed, squeezing his arm.

"That's wonderful news, Daniel, it really is. Thank you. Thank you for telling me."

She wouldn't be pathetic in front of him; that wasn't how she wanted him to remember her. "But does she know how lucky she is?" She narrowed her eyes on him. "Promise me." She looped her arm back through his until they reached the Mercury Fountain in the rotunda. Fitting that they end here. Not the message she wanted, but she had to accept it.

Once she had heard a story in which everyone was told to put all their troubles inside a sack and put the sack in the center of the room. Each person could choose any sack to take away, but everyone chose their own sack of troubles.

Not her. Not this sack.

34

On a summer afternoon, Lake out of kindergarten and Ben home early, he found Audrey alone in the basement. She was standing in her bare feet, cool against the concrete floor, flipping through a book on Goya. "What are you doing? Where's Lake?"

She answered with half-truths: "Trying not to melt. I hope she's napping in her room." Not *Wishing the hours away. I could not play one more round of Old Maid.* This was where she hid to escape the heat and tedium of homemaking. There was a little drawing board on the floor, white paper clipped to it, but Ben hadn't noticed that. She had been thinking of a self-portrait, but hadn't decided between leaving the page blank—because she couldn't find herself—or blacking it out with charcoal for the same reason.

Did he tire of her recurrent retreats and turn his focus on Lake? To Audrey, it seemed that way, at least for a while. He offered to take Lake on weekend walks, giving Audrey time to paint, and the two returned talking of things Lake couldn't possibly understand. "The prevailing wind comes out of the southwest here, Lakie," he said, then asked her if she remembered the Latin for a white oak.

"Corky lala," she tried.

"Quercus. Quercus alba."

Audrey rolled her eyes but was grateful for the time. When he took Lake to the county fair, Audrey tagged along with her Leica, holding her nose against the smell of manure. He held Lake's cotton-candy-coated hand. "I can feel the friction of her little wrist bones; they're growing," he said, sounding amazed. Maybe he held her a bit more gently. From behind, Audrey watched their private conversation, each of their profiles a riff on the other. When he bobbed alongside Lake on the merry-go-round, the shape of her face, outlined by the curve of her hairline, looked just like his. Her smile had the same full-cheeked expectancy, and her color was filling in, darkening, to match his. Audrey photographed the resemblance, their faces crisp at the outer edge of the picture, other faces blurred in the center. Father and daughter, together. Audrey had enabled that.

But he worked most days, and Lake soon made her own retreat, into books. While reading opened one world, it shut another. She no longer drew alongside Audrey or needed her to read stories aloud. Once Lake learned to decode words and was tall enough to peer into the mirror above her bureau, she preferred to inhabit the characters—Queen Crosspatch, Meg and Peg and Kilmanskeg, and even Peter Piper—throwing her voice down an octave. She liked to be watched, or to watch herself behind her closed bedroom door. The sound of her voice broke the house's long silences. "'Dear me, Duke, what are you doing here?'" she read from *Racketty-Packetty House*.

"'I am looking at her... I'm in love. I fell in love with her the minute Cynthia took her out of the box. I am going to marry her.'"

Sometimes Audrey stopped outside Lake's door to listen, amused and relieved. The child could entertain herself.

On a crisp fall day when Lake was nine, she ran into the house after playing a game of capture the flag in a neighbor's yard. She looked as though she'd been captured herself, her face flushed and teary, knees muddy, grass stains down her backside. If Audrey hadn't been on her way out the door, she might have missed the disturbance, but she broke Lake's stride before she started up the stairs. "What happened to you?"

"I hate Mel Dudrow!" she screamed, sobbing. "He's an imbecile." Audrey went to hug her, but Lake forced her way out of her arms. From what Audrey could make out, he had pinned Lake down on the ground, straddling her waist. Lake tried to buck him, without success. With his eyes bulging over her and his palms flattening her arms, he yelled at her, spit falling on her face.

"What did he say?" Audrey asked.

"He talked about that painting, the woman in the picture."

"About Lucille, my friend from the war?" She felt her face burning.

Lake didn't answer; she was gasping for air, still bawling.

"Did he say anything else?" Audrey smoothed Lake's hair.

"That his mother told him all about it. About my mother."

"He shouldn't have done that. I'm going to call Mrs. Dudrow." The voice she used—it didn't sound like her own at all. She looked out the windows, where trees filled in much of the Dudrows' front lawn. She could barely make out the house.

"Don't do that!" Lake pulled away, her face suddenly impassive. "You'll make it worse."

"But you know about Lucille. We've talked about her." Audrey started to recount the visit, the music box, a packet of seeds she'd sent not long ago—

"Where is she? She's not real! I don't believe you. She's some dumb lady in a picture."

"You really need to speak to your father about this. He should be the one talking to you."

Just then Ben walked in from the yard, saying, "What's all this about?"

When Audrey told him what happened, he said, "The boy probably has a crush on her."

Lake pinched her face into a scowl. "Like you had a crush on *her*?" She pointed to Lucille's portrait before running up the stairs.

"You've got to talk to her," Audrey said, "tell her more about Lucille and you."

He was already on his way back outside as though he hadn't heard her. She pushed again. "Maybe the problem is that there is no story to tell about you two. Can't you just make one up?"

"Back off, Audrey," he said, turning with his palm raised at her. "She's still too young to understand. I'll talk to her when the time is right."

After that Audrey often found Lake staring at the painting. "Any good piece of art deserves a close look," she had told Lake often. "Noticing everything can take hours." But not this painting. Lucille, in a red chair, leaned into the viewer's space. Her brassy hair swirled, as did the green background. She didn't look happy or sad. There was a tension in the one hand that gripped the wrist of the other, which lay curled open, palm up.

Lake looked and looked. "Why doesn't she look back at me?"

"She didn't look at me when I painted her. She was looking behind me."

"Maybe at someone else?"

It was as if there had been a third person in the room, to the left of Audrey—this was where Lucille's gaze went, just over the viewer's shoulder.

"Maybe me," Lake added.

"But you weren't born yet."

"But maybe she knew I was going to be born."

"She did. You're right about that."

Audrey was the one who called first, dialing the number that Lucille had included in a letter, alongside days and times when she was most available. Audrey closed the kitchen doors and stood pinned against the wall, holding the phone under her chin, her fingers gnawing at the cord. No one answered the first few times, and then a young boy picked up, another time a woman. When Lucille finally called back, she hardly eked a sentence out before going on a crying jag and then hanging up. Over time they tried again, Audrey speaking gently: "We really want to see you. I'll send you train fare." Lake was going to be in a recital or a school play, or maybe the May Day celebration would be fun. But at each suggestion Lucille went on long digressions about what was happening at the nursery and how she could not find a way to visit. "Why don't you just talk to her?" Audrey prompted. No, she couldn't possibly talk now, she would go to pieces, but yes, thank you for mailing the school photos, sharing the teacher's comments, telling me the funny thing Lake said to the dentist. After these calls Audrey hung up teary too. The last time, Lake, who had probably been listening through the door, asked for a drink of milk and looked at her questioningly, as if to say, *Am I not the one who ought to be crying?* "Farming is hard," Audrey finally said. Flowers, fruits, floods, droughts. Arthur was not always well.

"Lucille wants to see you, she does." She couldn't explain how sadness or weakness cumbered a person from doing what they most wanted.

But once they started using the telephone to keep in touch more, Lucille checked on Lake every three months. Audrey could almost set her watch by it.

The following spring Lake was to dance the role of Persephone in a recital, and she took her rehearsals seriously, all over the house. Wrapped in a yellow sheet, she pantomimed picking flowers in the meadow—the living room rug—until she fell, wailing on the floor, into the imaginary chasm that took her down to Hades.

"Goodness." Audrey laughed.

At once Lake was Demeter, morosely swinging her head and arms into every room on the first floor, searching for Persephone under every pillow and table, despairing, but not quite as hysterically.

"What's next?" Ben lowered his newspaper for this spectacle.

Lake kept looking, opening drawers and searching behind books on the shelf, rolling the carpet up, peering between the wall and the sofa, determined to find Persy, as she was calling her.

"I don't think she's here," Audrey said.

Lake reverted to Persephone, crawling on her knees to demonstrate a younger being, tempted a final time by those seeds beneath the pomegranate tree. And then she reenacted her reunion with Demeter with more cries, her arms wrapping around her torso like a lover's.

"A whole lot of carrying on about nothing," Ben said. Audrey didn't challenge him then. Couldn't he see this was a clear reflection of Lake's own desire to reunite with her mother? But he had been morose since the weekend started, after performing a routine gallbladder removal and finding the woman's cavity riddled with tumors. She didn't want to aggravate him.

If Audrey and Ben went out for an evening, they left Lake with an older lady, Mrs. Blue. The first time she showed up, her stockings rolled down around her ankles, Lake asked her why she was wearing doughnuts. But Mrs. Blue could handle that. "Just don't you try to eat them!" She laughed and laughed.

"Don't mind Lake," Audrey told her, "if you hear her talking to herself in her room."

She liked these nights out, to a concert and reception or a fundraiser. She liked Ben best when they were in a group of people—his height, his charming humor, his intelligence emerging from the gloomy mists that hung about him at home. He was careful never to drink too much in public. Home was where they scraped and dug at each other with Lake as their only witness. He had told her once, "Something about your seriousness doesn't draw me to you," so she knew he too probably preferred her when she smiled more, grew garrulous, lightened up, things she did for the benefit of others. She flirted, tossed her head back laughing, planted exuberant kisses on cheeks. Even their dancing seemed more an exhibition for everyone else, though with certain rhythms an old joy flickered between them.

But after a while, she dreaded the outings. When they returned home, Mrs. Blue often reported that Lake had given several performances, which explained why she was never asleep when Audrey went to check on her. She got too excited after being "on stage." And many nights Lake's face was wet with tears.

"What's wrong, baby?"

"I had a bad dream."

"What about?"

"I dreamed I was being born. It was scary, like falling a long way in the dark. When I woke up you still weren't home. I was afraid you weren't coming."

"Oh, Lake. Why?" Audrey lay down beside her.

"Something might happen to you."

"Nothing's going to happen to us."

"You might decide to go away."

"We'll always come home to you."

"But what *if* something happened? What if you're in a car crash. Who would take care of me?"

"You'd go to Ridgelea, or Aunt Viola would take care of you." She put her hand on Lake's forehead.

"What about my real mommy?"

"Lucille? Yes, she would come then." But this made Lake cry more, and Audrey rocked her harder in this irreducible truth, a piece of grit that couldn't be pierced: to separate a mother and a child is a terrible thing.

"I want her to come," Lake said. "But I don't want you to go."

When Audrey went to tell Ben what Lake had said, she found him opening a new bottle of bourbon. It was almost midnight. She covered the empty glass with her hand before he started to pour. "Can you stop?" she whispered. "Won't you ever quit?" He pulled the glass away, held it in the air like a taunt, and poured a double.

Lucille had become like that scent in the woods, but it was everywhere, filling their house.

35

By junior high, Lake loathed school. She feigned upset stomachs and sore throats to stay home. Audrey sent her anyway but then suffered Lake's morning tantrums. Soon the school was calling regularly to say she hadn't shown up. The only thing she'd ever exhibited any interest in was the stage, and the only time she seemed happy at home was when she was singing.

Audrey called the Conservatory, thinking Prudy might be a good teacher for her, but the telephone number was no longer in service. She found her in the telephone book under her last name, but a man answered. Lon, Audrey thought. They must still be together. "I've thought about you so often," Audrey said when Prudy came on the line, and Prudy told her the school had gone under. "Broke my heart." After she earned her degree, she'd taught there for more than ten years. Now she was taking students, trying to teach full-time on her own. Audrey had found an upcoming production of *Guys and Dolls*, and Lake wanted to audition for the company. A regular lesson time was scheduled, and Prudy and Lake began practicing.

Audrey worked distractedly during these years, finishing little. Eventually she enrolled Lake in a new high school, one affiliated with a junior college. Lake joined the makeup crew for one of the college productions, where she met Mary Ann, penciling in brows that ran underneath her broom of bangs, and Gretchen, drawing little black wingtips at the corners of her bell-shaped eyes. Lake had told Audrey she lived in the certainty that everyone had former, secret knowledge of each other. "They're like a school of fish, I'm like a water buffalo," Lake said. But when Audrey picked her up from rehearsals, she noticed these two older girls walking around her as if she were a Greek statue, their sentences overlapping, "Adore your pea coat… your baby-girl wrists… when are we going to see you onstage?" They came over in the afternoons, clinking glasses in the kitchen, scraping chairs as they tumbled into each other's laps, giggling endlessly. For once Audrey didn't mind her focus disturbed—Lake had friends.

"Next time I have a friend over," Lake said, after one of these visits, "come downstairs and introduce yourself, why don't you? You're not my mother. But at least act like you are."

She was used to bearing the brunt of Lake's moody teenage ways, but this charge was new. "I've seen them at the theater. I know them."

"They have no idea you exist."

Audrey planned to introduce herself the next chance she had, but the girls stopped coming around. A boy with a ponytail, Louis, seemed to have taken their place.

No one in Lake's school knew who Audrey Bray the artist was. Years earlier, she'd been part of a joint exhibition that warranted a write-up in the paper; a few commissions for her "cubist portraiture" and her "lyrical abstracts" followed. Now, with Lake socially preoccupied, Audrey's steady mundane attention went to art all day. In the cooler months she sometimes worked in the finished attic space of the third floor where she painted on larger canvases. If she ever closed the door from the top of the stairs—hardly ever the need because no one but Audrey made the climb—a sign on it read: *Do Not Disturb.*

Under the spell of a new work, she flattened her brush so the oils ran in one quadrant, but in another she bulked up the pigment to three dimensions. The process felt tedious at first, but then hours passed without her awareness. This was bliss. She knew what was in front of her was singular; it held the exact motions of her wrist, every caress, in colors whose perfect adulteration would never be replicated again. The painting was an extension of her; it had come down her arm and now lay like raw nerve exposed to air. And yet it exceeded her. She was not beautiful, nor could she have articulated her intense feelings in words, but the painting before her—it was, it did. When she stepped back from it, she felt a febrile rush.

Still entranced, she went to the kitchen tap for water, then followed the sound of shrieking in the street, children playing a game of kick the can. She hadn't noticed Lake, who had come downstairs after her.

"Interrupting your work, are they? You never have liked children."

Audrey flinched, slapped out of her daze.

"What?" she snapped. "What did you say?" She turned on Lake quickly, gripping her lean, ropy arm, but Lake shook her loose, raising her hand as if to strike. Audrey took an appalled step backward, stunned by their capacity for rage, or how her own passion had wheeled to rage.

When Lake stayed away from the house until long after dinner and Audrey threatened to take the car away from her, Lake yelled, "I hate you! You're trying to ruin my life!"

"You don't know anything about a ruined life."

This was their only intimacy, saying whatever came into their heads.

Audrey now felt strangely subsumed by whatever she was working on. Not that she was physically part of a painting, but that she had no separate self from it. Not even completed work grounded her. Finishing was terrifying for this reason. A small side-street gallery in Dupont Circle had offered her a slot during the coming summer. Who cared that it was three days between two month-long shows for men? After her work was taken down, the space would be painted for the next artist, but not before. She wouldn't mind blemished walls. She was thrilled for this chance.

Gone was any lyricism from her brushstrokes. These were frantic, bold compositions titled "Works Alone." She needed five more and had just begun a new one—quick, immerse! she told herself—the day Lake walked out with a backpack and a sleeping bag and got into someone's car. Ben later recalled it was a 1957 Packard. Audrey vaguely remembered Lake's mention of a weekend camping trip with Mary Ann and Gretchen, how she would call on Sunday to let them know what time to expect her.

But a call didn't come.

By Monday Audrey and Ben were pacing the house with worry, every look between them an accusation. Lake had missed a voice lesson with Prudy. Ben thumbed through the telephone book, searching for the numbers of the girls' parents. When finally he reached Gretchen's father, he was told that the girls had graduated from the junior college and moved out west for the summer, with plans to finish their bachelor's elsewhere. "They're going to throw some pottery," the father said.

"What the hell?" Ben shouted. "You've got to be kidding me. Do you know they've taken a seventeen-year-old girl with them, a senior in high school? She's a minor, they could be arrested."

"Ben," Audrey urged in the background, "hang up the phone."

Eventually Lake called them—after a week of silence, of absolute grief and certainty that something horrible had happened to her. She had reached New Mexico, her destination. "The salt baths," she said, slurring her words. "We've been there all day."

"I know you don't care about us, but what about Prudy? She's been worried sick."

Lake went quiet at this. "Tell her I'm sorry—"

"No, you come home right now and tell her yourself. Is Louis with you?"

"I'm fine. And yes, he is." She said this with a dreamy gloat. Drugs must be involved.

"Are you trying to kill us?" Ben was on the extension.

"I'm calling the police," Audrey said, and at that Lake put the receiver down—left it on a table or counter so Audrey could hear music, distant voices and laughter, strange yelling. The call was expensive, but she listened for more than an hour to these sounds until someone apparently needed to make a call and hung up the phone.

Audrey didn't follow through on her police threat. She was too afraid of getting Lake into serious trouble. Instead, she attended to Lake's memory in a way she never had in person. She wrote down a list of all the characters Lake had played in school, lines she remembered. She kept returning to an image of her rooting for strangers when she saw them late for their buses, the buses pulling away from the stops. "Go, go!" she would shout. And when they succeeded, "You did it, hooray!"

Audrey had planned on doing the same when Lake walked across the stage to receive her diploma. She was proud of that—as proud of herself as she was of Lake. She had helped make that possible, hadn't she? Any satisfaction to be had—well, it was gone now. Lake missed her exams, her graduation ceremony. Ben and Audrey dwelled with their fear and helplessness in different rooms of the house, on different floors; on the weekends, she held herself fixed in front of a floor fan, he sweated under the mulberry outdoors. Now all Audrey cared about— prayed for, as she also had never done—was Lake's safe return.

Guiltily, she recalled the many times she'd used Lake as a subject when she was little. In her high chair Lake sat willingly, probably because she couldn't get out by herself, or because this was the only way to hold Audrey's attention. She banged a toy teapot on the tray like a gavel but Audrey never stopped drawing. If she studied how one of Lake's eyes was slightly weaker than the other, or the little stripe of birthmark near her hairline, or the slight overbite that made her upper lip protrude, wouldn't she recognize Lake as her own?

All that obedience—used up. But the trick had its effect, as did Lake's absence now. She filled Audrey's thoughts. There wasn't room for anything else. For the two months Lake was gone, Audrey painted nothing. Her exhibit was canceled.

1973

36

Audrey's injured leg is exposed to the air; the rest of her lies under a sheet and blanket. Lucille is changing her bandages, a nasty job Audrey is relieved Lake doesn't have to do. Gently rubbing oil to loosen the adhesive around her knee, Lucille says, "Doesn't look as angry today."

She rolls Audrey onto her side, "like one of your bales of hay," Audrey says, laughing. Lucille flushes the wound with alcohol. Audrey flinches first at the cold, then the burn. "I had a nice little nap while you were at Ben's, but now I'm wide awake."

Outside rain bears down.

Since the surgery on her pelvis and knee, each bedridden day has blurred into the next, leaving her suspended in a kind of helpless peace. For so long she has wished for a reckoning from Lucille, but the past seems more and more contained, like a tiny remote island, uninhabitable. Now she can't manage without her. Lucille succeeded in bringing back every item requested from Ben's house, from right under his nose. And it amazes her how much Lucille's opinion—her judgment of Audrey's art—still matters. When she pulled out a portfolio of old sketches of Japanese soldiers, Lucille said, "Whoa, look at these. You should sell them."

"To who?" Nobody would want those. "The Japanese?"

"I don't know. Why not Americans? Hasn't enough time passed?"

"Has it? How much is enough time?" They looked at each other blankly.

She wishes Lake could see them together. "Did you have any luck talking to Lake?" she says now. "Did she say she's coming by today?"

"I said you were expecting a visit when I gave her your number, but Ray came by just before I left. It looked like she was patching things up with him, so that's good."

Audrey squirms. That can't be right. "I don't believe you. Patched things up? He's no good for her, you know that, right?" She pulls herself up to her elbows, but Lucille urges her down again.

"There, there, Lake is fine. She was talking nonsense about going to

Russia, and I hope he's able to talk her out of that." She laughs lightly, screwing on the tops of alcohol and ointments.

Audrey's chest tightens. It's hard for her to breathe. When Lake last visited her at the hospital, she was going to stay at Ben's. They never had the chance to plan her move here, where Ray couldn't find her. "If everything is fine, why isn't she here yet? She said she'd be here before one and it's going on one-thirty."

"She's just running behind. Between teaching and caring for Ben, trying to find another acting role, the girl has got her hands full. Don't try to get up, you're going to hurt yourself."

"Don't tell me to lie down again." Audrey flings off the blankets. "Hand me my crutches."

"What are you doing?"

"I'm going to find her. And help her. I am her *mother*. And you're going to drive me."

She's nervous being in a car, her first time since the ride home from the hospital. She shivers, wearing only a light sweater. Ben said she was a cold fish. Worse than that—bloodless. She doesn't want to see him, but she has to know that Lake is all right.

"What do you mean 'he's no good for her'?" Lucille asks. "You said Ray was crazy about her."

"I thought he was. But I've been hearing things from Lake I don't like. He has a scary temper." She raises her voice to be heard over the pouring rain and windshield wipers.

"Now you have me worried." Lucille is gripping the steering wheel, giving it little squeezes. "I had no idea."

"She's been trying to give him the shake but he won't have it." Audrey tells her about Lake's bruised foot and Ray's jealousy of another actor, how Lake had been spending more time at Audrey and Ben's house before Ray showed up at her school uninvited.

Hunched over the wheel, focused on the blurred-out cars ahead and their intermittent brake lights, Lucille says, "I don't even want to tell you." She takes a deep breath. "I feel awful about this. I'm the one who told him to come over today. He and I had talked about how neither of us could reach her—"

"You did what?"

"—and he seemed so devoted. She wouldn't see me. I thought we could help each other."

"Just drive. Get us there."

"Why do I always do the wrong thing, never what I should do? Not even what I want to do."

"Stop talking. You've always done exactly what you wanted."

Audrey's chest is swelling with panic by the time they arrive.

At first, the house seems empty, but Ben is in the backyard, picking up fallen branches. All of him is drenched.

"She was here earlier," he says, lifting his cane toward Lucille, "cleaning out every last cotton swab. What more could you possibly want?" He laughs, trying for a smile from Audrey. But she's scanning the kitchen for evidence of his drinking. Nothing is obvious. Lucille is dialing the telephone. Audrey feels his eyes on her and she thinks an apology is coming, but none does. He dries himself off with a dish towel. Lucille is asking Eva, her sister, about a spare key to their house.

When she hangs up, Lucille apologizes for the long-distance call.

"What was that about?" Audrey says.

"I'm worried." She squeezes one hand in the other. "You know I've had this idea for Lake to visit Pomona. For real this time, not like the last disaster. And Ray kept talking about wanting to get away with her, just the two of them, to mend things. I'm afraid I told him where the key to my house was. I didn't think he'd ever use it, especially without asking. But I don't know now. I was pretty specific about how to find it, but only to convince him I wanted to help. I wanted him to trust me."

Audrey leans her crutches against a chair and sits down. She digs the fingertips of both hands into her closed eyes. She is so livid she cannot speak.

"I'm calling George," Ben says. "He'll know where his son is."

While he uses the phone, Audrey says, "I can't imagine she would go all the way down there."

"I don't think they would ride his motorcycle in the rain."

"So they might be on his motorcycle? You didn't tell me that," Audrey nearly shrieks.

"They could be in his car by now."

Ben returns. "He says Ray was headed to a wedding this weekend, maybe in Baltimore. But when I told him he was knocking on my door this afternoon, he didn't like the sound of that."

"Maybe they went back to her place," Audrey says. "I can't sit here, doing nothing." She looks at Ben, wishing she could get in the car with him and leave Lucille behind. But that's impossible. "Stay here in case Lake calls."

"I don't see his motorcycle here," Lucille says, pulling in front of Lake's apartment. "Maybe that's it around the corner."

Something else has caught Audrey's eye. A black helmet lying on the ground, in the middle of the walkway. Closer now, she sees the helmet is filling with rainwater.

Everything that happened on the trip to Pomona years ago rushes back to her. She turns to Lucille. "This is your fault. Whatever is going on here, it's all on you."

1963

37

When Lake returned from New Mexico, Audrey hoped she would get a job, work on her GED, take up astronomy—anything to resume her life. But she lay in bed most days, hardly eating, staring into the mirror. Whenever she appeared outside her room she looked stricken, on the receiving end of bad news. There was plenty that summer—Medgar Evers had been gunned down in his own driveway, and Jackie Kennedy had just lost her two-day-old son. A few times each week, Audrey collected a dozen half-empty glasses and plates from Lake's room. She didn't scold her. She didn't want her to leave again.

Prudy was the one who approached Audrey and Ben. "She's not right," she said, her mouth pulling to one side. "She needs help."

"I'm taking her South," Audrey told Ben. "To Lucille's." She had considered this while Lake was gone.

"Little too late, don't you think? Could be a really bad idea," said Ben.

"I'm just doing what you two have never had the courage to do."

She packed three days' worth of things for herself and for Lake but didn't tell Lucille they were coming. They wouldn't stay long, or they would, impossible to know. But three days—that was long enough for something to transpire. Just before dawn on a late August morning, summer's heat broken, Audrey woke Lake, who seemed to sleepwalk to the car. But as soon as the engine started, she ranted: "How dare you insist on a trip now. I'm an adult. You can't order me around." When Audrey told her that Lucille's was the destination, Lake withdrew into the corner of the back seat and went mute, like a slug with salt thrown on it.

A long line of white buses was forming along Constitution Avenue as they were leaving town. "What in the world?" Audrey said.

"It's the March on Washington today," Lake said. "Don't you keep up with anything? 'Liberator Freedom Bus,'" she read aloud. "I have friends who are going." She leaned her head against the window. "I should be going."

"Will Prudy be there?" Audrey had forgotten the march was today and hadn't turned on the news this morning in her rush to leave. She didn't point out that Lake didn't remember either until they saw the buses.

"Yep. And wherever she is in the crowd, she'll be singing."

"I just hope no one gets hurt."

"They're already hurt, that's why they're marching. Don't you get it?"

"I do, I do." Audrey tightened her lips. Better to say nothing than to argue the rest of the way.

A couple of hours passed and Lake dug out an egg-salad sandwich from the hamper and ate it quietly, her gaze alert out the window. "Can I eat half yours?"

Audrey laughed. "Of course."

"The automobile has ruined the countryside," Lake said. Cars and pieces of cars seemed to litter that part of the world. Audrey was quick to agree with her on that.

A sadness overcame her when she reached the lonely white-frame house, taller and thinner than she'd supposed, like an old man she'd not seen since he was a young boy. Time had either ravaged it or forgotten it. All it really needed was a coat of paint, but it looked woeful, on a plot of land that sank slightly under its weight. She couldn't see any rolling farmland behind it—though it might have been there past the trees surrounding the house. She saw in Lake's face the same disappointment. Perhaps they'd both come to the end of their imaginations. What world had Lake built of words said, rooms she'd walked into, doors opened, windows seen through, love called out? Would this count as one more loss?

What kept Audrey moving toward the house in that moment, her hand at Lake's back, was a collie, bounding at her, jumping and licking her legs. To turn away seemed a worse provocation. She murmured sweet appeals to the dog, "Shh, shh, shh. Good boy, good doggie." The sun was lower in the sky than she'd hoped, but they had a few hours yet. The porch softened under their weight. Against the screen door, she framed her eyes with her hands, seeing down a dark hall to the kitchen. She smelled meat cooking, heard a voice, and knocked.

A boy answered, maybe twelve years old, wearing twill work pants and a red neckerchief. She knew he must be Clark, but she didn't want to get into introductions yet. He lightly kicked the door open wide with his foot. His expression was unmoving but not unwelcoming. The dog had lost interest in her and Lake, and now its nose trailed every gesture he made.

She asked for Lucille. "Friends, passing through town."

"My ma's fishing."

"Fishing now?" Audrey said.

"Sun needs to be coming up or starting to go down before they'll bite." He smiled, showing yellow teeth.

"Maybe you can tell us where to find her."

"We should leave," Lake said.

"That's easy enough," he said, ignoring Lake, eyeing the vehicle over their shoulders. "It's faster to walk but it'll only take you about fifteen minutes if you want to drive." He let the screen door smack closed and in a minute returned with a page torn from a calendar. May 1958. On the back he'd drawn a little map, taking up only a corner of the paper. "Here you go. Start off to the right out of here." He waited a minute, patient as Audrey and Lake read over it, and then said, "I'll have to be getting back to the kitchen, stove's hot."

They found the cut-in through the tall pines to the lake without a problem, and their car fit snugly in it. Lucille must have walked because there was no other vehicle around. From the shore they saw her rowboat. Her faint frame in the stern, steering with one oar, gained on them. If Audrey had run into her on a random street, she might not have known her. Even in the day's late shadows, her hair was brighter, bottle-blond. Her expression was determined, her jaw clenched, as if everything in her life had been building to this moment.

She acted as though she'd been expecting them, no surprise at all in seeing the nose of their steel-blue Chrysler almost at the water's edge and their figures on the pebbled and sandy shore, Audrey in her skirt and pumps, Lake in her teenage jeans and shirtsleeves cuffed on her upper arms. Maybe Lucille had gone mad. She was unreliable, to say the least—hadn't Audrey learned that already? But she was desperate to trust her. Lucille wore a dress, her apron tied on, no fishing attire, though Audrey wouldn't know what counted as such. She must have looked wary because Lucille called out, "It's okay, Lake can get in. Take off your shoes first."

"What did she say?" whispered Lake. "Her accent."

Lucille was still thin as a matchstick. Her nose tip, slightly squared, and the dip of the cleft above the center of her mouth closely resembled Lake's. The likeness gave Audrey a jolt.

"I'm going to let you take her. I'm going for a little drive by myself." Audrey had no idea where she would go, but the plan all along had been to leave them together for a while. She might trace her way back to the town center for an early dinner alone, or walk along Lucille's property, studying the fruit trees she'd heard so much about. "I want you to help this girl. You might be able to make her come to her senses. I can't get through to her. She gave me the scare of my life when she didn't come home for two months—"

"I can't swim," Lake interrupted.

"No, I suppose not. Where would you have learned? Leave your shoes," Lucille repeated. "You don't need them, and you don't have to swim to the boat. Wade out here." Lucille raised an oar. Audrey saw a rod then, a tackle box, a pretense of fishing at least. "No one's gonna drown out here." Lake obeyed, first rolling her jeans up to her knees. With both hands Lucille helped guide her over the side of the boat.

"I'll be back in an hour," Audrey called out.

Lucille held up a lantern. "Wait till dark. Give us till dark."

Lake's pair of leather moccasins lay on the shore. As Audrey drove off, she thought to herself, *I'm the crazy one.*

∽

People had drowned, mysteriously, over the generations in Lake Opora, often when they were boating alone, as Lucille had been. In her lifetime the water had claimed an older man who'd fished alone and tipped out of his small boat either from fainting or a heart attack or the carrying off of his own life, no one ever knew. She came out here frequently, drawn to the water as if she were the embodiment of thirst. What moved her was the miracle of being held by something inapprehensible—she could not cup water in her hands for any reliable length of time, yet she had floated on it for hours. She had lain on it like it was a mother's breast, more times since her own mother passed, craving the nearness of something elemental, solaced that this could be the same water all mothers before her had bathed in, drunk, been baptized with, or cried. Alone as she felt in her sorrow, here she was not. She sat down on the front wooden plank and rowed to the center of the lake so the land behind them gave the illusion of spilling away.

"You're good at this," Lake said. "You don't look like you would be, but you are."

"Here, you take the oars. All you have to do is not let them slip."

They switched seats. Lucille knelt behind the girl and began stroking her head. Near her crown was a patch of sharp-pointed hair growing in.

"I got into a habit this summer. Pulling it out."

Lucille divided the hair into locks and braided them. She smelled burning wood in the air, proof they weren't alone. She had imagined something like this, but different, a scene she relived again and again in her mind. From her kitchen window she would spot a girl with smooth oaken hair walking up the drive toward her, and the swing of her arm, a certain poise in the angle of her head, Lucille recognized as her own. Their eyes caught through the window, piercing as light reflected off water, and she ran to her ever-lost child. No, she wasn't surprised to see Lake, who was always sliding in and out of her view.

"Tell me why you aren't well."

"I hate school, I had to get away. Went to New Mexico."

"Why'd you come back?"

"I ran out of money."

"You couldn't find a job?"

"I got fired from my last one. Housekeeping. I lay down for a rest on the cool tile bathroom floor and the hotel guest found me. And a boy I—"

"A boy what?"

"A boy," she repeated.

"Where's he now?"

"Too many questions. I'm very tired. Let's not talk."

At some point Lake said, "Do you have anything to eat?"

Lucille reached into the mostly empty tackle box and pulled out a sack of bread, the morning's bacon, two peaches. She pulled in the oars and they moved seats again. Lake quietly ate.

They drifted. For a time it was as if they had always lived in this vessel together, had tracked how the sun, depending on the season, moved closer to the horizon across the sky, or higher. Birds warbled, coming in to roost for the night.

"Have you ever seen a sunset like this?" The sky had filled in a deep periwinkle.

"From the highest points in the city, sometimes you can catch a glimpse. And we have a river, you know."

"Humph," Lucille said, doubtful of the comparison.

Light drops of rain fell. She saw no discernible cloud above. Dankness, the smell of water and soil, must be the oldest odor in the world.

It was twilight now, between light and dark, when the distinct shapes of trees solidified into one, and lightning bugs fired against them. The sky still hovered bright above. Lucille couldn't be sure this was happening, any more than she could be sure Lake existed outside her own mind. She couldn't tell where she ended and Lake began. The girl might have been fitted inside her again, inviolate, curled up in that hollowed-out place.

"See the rabbit on the moon?" Lucille pointed. "Its ears up top, in profile."

"I see it."

They were a good ways from shore, its edges soft in the distance. Lucille dipped her hand into the lake water and spread the wetness across Lake's forehead. "Bless you."

"Lucille," Arthur called from far away. She didn't move. His calling continued, and she dropped the oars back in. She whispered to Lake, "You must be very quiet. I'll lead you into the marsh and I'll step out. Wait for me. I'll return."

Lake did as she was told. She lay down at Lucille's feet, in the water that had splashed over the gunwale. Lucille beached the boat and stepped over her onto shore, where Arthur was chiding her. "What is wrong with you, woman? Out like this past dinner, expecting your children to do everything for you. Where is your head?"

Gravel and sand abraded her bare feet as they walked to the car, Arthur carrying her shoes. The dream was over. Reality snapped into focus with the slam of the truck door. Did Arthur know about her dream, and in the ongoing dream, was Audrey on her way to get Lake from the boat? Audrey would be there, she always was. Lucille had never had a friend like her. Not even her sister could be counted on the same way.

Outside the dream, Arthur was complaining about their son shirking his work again in favor of a baseball game. They passed another car.

She turned, watching it recede. "What," said Arthur. "What are you looking at?"

"Did you see what kind of car that was?"

"No, but there's a doe, look at her." He slowed, pointing. The animal stood on the side of the road, unblinking. A shiver ran down Lucille's legs, but she told herself that Audrey was in that car. She would find Lake in the boat. She would know Lucille couldn't tell Arthur. She had always known.

But why couldn't Lucille tell him? What was she afraid of? Not his anger—that couldn't touch her now, nor could his disapproval. Perhaps it was the possibility of his disbelief. That might defeat her.

She wrapped her arms around herself. Giving up the knowledge of Lake to Arthur would be like giving up Lake all over again.

Inside their warm house, lamps glowed and plates thick with food lay on the table, the smell of yeast rolls and roasted corn in the air. There was Martha, who was never home for supper these days, always at Eva's, now sitting beside Clark—this too was almost out of a dream. Martha was the child Lucille had never heard cry at night when she was a baby.

"Are you gonna get up?" Arthur had said that first night home from the hospital, shaking her awake in their bed.

"What?"

"Don't you hear that?"

"No."

For a few nights he brought Martha in for her to nurse, sometimes twice. But finally he said, "I can't get up and work all day if I have to do this too. The baby has to sleep in here, and I'm going to sleep in the baby's room."

It was as if all Lucille knew of mothering was how to give birth, nothing more. When Martha cried during the day, her face wrinkled and wet in distress, Lucille's feet went heavy as cement, weighted with a longing for what she couldn't have. *I can't have that! I can't have that!* But she must have managed to quell the voice and hold Martha, for she was sixteen now, thriving, her blond hair in ringlets that bounced and blew in her boyfriend's convertible on Friday nights.

Sliding into the cane seat, Lucille had a different urge, to slip quietly upstairs to her room. That was what she did when the children were little and Eva arrived home from school. While her sister cared for them, Lucille retreated to her room, where she rocked, conversing in her head, an occasional declaration on her tongue, but her gaze on the floor, following a grain of pine till it met an end and turned back the same way or swirled into a dark knot and stopped.

She was looking down at the knotty pine floor now when Clark said, "Where have you been, Mama? Folks came by asking for you."

She stiffened, moving her eyes to the baked yellow squash.

"Who were they?" Arthur asked.

"Said they were friends but they weren't from around here."

"What did you tell them?" Lucille said quietly.

"I gave them directions to the lake. I don't see how they could have gotten lost."

"Maybe that's because you've never been anywhere else in your life to know what it means to get lost," Martha said, smirking.

Arthur called her out. Having more children—one to make up for his loss, a second for good measure—had affected his heart. And he had more farmland than he ever dreamed of owning. It seemed his heart was so full it might burst, his doctor cautioned. Lucille saw it now, around the table, his face rosy with adoration; he didn't like to see either child criticized.

"You don't know what you're talking about," Clark said. "I climbed my way out of Hanging Rock without a compass last week. You couldn't have done that."

"Maybe I should go find them." Lucille placed her napkin by her plate. "I don't want anyone to be out there looking for me."

"Oh, this was two or three hours ago, they must be long gone by now."

When the dishes were cleared, Lucille walked to the mailbox at the end of the long drive and stood under oak boughs, listening above the country sounds for an engine, tires on the road. Somewhere far off frogs croaked; cicadas hummed in the trees beside her. She clutched the mail—illegible now with the sun fully set. Waiting, turning, she heard in the distance what she did not want to hear this late, another car. There it was—the Chrysler, pointed toward the lake, Audrey's silhouette on the driver's side.

It passed, the cicadas started up. There was a rustling in the leaves. The doe, so close she could touch it.

Lucille spent the night, and several following, in fits of compunction, tossing and turning next to Arthur and his rickety breath. He sucked and shuddered from one to the next. The wavering reflection of her and Lake in the water held still now, solid in its insistence.

One morning, thinking that Arthur was in the barn where the grader would be running, she walked down the service road in her galoshes, the ground soggy from last night's storm. He wasn't there. She happened to pass the open door of his small toolshed, a wedge of light across the threshold. He was singing.

The longest train I ever saw
Went down that Georgia line
The engine passed at six o'clock
And the cab passed by at nine
In the pines, in the pines
Where the sun never shines
And we shiver when the cold wind blows
Who who hoo hoo hoo hoo, who who hoo hoo hoo hoo hoo hoo

"Arthur," she called.

He always waited before answering, as if she were a teacher and he the pupil. If he waited long enough, she might move on to someone else. "Yes?" He was standing over tools laid on a work table, oiling them, the grime on his hands visible even in this light.

"Do you know why I was such a mess when Jimmy died? Do you know?"

"I expect so."

"It wasn't all because of Jimmy. No, it wasn't that. It was because I had a baby." She felt all of it, like a brood of cicadas that had been waiting underground for years, coming to the surface. "I'd left a daughter in Washington. I don't know why I'm telling you now, except she came down here and once again I did the wrong thing. All because I didn't want you to find out."

He still hadn't looked up from his tools to see her standing in the lit doorway, but a planer fell to the ground now.

"Arthur Lind, are you listening?" She used his full name often, as if he were someone who was the subject of gossip, not an intimate.

"All right, Lucille, all right." He turned around in the toolshed's scanty light.

"You should have seen that girl. She was a wreck, a heap of bones when she came to me that day. What is wrong with me?"

He folded his arms, sucking his teeth. "You didn't do anything to her," he said. "You gave her the best opportunity you knew."

"Leaving her with her father—who didn't even know she existed. *Opportunity*—that's a silly word."

"It's all right. You don't need to tell me. After all this time. Don't get yourself worked up."

That was one of his favorite expressions, like she was a horse or a machine.

"But I do need to tell you. Look at me, Arthur Lind. I'm walking through the mud to tell you. Someone," she cried upward, "hear me!" She banged her fists on his chest.

*

Less than an hour after Arthur retrieved Lucille from fishing on Lake Opora, Audrey's headlights shone on the rowboat. Its emptiness didn't alarm her at first. Maybe the two had walked back to Lucille's. She began backing away when she saw Lake's shoes on the ground. Fear singed through her. Lake wouldn't have walked anywhere without those. She shined the lights on the boat once more and got out to inspect.

"My God," she cried, seeing Lake curled on her side in the hull. She couldn't tell whether she was asleep or worse. "Lake, get up, child. Get up." Her clothes were soaked, her braided hair dripping at the ends. She lifted her under her arms, but Lake lay slumped. "You've got to wake up. You'll be all right." Slowly Lake stood, leaning on Audrey as they walked back to the car. Audrey had brought a sweater and laid it over her in the back seat.

"Lucille," Audrey cried, talking to herself, thumping the steering wheel. "How could you? How could you?" That was how they traveled all the way home, six hours on the dark highway.

The first thing she did, after putting Lake to bed, was take Lucille's portrait off the wall. She wanted to slash a knife through it. But instead she took it to an old consignment store that sold art. "What are you hoping to get for this?" the owner asked.

She nearly laughed. "I should pay you for taking it off my hands." She never wanted to see that face again.

1973

38

Audrey shrugs off Lucille's attempt to help her out of the car, swinging herself forward on her crutches. Her fear for Lake has eclipsed any pain.

"We have to work together," Lucille is saying, her voice raised against the sound of rain cannoning down. "Lake needs us." She steadily guides Audrey up the staircase, but then something seizes her, and she takes the last steps two at a time. Once at the second-story landing she doesn't wait, she charges toward the door. "Lake," she calls, "it's Lucille. Let us in." She tries the handle and the door opens easily.

Sick, is what Audrey thinks. *I'm going to be sick.*

Ray is pulling Lake across the room with such force that her arm might come loose from its socket. She's crying. His face is full of rage.

"Let go of my daughter!" Lucille cries.

Ray looks confused, turning from Lucille to Audrey, and in that still moment Lucille tackles him. Audrey sees her incredible arm strength, how she must have gained it by hoisting her aging patients around day after day. Ray, too stunned to resist, drops Lake's hand and falls to the ground. Audrey goes to her, checking for any sign of injury, but neither of them takes her eyes off the spectacle of Lucille holding Ray down. With his hands free, he squeezes her arms, trying to push her off.

"Stop it," Lake yells. "Don't touch her!"

A voice comes from somewhere deep in Lucille, a tone Audrey almost doesn't recognize.

"Ray, I know you care about Lake. You're a good man. The best thing you can do is leave her alone. You need help. Lake here is going to Russia. I know she's going to win that role. You're going to stay here and get better."

He's wild-eyed, but in the silence that follows, all three of them looking down on him, he releases her, then shudders, covering his eyes with his elbow.

"Come on. Leave now," she says gently. She helps him up. "There we go. I'll go with you. We'll leave them in peace."

She looks back to Lake and Audrey, who haven't let go of each other.

"You're all right? I hope he didn't hurt you," Lake says.

"I can take it," Lucille says, still firmly gripping Ray's arm. "I'm just sorry for all of it. Everything I've done—and so much I haven't."

For the next few weeks, Lake stays at Audrey's. They're giddy as children about the prospect of Lake abroad. "Do you know how amazing this is, performing in the USSR in 1973?" Audrey says. "I don't even know anyone who's visited, and you're going to be onstage!"

Past nightfall, the two of them stretch out on Audrey's bed. Lake lies on her stomach with her feet kicked up behind her. After reading some of her lines aloud, Audrey interrupts. "Do you think people can take in life like that? Really be alert to everything, all the time?"

"No," Lake says. "We're too busy thinking about ourselves."

"Not loving enough," says Audrey. "That'll be the one regret for all of us, won't it? I can feel it already, in my aging, decrepit body."

"Don't talk like that," Lake says, tucking a quilt all around Audrey. "The only time I fully pay attention is when I'm onstage, inhabiting somebody else. That's when I see everything. And use everything I know. That's the only time I can share"—she pauses, resting her chin on her hands—"what I know."

"All your passion, all your youth and desire—those Soviets in their cold city, covered in snow, they're going to melt watching you. You're going to touch them. And when they're touched, they start to heal. You too, you'll see."

Audrey rides with Lake to deliver groceries to Ben but avoids him by waiting in the car outside. She stares for a long time at the house across the street, the Dudrows' moss-covered roof, sad looking through the trees. For years the house has been in ill repair. She can't remember the last time she saw Nancy. "I've been wondering about Mel Dudrow," she says when Lake returns.

"Do you know where he is?"

"He went to Vietnam. I don't know how he's managed since."

"Maybe everything started with him. I mean it began with Lucille, but then the way he hurt me—"

"He was vicious."

"—the way those two things came together. I haven't thought about that till now. I've been so mixed up..." Her voice trails off.

"Oh, Lake. I didn't do nearly enough."

"You stayed. You did that."

"Remotely," Audrey says, tilting her head and rolling her eyes.

"Usually out of sight."

"Letting you get around town by bus before you even learned how to ride a bike."

"Forgetting to pick me up at summer camp." They're laughing now.

"I had the day wrong on the calendar!"

"They knew where to find you," Lake says, pulling away from the curb. "They had your number."

Lucille calls every so often from her apartment. "A lot of hours over here with these rabbit ears," she says, referring to the antenna on her television.

"Lake's feeling better. I'm down to one crutch."

"No sign of Ray?"

"Nope."

"Can I speak to her?"

Audrey hands over the phone.

Long pauses and affirmations ensue. "I forgot to say," Lake goes on, "I won the role a while ago. I'll play Emily Webb in *Our Town*. I'll be leaving for Moscow soon."

Audrey remembers the sounds that came from Lucille's room each night when they stayed together after the car accident. The door cracked open between them, Lucille moaned and mumbled indecipherable words while she slept. Audrey wanted to comfort her but knew she shouldn't get up without help. Calling her name quieted her. Lucille began each morning smiling, doing "bicycle legs," jumping jacks, stretches, as if the night had been no trial at all. The cheery façade saddened Audrey, as does the faint pitch of desperation she can make out in Lucille's voice now.

"I've got rehearsals," Lake says, "so I don't know when I'll have a chance. But yes, I know how to reach you."

After she hangs up, Lake looks very sad. "I feel for her. I do."

39

Lucille is relieved that Lake is at least talking to her on the phone. But she still hasn't gotten beyond brief pleasantries with either her or Audrey, and even these are chilly. There have been no acceptances to her invitations, and no invitations offered.

She's been here fewer than three months, she tells herself.

But when she comes home from her elderly client—her dying client—even her apartment feels hostile. She always turns the television on when she first arrives, easing the transition to solitude, and tonight a surge of electricity shocks her fingers when she pulls the knob. Her only choice is to watch Jerry Reed or *Bonanza*. She turns the TV off. Adorning the shelves of her Connecticut Avenue high-rise are traces of Pomona: dried leaves of fruit trees pressed into clay, woody stems of raspberry bushes lying about like sculpture, peach pits lined up by size, some darker, others sun-bleached. They collect dust. No one has ever visited to see them. Her fourth-floor view is of storefronts. Her windows, when open, let in air polluted with exhaust and horns.

This week—and maybe it accounts for her mood—marks five years since Arthur died. His final illness, not a thing to do with his heart, came on abruptly. Martha found him slumped over his ledger books that were full of beautiful script, numbers in parallel slant, crisp lines of black ink. There was no red, ever. An immaculate universe he'd created. He told Martha he couldn't swallow. "Go ge ya mudah," he rasped. He didn't walk for four more years, the remainder of his life.

Lucille was wallpapering the dining room walls when Martha called to her. Persimmons and birds against a blue background—only two strips of the paper up. It hung like that for years. There was something Lucille liked about caring for Arthur on his back. It reminded her of Mrs. Causey and how she first met him. He had the same give now as a willow branch, soft all the way to its downy tips. If his smooth, hairless head had once indicated a full-stop brand of firmness, it now revealed him raw and tender.

"We were even then, fox," he said one day, using her old name. She'd never escaped from him, never outsmarted him. He reached playfully for her leg, but she skittered away. She thought of how she used to yield to him, to her own flesh with him, and not so long ago.

"How do you figure that?"

"I'd lost something. I knew you had too. I waited for you to tell me before we married. All I know is that your need finally matched mine." She didn't respond and he went on: "You shouldn't say what I would have done. Don't put that on me. I know what it's like to want something so badly. And not want to do the thing necessary to have it. I'd lost my boy. I would not have wanted you to suffer the same."

"Oh, you're the hero in hindsight, are you, Arthur? You would have saved the day."

"No, no. I'm just dying."

She welled up with tears then. And now.

In the next day or two, Mrs. Ordway will die. Lucille always wants to stay till the very end with her patients, not wanting to have been dragged through the dismal, dying part and then miss the death. Death is the mystery she wants to look into, where the abyss shimmers and waves. But the extended family is on their way, and they will want this privilege for themselves. Understandably.

By the time Arthur finished dying, her children no longer relied on her for anything. Clark was eighteen, Martha twenty-one. Lucille felt freer to assume herself again. The easiest thing in her life had been conceiving, and by that measure, only two more children, she had denied the truest part of herself. Caring for Arthur was what enlivened her once more. And since then she has tended to many people—fed, caressed, bathed, and buried them. Picking up a dried peach pit, rubbing her finger over its grooves, she has the sense of having held on to all the wrong things. Arthur is gone, and their children—she will never be able to make up for what she wasted. Same with Lake, her child who cannot leave fast enough.

40

Dulles Airport is smaller than Audrey expected and more beautiful, like something in flight itself. The ceiling is so high that she half expects to see birds flying above. It takes a moment for her to get her bearings and realize that Lake has to take a lounge, a mobile lounge, to where the plane waits. "I've got butterflies for you," says Audrey. Neither of them has ever flown on a plane. Mostly men with briefcases and large tour groups are in the waiting area, no one Lake recognizes from her company. The plane doesn't board for another hour. Everywhere are paisley prints, tinted glasses, beige suits. Lake wears a long sky-blue coat that mostly covers her bell bottoms. Her eyes loom large, thick-lashed, under a beret.

After Audrey tips the porter for checking the two suitcases, they walk toward the wall of windows. A plane is taking off, and she holds her breath at such a marvel, the noise of it penetrating the glass. She said "butterflies," but she feels an aching pit in her stomach, imagining Lake aloft, gone.

"You have some rubles to get you started, for tipping? Maybe they don't tip over there. You have your traveler's cheques? Oh, what haven't I thought to tell you? Stay in a group. Be chaperoned. Don't go anywhere alone at night." Audrey loops her arm through Lake's.

"I know, I know. Listen, you need to check on Dad while I'm away. Someone does."

It's a weekday, Ben's working—at least Audrey assumes that's why he isn't here.

"Has he had any visitors?" She wonders about Jeanne, his nurse, how long it will take her to show up at his front door after hearing he's a single man.

"He asks about you every day. It's become a joke. When you last called, I hadn't put the phone in the cradle before he started begging me to beg you to come home. I just put my hand up. 'Don't start.' Jeanne has brought a few meals by. I didn't recognize her at first, with her white hair and skin so wrinkled and tan. Frosted-peach lipstick slathered on her lips. Ick."

"I knew it!" But from the way Lake draws herself up, Audrey realizes this isn't for her to say.

"You like thinking he's been unfaithful. You want to believe that, but I don't think it's true. He says she's his only friend. Besides, she finally married a few years ago, some retired general."

Audrey follows a plane's descent in the distance. "And his drinking?"

"I'd say he's nearing pre-crash levels. Last night I unlaced his shoes, covered him with a blanket in his chair." It's mid-March, more than a month since Audrey has seen him.

"I'll check on him." Just yesterday she wanted, fleetingly, to talk to him, tell him how an art-fair curator had turned down her work. He might have made her laugh about it. But she feels a pang in her chest with the image of this sorry state—how he seems to be out-suffering everyone. "Don't worry about him; promise me you won't. This is going to be such an adventure for you—you'll have stories to tell the rest of your life. Maybe just don't fall in love with a Russian."

Lake laughs. "You're probably right. There's been enough falling from me already. I'm hoping there's more to life."

"Yes," Audrey says slowly, nodding toward the planes outside. "And no. If I hadn't been so determined *not* to marry, maybe Ben wouldn't have snuck up on me like he did. I would have picked somebody out, instead of being picked. That and the scarcity of men back then—that's how I wound up with your father."

"I'll see how getting married feels onstage as Emily Webb. I'll try it out." Lake smiles, adding, "You'll get married again. *You'll* find someone else." She squeezes Audrey's arm.

"I don't know," Audrey says. "There are worse things than being alone." But she called Daniel a few days ago, and his voice plunged into a drawl when she announced herself. Almost at once he asked her to dinner. She has much she wants to tell him when they meet next week.

She looks down at her mottled fingers, paint flecked across her knuckles. Feeling the indentation where her wedding rings used to be, she knows what she wants most is to create. She has lately come into possession of an etching press, storing it on her one square of kitchen counter. She used it to collage the Japanese portraits in a massive format, the largest she's ever created, more than eight feet high. The men's faces are amended with her drawings of them in nature, gardening, with children on their shoulders, in the arms of lovers, painting. While studying the piece on her studio wall, the curator had flirted with her, asking her to dinner, and this chafed her more than his refusal to take it on. He didn't outright reject it; he was intrigued but noncommittal. Her mind drifts there now, to drawing more of the figures—on the telephone, swimming, bathing, wounded.

A voice comes over the loudspeaker. "I should probably look around for the cast," Lake says. They turn from the window and that's when Audrey sees her, just a dark, diminutive shadow at first, against the light of the main entrance doors.

Lucille. She is running toward them. She wears a bright-yellow pleated skirt, her hands are full. Her figure grows larger until her outline fills in—it's her all right, her glasses crooked, a purse bouncing on her hip.

"My life," Lake says, shaking her head.

Flustered, with a sheen of perspiration across her forehead, Lucille holds out a bouquet of pink blossoms and green leaves. "Something to take with you," she says, out of breath. "Like Audrey's camellias. On the train to Washington."

Lake takes the flowers, leaning in to smell them.

"Oh, camellias don't smell." Lucille laughs nervously.

Lake shrugs, almost an apology. "Thank you."

"But they'll keep on your flight. Maybe longer. To remind you of home. I stopped by on my way, got these from the camellia bush in front of your house."

Audrey has never seen her with lipstick on or this much rouge.

"If I called Ben's number once, I called a dozen times. It wasn't till yesterday he picked up and told me all about your rehearsals at night and gave me your departure time. I wouldn't have missed this. But who knew it was so long a drive out here." She takes a breath, her voice still trembling a bit. "Can I get us some tea?"

Audrey pulls out money, but Lucille resists. Audrey presses the coins into her hand. The trespasser and the one trespassed on. They may never stop working it out.

Lucille wins. When she walks away, Lake says, "Did *you* know she was coming?"

"No idea. She won't give up."

When Lucille returns with the three teas, Lake starts searching the crowd for people she knows. "Wait, we haven't talked about how we'll be in touch," Audrey says. "Call me collect—Sunday afternoons, I'm always home then."

"I'm only gone six weeks."

"You don't really know that. They haven't scheduled the full tour." More flight numbers are announced. Audrey suddenly wants to cry at how fast this is all happening. For every painting she never made, it wasn't Lake who got in her way. It was love. It's true that at first the demand to love stymied her. But the demand faded. Love remained.

Lake reaches into her purse and pulls out handkerchiefs. "Three new ones, a going-away gift from Prudy. You two need these more than I do." She hands one to each of them.

Audrey runs her finger over the embroidered notes on the corner, three flats on a staff. She points to them. "What's this?"

"The song Prudy always sang to me, its key signature." Lake smiles, tucking her handkerchief back into her purse.

A large bearded man comes up to her, a spot of red tie showing above his sweater collar. "I didn't see you huddled over here. I thought you hadn't made it. Time to go." He grins, clearly smitten with her, not so much as a glance toward the other women. A new kind of worry hits Audrey.

When he moves into the line, Lake says, "The director has given his command."

Lake hugs Audrey first. Then she turns to Lucille, awkwardly opening her arms, but her shoulders, always so rigid, let go. Audrey sees it, how Lake closes her eyes as they embrace, trusting, at least for this moment.

Audrey pulls out her clunky Polaroid and snaps a picture of Lake and Lucille, their faces lit brightly by the big window. She flaps the developing photo in the air, hands it to Lake. "Flowers, photographs. What a ceremony." The image is still only a cloud with color at the edges. One more hug from Audrey, and then Lake heads to the line.

"I don't want her to hurt herself in those wavy-soled shoes," Lucille says.

"Isn't that what she's supposed to do? Break a leg, Lake!" Audrey calls, laughing.

When Lake reaches the end of the line, the company absorbs her. She turns around for one last wave, blooms in hand, a ray of light hitting her hair.

"She's really something, isn't she?" Lucille says. "You only have to look at her to know she was raised by a mother who loves her."

They return to the window—as close as they can get, their breath fogging the glass—and the lounge starts on its way. Silent and separate as they are, no one else would recognize them as friends.

"Mothers," Audrey says. "You, me, Prudy. She has us all."

They watch, riveted, as the lounge arrives at the jetway, and later, farther in the distance, the plane sails along the ground and soars upward, and then, small as a bird, disappears into the clouds.

Acknowledgments

First and always, my love and gratitude to Carter—without whom, nothing—and to Amelia. I could not have written this book without your love, wisdom, and support.

Immense appreciation goes to other readers or editors of the manuscript: Jay Schaefer, who approved first, launching my own faith; Susan Shreve, Leslie Williams, Diana Oboler, Alexandra Zapruder, Mary Kay Zuravleff, Jessica Francis Kane, Sarah Hollister, Caroline Altmann, Margaret Rubino, Joy Johannessen, Andrea Chapin, and Molly McCloskey—your fingerprints are all over these pages and the novel is better for them. Same goes to Laura Scalzo: I am forever grateful. Many of you are in this wonderful DC community of writers—one of the reasons I love this city.

Thanks to the hospitality of people who lent or shared their space while I wrote this book. Susan Shreve, your company and studio have been the gift of a lifetime. And Sarah Hollister—from Sycamore to Fredericksburg, thank you. Much gratitude to the McElroy-Rietano family whose Fair Hope Farm was the site of my first full-draft reading. And to Green Bough House of Prayer—early outlines scripted within those blessed walls were the scaffolding here. A general thanks to libraries everywhere—the seat of my childhood desire to write—and specifically to the American University Library.

This book began long ago with interviews of women and men who worked in or had knowledge of 1940s Washington or wartime: Thanks to the late Nancy Montgomery, Betty Hennigan, Emily Gilbert, Margaret Sparks, George Timberlake, and William Hollister. Eric Spaar was a patient resource for my questions on the military. Thank you to Sabrina Cabada for sharing her knowledge of art gallery operations in the 1960s and 1970s. Charles "Buckey" Grimm gave me important background on the National Archives and Records Administration's role in cataloging captured war film. The moment I read Nan Knight's piece on "a secret workplace tradition" in Washington, I knew I had at least one setting for the novel I would someday write.

I'm grateful to the editor of *The Antioch Review* for publishing my story, "Bride," now more backstory than excerpt; but it too, was an acceptance that propelled me forward. And I'm forever thankful to Jaynie Royal and the team at Regal House Publishing for bringing this book into the world, alongside so many other wonderful ones.

Dearest family and friends, you've supported me for years in this endeavor. Every kind word, show of interest, and enthusiasm for my work carried me here. Endless thanks to you all.